LaRosa Chronicles

Yesterday, Tommy Gray Drowned

K. Spirito

First published by Writer's Showcase; an imprint of iUniverse, Inc; 2000
ISBN: 0-595-13767-9 (print)

Produced on CD by A Snowy Day Distribution & Publishing
ISBN: 978-1-936615-07-0 (audio)

Produced by A Snowy Day Distribution & Publishing
ISBN: 978-1-936615-08-7 (e-book)

Revised and Re-published 2011 by:
A Snowy Day Distribution & Publishing
P.O. Box 2014
Merrimack, NH 03054
(603) 493-2276
ISBN: 978-1-936615-06-3

Cover Design: Sal Spirito Jr
Drawing: Josephine LaFrazia

Printed in the United States of America

LaRosa Chronicles

Father Sandro's Money (available)

Kathleen (work in progress)

Roses Falling (work in progress)

Time Has A Way (available)

Everything Happens To Margi
(work in progress)

Yesterday, Tommy Gray Drowned (available)

Tomorrow Is Promised To No One
(work in progress)

CANDY-COLORED CLOWN (available)

Spiderling (available)

P I S C A T A G U A (available)

Summer And August (available)

Adriano Saves the Christmas Stroll
(work in progress)

Visit: www.kspirito.com

To playmates lost…

April 1959

"There outta be a law against makin' kids go to school on such a nifty day," I grunted. It was that last bell on that Monday morning that finally squelched my spring fever and bullied me into putting my dawdling rear in gear. I traipsed up the macadam driveway to the white five-room schoolhouse that overlooked the Village of Echo Lake, Massachusetts. Then I took up my usual spot in the fourth-grade line - last.

Anne Ford and Mary Mason were nose to nose at the front of the line. Their hands covered the sides of their mouths, so the rest of us peons could not hear their nasty secrets.

"Dirty birds," I snickered under my breath. "Those two are always ripping some poor slob to shreds." My insides curdled. "Hope that slob isn't me..." I gave myself the once-over. "Gee whiz..." My biggest flaw could not be denied - my clothes. By this time in the school year, every one of the three outfits Mother bought for me last fall was in real sad shape. The one I had on today was as ratty as last week's hobo. "It's not fair," I groused, kicking the ground. Anne and Mary always wore the coolest dresses - a different one each day of the week. I leered at them. Needless to say, fancy lace slips were underneath those pretty dresses.

But then I could just see my arms stretching up to the ceiling. All that silky pink gingham slithering down over my naked body... Making prickling goose bumps... The smell of sugar starch wafting up my nostrils, making me sneeze as the frock sheeted over my face. My hands would smooth out the crispness while Mother happily tied the wide satin ribbon into an opulent bow behind my back. After adjusting the white lace collar, Mother would pat my butt, smile at me, and send me on my way.

I sighed. "Oh well, that's not about to happen..." I gnawed the inside of my cheek and ogled Anne. She really was quite pretty. Too bad she was such a witch. Gosh, look at her hair... So clean and shiny in the sunlight. Bet dollars to donuts it smells like her mother's perfume.

I pictured Anne chattering on and on while Mrs. Ford artfully braided Anne's brunette spirals - a different style and a different ribbon for each day of the week. My fingers explored my own sheered locks, which Mother had recently taken upon herself - for the umpteenth time - to chop. Some rare form of pageboy evolved, which all the kids - especially Anne Ford and Mary Mason - poked fun at - much to my embarrassment.

Eternal moments passed. I fidgeted.

At last, Mrs. King, our fourth-grade teacher, opened the big blue door. Her chestnut hair, short and curly and combed just so, accentuated her chocolaty eyes, which were drawn slightly out to her temples. Her lips were only scantily tinted, because teachers were not supposed to promote makeup. The mother of two always looked so neat and composed; yet she was not the classic schoolmarm either. Slim and athletic, she was a popular teacher who played dodge ball quite often with the students during recess. She related well to her charges and always found ways to motivate even the rowdy ones in a strong but kindly manner. On the other hand, Mrs. King did not dote on any of us. No, she made us do what we were there for without any ifs, ands, or buts.

As twenty-eight fourth graders filed into the classroom, illuminated by towering windows on three sides, hard-soled oxfords and buckle shoes shuffled noisily across highly polished oak planking. Some of the soles imparted black scuffmarks; and that made the janitor mad. Energetic adolescent activity filled the sun-streaked room where only moments before silence reigned.

In unison, voices recited the Pledge of Allegiance to the Flag. Then Mrs. King read the Twenty-third Psalm. Every day she recited a different Bible verse - that was before such things were against the law. The Twenty-third Psalm was one of my favorites - especially the part about lying down in green pastures beside the still water. Wait a minute. Mrs. King read those very same words just the other day. Psalms were supposed to be recited in sequence until completed, whereupon, they were read from the beginning once again. Well, maybe the Twenty-third Psalm is one of her favorites, too, I thought. I nodded. I'll have to ask her about it at recess.

I joined in with the class already reciting the Lord's Prayer. Getting that over and done with usually signaled the start of daily lessons, but not on this sunny Monday morning.

Mrs. King just stood there. Something was wrong. She was not at all the self-assured teacher I was used to. Her troubled eyes wandered the faces of her young charges. When she came to mine, I quickly looked down at my hands, which were still folded from prayer. I heard her take a deep, labored breath. I looked up. What was the matter with her?

She straightened herself. Her mind certainly was on something else. Her voice came out kind of sad: "Many of you have already heard…" She faltered. Her eyes rolled. She was trying not to cry, I could tell. "But there may be some of you who may not know…as yet…"

The classroom had never been so quiet. Complete attention was upon Mrs. King. I swallowed hard.

And then…then like red-hot grease in a frying pan, those dreadful words spattered out her mouth: "Yesterday, Tommy Gray drowned."

My mouth dropped as my ten-year-old body recoiled. My brain grappled with her words. What in the world was she talking about? Dead? Tommy? He's dead?

Death was something I never experienced before that morning - well, except for the times when Father killed a chicken for Sunday dinner. He didn't like me to watch, but sometimes I did anyway. But a dead person? I didn't know any dead people - especially Tommy Gr…

Yesterday, Tommy Gray Drowned

My breath seemed to cease as somewhere, far off, I perceived Mrs. King's voice, "Let us bow our heads for a moment of silence." However, my eyes were in the middle of darting to the opposite side of the classroom. The second desk in the row next to the massive windows was… My head jerked back as I gasped. Tommy Gray wasn't there! No! That can't be!

Golden sunbeams reflected off the shellacked pine surface of his desk. Black dots from the glaring light floated in my eyes as I turned away and lowered my head.

The silence was ghastly. A shoe scuffed the floor, making the hair on the back of my neck bristle. Somebody choked back a cough - maybe it was me.

Shallow breaths dizzied me as I gawked out of the corner of my eye, back at his desk. The seat was still empty. I told myself that at any moment now, I was going to hear the big blue door groan open and then his head would poke through the classroom door. Yes, I was going to see his pudgy body squeeze through the skinniest of spaces in that door. Careful not to attract attention, he would tiptoe to his desk. Yeah, any moment now; I just knew it. This was all just one big mistake - someone's mean joke.

Desperately, I tried to justify Tommy Gray's absence. Wait a second… Tommy's got the measles! That's it! They're going around, you know.

"All right now, class…" Mrs. King sucked in a deep breath and straightened herself again. "When I find out the arrangements, I will let you all know immediately. Principal Cole has informed me that she will allow us to go to the wake and funeral together as a class. However, if any of your parents do not want you to go, you may stay with Miss Carter's class until the rest of us return to school."

Okay, I knew what funeral meant. I had seen cars lined up outside the church in the middle of the village - once in a while - on weekdays - whenever school wasn't in session. I had heard the steeple bell toll as cars with headlights on passed slowly through town. But wake? Well, that was entirely new to my ten-year-old vocabulary. I thought wake was what a person did after sleeping at night or taking a nap or…

At recess, I discreetly wormed my way through the assemblage of kids surrounding Anne Ford and Mary Mason at the monkey bars. For sure those two know-it-alls were babbling on and on about Tommy Gray. I was going to find out from them what all this wake and funeral stuff was all about. But then I heard some other ignorant fool spout out the question burning in my soul. Thank God, that ignorant fool wasn't me!

"You're so-o-o stupid!" Anne sneered. She stood there, hands on hips, and proceeded to sanctimoniously ridicule that poor fool. She even scrunched up her nose right smack in that drooly mouth's face. "Don't you know anything, dummy? A wake is when the undertaker man washes up the dead body and puts clean underwear on it - and Sunday best, too. He even paints make-up on the face - doesn't matter a particle if it's a boy or a girl."

"And then..." Mary chimed in while dangling by one arm from the bar over Anne's head, "...the undertaker man squashes the dead body into a gasket 'cause it's stiff and won't bend 'cause o' rigamutus."

"And then..." Anne cut in. She gave Mary the evil eye for having the audacity to interrupt. "Then everybody prays over the dead body for three days. A-n-d as you a-l-l know..." Her voice was singsong. "...a dead body is never *ever* left alone at night. So after that, everybody gets in their cars and they all follow the hearsh to the cemetery - and they keep their cars' lights on even though it's daytime. And of course, everyone knows it's against the law for any other cars to cut off the funeral possession. Well then, when the whole bunch of 'em finally gets to the cemetery - 'cause they drive so slow, you know - the priest reads some words outta the Bible 'n' sprinkles holy water all over the casket. An' then, the pole bears lower the casket into a big hole in the ground with ropes and everyone throws dirt on it. And that's the end of it!" Anne slapped her hands together as if she were brushing off dirt.

I was going to puke. Such things were beyond all comprehension as far as I was concerned. On top of that, I could not imagine a thing like that happening to me. My body shuddered like the last leaf clinging to an oak tree in a blizzard. No one was *ever* going to put me in a hole in the ground like that! No way! No how!

Though all this newly acquired knowledge scared me to no end, curiosity took over and decided for me that I was going to the wake and funeral with my classmates. This wake and funeral business was big stuff.

Mother and Father made no objections to the excursion. They sloughed the whole thing off by merely saying that I had to find out what it's all about sooner or later. Of course neither one of them went. If they had, it might have helped me to make sense of Tommy Gray's death. If only Mother or Father had talked to me about it - that plus other growing-up experiences that did not set right in my immature brain during sleepless nights. So many of those experiences reverberated throughout my life. But they kept everything to themselves. I had no right to question. I had no right to know. Just keep my mouth shut and do as I was told.

So a sense of isolation took root in me. It spread like crabgrass, strangling me - even as an adult.

That afternoon I hastily delivered my newspapers, taking the shortcut between Echo Lake and the backwash where high water accumulated every spring. I usually did not risk this route so early in the season. Sometimes water covered the dip in the trail and I had to turn back. Luck was with me. The path was clear - or so it seemed. I should have realized that last year's leaves were concealing slick gunk. Much to my chagrin, the back wheel of my blue twenty-inch bike mired in that gunk. "It's all my fault," I sniveled. "I shouldn't have taken this trail in the first place. How dumb can I be? Why did I have to ride through here anyways? I should've walked my bike across this stupid dip. Well, I just can't leave my bike here."

Straddling the front tire, I gave several teeth-gnarling tugs. I didn't expect the rear tire to free itself quite so quickly. Before I got the chance to catch myself, I landed smack on my butt, right in that gunk. "Aargh! What a stupid dumb mess!"

"Dumb mess," Echo Lake repeated again and again.

"Humph," I muttered, smearing muck off the seat of my threadbare corduroys. I swished my hands in the lake and of course, the water froze my fingers into popsicles. I shoved them into my pockets and made tight fists. That did no good at all, but there was no other way to try and warm them, since I had left my only holey mitten at home. The other mitten came up missing a while back. So instead, I shrieked, "To heck with it!"

"Heck with it… With it…" Echo Lake taunted.

I scrunched up my face and stuck my tongue out at the lake. Then I yanked my filthy bike upright and continued my quest. My feet were heavy and with every step I took, my gunk-soaked pants rode up the crack of my butt and my waterlogged boots farted.

At the edge of the clearing, I crept up behind a stand of budding maples. I peeked out at Echo Lake. The chilly breeze swept dirty blond strands into my eyes. I brushed them away.

Wispy clouds streaked across the robin's egg sky, shadowing the water's surface like spirits. Careful. A dead body might float up any second now and get me.

For the first time in my whole life, I felt my heart throbbing in my throat; its thunder boomed in my ears. Liquid terror coursed through my veins as I inched out into the clearing, wary of anything and everything that might be lurking about the deserted beach.

Nothing - anywhere.

I let my bike drop to the ground and jammed my hands into my hipbones. I scanned the recreational area, which the residents of the Town of Echo Lake constructed years ago.

White sand had been broadcast across the bulldozed shoreline and into the lake about twenty feet. Through the years, the sand crept towards the depths that were freezing dark, no matter what time of year. Off to one side, a narrow dock made of oak logs dipped in tar jutted out into the water. Many a lethargic summer day, I lay across the roughly hewn logs of that dock. Once in a while, I got slivers, which I had to pick at all night long, because if Mother ever found out I was dallying on that dock, she would blow her stack. But none of that mattered, because hundreds of silvery minnows schooled in the crystal water below the dock and nibbled my fingertips. It tickled and I tried not to giggle - what if somebody heard me laughing? Sometimes I didn't care and forgot about everything. I laughed like crazy. And then I hummed *Mr. Sandman.* Not too loud though. My voice sounded real dumb.

Well, anyways… I snuck up to the sandy shoreline. "Humph. No dead bodies."

Only the water, barely ruffled by the early springtime breeze, was lapping against the shoreline. This gentle water actually killed somebody? Somebody I knew? It killed Tommy Gray? My friend? "Gee, that's not right." I squinted at Echo Lake. Well, that bugger certainly betrayed *my* trust.

"Wonder what it feels like to drown?" I whispered. "Maybe Echo Lake wants to kill me, too. Don't know why… After all, I love the water. I practically live in it the whole summer long. I consider it my friend…as much as…as much as Tommy Gray."

April 1989

On a pretty Sunday morning, I returned to the cemetery where Tommy Gray lay at rest. Only the muffled sounds of my unsteady footsteps on the grass, still brown and matted from winter, violated the quiescence. But if I looked close enough, spikes of green had begun to shove their way up, through last year's sheathe, grabbing at the warmth of the early spring sunshine.

The thought of why I came to this cemetery on this pretty Sunday morning never consciously crossed my mind. Guess I felt some sort of need for rejuvenation, for happenings that would take me away from all I usually did, away from the life I usually led, away from the stifling emptiness Peter left behind when he tramped off for Vietnam for the second time in our lives - the purpose of it all. Books, movies, and lunch or dinner with friends seemed to lack all reason – never mind exercise, sailing, or going to the gym. I didn't have a job - I gave up nursing just after Peter came back from Nam the first time. So, it seemed, the unexpressed urge to do something for no reason at all egged me on. One way or the other, who would ever go to a place like this merely to get away from it all?

The grave of my fourth-grade classmate remained elusive. I jammed my hands into my hipbones. "I swear I know exactly where you are, Tommy. How can I ever forget?"

After Tommy Gray drowned, I began to sketch him and me on scraps of paper during long, lonesome nights. I drew sketches again and again and then made sure to throw away each and every one into the trash barrel outside of Pierce's Grocery Store. Mother didn't approve of me "drawing pictures" or engaging in any "artsiness" at all.

Yesterday, Tommy Gray Drowned

As years went by, the scenes in my sketches became bigger, more graphic. Then, as Peter and I plied the salty waters off New England in our sailboat, Tommy Gray's face seemed to float up to the surface from the crystalline depths below - as if from Echo Lake. All too often, his hazel eyes, so incredibly sad and sequestered behind that sandy mop of his, fixed upon mine. Rippling back and forth, his eyes mesmerized me, leaving my entire being restless, uncertain. I always shook it off, never daring to make sense of any of it. Nor did I speak of it to anyone - even Peter.

A car passed the cemetery, catching my attention. My eyes followed it until it rounded the curve and disappeared beyond a stand of pines. I saw myself on that road, a child speeding past this place on my blue twenty-inch bike, delivering the last copies of the *Evening News*. Only, at that curve I skidded to a stop. My bony knees straddled the metal frame as I glanced over my shoulder. "Tommy?"

A tremendous energy had filled me, almost overwhelming me, and it made me restless. Did I really hear his actual voice? I thought about it. Nah, not his voice; it was just...well, you know, like maybe an illusion - something like that. Like when you looked at somebody and got the illusion about things going on with that person or what that person was thinking?

I struggled with my fears and limitations, but still I felt tingly - as if tiny fans were blowing all over my body. I looked around. Nobody in sight. I glanced up at the cemetery. A creepy sort of obligation to learn whatever I was able to learn came over me. Why not; I was here already; may as well go check it out. I hopped on my bike then circled around and headed to the cemetery.

His gravesite was peaceful, the atmosphere sweet and thick. I felt immersed in it - as though I were sitting at the bottom of a jar full of maple syrup.

I squinted up at the sky, yearning to know if he was looking down upon me. "Won't you tell me everything's okay between us, Tommy?"

It seemed as if a boulder crushed my chest when Tommy did not answer.

Right away, I regretted my words. I looked around, making sure nobody heard me standing there talking to a piece of rock. Geez, I thought, I really blew it. Why did I have to go and ask a dumb thing like that? My one and only chance; and I blew it! Now Tommy was never going to talk to me!

I hated the way I felt. I hated the powerlessness. And I couldn't think of anything to do about it.

And so his silence triggered the replay of that day our friendship turned to dust in the March wind: "Hey! Gimme the paper 'Lizbeth!" Tommy Gray reached into my paper bag for a copy of the *Evening News*. His round eyes narrowed as his brows fused into one straight line. Wrinkles corrupted his impish nose and his chin drew up so tight it looked like a pulpy crabapple hanging off a tree branch in January. "Now you don't hafta stop at my house! So there!"

Unwittingly, he had snagged several copies, which the raw March bluster seized just right and then blasted to smithereens. An explosion of newsprint swirled down the remote country road.

I knew right away that my scrawny legs could not carry me that fast. Yet I had no other choice. So I dropped my bike. Metal grated across the blacktop as I took off after those pages.

I rescued one page impaled on a branch then stuffed it under my arm. I jumped for another page spiraling above my head. Missed it. I jumped again, stretching higher. My fingertips brushed the corner of it, but before I got a better grip, that invisible scoundrel - namely the wind - swiped it away. "This is useless!" I shrieked, upon landing. I stomped my foot and flailed my arms worse than willow branches devoid of greenery. "I'm never gonna find all the pages! Much less catch them! Geez, Mother is gonna kill me! I can just hear her now, hollering and carrying on, 'You should have paid better attention! You know full well you can't trust a stinking soul in this cesspool of a town!' She is never gonna give me a chance to explain!" I turned and scowled at Tommy Gray.

Yesterday, Tommy Gray Drowned

He stood there, in the same spot; arms limp at his sides, right hand clutching a page of the want ads for dear life. The wind was whipping his hair like leavings of straw in a new-mown hayfield before a rising thunderstorm. He looked like an overstuffed scarecrow in a faded plaid overcoat with frayed cuffs and patched elbows. His skin was poking through the threadbare distended knees of his baggy home-sewn overalls, which were devoid of blue coloration and sizing due to endless washings.

What possessed Tommy Gray? He never did one single mean thing to me before that fateful day in 1959. Somewhere within me, I should have known he was up to no good. But my heart would hear nothing of it. If anyone else had ambushed me in such a manner, I would have shielded my precious cargo like a grizzly bear. Fending off Tommy Gray never once entered into my mind - not for one blessed second.

I set my jaw then stomped over to him. Words began to tumble out my mouth: "What is wrong with you, Tommy Gray?" I snatched the newsprint from his grubby paws as hot angry tears smarted my face that was chilled by the brutal March wind. Stupid dumb sniveling. I hated when that happened. I dug my fingers into my hips - as if that would stop me from being such a crybaby. "I thought you was my friend…"

Dumbfounded, Tommy said nothing - although his facial muscles drooped and his round eyes sagged. When his head slumped, it dawned on me right away: He was just as unprepared for those newspapers exploding in our faces as I was. Eyeball-to-eyeball, my facial cast spat at him: Well, you should have known better.

No sooner did his eyes read mine than my immature assumption about friendship hit the both of us like pins popping balloons. Our unspoken friendship had been hung out to dry for the entire world to see - like underpants pinned to a clothesline on a sunny day. Plain as the nose on your face, Tommy deeply regretted his transgression; however, this friendship thing… Well, that was another matter entirely.

We spun away from each other. That's when I caught sight of Mike Anderson lurking off in the distance, one lanky leg propped up on the wooden guardrail. That showoff was wearing khaki chinos, a brown bomber jacket, and the grin of a sadistic hyena. His slicked-back crew-cut gleamed in the sunlight like black coal. Why, that son-of-a-gun. He put Tommy up to this. I just knew it.

A few weeks ago, Mike Anderson turned thirteen - a teenager. So now, he thought he was better than anybody else. I rolled my eyes. Big Deal. What a disgusting showoff.

Tommy Gray glanced sideways at Mike Anderson then back at me. Unsure of what to do, he faced the unhappy choice between that teenager and me - a silly twerp from his fourth grade class. Since the company of a real teenager showed status within the Town of Echo Lake, Tommy abruptly scoffed at me and then sidled up to that showoff.

A smirk plastered Mike Anderson's puss. His defiant eyes needled me one last time before he strutted away shoulder to shoulder with Tommy Gray. "She's such a sissy."

My heart broke when my secret friend nodded agreement and then his laughter blended with that of the troublemaker mocking my helplessness. The naive child within me could not figure out why Tommy turned against me. So many times before that day, Tommy Gray had met me at the gravel lane that skirted the broken-down red shack in the woods where he lived with his parents and little sister Becky. Always polite, he would take the evening paper I handed to him. A time or two, he actually mumbled a fleeting hi. Most of the time, he timidly turned away without uttering a single word. Once or twice, I thought I caught a hint of a smile, but I wasn't sure it was intended for me or not. Tommy Gray was not much for smiling. No, it was almost like...well, you know...like he was afraid to or something. But let me tell you, when he did smile, it was like sunbeams raking across my slumbering heart, making it swell with wakefulness. Happiness sheeted over me like rain on a muggy August afternoon.

His smile involved only half his face; the other half remained frozen in a weird sort of passivity. Half his lips lifted his pudgy jowl into a ripe Macintosh and smack dab in the middle of

13

it, a dimple drilled so deep I thought a hole had sprung right through his cheek and any second, spit was going to ooze out.

Yeah, before that day in March 1959, Tommy had always been nice to me - more than most other kids I went to school with in Echo Lake, Massachusetts. In this one-horse town of about three hundred families, unforgiving gossips raised up snot-nosed brats to be just as narrow-minded and unjust as they were to those they deemed different - and there were always differences - they made sure of that. After all, blackballing was one of their favorite sports.

Still, it was not my fault that I delivered newspapers since I was six years old. It was not my fault that my name was not Jane or Mary or Patty. No, I was a skinny dirty-blond girl, doing a boy's job with a dumb name like Elizabeth. To top it all off, my pea-brained parents insisted that in school I should be addressed as Elizabeth. It didn't matter that at home they called me Beth.

So my peers picked on me unmercifully. A runt with an uncommon, elongated name was much too much for those small-town brats to accept. Yup, more times than I cared to admit, I heard that poem: Lizzie Borden took an ax...dah ta dah ta dah. And when the word lesbian entered those discriminating brats' vocabularies, whew! You bet your britches they slurred Lezzie all over me! And don't forget: I also delivered newspapers! Sheesh... Was I ripe for the picking or what?

True, the offspring of Echo Lake did dish out shameful cruelty, but it always seemed to me that Tommy Gray was different. Something clicked between us - but I don't remember when or how. He sensed things were tough for me - and I sensed things were tough for him, too.

We lived across town from each other - on opposite edges of civilization as it were. The difference was: his playmates always returned when the warm weather drew them back to the lake. I did not have that luxury. Skunk cabbages, jack-in-the-pulpits, and poison sumac ruled the forbidding swamp beyond my house. Nobody ever wanted to go there.

Far away from playmates of my own age and gender, I spent endless hours all by myself staring out my bedroom window. Nighttimes were the worst. How often did I yearn for the friendly breeze to take me aloft, above the white pine across the way, where the wind whistled and moonlight pinned diamonds of dew upon the needles? Imagine me: soaring through wisps of clouds; free from care; mist peppering my skin.

After Tommy died, I daydreamed of meeting him up there. And you know what? He smiled, big and toothy - from both sides of his face! And that smile warmed only me. His hand would enfold mine and then we scattered white puffs, skimmed glittering oceans, and arced high above spiky snow-capped peaks where the air was brisk and invigorating. Yet we never needed jackets. We circled the world once…twice… He always left me at the sill, always promised to return.

Anyways… Where was I? Oh, yeah… Well, after Mike Anderson and Tommy Gray swaggered away like that, I got to thinking and little by little, the whole thing just got my goat. "The nerve of that bugger plundering my paper bag that way. Well, you know what, Tommy?" I gathered myself together then stomped to the dingy red shack where the Gray family lived. My puny fists bashed the door with all their might. The rotten casing griped. Paint flaked from the rippled plywood where a single haphazard coat feigned protection from the elements. Fright knifed my gut: What if that moldy door caved in, because I hit it too hard? Geez, then I'll be in even bigger trouble!

My knees quaked as I envisioned my bare butt slung across the kitchen chair and Mother's arm arching high into the air - in her hand that dreaded switch.

Hinges creaked on warped unsecured screws as the door teetered open. Mrs. Gray, calmly folding a dishtowel, was standing before me. Her dark eyes fell upon me. Her placid demeanor instantly mutated into unmistakable consternation. What a dreadful sight I must have been - a convulsing ragamuffin on her termite-eaten stoop, tears flooding down a red swollen face, scrawny bones shivering in the March blow. Why, any second now, those knees were going to buckle and that ragamuffin was going to find herself writhing on rock-hard ground.

Yesterday, Tommy Gray Drowned

Well, it's now or never, I figured. So I gasped for air then belted out, "Tommy... He... He took m...my papers...an'...an'...the wind..." My jaws clamped shut, refusing to open - even if somebody pried them with a crowbar. Frigid air whistled through my clenched teeth. That was the only way for me to draw breath since my plugged-up nose overflowed with gooey snot. I swiped the tattered sleeve of my winter jacket to catch it. Dried remnants of similar actions gored my upper lip.

"Tommy!" Mrs. Gray bellowed, at the top of her lungs. "You get yourself home here right this instant, young man! I know you can hear me!"

Electric terror surged up and down my spine. I just about jumped out of my winter-bedraggled boots. Never before had I ever heard her holler like that. Worst of all, her hollering vomited back at us from beyond Echo Lake: "You can hear me! Hear me!"

Now, Mrs. Gray was no towering giant - a bit on the stocky side with short dark brown hair - ordinarily I had no concern - yet at that moment, those black eyes of hers blazed with white-hot fury and her stance appeared larger than life. Holy cow! That woman meant business!

From the dusty corners of my adult mind, I could still see Tommy Gray, head bowed, shuffle up next to my ten-year-old quivering exterior. His face contained not the vaguest hint of the abject fear that I would have felt if it were my mother hollering at me like that. No, only remorse had taken root on his face. Obviously he knew that showoff Mike Anderson high-tailed it out of there, leaving him to face the music alone. But that didn't seem bother Tommy Gray. He was ready to take whatever he had coming and was not afraid of his mother. I got the sense that Tommy knew his mother would never hurt him. No matter what, she still loved him. His shoulders shrugged as hazel pools peered at me through straight flaxen locks. His lips barely moved. "Sorry, 'Lizbeth."

"Now, you go help this poor girl round up her papers, young man," Mrs. Gray commanded. "Get on with it!"

Tommy and I never did find all those pages of the *Evening News* - though I never told him that. He felt bad enough as it was.

Sadly, from that day on, the unspoken friendship between us vanished like March winds in August. Tommy Gray never spoke another word to me. Ever. No, he avoided me like the plague - I could tell - and never came to take the newspaper from me again. When I did see him, he peered at me the same way he did on that wicked March afternoon - then he turned on his heel and took another path.

And my insides ached, hollow. More than anything else in the whole wide world, I wanted to forget the whole calamitous episode. I wished away that day, time and time again, and tried to deny it ever happened. But wishing didn't make it so.

Yesterday, Tommy Gray Drowned

IMAGES

I rubbed my face, trying to erase the past. I squeezed the fingers of one hand and then the other, forcing a vision of the plot of ground on a small grassy knoll where Tommy Gray lay. My heart broke - like so many times before - thinking of him lying in that dreadful place. Yet this day, the stone that bore his name was nowhere to be found.

I roamed about the surrounding lanes. So many markers. Some big. Some small. Some fancy with scrolled lettering. Some only numbered.

I snapped my wrists a few times, as if shaking off droplets of water, and then doubled back to the place my mind insisted he was. At long last, I spied it - a flat granite stone, obscured by a maze of last year's crabgrass. "Oh... I thought you had a monument, Tommy."

Emotions unraveled. Savagely I tore at the offensive crabgrass. "Stupid junk! You have no right to be here!"

I stood back, brushing my hands together. "There! Now everyone can see your name!"

My victory soured, for inscribed on the granite marker was Thomas Gray 1949-1959. My eyes were like restless ocean waves washing back and forth across the engravings. I knelt down - the way one does on velvet church kneelers - and blessed myself. My fingertips reached out to the marker. Seeking to find my childhood friend within the cold polished granite stained with grass and moisture, I failed miserably.

As ancient grief consumed me, my hands flattened across my breast. The throbbing in my throat chopped my words: "I never came to terms with your death, Tommy." My tears swelled.

Yesterday, Tommy Gray Drowned

"Ten years old... Why, Tommy? You - the best swimmer I ever knew."

Everything was so hushed up back in those days, I thought. Grief, death, funerals, all that stuff...taboo. Kids don't feel such things. But if a kid did, the kid got over it soon enough. I sighed. "Well, that's what the big people of Echo Lake preached. So, what in God's name am I doing here, Tommy?" I blinked up at the cloudless sky, so incredibly blue. I still did not see his face looking down on me.

Emptiness constricted my insides already crushed by the vacuum Peter left behind when he tramped off to Vietnam for the second time in our lives. I resented that God-forsaken country for stealing my husband away from me again. "I cannot bear to go through all that loneliness again, Tommy. The uncertainty... What am I going to do?"

In the late sixties, the United States government, in all its infinite wisdom, drafted Peter. Then, just a week after arriving in Vietnam, his platoon was ambushed somewhere near the Cambodian border. Scores of young men died that day, others went missing in action - including Peter. I refused to go on living until he returned. Days turned into years as over and over my mind replayed that last evening we spent together, strolling along the Charles River to the place where we first met. By the time I unlocked my apartment door, the city had long since been illuminated. We gave ourselves to each other in anguished tenderness and then at dawn, my world came to an end as he called over his shoulder with that silly grin of his: "Don't worry, Bethie. Nothin's gonna happen to this bod'! I'll cherish you in my heart, my little morning eyes, forever."

Nine months after he left, Julie was born. He never knew.

Yet even having his child did not shake me from my self-imposed isolation and rejection. Just when I gave up the thought of him ever coming back, there he was. We married soon after, and last Christmas Julie married Ken Waters. "I finally have a family to call my own, Tommy. But now, Peter is gone... Again."

In the shattered silence, I covered my mouth as if that might stop my thoughts. Cold metal etched my lips, causing me to gaze at my hand and the diamond encrusted wedding band. Its glitter seemed to mock my pain. I squinted at the pinkie ring on my other hand. Peter had fashioned it from buss wire back in the '60s. The peace sign was gnarled, pitted, and tarnished.

"I keep telling myself that Peter is doing a wonderful thing by going back to find MIAs. He might be able to influence the Vietnamese government to cooperate. If anyone can do it, he can. Several congressmen and dignitaries and the press went with him, so he should be safe...this time..." That thought gave me no solace. I sighed. No, that thought just didn't suit me at all. "I just can't shake the nagging feeling that he's not coming back to me, Tommy." I glanced down at the grave. "How long am I supposed to wait for Peter this time? When does my life start?"

My thoughts suddenly scattered. I trembled, but not from cold or fear. Images...images in my head...that's what made me tremble. Images were struggling to make themselves known. Suddenly, I needed to retrieve my sketchpad and pastel chalks from my car. I just had to.

I dashed to my car and then back to Tommy Gray's grave. I dropped to the ground, Indian style, and began to draw Tommy's grave. Strange how the scene materialized off to the left side of the sheet... I held the sketchpad at arm's length and cocked my head. "What in the world... I usually do a better job than this."

The sketchpad flattened on my lap - as if guided by unseen hands. Then my hand began to add something to the right.

I gave myself up to the mystique, my eyes drifting to the right of me. It's the grave of Gerald Gray.

I squinted at my hand and then at the grave of Gerald Gray. "How come I'm drawing your father's grave, Tommy? Hmmm... 1909-1969... Your father died ten years after you?"

Taking control, I held the sketch at arm's length. Tommy's grave appeared clear, easy to see, and yet his father's grave was dark and shrouded in ominous chaos. I endeavored to clear up the letters and date.

However, my hand refused to do what my brain dictated.

Yesterday, Tommy Gray Drowned

"I give up," I huffed, slouching in utter bewilderment.

After a while, I attempted to get to my feet, but spasms electrified my legs. Forty-year-old arteries and veins did not appreciate my sitting cross-legged on the April ground for what must have been an hour or more. I staggered back to my car, kicking my tingling legs this way and that, trying to restore circulation. Upon opening my car door, I slid the sketchpad behind the driver's seat. I got in and started the engine. Driving out of the cemetery, I got the feeling that more than the memory of Tommy Gray was going with me.

BURDENS

At the four corners that overlooked the Village of Echo Lake, the blinking red light prodded me to make up my mind: Going straight across? To the lake? Going right will take you out of town. Come on, lady.

I frowned at the main drag on the left; the millhouses huddled in the hollow. All appeared much the same as years ago. No shopping malls. No skyscrapers. No McDonald's. Nothing replaced the small-town uniqueness. More than likely, townsfolk still considered two cars cruising Main Street a traffic jam. They were known to flock out of their homes to view any minor occurrence, especially on Friday and Saturday nights when there was nothing else to do anyways.

I zeroed in on the white steeple of the Catholic Church that pierced the heavens. Emptiness built within me as I recalled attending the funeral service for Tommy Gray. I looked away.

Just beyond the church was the abandoned woolen mill, which was constructed out of granite blocks. The textile industry had been the backbone of the town's economic base during the first half of the 1900s. Echo Lake failed to recover from the mill-closings and subsequent relocation to the South. Many people migrated to greener pastures while others resigned themselves to welfare or commuting out of town to work. The town stagnated, but despite that, one gas station and a mom and pop grocery store hung in there while I was a kid. They supplied the everyday needs of about three hundred families.

I scratched my head. If I ventured into the village, was I prepared to run into anyone from the past?

Yesterday, Tommy Gray Drowned

The rumble of water caught my attention. I zeroed in on the pocked cement bridge across the intersection. A river meandered beneath it. Just beyond eyesight, a barrier of concrete held back the river, which created a lagoon of sorts. The woolen industry had left behind its power sources - a series of dams, which held back bodies of water that spilled over in the form of gorgeous waterfalls. The largest body of water was Echo Lake.

An air horn ruptured my introspection. My eyes shot to the rearview mirror. A hair's breadth from my bumper was a dingy black pick-up. It was inching closer by the second. Plain as day, I could see every rust canker - plus the irate driver who was mouthing words I was kind of glad I could not hear. His hair was dark - I couldn't tell the exact color, but it was slicked back, kind of pompadour-ish. A glowing cigarette was suspended out beyond his lips, jouncing with every utterance. Huge hands were flailing, hammering the steering wheel, jamming on the horn.

I squinted into my passenger-side mirror and spotted a slicked-back carrot-top bobbing in and out the pick-up's passenger-side window. That guy was also issuing a barrage of obscenities both verbal and non.

Obviously, those two hotheads were in one big hurry. Instinct told me hanging around at that stoplight was not wise, so I stepped on the accelerator, steering straight across the intersection. On the other side, I slowed to a crawl and watched the pick-up fishtail into the intersection. Tires smoked up the pavement. As the rust-bucket headed down into the village, I shook my head. "Tsk, tsk, tsk. Some things never change."

I did not let those two ignoramuses get to me. Driven by some sort of mystic necessity, the only thing on my mind was the beach at Echo Lake. I stepped on the accelerator and eased away from the intersection.

Sunlight filtered through the trees, striping the country road in gold and black. Eons ago, I delivered newspapers along here. Several new homes commingled with the ones forever chiseled in memory. About half of the old homes were modestly maintained. Some owners had hot-topped their gravel driveways. A garage or two had also sprung up. Other places were rundown and brush grew at will; a few prehistoric vehicles with flat tires and some without tires were suspended on cinder blocks, wasting away in side lots.

I found my way to the lake as if I never left. No big feat - only one road went in that direction. I stopped at the overgrown gravel lane that meandered through the woods to a small beach - the place where Tommy Gray lost his life thirty years ago this month. Heavy-gauge chain, rusted with age, sagged across the lane. An unreadable metal sign nailed to a hundred-year oak probably at one time indicated no trespassing. Nevertheless, I pulled my car off the road and into the trees and put it in park. "If the numskull who owns this property doesn't care enough to replace that rusted sign and chain, he certainly doesn't give a hoot whether I take them seriously or not."

I got out of my car and stretched the journey from Brighton out of my bones. I stood there for a moment. Did I really want to set foot in such inhospitable surroundings?

Next thing I knew, my sketchpad was chucked under my arm and my fingers were gripping corroded links, holding them down as my right leg swung over the chain and then my left leg. Brushing grains of rust off my hands, I began the hike to Echo Lake.

Sadly, the washed-out lane was barely passable. The footing was frightfully tricky in spots - to say the least. At one point, slimy half-thawed earth gave way beneath my feet. I stiffened while slithering into a channeling rut and caught myself just before my right ankle gave way. "Whew. The last thing I need now is to fall and break something." I scanned my surroundings. "Imagine lying here, stranded, alone. Curious forest creatures closing in on me, taking a look-see at my unholy predicament. Nobody is going to come looking for me - especially here of all places. Why should they? Even *I* didn't know I was coming here." I shivered. "Wait... Something is different... Yeah, over there. The red shack where Tommy Gray lived..." I gasped. "It's gone!"

I stepped over to the spot. Oak and birch saplings grew through the decaying junk. Several white birches had yet to right themselves from the weight of the winter snow - although tiny green buds on their branches were ripening.

My foot skimmed back and forth across dry leaves and twigs. Numerous past autumns were concealing all evidence that a family had lived here.

I took a step. Something pricked my heel. I leaned against a tree and twisted up my foot to see what was going on. A wood screw had impaled the sole of my sneaker. Attached to it was a strip of red plywood. I slipped off my shoe and fingered the decaying piece of yesterday. The wood disintegrated and fell into dust on the ground - brittle as my insides.

I wheedled out the screw. Then, while putting on my shoe, I heard rustling above my head. I squinted up through streaked sunlight to where a large crow was pacing back and forth on a tree limb. Its jet-black head cocked sideways at me. One eye seemed to penetrate my soul as his feathers and wings brandished threats. Caw! Caw! The crow seemed to be demanding: How dare you come here, woman!

I thought about throwing a stick to scare off the noisy demon and restore the peace. Yet I knew very well that I was the interloper here, not that crow. As if I were that crow, I surveyed the barrenness. History had been forever erased here. It was as if Tommy Gray never existed. How sad. How tremendously sad. I wanted to run. Hide. But that would not change things. That would not stop the need inside me to unearth who I was, why I was, why I came here in the first place.

Trudging onward, I finally stepped into the sunlit clearing, shielding my eyes from the sudden brightness. A pair of Canadian geese glided across the lake, leaving barely a wake to disturb the reflection of marshmallow clouds that sweetened the sapphire sky.

Off to the right of me, someone had been building a house - for quite some time, so it appeared. Age discolored the weathered plywood walls. Only black tar paper covered the roof. Piles of lumber and construction debris littered the surroundings. "So much promise going to waste," I muttered. "More than likely, nobody's home. Good, I want the beach all to myself anyway." I squinted at the lake. "All to myself?" I yanked my eyes away, but they were pulled back to the beach. I stared at it. "What in the world am I doing here?"

The answer came back to me: Pining away my life because Peter took off again. Or getting Tommy Gray's death straight in my mind thirty years too late?

The tranquil water still did not fool me one bit. It continued to be an untrustworthy enigma. How could it have been so heartless to kill my classmate? Throughout my adult life I continued to suspiciously deliberate the fickle water while sailing Lake Winnipesaukee and the New England coastline. So many times, the face of Tommy Gray peered back at me.

I scratched my head and cleared my throat. Spring was early this year - the same as 1959. Through the years when the snow began to clear, I wondered if that was the case back here on this beach - and every time I wondered that, a terrible Monday morning seemed to stop the beating of my heart. How long did I sit there that afternoon, picking up handfuls of sand, the color of Tommy's hair? The damp grains ran out between my ink-stained fingers. Some of it stuck. Indeed, the memory stuck.

Tommy Gray had always tried to hide the fact that he was looking at me, but that afternoon, I saw his round hazels peeking out of that mop of his - in the water.

I recalled the time he hid in the trees and watched me lying on the dock, playing with the minnows. I caught him at it, because I heard him humming *Mr. Sandman* along with me. Trapped in my mind, his face, clear as if he were alive, right there - right there in front of these forty-year-old eyes.

I stepped over to the beach then knelt down on what remained of eroded sand, pine needles, dried leaves, and streaks of black earth. I opened my sketchpad to a clean sheet then began to draw Tommy Gray. I went for chalks to create orbs of hazel peeping though jagged straw-colored strands raining upon his round face - but the chalks created an eerie colorless transparency. I could not clear it up or draw it out. Something I could not see was guiding my hand. The beach appeared on the sheet, but not in the sad shape it was right now. It appeared as it

27

Yesterday, Tommy Gray Drowned

existed that Sunday long ago when Tommy Gray drowned. And his face was half submerged in Echo Lake.

While struggling to figure out the meaning of this peculiar picture, my brain unexpectedly cleared. Images of utmost importance, long forgotten, struggled to make themselves known. Good heavens, was I relieved when the sensation eased. But sure as shootin', I wanted to know what was going on with me. Was I having a nervous breakdown because Peter took off? Was I sliding into senility or something?

Totally agitated, I folded up my sketchpad and pastel chalks and plodded back up the rutted lane. At the place where Tommy Gray's shack once stood, I drew the sorry excuse for a home as it appeared when he lived there. The crude structure sagged to one side, and the roofing paper had come loose in the March wind. When I finished, I hesitated. There was something about that place I just could not put my finger on.

I headed back to my car. Climbing over the rusted chain. I intended to leave, but then my footsteps veered off in the opposite direction. Down the country road a ways, I found myself standing in front of the location where in March 1959 Tommy Gray snatched several evening newspapers out of my paper bag. The lonesome stretch of road hadn't changed. I doubted if it had even been paved since then. The oak trees that framed both sides of the road had become bulky with age, and the wooden guardrail, which Mike Anderson leaned upon thirty years ago, was still there - although its usefulness if a vehicle were to ram into it was entirely doubtful.

A tidal wave of emotion swept over me, dislodging bitter tears of repressed grief that splintered the walls I had built to keep out reality. What could have been if Tommy didn't drown? If only I didn't lose his friendship. I should have made things right. I collapsed on a decaying tree stump.

Once again, my hand began to sketch. Bathed in amber light, Tommy and I were picking up runaway pages of the *Evening News*. My blue bike was lying on its side where I dropped it then raced after windswept newsprint. Its front tire pointed up towards the heavens.

Once again, frigid air bit my unprotected face and hot tears stung my frozen cheeks. My body felt so heavy, unable to move, burdened with life - burdened with Tommy Gray - burdened with Peter's absence. "Why do I always end up like this? Alone. Empty inside."

"Empty inside," came back from Echo Lake.

I jumped to my feet. "I have to get out of here!"

"Get out of here! Out of here…"

My fists clenched as I stiffened. "You're nothing!" I bellowed. "Just an echo!"

"Just an echo! An echo…"

"Sheesh," I huffed.

My stomach churned.

I glanced at my watch. "No wonder I'm such a freak. It's well after noon, and I haven't eaten a thing all day." Only a cup of coffee had sustained me on the journey from Brighton. "I better go into the village and see if I can get something to eat."

I trudged back to my car, got in, and turned it around. I started toward town. Half a mile down the road, my foot stomped on the brake. Tires squealed as my hands yanked the steering wheel to the right, veering into the graveyard that overlooked the lake and the backwash. Another place I was not intending to go - yet here I was. My car threaded through the overgrowth that used to be a horseshoe lane - once upon a time. Winding up nearly back at the road, the car stopped.

I sat there for a moment. "Humph." I got out of my car. With my sketchpad and pastel chalks chucked under my arm, I traipsed through overgrown thicket. Stepping over a shattered headstone, I was about to sit on the base of it when I caught sight of a black and yellow spider going about its business of weaving its first web of the season. Shivers pricked my flesh. "I hate spiders!" I backed off to a safe distance then sat on the base of an overturned headstone.

My hand instantly sketched the graveyard as the ten year old child inside me dictated - as it was thirty years ago: red geraniums; tiny American flags decorating graves of war dead; lush carpet of Sherwood green revealing the tracks of a hand mower. The smell of cut grass seemed to intoxicate me. Beer cans littered the grass at the edge of the woods.

"Huh? Beer cans? What on earth possessed me to draw those?" My face scrunched up and my shoulders slumped. "I can't make heads or tails of this - or any of the other sketches I drew, for that matter. Good heavens, my mind is mush…" I whipped the cover shut and got to my feet. I shook myself out. "That's it. I am out of here. I'm too pooped and hungry to think about this baloney one minute more."

DON PIERCE

The window of Pierce's Grocery Store mirrored my car as I drove up and parked. Glass shelves, stacked with cereal boxes, soda pop bottles, and cosmetics muddled the view of the inside. An American flag rumpled outside on the right front corner of the single-story building. Ivory paint, slapped on numerous times throughout the years, plus a neon sign seemed to be the only major differences. The store used to be federal blue, and the white block letters, outlined in black that once emblazoned the overhead facade, were now mere shadows beneath the paint.

I shut off the motor and sat there, unsure if I wanted to go in or not. "What if I run into somebody I used to know?" I chewed over how the people of this town had always been so hardhearted. "Maybe things have changed." I rolled my eyes. "Not at all optimistic about that." I remembered those two idiots who blasted their horn at me earlier. They were the first human contact I had in this hick town in more than twenty years.

My gnarling stomach put an end to my indecision. So I bit the bullet and avoided my reflection in the store window while getting out of my car. I tramped to the front step then stepped up to the door. My hand gripped the knob. I took a gutsy breath then turned it. I nudged open the door only to cling to the inside of the knob until the frame made contact with the doorjamb. A small brass bell tinkled ever so slightly overhead. With each indecisive step I took, floorboards tattled on me.

A white-haired clerk standing behind a vintage cash register peered over the rims of half-glasses at me. He was handing lottery tickets and change to a customer.

I pretended to look for something on a rack opposite the deli.

The customer turned and headed my way. His eyes pawed me, I could tell, prying, making assumptions as to who this strange female was and why she had the audacity to invade his private realm.

Relief sheeted over me when the bell jangled wildly and the door closed with a thud. I channeled my attention to the deli case. My eyes widened. That case was so meticulously arranged - just for the sole purpose of driving me crazy. I could have eaten one of everything in that case without a second thought.

The roly-poly clerk shuffled to the deli.

My gut squawked. I coughed to cover up the racket.

"What cain I git fer ya, young lady?" His voice was surprisingly mellow, fatherly - and distantly familiar.

"How about a cold cut sub?" I said. "Everything on it. Please. Hots, too. And lots of mayo. Oh, yeah, and one of those pickles in the jar over there."

"Ayah."

I squinted over the deli case at the benign old man fussing with my sandwich. I picked up on his soft humming. He seemed to be enjoying the task. His face was smooth, milky with age and lack of exposure to the elements. I bet if I touched his cheek, it would feel like satin - just like my father's did just after shaving and patting on spicy cologne. A hint of natural blush accentuated the tip and bridge of the clerk's nose. His friendly bearing made me feel instantly at home. Hey... I knew this guy! A bit shorter in stature... But then I was a kid the last time I saw him. Everyone looked bigger back then. Could it be that the same guy still owned this store? After all these years? Almost afraid to ask, I stammered, "Are you Don Pierce?"

"Shur am." He slurred his words. "Who's askin'?"

"Elizabeth Blair. I grew up here." My enthusiasm surprised me. "My maiden name's Spencer. I lived in the last house at the far end of town - close to the Fox Creek town line."

"Name sounds a bit familiah," he mused, eyeing me and then the ceiling. "Cain't seem ta place..."

"Sure you do!" I insisted. "I pedaled the *Evening News!*" That old dude just had to recognize me. "I rode a little blue bike and…"

"Well, by Jove, shur!" His face lit up, and there for a minute, I thought he was going to dance the jig. "Li'l 'Lizbeth, the papah girl! Well, I'll be. Shur, shur, I remembah ya. What braings ya 'round these here parts?"

I skirted the question: "Seein' how much the ol' town's changed since I left." No way was I ever going to divulge that the bothersome memory of a dead classmate lured me back to Echo Lake. Furthermore, discussing Peter was out of the question - that would certainly ruin the moment.

"Ever'thin's 'bout the same," Don said. "Out-o'-towners built themselves fancy houses up there bys the lake. That's 'bout it." He handed me the sandwich and winked. "Gonna draink somethin' wit that? Ya knowd, I still makes dem cherry cokes ya took to so."

My mouth dropped. Not only did the old geezer still make cherry cokes, but he also remembered I had a thing for them. "No kidding?"

He nodded.

"Well, whip one up for me, Don!"

With a quick thumbs-up and a wink of an eye, Don entrenched himself in formulating the vintage concoction at the same soda fountain he used way back when. A droll smile erupted on his impish face, which tickled my insides. Using plastic tongs, he plucked three cherries from a huge apothecary jar then dropped them into the coke. Fizz bubbled over the rim of the glass as he peeked at me over the rims of his half glasses. Mischief besmirched his pudgy wintry face then a hearty chuckle burst forth. He winked again then threw in two more cherries. More fizz. "Here ya go, Li'l 'Lizbeth. Special made fer ya." He slid the glass across the counter then anxiously wiped his hands on his starched white apron, awaiting my reaction.

Seizing the glass, I shrieked like a schoolgirl, "Thank you, thank you, very much, Don!" I chugged down several gulps. Effervescence inflated my cheeks and imbedded in the crevices of my throat. It bubbled up into my sinuses. My eyes watered. I hacked to clear my throat and managed "M-m-m." My fingers roughed up my nose then plowed moisture out of the corners of my eyes. "You still got the touch, Don."

Beaming with pride, he turned to clean up the deli counter. Bright red painted the tips of his ears.

I tossed a ten-dollar bill on the counter and said, "Sure is nice seeing you after all these years. I think I'll go out and sit in my car while I devour all this."

"Ayah," he said turning back to me. "Don't blame ya one iotah." His hands swiped across the front of his apron then he picked up the money. He jammed down the keys on the vintage cash register. The drawer spat out with a loud clang. He handed me my change, saying, "A corker of a day out there. Early sprang fer shur." He took a snow-white cotton handkerchief out of his back pocket and began to clean his half-glasses. I thought men didn't carry cloth handkerchiefs anymore. He squinted out the window and said, "Got yerself one o' dem snazzy ragtops out there, I see. Y'oughta roll back that there canvas 'n soak up the sunshine."

"I just might do that, Don." I gave a decisive nod. I took one last eyeful of him, implanting his image firmly into memory. I fully expected not to pass this way again for a very long time. "Take care of yourself."

"Nice chattin' wit cha, Li'l 'Lizbeth." He waved a fond farewell - just like royalty.

Totally psyched, I bubbled with glee when the bell over the door tinkled. As I hopped down the cement step onto the pavement, my candy apple red convertible glittered before me. I felt myself smiling. I had not felt this exuberant since before Peter left for Vietnam.

I lowered the white canvas top then made quick work of the sub and cherry coke. However, when it came to the succulent cherries, I savored each red orb. "A jillion calories each," I mused while lifting my face to the radiant sunshine. "Oh well…" Wallowing in the radiance, I felt full in my stomach and happy in my mind. Good ol' Don Pierce certainly made my day.

Contentment was short-lived, however, as like waves upon a stormy ocean, the sketches I had drawn rippled across my slumberous brain, urging me to retrieve the sketchpad from the back seat.

I flipped the pages, one by one: Tommy Gray's grave; Echo Lake; the shack where Tommy lived; the day the newspapers blew away; the decrepit graveyard as it appeared back in '59. No matter how much I mulled over the bizarre sketches, I could not make heads or tails of them. Why did I draw them?

I heaved a sigh then flipped to a clean sheet and ejected a chalk from the box of pastels. I molded Pierce's Grocery Store. But the year was 1959. A group of kids were loitering outside that day. Butch cuts. Pompadours. Ponytails tied in wispy scarves. Jeans. White tees. I still recalled some of their names; others reposed in the dark abyss that time had left behind. Odd how I remembered the day – Monday - the afternoon after Tommy Gray drowned. I had just gotten back to the center of town after lollygagging - as Mother labeled such actions - at Echo Lake. Rick Morton, seventeen at the time, was leaning nonchalantly against the front quarter panel of his black Dodge coupe. His legs were crossed at the ankles. Rolled-up blue jeans exposed white crew socks. His arms, folded across his chest, made his biceps bulge.

A voluptuous floozy with bleached stripes running through her teased blackened rat's-nest had slung herself supine over the hood of his car. She was staring at the heavens while chewing gum the same way a cow chews its cud. I squinted up at the sky. I saw nothing - only cloudless blue.

Kids of all ages surrounded Rick Morton who may have been a member of the volunteer fire department. I eavesdropped and was awestruck at graphic details of Sunday afternoon at Echo Lake where ice had only recently cleared. It seemed that Gerald Gray had just plucked his only son out of the water when Morton arrived. Tommy's eyes were glazed, his skin blue - except for crimson and purple splotches - evidence of poison sumac and the quick fix to stop the itching.

I lingered off to the side, my skinny body plagued with the horror of it all. As a child of ten, I learned a lot about death that April Monday in 1959. But that's how I learned just about everything. When unforeseen events in life smacked me in the face, secondhand information explained it away. My parents never discussed anything in front of me - although Mother usually beat her gums about her lot in life at Father who was off in another world.

Guess who was with Tommy Gray that day? Yup, Mike Anderson. Ironic, huh? Wherever that showoff went, some sort of catastrophe followed. He was the one who summoned help that came too late for Tommy Gray. He even admitted to Chief Briggs that he delayed running for help because he thought Tommy was playing games; after all, Tommy was a great swimmer; there was nothing to worry about.

Yet even Mike Anderson knew when Tommy stayed underwater too long. In which case Mike waded way out into the water, which was so painfully cold that he retreated to shore real quick. He searched the tree line and then behind the logs of the boat dock, hoping against hope that Tommy was hiding. No luck.

Panic struck Mike Anderson. He charged up the narrow lane to the red shack and pounded on the wobbly plywood door, screaming bloody murder, "Tommy's at the bottom of Echo Lake!"

Gerald Gray, a merchant marine, rammed open the door. Shoving Mike aside, Gerald made a mad dash to the beach.

Meanwhile, Mrs. Gray called Chief Briggs. Within moments, the siren blasted atop the roof of the fire station in the village.

The few people who were hanging around the town on that beautiful Sunday afternoon raced hell-bent for leather to Echo Lake. Among them was Rick Morton who arrived just in time to see Gerald Gray, dazed and half-frozen, slog out of the icy lake, the lifeless body of his son slung across his long arms. Over and over again, Gerald Gray lamented, "I couldn't find him... I just couldn't find him..."

Some guy, whose last name was Murphy, snatched Tommy away from Gerald and placed him face down on the sand. Frantically, Murphy pumped Tommy's chest. Lots of water came out, but it was too late. There was no bringing Tommy Gray back.

As customary in those days, the siren blew continuously for ten minutes to let townsfolk know that one of their own had accidently died. The plaintive wail never reached my ears. As it was, I had gone off to Worcester with Father and Brother that Sunday. Father had to drop off some tools he needed at a job site the next day. I got home after darkness spread over the Town of Echo Lake.

Mother never uttered one single word about what had happened, so I knew nothing until I got to school the next morning and Mrs. King spoke those heart-stopping words: "Yesterday, Tommy Gray drowned."

Yesterday, Tommy Gray Drowned

COUSIN RUTH

"Bethie? Bethie Spencer?"

Bethie? Nobody called me by that name - well, except for Peter. Bleary eyed, I looked up at a slender, slightly graying brunette. Her shoulder-length hair was combed into a loose wavy style and large mint green glasses framed her soft coppery eyes. Pearl pink lipstick tinted a small but sensual mouth. The spunky forty-something-year-old was wearing no other makeup - she really didn't need any more.

"You're really Bethie Spencer? Aunt Joanie and Uncle Bob's daughter?"

"Yeah, yeah," I muttered. "That's me. Although my last name is Blair now." I didn't even try to hide my expression, which demanded to know who she thought she was bugging me like that?

"I'm Ruth! Your Aunt Irene's daughter! Gosh, I couldn't believe it when Don told me you were out here!"

I studied her face. Family resemblance was distinct: the nose; the wide-set, walnut-colored eyes…well, hers were copper-colored. She had the dark arched eyebrows that made family members look angry even when that was not the case.

Even though Aunt Irene - my father's sister - lived in Echo Lake, there had been little contact when I was a kid. Mother did not get along with Aunt Irene - or Uncle Bob, for that matter. Contact ceased entirely after my family moved to Boston.

But as it was, Cousin Ruth was several years older than me, so we were not meant to be close anyways, because an unwritten law back in those days dictated that one did not hang

39

around with anyone older or younger than oneself. Time, the great equalizer, now put a new spin on things.

"You still live around here?" I asked.

"Guess I'm destined to live here all my life," Ruth said whimsically. "I married Wally Murphy, you know. Remember him?"

I thought for a moment. I shook my head no.

She gave a light one-shoulder shrug. "So what about you? What brings you here?"

"Just visiting," I said. Imagine that, I thought, I actually ran into someone related to me. All at once, I felt alive. Connected. I perked up. "Thought it was about time to check out the old metropolis."

Ruth giggled. "Metropolis, yeah, right." She pointed to the sketchpad on my lap. "I like your drawing." Her finger began to wag back and forth. "Hey, I know those kids! Rick Morton's the one leaning on the car. And that was his latest flame sprawled on the hood. Now, what was her name... She came from Milford... I forget. Anyways, it sure didn't take Rick long to replace Linda Benson after she ran off. A hot item, Rick and Linda... Always thought someday they'd get married. Just wasn't in the cards, I guess. Rick hitched up with a widow from Fox Creek - name's Jenny - about ten years ago. Been separated for quite some time, so I hear. Maybe even divorced by now for all I know. That overgrown teenager is not about to settle down. I don't think he ever did an honest day's work in his entire life. A real wil' chil', I tell ya. You know, Rick Morton still wears black penny loafers - complete with pennies let me add - and jeans turned up at the cuffs to show off his socks - just like in your drawing there. See that tee shirt with cigarettes rolled up in the sleeves?"

"He still does that?" I asked.

Ruth nodded. "And combs his hair into that same silly pomp, too. It's so hilarious. His hair is much too thin now to stay put. He goops it up wicked bad, stiff as a board. I feel like telling that overgrown teenybopper, 'Hey, get over it!'" Ruth giggled, sounding very much like a teenager herself.

Before I could get a word in edgewise, she babbled on: "Say! Why don't you come over to my place? We'll have ourselves a nice glass of ice tea and catch up on old times. I know Wally will love to see you again. Whaddaya say?"

I thought for a moment; nobody was waiting at home for me. So I said, "Sounds like fun."

"Mind if I hitch a ride?" She skipped around the other side of my car, not waiting for an answer. "I walked down here - it's such a terrific day, you know."

"Hop in," I said, even though she was already in the car and buckling up.

"I love this car!" she said as I backed away from Pierce's Grocery Store. "I was going to tell you that before going into Pierce's, but I noticed you was sleeping. If I had known who you were, I would have woken you up right then and there."

I wished she had; then I would not have had those fleeting visions that messed with my mind; visions that reared up again as I drove back toward the lake. It was so hard to block out the visions; especially when we passed the rundown graveyard, which I drew earlier.

A short distance from there, Ruth motioned for me to turn into a driveway that led up to a modest ranch house, white with brick-red shutters and trim. The grounds were impeccably groomed. Obviously, Cousin Ruth and her husband were avid gardeners. Getting out of my car, I sucked in the fragrance of multicolored hyacinths and yellow daffodils drifting on the late afternoon breeze. "Nice," I said. "I can't get over your front lawn. How incredibly green and lush for this early in the spring."

A plump robin swooped down and then cavorted across the gentle slope. Abruptly it stopped and plucked a worm out of the ground. Its victim stretched thin then sprang from the ground like a rubber band and wrapped around the yellow beak, writhing wildly. The battle was lost when the robin gave a jerk of its head and choked down the succulent morsel. Puffing up its red breast, it momentarily savored the victory. Then once again, the robin cavorted across the lawn in search of another victim.

Yesterday, Tommy Gray Drowned

As Cousin Ruth showed me around her house, I speculated that she had nothing better to do than to clean. The colonial style furniture looked as if it just came off a showroom floor even though the style was decades old. And then there was the fact that the place never knew the touch of a child.

On the back porch, Ruth invited me to sit on a wooden glider. She disappeared inside as I surveyed the backyard. A white wrought iron loveseat invited visitors to linger in shaded sunlight and renew themselves among azaleas, rhododendrons, and other lush greenery. Songbirds filled the air. I was surprised to see, off to the right of the backyard, a satellite dish aimed towards the western sky. Echo Lake was not lost in a time warp after all.

Ruth hollered from the kitchen: "So, what do you think about the town?"

I hollered back, "I noticed a couple of changes."

"Like what?"

Put on the spot, I did some quick thinking. "Well… That mill block across the street from Pierce's Grocery is gone."

"The town condemned that fire trap," Ruth said, coming out of the house with a tray in her hands. Her voice moderated. "For decades, all kinds of disgusting vermin and termites helped wreck that place." She set a tray on the table near the window. "Nobody wanted to live there anymore. It was awfully ramshackle when my family rented a flat there. Remember? Thank goodness, we didn't live there very long. That was when we first came to town, you know."

Ice cubes cracked as Ruth poured iced tea into two tall glasses and garnished them with lemon wedges. "Anyhow, one day, a bunch of chuck-wheats got to goofing off with matches and torched the place. Half of it went up in flames in a heartbeat, so town fathers decided to tear down the rest before somebody got hurt. Belonged to the town anyway. Mill owners hadn't forked over taxes in years." She handed me a glass and pointed to the sugar bowl.

I shook my head no. "I went to the lake," I said. "Looks like nobody swims there anymore."

Ruth shook her head. "Echo Lake supplies the town's water now. Besides, most of the land around the lake is privately owned. Posted, too. You can't put your big toe in the water even if you wanted to." She stroked her chin with her thumb and forefinger. "There's a public beach up past the Fern Cove Waterfall. Everyone swims at the Cove now. Isn't that the dumbest thing you ever heard? Fern Cove dumps straight into Echo Lake - so much for a clean water supply."

"Does seem kind of dumb." I said. I changed the subject. "Hey, remember when we used to swim at the beach down past the Gray's shack? That was such a nice spot."

Ruth tisked. "Sure is a mess there now."

"So I suppose nobody puts the raft out in the lake like they used to every spring," I said.

Ruth giggled. "Cannon-balling off the raft was such a hoot." Her merriment was fleeting, replaced by a frown. She took a whimsical breath. "A raft hasn't been out there in ages. Boat dock's gone, too. Got all rotten and waterlogged. Little by little, the whole thing caved into the water."

A door slammed. Ruth was instantly on her feet. "Wally's home!"

The screen door screeched open then slapped shut. I could tell the worn-out spring had been recently replaced - I had heard similar sounds when I was a kid after Father replaced the springs on the backdoor. New ones took a while to loosen up.

Ruth reappeared, husband in tow. "Wally, you remember my cousin Elizabeth, don't you?"

Wally stood about five-foot-eight with the build of a carpenter, which he was. His hair was nearly all gray. His laughing root-beer-colored eyes and wide toothy grin made me take to him immediately.

"Well, don't this beat all," he said. "I certainly do." He shook my hand so enthusiastically that I swore even my brains jangled. "You're that skinny little runt who delivered the *Evening News* all over town every afternoon, rain or shine." His teasing voice was deep and raspy. "We could almost tell the time of day by when you dropped off the paper."

"Yeah, I was like the mailman all right," I said dryly. "Mother insisted customers get their reading material no matter what, each and every day." I bit my tongue to stop from adding: Worst part about it, most people in this dumb town probably never even read the paper. And if I wasn't home at the precise time, which only Mother covertly determined, all Hades broke loose. Why I had to go home so soon was beyond me. I always ended up alone in my room anyway. But I did as I was told - or else.

I remembered one day, I was skipping rope in the yard - all by myself - thinking about a bunch of girls I saw earlier on my paper route. They were skipping rope, too. How come they didn't have to deliver papers or do so something to earn extra pennies like I did? They played while I worked - yet I was the one poked fun at or completely ignored. Their clothes were worse than mine, plus they played in the street because the place their parents rented had no yard. At least my family owned our house and I had a yard to jump rope in - all by myself.

"So where ya livin' these days?"

Wally's voice shook me out of my feel-sorry-for-myself moment. I cleared my throat then said, "Brighton. With Peter, my husband. We have a daughter. Julie. She and her husband Ken live in Cohasset."

"Man, it sure is great seein' ya after all this time. Ruthie and I are just about the last of the ol' gang still hangin' 'round these parts."

"You got a gorgeous place here," I said.

"We're kind of fond of it," he said. "Built it ourselves about fourteen years ago." He spied my fingers twisting my wedding band. "What's your better-half up to? I'd like to meet the man."

"Vietnam."

"Nam?" He and Ruth exchanged puzzlement.

"Trying to locate MIAs," I muttered, gazing at my ring. "Peter was missing in action himself in the late sixties, for several years, so he feels pretty strongly about MIAs."

I hated to think about Peter. It was my way of punishing him for leaving me again. And yet the emptiness that gnawed at my gut seemed to punish me more than it did him.

"Mm-mm, tough job," Wally said. "Pete must be quite a guy." Wally's brows knitted as his lips pursed.

"Quite a guy," I echoed. I drew a deep breath. "Anyway… I got bored at home, all by myself, and so here I am." I looked at my watch. "But, I really should get going. It's getting late and I don't like driving after dark."

"Oh, stay for supper," Ruth begged. She looked like a child who just had her lollipop taken away.

"I really can't," I said, lifting myself off the glider. "You should've seen the cold cut sandwich Don Pierce made for me." I chuckled and rubbed my tummy. "And the cherry coke was incredible!"

"We're lucky to still have that old dude hangin' in there," Wally said. "He's a bit of a father figure to everyone in these parts."

"He never married?" I asked.

Wally shook his head. "My Pop says Don got jilted shortly after buying the store - Lord only knows when that was."

The three of us laughed. Then I said, "Too bad. Don is such a great guy."

"Listen, why don't you come back sometime?" Ruth pleaded. "Stay a few days, okay?" She looked at me, expectantly. "I'd love to have the company. And I'm sure we can get ourselves into some sort of hot water."

I didn't think I'd ever be back. Funny thing though, I got the distinct impression Ruth and her husband really understood me - and I understood them. That was somehow overpowering. I felt kind of sad to leave them - like I was awakening from a pleasant dream. But it was someone else's dream. So I had to go. But then unexpected words poured from my lips: "I just might do that! Yeah, I will! Real soon!"

Yesterday, Tommy Gray Drowned

DREAMS

Staying awake on the drive back to Brighton was next to impossible. Not only had the early spring sunshine and fresh air zonked me, but the return to Echo Lake had also caused old memories and new knowledge to stray across my brain like phantoms. I fretted about that. I should have been happy about running into Don Pierce and Ruth. She and Wally were so clearly genuine, so stable and straightforward. I had a nice time with all of them.

As it was, by the time I hit my bed, my haggard body deflated like a punctured balloon. And like the air that transfigures a flaccid balloon into a thing of beauty, my absent spouse was not there to fulfill me. I missed him so much and yearned to tell him about my day. "Come back, Peter. Please, come...back..."

...Nearing Minot's Ledge...tucked safely under his arm... I snuggle in the safe harbor of his muscular nearness, soaking up his warmth and strength. Swells rock the boat. Our tee shirts are almost dry from the tropical rain that drenched us as we sailed out of Plymouth. I gaze up at him manning the helm with all the magnificence of the greatest of sea captains. Nobody can hurt me.

Minot's Light beckons. Its rhythmic beam appears to be an extended arm: Here... Here... This way... I am here...

Gee, I thought Minot's Light signaled, I love you... I love you...

I blink. So hard to see... Hazy... What's that? Is that...Tommy Gray?

Yesterday, Tommy Gray Drowned

Yellowy mist engulfs him. Come... He gestures. ...here.

My mind delights. It is Tommy!

A petite maiden materializes. She stands beside Tommy. Breezes tousle her hair, gold as sunbeams. The blueness of southern oceans infuses her eyes.

I blink. Is that me with Tommy Gray? No... I am here with Peter. That is not me. My eyes are not blue. And I am so much older... But age does not matter, because I am in the arms of my beloved. No, wait... My arms are empty. I am at the helm! Peter? Where did you go?

Storm clouds boil on the horizon. The sky blackens. Winds bluster. Titanic waves break portside. The boat pitches side to side...on the brink of capsizing... Peter! Oh no, I cannot hear my own voice. Peter! Come back! I can't do this alone! I slump against the helm. Oh Peter... Please come back...

Footsteps... Someone is coming up the galley way? Peter? I can't see... Rick? Rick Morton?

His unblinking bat-like eyes, black as deep space, are menacing, stupid. Still the neighborhood bully.

My alarm turns to laugher. Get a life, fruitcake! Nobody dresses that way anymore! I laugh and laugh and laugh... What? Is Rick stomping towards me? He is! His alcohol-fueled rage matches the raging squall. His finger spikes the softness of my upper chest, over and over again. Ow! That hurts! What is wrong with you?

His twisted mouth vomits foulness, but the tempest drowns out his words. His lips purse and then move no more. His body ripples, turns glassy. Raven hair fades to white - white as rime snow atop Mount Washington. Black eyes dilate, age, turn to blue-gray. Wretchedness sets in.

My hand covers my mouth. Gerald Gray! I track his empty gaze to the horizon. Tommy and a pretty girl.

Gerald's eyes ice, skewering Tommy...and the girl.

Fear cloaks Tommy and the girl. Phoof! The girl is gone! Tommy lingers, his face half-hidden in the water. Phoof! Tommy is gone!

Wait! Who is that? Tommy's mother? She's been there all the time? She's turning. Becky is with her. They're smiling. At me? Yes. At me! Benevolence intensifies Mrs. Gray's chocolate eyes.

Gerald Gray stretches out from the boat, elongated, rubbery, fibrous.

I grab for him. Leave them alone! I can't pull him away!

Gerald slips through my grasp. He slithers toward Tommy's mother and sister.

Stop!

Mrs. Gray arches backwards, pulling Becky with her. They hasten off beyond the horizon.

His decrepit form detaches from the boat and dissolves into the belching torrent.

Waves crest, sheering off like pages of newspapers in the raw March wind. The halyard clanks against the mast, metal against metal, again and again. The forty-foot sailboat is nothing but a plaything to Neptune. I quake. I cannot control the reefed main!

Who is that on the bow? Don Pierce? Yes! He's smiling at me - and waves like royalty. The corner of my mouth lifts.

The tumult lessens.

Peter's arm enwraps me. He is so warm. I am so cold.

I am a child. Safe. My cheek nestles into his shirt. Gross! The fabric is rough and acrid! I peer up at him. His eyes, cold and vacant, stare off into the distance. Slowly, he faces me. A black, lecherous grin. His breath rattles...heaves... You're not Peter! Get away from me, Warren Squire! Get away from me! Get...

"...Away from me! Get away from me!" I bolted upright in my bed, gasping for air as if submerged too long. My heart thumped like a base drum. Flogged by reverberating visions of that abysmal nightmare, I swiped my face. The salty moisture seeping into my mouth was my own sweat. I reached for Peter, but he wasn't there. And the bed was still made. I never did get under the covers.

Yesterday, Tommy Gray Drowned

I shook myself awake, my eyes scouring the bedroom. I squinted at the clock on the nightstand. Midnight. I fell back on the pillow and lay there for a while, wide awake. I sat up. "Where's my sketchpad and chalks?" I had to have them that instant. I groaned. "They're in the car." I fell back on the pillow. "No way am I going to go sneaking out of this house at this hour. That is ridiculous."

I lay there another while. I turned my head and squinted at the clock on the nightstand. 1:32 a.m. I scratched my head. "I am never going to get back to sleep."

Next thing I knew, I was groping about the darkness for my blue furry robe and fuzzy slippers - and of all things, I was calling to them, "Where are you guys? Ah, here you are." I put them on then stole out the back door, resembling a funky moppet from some kid's show I saw on TV. "Hope the neighborhood skunk doesn't catch me slinking about in the middle of the night in this get-up."

Jostling the key into the passenger-side door, I lifted the handle. "Ugh!" My middle fingernail bent backwards. The handle snapped back as I let go and stuffed my finger into my mouth. I did the soft-shoe across a blacktop stage, which wasn't even spotlighted by the moon. I restrained unholy vociferation while my tongue replanted the nail on its bed. My entire finger stung like the dickens!

Managing to get the door half open, I bashed my butt against it then snatched the sketchpad and pastel chalks out from behind the backseat. I attempted to close the door without making a sound - why I was concerned about that at this point was beyond me. I supposed I feared any further commotion at that ungodly hour would surely alert the neighbor's Pekinese.

Well, wouldn't you know, the door didn't close tight. I rammed my hip against it. The entire car rocked, but the door refused to latch. "Sheesh!" I rubbed my hipbone. "Black and blue by morning, that's for sure."

I scurried back into the house then kicked off my slippers and curled up on the beige recliner. The street lamp and LCD of the VCR clock on top of the TV illuminated the living room. No more light was necessary; my hands possessed their own sight. A new sketch emerged - Warren Squire's house. My stomach turned. Squire had not crossed my mind in years. I shuddered, trying to avoid the memory of him, but...

When I was a child, Warren Squire and his wife lived next door. They were friendly with Mother and Father, but that relationship came and went as swiftly as others. Protecting her self-serving opinions was more important to Mother than relationships, rolling with the punches and enjoying fresh experiences.

Was Squire still around? I wondered. Well, it didn't matter one way or another. Casting aside Squire and that dead-end neighborhood, I abhorred everything I tolerated there.

One by one, my right hand turned back the pages of the sketchpad. My left hand fingered the necklace and crucifix Peter gave me the day we married. "What in the world do these sketches mean? Pierce's Grocery Store? Ah, good ol' Don. That forgotten graveyard with the beer cans?" My teeth clenched with the thought of that nasty spider. "Tommy Gray and me, trying to catch runaway newspapers... I hate that day. The dilapidated red shack? As bad as it was, I wish it was still there. Tommy's transparent face half in the lake, half out? Geez, he was the best swimmer around. How could he have possibly drowned? His grave. Why hasn't my brain put you to rest, Tommy? After all these years?"

I shivered. But was I chilled from the night? All the way to my toes? Or was the chill more than just a chill? I reached for the afghan draped across the back of the recliner and then raised the footrest. I covered my legs with the afghan and stretched it up under my chin. I propped the sketchpad on my lap. The chill dissipated.

My eyes delighted in Tommy Gray: his round face, those hazel eyes, that unruly sandy mop cut straight across his forehead with all the precision of unsharpened household scissors. Forever bound within the fathomless reaches of my mind, his voice seemed to be singing to me: Mr. Sandman, bring me a dream...

Yesterday, Tommy Gray Drowned

Warm breath, like gentle surf murmuring within a pink conch shell, caressed my ear. Sweet words of passion: I'll never stop loving you, Bethie. I love you more now than I ever did before. Oh, my sweet morning eyes, I need you so much...

Oh, Peter...

Fingertips touch. His flesh cools mine, the burning, the yearning.

Intoxicating waves of ecstasy swell within me.

Gentle rise and fall brings him to me and me to him.

At the ebb we lie in each other's arms.

Gone away the world...

EMMA LAROSA

At seven thirty in the morning, hazel eyes penciled on my sketchpad lying on my lap coaxed me back to wakefulness. I smiled at the image of Tommy Gray, comforted by his serene vigil. "Somehow, our friendship goes on, huh, Tommy? Just like before. It's one of unspoken understanding, unacknowledged friendship."

I raised my knees and propped the sketchpad against my thighs. I touched his image. It felt warm, tingly, and I was okay with that, okay with the sense of personality that came from his image. "If only this paper were flesh, Tommy. So I might truly touch you."

As the early light flowed through the window, I skimmed through the sketches. Frustrated because I still could not figure out what they meant, I started to push the afghan aside. Abruptly I stopped. I fingered the afghan's dusty rose yarn. Emma LaRosa crocheted this afghan for me last Christmas. "Maybe she can help me sort out these weird sketches."

The air seemed to thicken around me. It was a very agreeable sensation - like sitting in Emma's kitchen where bread was baking.

Wasting time until a decent hour to call Emma, I took a shower and primped. I was being foolish; most elderly people, including Emma LaRosa, got up early. I concluded that my delay was coming more from self-consciousness than the clock. What if Emma thought my sketches were really whacked out? And me, too, for that matter?

Yesterday, Tommy Gray Drowned

Life certainly changed the day I met Emma LaRosa - and it did again, a little over a year ago. We had eaten lunch at Julio's Ristorante with Emma's daughter Margi, Emma's daughter-in-law Janice, and my Julie. Man, it sure was cold that January day. We had just left the restaurant and parted ways with Janice. Just then, down the street, some contemptible psycho decided to rob the Brighton Savings Bank. Emma and I were walking ahead of Julie and Margi. It was Emma and I who got caught square in the crossfire.

"Stop," the cop had barked. "Put your gun down!"

Gunshots! A bullet pinged off the parking meter! Excruciating pain in my gut!

I opened my eyes. Julie's terrorized face was looking down at me. I was lying on her lap. I felt a single teardrop spatter my cheek and then nothing but darkness after that.

I found out later that the fleeing robber had smacked head on into Emma. She sustained serious head injuries. For weeks, wicked black eyes, which turned into dreadful yellow, masked her face.

Anyways, the bandit's gun flew out of his hand and upon impact with the sidewalk, misfired. The aimless bullet took down the cop who was in hot pursuit of the robber.

Thank goodness, Janice was still down the street when it all went down. She was standing outside her car, rummaging through her pocketbook for her keys. Hearing the fracas, she sought us out, only to discover Julie sitting on the sidewalk cradling me on her lap; Margi was cradling Emma on her lap. Janice spotted the robber slithering to his the gun. She got to it first and aimed it straight at that robber. "Stop!" she bellowed. "Stay down or I'll shoot!"

That bank robber was not about to take a threat from a hundred-fifteen-pound woman seriously. Nope. He stumbled to his feet then lunged at her. Little did he know she was a black belt. One decisive kick to his groin put him in the hospital for several days. Later, he was arraigned at bedside, but of course, he plea-bargained, which meant the case never did go to court. Not long after that, his lawyer came up with some legal snafu that put the bank robber out on the streets again. Can you beat that? As it happened, a couple months later, the robber got shot dead robbing a convenience store - but not before taking out an innocent customer. Unbelievable.

Well, Emma and I almost didn't make it either. My mind still belches with the memory of it all.

After the ordeal, the two of us appreciated life more than ever. Relationships with family and friends intensified. That's when Peter showed up in the doorway of my hospital room. I had missed him so much - for so many, many years – that I didn't believe it was really him. Surely my eyes were deceiving me. I blinked, convinced that I was losing my mind. The slightly graying, clean-cut apparition was wearing a pale yellow oxford shirt open at the neck and a gold-brown v-neck button-down sweater. Creases sliced across the lap of his brown pants from the plane trip from Virginia where he had seen news coverage of the robbery on television. A tan topcoat was slung over his arm - later I found out that a prosthetic hand was underneath that topcoat. The stainless steel appliance replaced the hand he had lost in Nam.

Peter had spent four years in the Cambodian mountains, before being discovered. He was taken back to a VA hospital in Virginia where several lingering maladies impeded the return of his memory. To this day he still can't recall one single thing about Nam or how he lost his hand. But he eventually remembered me - that's the most important thing of all. Unfortunately for the both of us, he was afraid my life had moved on without him. He almost didn't come to Brighton after hearing about the bank robbery. He was so worried I might not want a cripple hanging around my neck. That didn't bother me at all. He came back to me; that's all that mattered.

His eyes pledged that we would never be apart again. Well, guess what? Here we go all over again! He's off to Vietnam and here I am alone – again.

I glanced at the clock. Nine-thirty. I called Emma.

Yesterday, Tommy Gray Drowned

"Well now, hi there, Elizabeth. Haven't heard from you in quite some time. Julie called yesterday. She tells me Peter is off to Vietnam. Any word from him?"

"No," I brooded, wanting to complain that Peter was always thinking of everybody else and not me. It's just not right.

"Now don't go fretting your pretty little head about Peter. He is just fine. All those high mucky-mucks with him are guarded to the hilt and that will keep him safe. Plus with reporters and security people buzzing about all the time, nobody will dare mess with any one of them. They probably don't get a moment's rest."

"I guess so," I muttered. "It's just that... Well, I wish he didn't go back there."

"Can't blame you for feeling that way," Emma said. "You two were separated far too long the first time. Aargh! Such a dreadful war... Still, we are all so proud of Peter. Someone has got to find out where all those missing young men ended up; they deserve to be home where they belong."

I winced. "How in the world will he and those Congressmen ever find all those MIAs? After all these years?"

"To top it off, identifying what's left of those poor souls is going to be next to impossible," Emma said. "It's all just too sad."

I kicked myself for being so self-centered. Truly shameful. Others needed Peter right now. Yet a tremendous hole existed in my heart where only he belonged. More than life itself, I needed his warmth, his touch, that silly grin of his. The sight of him, the sound of his voice, the smell of him always made me feel better. If only I could tell him about my bizarre rumblings in Echo Lake, my bizarre sketches. He'd help me put it all into perspective. I just knew he would. He looked at things much more logically than me.

"Elizabeth? Are you there?"

"Uhm, yeah. I'm here, Em. Say listen, if you're not too busy, is it all right if I drop over for a few minutes?"

"Why certainly, dear. You come right on over. I will put on a pot of coffee." Emma sounded so thrilled to have my company - I hoped to live up to her expectations.

"And don't eat a thing," Emma added. "I am just about to pop a sausage and spinach calzone into the oven. I will put some extra cheese in it, just the way you like it."

I laughed. "How can I resist?"

That feisty lady was going to be scurrying about her kitchen, cleaning things that didn't need to be cleaned up until the last the moment I got there. Everything must be as perfect as humanly possible. Her spunk was legendary and everybody loved her cooking. Her spirit continually awed and inspired me, not to mention others. I will never forget her words to Peter just before Margi wheeled her out of my hospital room: "Through all these empty years, your family never stopped needing you. Nothing has changed that, so go ahead, throw all those self-doubts and fears of yours to the wind. You are home now."

Yesterday, Tommy Gray Drowned

PURPOSE

Just before 11:30, I steered my car onto a tree-lined street bordered by awakening privet hedges and postage-stamp lawns. The house that Emma lived in was also in Brighton, about a mile from my place. Her husband Seth passed away about two years ago, shortly before Julie and I met Emma. He and Emma were married for over fifty-two years. Everyone said Seth was quite a guy with easygoing charm and looks to match. I wished I had known him.

Scores of red and yellow tulips welcomed visitors to the LaRosa property while numerous rose bushes had yet to stir from their winter hibernation. When I got out of my car, the delicious aromas escaping the Italian kitchen just about bowled me over.

I tapped on the back door then nudged it open. "Em? It's me. Elizabeth."

"Come in, come in," came a cheerful yip.

I went in, wishing Emma was more concerned about unlocked doors. She never worried about anything. She refused to be worried. If something happened, well, time had a way of fixing it as it was intended to be fixed.

I rounded the corner to the kitchen. Emma was putting the finishing touches on the table covered with a starched ecru tablecloth, one of many she had crocheted through the years. I couldn't imagine my bungling fingers doing something so creative. She was humming airily, totally engrossed in the task at hand, seemingly without a care in the world. Her serene face bloomed with beauty that only age and love could sculpt. It didn't take a philosopher to recognize that her task was a labor of love. Her ebony eyes, faded with the years to a greenish-brown, sparkled behind silvery-blue bifocals. Her salt-and-pepper permed hair had been roller-set at the hairdresser's on Thursday. A pale blue apron, emblazoned with black-faced sunflowers, shielded her green-print dress. She smelled like a host of honeysuckle blossoms when she hugged me.

"Look at this sumptuous feast," I said, my arm arcing over the table. There's enough food here to feed ten people." I shook my head. "I don't know about you, Em. I don't think you'll ever change."

"And why should I?" she said, her chin taut and levitated. "I am happiest when my hands and mind are busy. It makes me feel useful and keeps my mind off my troubles." Her infectious enthusiasm made those around her forget their own troubles and I was no exception.

Needless to say, I stuffed my face. "Mmm, mmm, Em! This calzone is delicious!" I licked my fingertips, slurping, "You ought to open a restaurant!"

"Well, thank you, dear."

And then what do you know? She leaned over towards me and offered more salad. Big surprise, huh? Well, by this time, I definitely had to beg off. "I can't eat another bite. But you know what? Write down the recipe for that calzone and I'll practice making it. I'll surprise Peter when he gets home. He'll have a heart attack when he sees I actually cooked."

Emma laughed. She told me once that life had taught her to laugh and not to take herself so seriously. Moaning and groaning didn't do any good anyway. I should have taken heed of that.

She eyed me up and down. "I don't think you are eating enough, dear. You must come over and eat here while Peter is away." She knew he did most of the cooking - since I was known to burn peanut butter and jelly sandwiches. Well, I was never much into cooking anyways. Maybe that's because Mother detested the kitchen and that rubbed off on me. Although it was quite interesting how much Julie loved to cook. With Julie and Emma spurring me on, I had to admit I was making moderate progress in the kitchen.

"Don't worry about me eating," I said, waving her off. "I'm doing okay. You don't see me wasting away to nothing, do you?"

Emma ignored the question. "I see you brought your drawings." Her eyes were glued to my sketchpad leaning against the leg of the table.

Merriment collided with stark reality - it was so easy to become distracted by her zest for life and culinary delights. Still, I wished to remain in the safe harbor she so expertly created and not trash it all over Peter, Tommy Gray, and a bunch of sketches.

I pushed back my plate. "I didn't know anyone else to go to, Em. I sort of figured that you and I... Well, after that awful bank robbery and all... Maybe we can put our heads together, because something is happening that's making me crazy." My whole body seemed to sag, which included the muscles in my face where only seconds before delight was plastered all over it. My hands were clasped so tight my knuckles turned white. Stress turned to nausea, twirling the room. Suddenly I wished I hadn't eaten so much.

"Well, for heaven's sake, dear, I am glad you came to see me." She looked worried.

But Em never worries about anything, I told myself.

Her breath quickened. Her chest heaved.

Suddenly, it dawned on me that my elderly friend might not be capable of handling my problems. Coming here had been a bad idea.

But then she said, "I hope I can help. What is the matter?"

I hesitated, peering sideways at her. Something inside me told me she was okay with this. I picked up my sketchpad and flipped the cover. "This is the grave of one of my fourth-grade classmates. His name was...er...is..." I swallowed hard. "...Tommy Gray. He drowned...in Echo Lake."

"Uh-huh." Emma pulled her chair closer to mine for a better view. "Julie told me you went back to your hometown."

"I haven't been back there in more than twenty years."

Yesterday, Tommy Gray Drowned

"Most people want to go back to where they grew up - sometime or another," Emma said.

"I never wanted to." I shrugged. "There must be something wrong with me. But you know? Right after Peter left for Nam, something began to bug me about Echo Lake; and now, for the life of me, I still can't figure it out."

Emma examined the sketch, her eyelids wrinkling into mere slits. Her lashes looked like fuzzy little caterpillars. She tilted her head this way then that way. "You went to the boy's grave first?"

"Yeah," I replied. "I was standing there, looking down at the marker; and all of a sudden, I got this weird sensation to sketch it. Look. Crabgrass has taken over the gravesite and the marker is stained; yet you can still see it ever so clearly - even his name, see? But look over here, Em. His father is buried here. He died ten years after Tommy. Look at his marker. You can't read the name or the date, which is actually quite clear. I tried to make it readable, but something got in the way. That part of the sketch is smeared on purpose and I had nothing to do with it."

"Oh, my." Reverence shadowed her voice as Emma tapped her index finger on her upper lip. Her brows were furrowed. Fixated on the illegible marker, she asked, "You sure you didn't move your hand, dear? Perhaps the wind smudged the chalk…"

"No, Em," I huffed, chiseling my fingers into the pages and flipping to the next page. "This is the beach where Tommy Gray drowned. Again, I felt as if something took over my hand and drew this sketch. See how nice the scene looks? The white sandy beach? The boat dock off to the left? It's private property now and has gone to hell - pardon my French. My cousin Ruth still lives just outside the Village of Echo Lake, not far from the lake; and she says the boat dock rotted away a long time ago. Em! This is how the beach looked in 1959!"

"How come the boy's face is half in the water, half out?"

I winced. "Beats me." I waved my palms in midair. "Why on earth did I draw Tommy like that? It doesn't make a lick of sense. And look at his face."

"It is hazy," Emma said. "Not much color."

"Come on, Emma. You've seen lots of my sketches. Nothing ever comes out like this."

She silently concurred.

It bothered me that she was so calm. Her reality was different from mine - I knew that – so maybe she saw no reason to be worried. On the other hand, I thought I had good cause to be worried. These sketches were weird.

We deliberated the sketch for several moments then glanced up at one another. Both of us were stumped.

I flipped the page. "Look at this next picture, Em. Tommy Gray lived in this run-down shack thirty years ago. It was a stone's throw from the lake. But it's gone now. Torn down." My voice got louder and more urgent. "The site is all overgrown and saplings grow at will. There's no way I remember all the details you see in this sketch."

"Now don't go getting yourself upset, dear." Emma patted my hand. "There has to be some sort of explanation."

I gazed at her wrinkled ivory hand, gnarled by thickening arthritic joints, resting upon mine. How many individuals did this weathered hand comfort through the years? I looked up at her face and met her eyes. I smiled thinly then turned the page. "A month before Tommy Gray drowned – it was March - he snatched some newspapers out of my paper bag and the wind blew them to kingdom come. This is where it happened; and this sketch shows that very day." I flipped the page. "Here's another sketch - a graveyard that overlooks the lake."

"Well, that seems like a nice spot - except for those beer cans strewn all over the place."

I was pleased that Emma noticed the oddity as quickly as I did when I drew them. "That graveyard is not like that anymore," I said. "It's not kept up at all."

"What a shame," Emma said, shaking her head.

"Gravestones are overturned and shattered," I said. "Bramble bushes have taken over; and brush and garbage is strewn all over the place. Getting around is nearly impossible. This is the way the graveyard looked thirty years ago - except for those beer cans… I certainly don't remember those." I was vaguely aware of Emma, ever calm, looking at me to see how I was taking all this. All I saw was the beer cans.

"Heavens to Betsy, I don't know what to say," Emma said.

"And you know what the eeriest thing is, Em?" I didn't wait for an answer. "At Tommy's grave and the lake… actually, every place I drew a sketch I sensed someone else. It was like…well…like someone was talking to me…only, inside my head, you know? But the words were all fuzzy. I didn't understand at all."

"How about taking the drawings out of the binding?" Emma suggested.

I eyed her and then the sketchpad. "Well…uhm…sure… Why not?" I opened the clasp and handed each sketch to her. I couldn't believe it when she bent at the knees then one by one arranged the sketches on the kitchen floor. In the top row to the left, she placed the one of Tommy's grave, next to it, Echo Lake, and lastly the dilapidated red shack. In the second row she set the picture of Tommy and me chasing after the *Evening News;* next came the graveyard littered with beer cans; and finally the scene in front of Pierce's grocery store.

"What is this one?" Emma asked, holding up the seventh sketch.

A tremor shot through me. "Uhm…that's…uhm…my neighbor's front porch." I couldn't bring myself to say his name - I couldn't even remember sketching that.

"What does it have to do with Tommy?" Emma asked.

"I have no clue," I said.

She squinted at the sketch for a moment and then at the two rows of sketches. "There doesn't seem to be a proper place for your neighbor's porch."

The front porch - Warren Squire's front porch - ended up in a row all by itself.

Emma stood up and arched her back. She sagged onto the chair beside me. Never once did her eyes leave the sketches. Every minor detail of each one was thoroughly dissected.

I leaned in closer, trying to see though her eyes. Did she see something I didn't? "What do you think, Em?"

"Well…" She hesitated. "You say you sensed some sort of talking, but didn't actually see or hear anyone." Her eyes met mine. "You felt almost serene, didn't you?" She nodded.

"I guess so."

"And you were not the least bit frightened, am I correct?"

My fingertips fled to my bottom lip. "That's right. That's exactly how I felt. But afterwards, whoa, I thought I was losing my marbles."

Emma scoped out the kitchen as though making sure nobody else was listening.

I did, too.

She leaned in close to me.

I almost pulled back away from her.

"Not too many people know this," she whispered, "but that very same thing happened to me when my Seth passed. It gave me great comfort to think he found a way back to me; that he never really left me. The day that evil man robbed the Brighton Savings Bank, I knew for sure Seth spoke to me." Her voice trailed off. Her eyes seemed to focus on some distant place and time - a place neither I nor anyone else could go. Contentment stole across her face. For several moments, she left my presence.

The room felt so incredibly empty. I needed her back. "Em?" I patted her hand. "You okay?"

She took a deep breath then smiled at me. Her hand grasped mine and squeezed reassuringly.

I felt a whole lot better.

"When that dreadful man smashed into me," she said, "I was dead - I am convinced of it - but you know what, Elizabeth? I don't think God wanted me yet. He sent Seth through beautiful puffy white clouds. Everything gleamed so brilliantly." Her hands were painting the scene in the air as she spoke. "And then… Well, then I saw Seth." She clasped her hands to her chest. "Oh my dear sweet Seth. He was everything I knew him to be in my heart. But then he told me I must go back; that I was still needed here." Her hands reached out to him. "Oh, Seth, I don't want to go... Well, you know, I cried and cried and carried on so. I begged him to let me stay with him forever. I don't know how he did it, but somehow, without even touching me, he forced me to look down at Margi and Julie suffering so terribly there in that sterile Emergency Room. And all the others, too, suffering. Margi was all splattered with my blood. Don't know how I knew it was my blood, but I knew it was. Margi was swaying to and fro in the corner - and I just couldn't stand to see her like that. She had not fully accepted her father's passing and now to lose me? To lose her mother, too? It was at that very instant, Seth took me in his arms and I felt myself breathe again."

"That is the most incredible thing I have ever heard, Emma." My tears overflowed. "You two must have truly loved each other."

"We still do, dear." Her tone was matter-of-fact. A contented smile painted her face. She seemed younger than I ever knew her. "Know what else?"

I got up and went for a paper towel. "What, Em?"

"At Julie's wedding last Christmas," she said, "Seth whispered in my ear."

I turned to her, dabbing away tears with the paper towel.

Emma nodded at me. "Seth said that Julie and Ken are almost as much in love as we are."

At first, I felt like bawling like a baby, but then my chin jutted out. "Geez, Em, how come nothing like that happened to me when I was unconscious?"

Emma shrugged. "I suppose that may be because Peter was alive. He wasn't dead like you thought at the time."

I pondered her explanation. "Mmm, maybe... I wasn't all that close to anyone else... Ever... Guess that's why there was only blackness for me while I was in that coma."

"Maybe," Emma murmured as her head tilted to one side. Her eyes narrowed, scrutinizing the rows of sketches lying on the linoleum floor.

I followed her gaze. Reading her mind, I gasped. "Em... You don't mean... You think..." I jumped up and went to the window. I paced to the stove then to the window, several times. I went to the kitchen counter, leaned on it, and bit my bottom lip. "Is Tommy Gray trying to tell me something?"

"God works in ways we don't always understand, Elizabeth. Perhaps, He is sending that boy back to you for a purpose - just like He sent Seth to shoo me back to where I belong." She chuckled. Her cheeks flushed slightly.

I didn't think this was a laughing matter at all. Once again I paced. "But, Em," I lamented, my arms stretching wide and jouncing. "This is much too weird."

"Look at it a different way, dear: Why is it that out of a clear blue sky, someone crosses your mind? You haven't thought about that person in God knows how long. Did your mind just short circuit in a spot where that person is held in memory? Perhaps. But I like to think it's that person whispering to me, reminding me that I am still as much a part of him - or her - as ever."

I stopped in my tracks, dropping my hands to my sides. "Tommy Gray? Whispering to me? Why me?" I scratched my head. "For the life of me, I cannot understand what he could possibly want from me." I searched her face for answers.

She shrugged. "Let's think this over for just a minute, dear. Here." She patted my empty chair. "Come. Sit down."

I narrowed an eye on the chair.

She patted the chair again.

I stepped over to it and slowly sat down.

"Now listen to me," she said. "My first thought is that you just were not - or are not - willing or prepared to listen. Relax, dear. Concentrate. Maybe then, you will understand. You are going back to Echo Lake again, aren't you?"

I rubbed the back of my neck. "I have to, Em. Whether I like it or not. Someone's hand has got a hold of my heart and grasping so tight that sometimes, I can't even breathe. Someone is dragging me back, Em. I don't have any choice in the matter."

"Well, then," Emma said. "It can only be that Tommy wants to communicate with you. That's the way I see it. I so wish

Yesterday, Tommy Gray Drowned

I could go with you, but this body of mine is too old for such an adventure."

It probably would not have taken much to convince Emma otherwise, but I had a sense that I should do this alone. "Don't worry about it, Em. I'll stay with my cousin Ruth. She asked me to come back to visit for a few days so we can catch up on each other's lives."

"Well, isn't that nice, dear. I feel so much better knowing you won't be there all by yourself. Just watch out though. I have this uneasy feeling in my bones I just can't put my finger on." Her voice sounded ominous as her eyes scanned the ceiling for elusive clues. Then her brows came together. She looked back at the sketches on the floor. "Now, let's see if we can figure these out. Seems to me there is something about that boy's father, especially because you could not draw his grave clearly. Maybe you didn't like the man?"

I swallowed hard. "I can't recall any reason not to." I sucked in a chest full of air. "I can only vaguely remember Gerald Gray. Tall, somewhere around six feet, I guess. A bit wiry. He had white hair and eyebrows. I don't recall if he ever spoke to me. I do know he was in the merchant marines and that's the reason he wasn't around much. You know what, Em? He must have made good money doing that kind of work; why did his family live in that dilapidated shack?"

"Doesn't make a lick of sense, does it, dear?"

"Imagine, bringing up children in a place like that," I said.

"Why on earth would anyone do such a thing?" Emma asked. "Especially when it is entirely unnecessary?"

Unnecessary, echoed a voice inside my head.

That's when it occurred to me: I didn't have to deliver newspapers; Father made more than an adequate living at carpentry, yet most of the time, brother and I looked like ragamuffins. Where did Father's wages go?

"What was Tommy's mother like?" Emma asked - but I didn't hear her. She poked my arm.

"Huh?" I blinked at her.

"Tommy's mother, dear. What was she like?"

"Uhm…nice enough…I guess…" I shook off bewildering circumstances of my childhood. "Mrs. Gray paid for the newspapers herself - and always gave me a nickel tip. A nickel was a lot back then. Come to think of it, I didn't see her much after Tommy died. On collection day, an envelope was tacked on the door. I almost knocked a couple times, just to see how she and his sister Becky were doing - but I was afraid to…"

"Afraid?" Emma asked.

"What if Mrs. Gray was mad at me for tattling on Tommy? Shoot. I felt so bad about that mix-up with my newspapers. If only I had known what was going to happen. If only I had kept my big yap shut. I shouldn't have told on him." I glanced up and was surprised to see Emma studying my face. For a fleeting moment, I wondered what she was thinking. Maybe it was better not to know. I took a deep breath and then continued: "Mrs. Gray was soft spoken…well, except for that day she hollered at Tommy for taking my papers. I'll never forget her voice. Man, did she holler! Scared the ever-lovin' poop out of me."

Emma looked amused. But then she turned sober. "Wonder what is listed as your friend's cause of death. Do you know if an autopsy was done?"

"Geez, I don't know, Em… I don't remember talk of any autopsy."

"That sort of thing was not done much back then," Emma said, peering at the picture of Tommy, transparent and half-submerged in the water. "Maybe he didn't die from drowning?"

I bit the inside of my lip then gave a skeptical nod. "Well, what about the shack? And the place where my papers blew away? There's got to be some kind of connection."

"You got me there, dear."

I bounced my hands out to my sides. "We're just not getting it, Em."

"You say this graveyard is a mess, but this picture shows just the opposite," Emma said.

Yesterday, Tommy Gray Drowned

"And that graveyard isn't even the cemetery Tommy is buried in," I said. "What does this graveyard have to do with him? Those beer cans in the background blow my mind. Why do you suppose I drew beer cans?"

"Doesn't make a lick of sense to me, dear."

Questions went unanswered as Emma posed more: "How about this last picture? Your neighbor's house? Did Tommy know him?"

"I-I don't think so," I stammered. "To be honest, I can't remember Tommy ever setting foot on my side of town. What did…Warren Squire…have to do with Tommy Gray?"

Emma heaved a sigh. "Wish I could be more help."

Perhaps the sketches were just short circuits of an unhappy childhood brought on by Peter's absence, I thought. But then, what if instead, they led to something weird about Tommy Gray? One way or the other, my gut told me all of this was going to lead to me to a greater understanding of what happened back then. It was going to lead me to the child in me, lead me to the adult in me. I decided it was time to go back to my house and call Cousin Ruth. I was going to take her up on her offer for me to stay with her for a few days. I had to get to the bottom of all this. I got to my feet and stretched. "I don't know Emma… I got the feeling you helped a lot more than either one of us knows."

MIKE ANDERSON

Bundling my fisherman's-knit sweater close to my body to ward off the April morning chill, I once again set off down the eroded lane to Echo Lake. The sun strafed the dew bejeweled landscape. If the temperature overnight had been a tad lower, an ice coating would have put tender growth in jeopardy.

At the place where the dingy red shack once stood - Tommy Gray's home - I stopped and flipped open my sketchpad to the image of what used to be. I dissected every minute detail. "There must be some kind of message, a hint, something. But what?"

My baffled grunt distorted the silence, reminding me of the crow that chewed me out the first time I stood here. I glanced up at the branch. Vacant.

I felt incredibly alone. I wished I were somewhere else. But where? That house I shared with Peter in Brighton was sheer torture for me; his ghost seemed to roam every room. I saw him chopping onions at the kitchen counter. I saw him sprawled across the sofa and laughing at some mindless sit-com. I saw him shaving in the bathroom mirror. Even the toilet seat, usually left up, bedeviled me with its incessant yawn.

I tramped onward. Stepping out of the woods, I shaded my eyes and scanned the shoreline. Maple branches speared the water where the dock used to be. Odd how I felt as though I were lying on that dock at that very moment; the summer sun scorching my back; minnows nibbling at my fingertips dangling in the lethargic current. Laughter of families and bawling adolescents roughhousing on the raft a short distance from shore seemed to reverberate against the timberline. I envisioned

71

toddlers scooping up sand with miniature yellow shovels then manipulating the loads into colorful little pails. Thoughts of open fires and searing hot dogs made my stomach growl.

My brain denied the reality of the debris that now littered the remnants of a pristine beach. I frowned at a wooden rowboat lying upside down, putrefied by years of inactivity and exposure to the elements. Even the trees suffered from neglect: broken by windswept time; membranes of branches clung to trunks like umbilical cords.

Somewhere within the caverns of my aching throat came the question: Where did those days go?

Lost.

My soul took pity on the unfinished wood frame dwelling that I noticed on the first trip here. Barren and debased, only tarpaper covered it. It appeared to be a wretched beggar wearing nothing but tattered underwear for the entire world to see. Why didn't the owner have decency enough to put siding on his own house? Anyone could see the potential. It was more than average in size. Plus the view of Echo Lake must be gorgeous from inside that splendid picture window. If that place were mine, I would get rid of that mess of building materials and trash and then clapboard the house and paint it white. Light green trim. No, sky blue trim. No, Sherwood green. Yes, Sherwood green trim. I'd make a garden path of zigzagged brick that would ribbon the yard. The path would wind through a carpet of lush green grass and end at a white gazebo. And everywhere roses - lots of fragrant roses. And other flowers, too - every color and description.

My fantasy ended abruptly the second my right foot sunk into muck. I had almost walked right into the lake. Backing away from water's edge, I stood there, looking out at the unruffled surface. My heart ached to tell Tommy how much his friendship meant to me. "Do you see me Tommy? I came back."

"I came back... Came back..." Echo Lake taunted.

Deceivingly calm on this cloudless spring morning, the monster seemed to be lying in wait, ready to pounce on its next victim foolish enough to venture out into its liquid deathtrap.

Without the slightest hesitation, it would snuff out another life - just like it did my fourth-grade classmate and his father.

If only I could go back. I wouldn't go to Worcester with Father. I'd stay behind and come here instead. Tommy stop! Stay away! My heart throbbed in my throat. He doesn't hear me! He's over his head! No! I spun around, hiding my eyes against my forearm. My horrified gasps were suddenly smothered by a low menacing snarl. I stiffened then allowed my arm to sag ever so slightly.

Flaming eyes penetrated mine. A Doberman! Its black and copper fur bristled. Its fangs glistened, vibrated.

Terror bolted through me, vaporizing the flow of blood within me. I dared not breathe. That Doberman was going to tear me to shreds if one single hair on my head moved. I was trapped. No wait... I could back into the water... Heartbeats thundered as I mustered up the courage to inch my foot backwards. Ice water cinched my ankle, numbing my foot that again mired in slime.

The Doberman matched my every step. It was determined to follow me right into that frigid water. Its gums pulsated, scarlet, which bleached out its canine teeth, making them look a lot larger than they actually were.

I had no weapon. The only protection was my sketchpad and box of pastel chalks. I raised them in front of me. Chalks dropped out of the box and into the water. Plop! Plop, plop!

The Doberman twitched. It all but attacked me right then and there. I had to get out of there. Perhaps I should dive into the lake... Yeah, right. Drown - just like Tommy Gray.

"Brutus?" A whistle.

My insides somersaulted. Someone's coming! Friend or foe?

"Brutus? Where are you, man?" Another whistle.

The Doberman's cropped right ear zeroed in on its master.

My eyes rolled in the same direction. A man's voice was coming from the direction of the unfinished house. My gut screamed: Go, you lousy mutt!

Yesterday, Tommy Gray Drowned

The Doberman stood its ground. I was its prey and it had a job to do.

"Come on, Brutus. Where on earth are you?" The man's voice grew louder, nearer.

Flaming eyes remained focused on me.

"Bru... Hey, what is going on?"

At last, he finally found his watchdog at water's edge, staring down a flagrant interloper. Me.

"At ease, Brutus," the man commanded; his tone too even for my liking.

The Doberman whipped around and dashed off, wagging the stump of a tail and yipping like an innocent puppy. It glanced back at me, red eyes much kinder now, a gentler shade of brown. Its tongue slopped out of its mouth, limp and pink as a thinly sliced piece of Easter ham.

When I started to breathe again, I found my lungs completely devoid of air. I gasped for air like a baby just expelled from the womb. My adrenaline-charged heart raced. My body went weak. I teetered towards the water.

"Much too early in the season for swimming," the man scolded, while latching onto my arm.

Between that red-eyed Doberman and that frigid water, I felt as though the great hand of God had just plucked me from the ugly grasp of the grim reaper himself.

"What are you doing here?" the man demanded - although his voice contained a certain amount of relief that I didn't fall into the lake.

"I...uh..." I stammered. My eyes never left that Doberman, even though it showed no further signs of malice.

"Didn't you see any of the private property signs?" the man demanded. "The whole lake is posted, for Pete's sake!"

For Pete's sake, Echo Lake belched.

"For Pete's sake," I mumbled. I battled to retain some semblance of dignity while extracting my arm from his powerful grip. "Well, yeah, I saw a sign, but..."

"But what?"

"I just wanted to see where I used to swim."

"Where you used to swim? Who are you?"

"Elizabeth...Blair... I grew up here...uhm...on the other side of the village and..." I felt so foolish, self-conscious. It was hard not to, standing there all mucked up. "Sorry for the intrusion." I wheeled around to put distance between me and that hideous place as fast as my wobbly legs could carry me.

"I don't recall a Blair family in these parts," the man countered.

I rolled my eyes and clenched my teeth. Was that guy calling me a liar? Of all the nerve! I spun around and glared at him. "Look, I just wanted to..."

His cobalt-blue eyes invaded mine.

My breath ceased - breath I just got back a second ago. Good heavens! Was this guy some kind of looker or what! Tall - at least six-feet. Athletic. In his late thirties or early forties. And look at those clothes: green windbreaker and gray sweats with Celtics embossed down those long powerful legs. I ogled him as if I were a teenager bedazzled by that all-consuming first crush. I couldn't help but envision that rugged well-built hunk dribbling a basketball down court, giving Magic a run for his money, the crowd going berserk. My jaw quivered. "Oh, uhm... I'm sorry...again... Uh...Spencer... Spencer was...uh...is...my maiden name. I delivered newspapers...when I was a kid and..."

The most exquisite smile I ever saw flashed across his face as he ran his hand through his thick, dark, wavy, untamed hair. Within me, long sleeping passion - lust - whatever you want to call it - erupted from a burgeoning volcano. He held me totally captivated. Moments passed and then his obvious amusement brought me to my senses. I glowed hot, embarrassed, and completely mortified.

"You're that skinny pip-squeak who rode that funny little bike," he said. "Yup, I can see that kid in your expression. I'm Mike Anderson. Don't you remember me?"

I gaped at him in disbelief. After all these years, I ran smack dab into the archenemy of my youth? And even his dog had designs of eating me for breakfast? I bit my tongue, but I was prone to say: I will have you know, buster, my blue bike was not the least bit funny! Why even when I forsake it for a bigger one, which got crushed by some old dude backing up at the post office, that *little blue bike* was there for me! Hunk or not, I defiantly rebuilt my grudge and pursed my lips. I knew the best thing for me to do was to get out of there before I got riled up more than I already was and things got a whole lot nastier. Holy cow, I could not believe Mike Anderson turned me on! I whirled around to go, curtly replying, "Oh yeah. I remember you."

"Stay… Please stay…" His voice was meek, a bit on the pathetic side. "Talk to me…for just for a little while, huh? I don't get much company around here."

My brows furrowed. Was he for real? I turned my head ever so slightly and sized him up out of the corner of my eye. His face was earnest; and he certainly appeared a lot more civilized than the thirteen-year-old I held in memory.

Suddenly, a voice within me: Hey, give the guy a break. People change.

I shook my head, clearing my brain, and then fumbled for subject matter. I ended up pointing at the unfinished house. "You live there?"

Mike glanced back at the house. "Bought this land ten years ago." He looked down at the ground. Then he bent and picked up a stone. He skipped it across the water. He didn't seem at all the self-involved punk I used to know. "Been putting that house together ever since. Other things got me bogged down, so finishing up the place gets the bottom of the list." He glanced at me. His eyes seemed to search mine for forgiveness for his procrastination, forgiveness for the past.

I shifted my weight, floundering, once again, for subject matter. "No more activity, businesswise, going on around Echo Lake than before?"

"Nah." He side armed another stone across the water. "Folks still commute to Worcester. Since 495 and 395 came through, everybody works if they have a mind to. My job at the Water Works is okay. Won't make me rich though. You an artist?"

I didn't hear a word he said, because I had made the mistake of watching the poetry of his movements, his full lips.

He pointed at the sketchpad and chalks I held crushed against my chest. "Those are art supplies, aren't they?"

"Huh?" I looked down at my sketchpad and the box of empty chalks. I looked at him and cleared my throat. "No...uhm... Well, I guess so... Just a pastime. Peter - he's my husband... He got sick of me using number two pencils to draw ocean scenes on scrap paper every time we sailed. He surprised me one day with all this stuff. Been into pastels ever since."

"Mind if I take a look?" he asked, extending his palm toward me.

I was not at all sure I wanted anyone to see the seven sketches, much less Mike Anderson. After all, he was at the root of what happened between Tommy and me. Plus, in some silly way, I did not want him to think I was whacked out for drawing such weird images. Yet the meanness I remembered no longer shadowed his face. He seemed entirely sincere, trustworthy. Strangely reassured, I showed him the first sketch.

His demure smile vanished. He seemed to sag as his face drained of color. His brows rumpled as his hands surrounded the sketchpad as if it were a sacred object. He took it from me then sank to the ground that was still damp from the early morning dew. It seemed as if he was hardly breathing as he scrutinized every feature of Tommy Gray. Were those tears pooling in his eyes? His bottom lip quivered ever so slightly. "This is Tommy Gray to a T. Why on earth did you..."

I shrugged. "I don't know... Guess I never got over what happened to him."

"Me neither," Mike murmured, running his hand through his hair.

I let down my guard. I actually considered telling him that I thought Tommy lured me back here after all these years.

"Part of me drowned with that kid. He's one of the best things that ever happened to me - the only one to keep me from being a total screw-up. If only I acted quicker, instead of being a know-it-all punk, he'd be alive today."

Yesterday, Tommy Gray Drowned

His confession stunned me. I blinked at him, trying to make sense of the past, trying to make sense of the way years changed people. Finally, I said, "We both carry that kind of guilt." I collapsed onto the sand next to Mike and wrapped my arms around my knees. Dampness infiltrated the seat of my pants. My feet were cold and wet from the unscheduled excursion into Echo Lake; so were my sneakers, which weren't so white anymore. Yet the fisherman's knit sweater suddenly felt much too bulky, stifling.

"You don't have anything to feel guilty about," Mike said.

I squinted at him.

A puzzled expression tightened his face.

"Yeah, I do," I said. "You don't know how much I regret that day Tommy and I got into that newspaper mix-up."

Mike cut me off, "That wasn't your fault."

My bottom jaw drooped. He actually remembered that day?

"Tommy was just showing off - for my sake," Mike said. "If I wasn't there that day none of that would have ever happened. Whether you know it or not, that kid had a thing for you."

"Come on," I said skeptically.

"Well, he did," Mike insisted. "Know why? He never said anything about you, that's why. When he didn't like someone, he let me know in no uncertain terms. But you, 'Lizbeth? You? Nah, Tommy never said one blessed word about you. Kind of made me jealous to see the look in his eyes whenever he saw you coming."

In an uncanny way, his observation comforted me. I believed he was telling the truth.

"Tommy never talked about anything he liked," Mike said. "He was very reserved about things like that. It was almost as if he was afraid that revealing something he cared about meant someone was going to come along and take it away from him. Though it is beyond me why he hung around with the likes of me. I was such a punk. Talk about opposite poles of the magnet."

"How come you two went into the water that day?" At last, I spat out the question that cycloned inside my head every year when April rolled around.

"Wasn't much else to do." A tisk escaped from the side of his pursed lips as his eyes scanned Echo Lake. "We were bored – plus it was such a warm afternoon - just like today is supposed to be. The water seemed so inviting." Mike appeared to be reliving that fatal day. "I don't know if you remember at all, but that year the weather was just what poison sumac thrives on."

"How can I forget?" I said, stepping back in time. "I got it wicked bad that New Year's Eve. That winter was so mild that poison sumac floated on the breeze for months. You didn't even have to touch a leaf to get peppered with it. Worse than poison ivy or any food allergy I ever had - and man, did I get real bad rashes from green beans. Thankfully, I grew out of that."

"Allergies didn't bother me," Mike said. "But that stinkin' sumac sure got to me. Tommy, too. The itch was sheer torture. We did everything to get relief. That's how we came up with the hair-brained idea of jumping into the lake. Stripped right down to our underwear, we did. Then we ran hell bent for leather right into that water. It was still much too cold for anyone to be in it, but the itching stopped, at least until we came out. To this very day, I remember diving in there. Hot dog, talk about cold! My frozen body shot out of that water like an iceberg lopped off a glacier. I was one giant goose bump, sucking for air." Mike chuckled. He looked at me. His left eyebrow angled as if penciled there by a child; his right eyebrow hooked up and down.

I burst out laughing. So did he. A moment later, we stopped laughing. It wasn't funny anymore.

He cleared his throat and stared at Tommy's picture. "So. The kid got to goofing off - just like he always did. He insisted that the water wasn't cold at all. He swam way out over his head - past where the raft always was in the summertime. 'Come on,' he hollered to me. He kept waving his hand at me, motioning to me. 'Not a chance,' I shouted. 'Freezin' my butt off ain't for me." No sooner did I get out and turn around, Tommy was gone. My stupid brain convinced me he was goofing off. Cripes, I hate

79

myself. To think how casually I got dressed - just buttoned up my shirt without a care in the world - and all the while, Tommy was out there...in trouble..."

Mike turned away, his shoulders heaving with deep, tenuous breaths. I spotted his finger surreptitiously flicking a bead of moisture off his cheek.

"I ran away, you know," he said, bowing his head, heavy with the burden of memory. "After I told his parents I couldn't find him." Mike waved his head side to side. "What a friggin' coward I was. I hate myself for that. I always started trouble and then vanished into thin air. I never took the fallout."

My anger towards the thirteen-year-old floating in memory dissolved into remorse that I wanted to share with him. What a tremendous guilt he carried. I placed my hand on his shoulder and said, "I never realized the deep friendship you and Tommy had."

"He was a great swimmer, you know," Mike said. "Everyone says that he might have been okay if he waited a half an hour after he ate. Just before it happened, he and I were up at the shack, swilling down pea soup and bologna sandwiches. Tommy wolfed down two bowls of that soup plus three sandwiches. And mayonnaise! Gadsooks! I never saw anyone put mayonnaise on things the way he did! That stuff gushed out the sides of the bread and slimed up everything. And then he dipped the sandwiches into the pea soup. What a mess! First thing I know he's smearing mayonnaise on his poison sumac! Of all things! Just to see if it would help stop the itching! I never laughed so hard in my entire life! Well, his mother came along and chewed him out and I laughed even harder. My sides hurt bad. She made Tommy clean up all the mayonnaise and then she put some purple stuff all over him. And me, too. She insisted it will ease the itching, but to be honest, nothing ever did...well, except for that ice cold lake."

"I remember that purple stuff," I said, scarcely letting Mike finish what he was saying. "What was it anyway?"

He shrugged while flipping to the next page of the sketchpad. "Certainly was a waste of time plastering that stuff on.

All it did was stain our clothes and turn our skin purple." He stared blankly at the sketch, fiddling with the corner of the page. "The shack... I tore it down; first thing I did after buying this place. The sight of it turned my stomach. How those people ever lived in that firetrap is beyond me. The roof leaked... Leaked? Leaked isn't the word for it! And the floor was so rotted out you fell right through it in places if you weren't careful. Didn't take much to catch a toe on those planks they put down to cover up all the holes. After old man Gray died - drowned out there in a boating accident, close to where Tommy drowned." Mike pointed out the spot. "After that happened, Tommy's mother moved out of the shack. Kind of weird how Gerald Gray turned up drowned almost ten years to the day after Tommy drowned, don't you think?"

We sat in silence, mulling over the coincidence, staring at the lake that seemed so placid, so genteel. The idea that such tragedies could occur out there seemed beyond all comprehension.

"Want to know something else that's weird, 'Lizbeth?"

My eyes met his.

"I was destined to buy this place," he said. "Every day I come down here with Brutus and sit here for hours gawking out over the lake. Tommy is out there. I just know he is. He's keeping an eye on me."

Words failed me. I wanted to console Mike - and myself. You would think I could do that; after all, I was forty years old. And Mike...forty-three? Wow... How strange the world turned. Up to a short time ago, the memory of him was not exactly the greatest – to say the least. And how funny to see Brutus, gentle as a lamb, lying on his side; Mike's foot gently stroking his velveteen belly. The Dobie loved every minute of it. Mike gazed at the contented Brutus, tilting his head to the side. Man and beast were anything but hostile.

"Not long after Tommy drowned, my parents moved to Worcester," he said. "But as soon as I could, I came back here."

"Oh, speak about coming back," I said, glancing at my watch. "I gotta go!" I scrambled to my feet, brushing off my pants. "My cousin Ruth is expecting me for lunch. I'm staying with her and her husband for a few days."

Mike jumped up. "Ruthie and Wally Murphy? They're friends of mine! Haven't seen those two since Moses was a pup. Tell them give me a call, why don't you? They have my number. Let's sit here and talk some more. How about tonight? I'll put out some lawn chairs - I made them myself. They're a lot more comfortable than sitting on this sand, that's for sure. You haven't forgotten how beautiful the sunsets are here, have you?"

"It's supposed to rain later," I said.

He was visibly disappointed.

I bit the inside of my lip and started up the lane.

"Maybe tomorrow," he said.

Brutus pranced ahead us - some difference from the man-eater that rudely introduced itself at water's edge.

Mike held down the chain that barred entry to the lane. As I stepped over it, I said, "Better replace this old chain and the rusty signs if you expect to keep obnoxious transients like me out of here."

That perfect ivory smile smeared his face.

My insides fluttered: Oh please, don't do that…

His hands enfolded mine. "Glad you came back, 'Lizbeth." His touch was firm, warm, and lasted much too long.

I looked into his intense eyes. As if struck by lightning, every bit of my remaining defenses blasted to smithereens. An awkward moment passed as his generous lips invited mine. Another awkward moment. Suddenly, guilt cinched my gut: What on God's green earth was I doing? I was betraying Peter! I broke for my car. Driving away, I waved a fleeting good-bye. Oh how I hated my wanton temptation. But it never would have happened if Peter had been there. Despair overwhelmed me. Was Peter ever going to come back to me?

INFERNO

"Sorry I'm late," I called as Ruth sprinted out of her home to greet me. I was yanking off my mucky shoes and socks, feeling scummy. She was wearing black jeans and a lavender button-down shirt tied in a square knot at midriff, looking perfect. "But I drove over to the lake and…"

She cut me off, "Think nothing of it." She leaned over the driver's side door and hugged me. The first thing that struck me was how loving yet down-to-earth Ruth was. I liked that.

She opened my door as I chucked my feet into flip-flops. She took hold of my hand and tugged me out of my car and into the house. "I've been running around like a chicken with its head cut off! I fixed us a great barbecue! First of the season! Wally's joining us, though we have to wait a couple more hours for him to get here, since he's working on a new house up past the lake - about two miles from Fern Cove. He says to me this morning, 'Now, Ruthie. I'll be home early, but only if I skip lunch.' So I says to him, 'Okay!'"

I could not get a word in edgewise. She was obviously excited that I was there, but even more so because Wally was coming home early. From the short amount of time I had spent with them, I fully understood how much they adored each other. They looked at one another the way Peter and I did - when he was around, that is.

"I marinated chicken breasts overnight," Ruth said. "Let's you and me make a giant salad and then shuck the corn - I think corn comes from Mexico this time of year. You think so?"

"Maybe Florida," I said.

"Who knows?" Ruth said. She rambled on and on gasping at times for air. "When you called, I couldn't believe it. I thought I'd never get to see you again. I am so glad you decided to come back. Now, we can get to know each other. We never did that when we were kids, you know."

"Kind of funny how age doesn't matter anymore," I said, feeling like I was going to pass out even though she was the one who wasn't breathing with all her yakking. She acted like a giddy schoolgirl. What a switch. I had always been the kid, but things were different now. I was more grown up, more sophisticated than she was - at least at this moment. "Sure would have liked a chance to see your mom and dad again."

Ruth nodded, momentarily refraining from talking as her thoughts reverted to her late parents. She cleared her throat. "I heard your father passed on and your mother remarried."

I nodded. "Mother lives in Arizona."

"Wally's lucky," she said. "His parents are still hanging in there."

"Living in the same house across the street from the Briggs' farm?" I asked.

"Yup," she said. "But Ray Briggs sold out after Chief Briggs passed on. Ray hated it here. He's somewhere out west, I think. Hey! Remember that January when the Briggs barn caught on fire? Wally's Pop still talks about it. That tremendous heat blistered the trim on his house."

"Good thing his house is made out of brick," I said, "or it would have burnt to the ground along with the barn."

Ruth twisted up her face in a silly sort of way. "Remember the smell? Like sizzling rancid steak."

I twisted up my face. "Skunked up the town for days."

"Terrible thing how the dairy cattle burned up in the stanchions," Ruth said. "And all the sheep, penned up in the cellar, too. Pop and some other folks managed to save the horses, but only after covering up the horse's eyes with jackets."

I rolled my eyes. "It's the only way to lead them out of a burning barn."

"By the time anybody got to the cattle, there was only time enough to release a few from the stanchions before the fire got too hot. Well, you know what happened, don't you?"

"The cattle stampeded right back into the fire," I said.

Ruth groaned. "Awful, huh?"

"What sparked that fire anyways?" I asked.

"Officially," Ruth said, "it was hay spontaneously combusting. Wally's Pop says otherwise. He saw a bunch of guys running out from behind the barn just before flames shot out the roof. Kids were always playing around there, too. Not only that, Chief Briggs got most of his farm hands from the state pen - bunked them in the hayloft."

"No doubt those convicts smoked up there," I said.

"Pop reported the fire, you know," Ruth said. "And he also told Chief Briggs he recognized the guys running from the barn. Chief never did one single thing about it."

The raging inferno had been virtually impossible to put out that bitter January day so long ago. Fire hoses, hydrants, tank trucks - everything froze solid. Thick ice layered everything. An enormous amount of smoke hovered over the village for days and soot dotted the meager snow that had blanketed southern Massachusetts just after Christmas. It looked as if someone sprinkled pepper from a huge shaker in the sky.

Instead of delivering my papers the next day, I leaned over the handlebars of my bike, mesmerized by the awesome destruction. It looked like bombing scenes I had seen in the TV series called *Victory at Sea*. That was the only show Father ever watched. Charred timbers stood like fleshless corpses. Icicles clung to them, crackling in the silence of subzero twilight. Grim reminders of what used to be bloated my ten-year-old body with hopelessness. In the weeks that followed, I sped past the scene, not wanting to see it anymore. After the frost lifted from the ground, Chief Briggs bulldozed the place - and I was glad. In the springtime, he planted grass. A lush green meadow in which dandelions, buttercups, and cornflowers took hold grew there ever since.

Yesterday, Tommy Gray Drowned

Ruth and I gabbed on and on about old times while preparing the barbecue. Before we knew it, we heard Wally's truck door slam. When he walked into the kitchen, Ruth rushed to him. Putting her arms about his neck, she planked a juicy kiss square on his mouth. Wally offered no resistance.

Jealousy stabbed my heart. I wanted to put my arms around Peter and kiss him like that. But no, my husband was slogging around some far off jungle. It's not fair!

"Food's just about ready, my love," Ruth said.

"Lemme get cleaned up a bit and change out of these stinky work clothes," Wally said.

When he returned, neatly dressed and freshly shaved, the dining room table was laden with goodies. "Holy mackerel! Look at all this!"

The three of us ate like porkers and then lingered over coffee. Attacking the dirty dishes was not on the agenda.

"You should see the drawing of Pierce's Grocery Store Bethie drew," Ruth said to Wally. She pried herself to her feet. "Get her to show it to you while I clear off the table."

I wanted to help - and did some heavy protesting to that fact - but it was pointless; I was outnumbered. So I slunk off to fetch my sketchpad from the backseat of my car. When I got back, I smiled self-consciously at Wally, hoping he was not going to think I was some kind of freak for sketching such weird scenes. I opened the sketchpad to the drawing of Pierce's Grocery.

"You do beautiful work," Wally said, taking the sketchpad from me.

"Thanks," I said with a fair amount of relief.

"The faces are so clear," he said. "I can tell who everyone is. The carrot-top there is Rusty Kane. And that's Rick Morton. Get a load of the duds. Oh... Elizabeth... Shame on you..."

"What?" I asked, leaning in for a closer look at the sketch.

Wally's left eyebrow twitched up and down.

Ruth came back just then. "For heaven's sake, Wally, what is the matter with you?"

He laughed while holding up the sketchpad and pointing at Rick Morton's crotch. "Look." Wally gawked at me. "You even made him stacked."

"Stacked?" Ruth and I said in unison.

"Stacked," he said. "Some guys wore jocks and stuffed them with socks or facecloths to make themselves look...well...stacked. Teen idols did that a lot."

Good heavens, I don't know when I laughed so hard! So hard that I started to cry. For a change, crying was not from sadness.

When the three of us finally pulled ourselves together, Wally asked, "All right to look at the rest of the pictures?"

I nodded.

He passed over the sketch of Tommy and his father's grave without seeing it. He gazed at the one of Tommy Gray half-submerged in Echo Lake. "Wow, this is a great likeness of the Gray kid. Man, what a tearjerker that was. Pop was there that day. He tried to bring Tommy back and was all torn up for the longest time, because nothing he did worked." Wally sighed. After a moment, he went on to the next drawing: the beat-up shack. His head cocked sideways as he squinted at it. He didn't say a word though. Neither did Ruth. He went on to the sketch of Tommy and me picking up newspapers. Again neither of them said a word. They just stared at the sketches. What were they thinking?

Wally turned the next page: the overgrown graveyard. Well, it wasn't overgrown in my sketch.

Ruth slammed her hand on the sketchpad.

Wally and I flinched.

"Bethie!" she exclaimed. "How on earth did you remember this? It's been years since that graveyard looked like this!"

"Geez, I don't know," I said. "I don't understand it either. Why did the town let that place go like that?"

Ruth shook her head. "Just gave up on it."

87

Yesterday, Tommy Gray Drowned

"Bunch of dumdums kept going in there partying and wrecking the place," Wally said, scratching his head. "Costs too much to continually upright headstones and fix the damage."

"Selectmen got on Chief Briggs about it," Ruth said, "but someone had to die in this town before that old geezer stirred out of his house after dark."

"Echo Lake needed better law enforcement," Wally said. "But Briggs was a bit of a fixture around these parts, and nobody had the heart to get rid of him." Wally flipped the page. His eyes rounded. "Whoa. Squire's house." Wally turned sullen, withdrawn, his pain clearly evident. "Nasty son of a gun."

Ruth reached for his hand. She knew full well what was eating her husband. I wondered what it was, but hesitated in asking.

When Wally spoke again, his voice was muted, tremulous. "When I was a kid…oh, about eleven or so…Squire tried one of his filthy games on me."

My mouth dropped open. Filthy games? Surprise lifted my brow. Though not at all new to me, that subject had always been a real no-no in Echo Lake.

"That pervert hung out at the bar - the one up the road from Pop's," Wally said. "One day, Squire spied me wearing a tool belt. That was just the opening he needed. He came up with this cock-and-bull story about a newfangled tool I just had to see. As you know, he's a huge barrel-chested piece of reprobate…"

"Not anymore," Ruth said.

Wally gave her a thin smile. "Not any more…" He cleared his throat then continued, "Squire's voice was so syrupy. He coaxed me into trusting him - enough to leave my wagon right there beside the road and scamper off after him - behind the bar. Without the slightest thought, I got right into his car. Talk about dumb, huh?" Wally glanced at me.

I pursed my lips, fidgeting. My stomach somersaulted like a gymnast. What was I supposed to say? Squire got me to do dumb things too?

Wally looked down at his hands, folded on the table. "Well, there I am sitting in the front seat and Squire pretends to search for the tool he told me about." Wally bit his lip. "The stench inside that car made my stomach turn flips. Musty and foul smelling - filthy dirty. Well, of course, he couldn't find that tool - though he did manage to wriggle up close to me. His mangy hand stroked my knee and like a bonehead, I just sat there. Suddenly, the door burst open and a hand reached in and yanked the pervert out the driver's side while another hand planted itself smack into his jaw. Squire lost a molar out of the deal - and got Pop's steel-toed work boot right in the butt. Pop cursed Squire up one side and down the other: If that pervert ever came near me again he wouldn't live to tell the tale of it. Those big burly arms of Pop's scooped me up and carried me all the way home. Imagine that? An eleven-year-old boy carried home by his old man? But you know what? Somehow, it was okay. When we came around the side of the bar, Pop spotted my wagon and pulled up short. He buried his head in my chest and cried like a baby. Sure was a good thing I left my wagon where I did. That's how Pop tracked me down back there behind the bar - just in the nick of time."

The dining room was dead quiet. Warren Squire was not a subject any of us could stomach.

Ruth gazed compassionately at her husband. She picked up his hand and rubbed the back of it across her cheek.

I shifted my weight.

Wally took a deep breath. "A rare bunch of people lived in this town back then. We kids didn't know who to trust. Folks wore blinders - nothing bad ever happened in their town. Shoot. They all knew about Squire, but nobody raised a finger to stop him."

"Lots of stuff that went on back then got swept under the rug," Ruth said. "Still does."

I cleared my throat. My mouth was dry and stale when I opened it to speak. "Respect for adults was absolute."

"If a kid did something an adult didn't like, justified or not, he got walloped good," Wally said. "Parent or not, anybody had the right to correct kids."

"And if you got a lickin' in school," I said, "You got one when you got home."

"But one time my second grade teacher spanked my friend Donna for something she didn't do," Ruth said. "Next day, Donna came to school with terrible switch marks. I know because she showed them to me during recess."

"That's why Ray Briggs sold out and left town when his father kicked the bucket," Wally said. "Chief Briggs used to holler at Ray something terrible - and shoved him around. Saw him with my own eyes a time or two. That poor kid never did one single thing right. Ray just sat there on the front stoop, his face in his hands, and look so down in the dumps. I know for a fact that Squire got it in his mind that Ray was one unhappy puppy and took advantage of that fact. The two of them came and went from the barn lots of times when the Chief wasn't around. There's no doubt in my mind that Squire was up to no good. Pop and I were relieved when that barn burnt down. But you know, Squire never left Ray alone either." Wally closed his eyes for a second, squeezing out painful memories. He took another deep cleansing breath then changed the subject. "Well, anyway... So much for scum of the earth... Ruthie tells me you went to the lake today."

I shook off the previous topic. "Uh-huh. The beach was a great place to go when we were kids."

"Not anymore," Ruth puffed.

"I ran into Mike Anderson," I said. "And good ol' Brutus. That dog had me cornered good until Mike came along."

Wally chuckled. "Mike did an awesome job training that pooch. Never seen anything like it. Did it all by himself, too."

Just then, a flash of lightning lit the backyard. Thunder followed. None of us had noticed the storm coming.

Wally and Ruth got up and peered out the window.

"Mike invited us to come over and watch the sunset," I said.

Ruth and Wally exchanged glances. Her right eyebrow arched.

"I told him no," I said. "Since showers were in the forecast and all." My eyes roamed across the ceiling. "It's raining already. Hear it?"

Wally and Ruth turned, eying me kind of critically.

Another bolt of lightning lit the backyard. Thunder rumbled, louder, nearer.

"Well, maybe tomorrow night," I said. "If you two are game."

"Uhm, sure," Ruth stammered. "Sounds like fun."

Yesterday, Tommy Gray Drowned

TOWN HALL

"You and Wally didn't see one of my sketches," I said to Ruth over coffee and homemade muffins the next morning.

"Oh?" Puzzlement sheeted her face.

I opened the sketchpad to the drawing of Tommy and his father's grave.

Her eyebrows lifted. Her voice sounded ethereal. "Oh my goodness." She set down her coffee mug and gingerly took the pad from me. Her fingertips skimmed the inscription: Thomas Gray 1949 - 1959. She contemplated the flecks of chalk that clung to her skin. Then she blew them into the air and brushed her hands together. I got the feeling the sketch bothered her - a lot. I wanted to know why. I wanted her to open up.

Moments passed.

I broke the silence: "The first day I came back to Echo Lake, I stopped at Tommy's grave before going anywhere else."

"How many of these did you draw?" she asked.

"Seven." The number distorted my voice like a wad of phlegm. I coughed to clear my throat then said, "Each an enigma in itself. And the power behind the chalk wasn't my own."

She frowned at me.

"Those sketches have something to do with why I came back to Echo Lake after all this time," I said. "I'm sure of it."

Ruth handed the sketchpad to me. "Geez, what are you going do about it?"

I shrugged while propping the sketchpad against the leg of the table. "A weird sensation keeps bugging me that Tommy's death wasn't all it seemed and I really have to get at the truth."

Yesterday, Tommy Gray Drowned

Ruth winced. "Gosh, after all this time? Where on earth do you start?"

"My friend Emma says the best place is Town Hall. Death certificates might reveal something."

Ruth gathered up our breakfast dishes. At the sink, she was pensive while rinsing off dishes. I took the dishes from her and loaded them into the dishwasher. Upon finishing, she turned to me, swiping her hands across a dishtowel. "Do you really think death certificates will reveal anything?"

"I haven't the faintest idea," I said, leaning against the corner of the refrigerator. I gnawed on the inside of my cheek. I crossed my arms. She was still looking at me. "Your guess is as good as mine," I said.

She tossed the towel on the counter. "Well then, I'm going with you. I got a thing for riddles."

"I was hoping you'd say that," I said. Relief settled over me. I was about to change my mind about going it alone. "Don't know why," I said, "but I got a feeling that poking around Echo Lake's past might not be appreciated. What if we dig up some dirty little secret that someone might just as soon be kept buried?"

Ruth giggled, her eyebrows jiggling. "I'll catch whatever you miss."

A short while later we stepped out of her house into the brilliant morning. During the night, the first boisterous thunderstorm of the season left the air crisp, a pleasure to breathe. Birds were celebrating the unspoiled day with a cacophony of songs.

"Let's put the top down," Ruth said as her fingers parted the moisture beads on the hood of my car.

"Sure," I nodded. "After the canvas dries off a bit."

Well. That woman pouted like a spoiled brat.

I cracked up. "Look, it won't take long to dry, once we get moving. Promise."

We started towards the village, and like I promised, my car shook off moisture - almost like a puppy dog after a bath. The windshield blurred with the moisture. Several times, I turned

94

on the wipers to clear the view. Approaching the four corners, I pulled the car over to the side of the road and stopped. I pointed to the button. "Go ahead. Push."

Sheer delight enveloped her. The second her finger pushed the button, hydraulics whirred and then the canvas top folded into the chassis behind us.

"Wanna drive?" I asked.

In a heartbeat, she was out the passenger door, around the car, and yanking me out of the driver's seat. I had to hurry to the passenger seat - she almost left me there on the road. So then, that cousin of mine ate up the openness and illusory stature, waving to everyone and his brother. As stone faces stared back at us, I shrunk down in my seat. "They must think we're a couple of lunatics," I said, feeling self-conscious for the first time since buying the convertible. Back in Brighton nobody paid attention to convertibles - or any other kind of car for that matter. People owned all kinds of cars, newer and flashier than any I saw in Echo Lake. Antique cars glittered from restoration, not rust.

Ruth laughed. "Who cares what anybody thinks?"

I thought about that. I sat up tall. "Yeah. Who cares."

We coasted into the gravel parking lot beside Echo Lake Town Hall. A minor dust devil followed us in. When it caught up to us, Ruth feigned several coughs.

I noticed two old codgers sitting on a park bench near the monument that honored the war dead of Echo Lake. "I used to deliver papers to them," I said under my breath. "Boy, they got old."

"How ya doin', Jack?" Ruth hollered.

Jack returned my cousin's greeting - somewhat weakly, I might add. Then he leaned over to the other old codger and said something. Whatever it was must've been humorous, because they guffawed. There for a moment, I wondered if that was good or bad. Maybe they were poking fun at me. Or my car. Geez, some things never changed - not even me. But like Ruth said: Who cares? Banishing the old codgers from my mind, I scanned the familiar locale. A patina cannon mounted on a granite base pointed ominously down Main Street, stalwart, guarding the

Yesterday, Tommy Gray Drowned

American flag fluttering in the temperate breeze above the grassy knoll. Behind the Town Hall to the right, I noticed the dam, one of several that controlled the water and had powered the woolen mills, now defunct. When I was a kid, a wheel-house hid the dam - plus the litter produced by nefarious activities.

"Nice park, huh?" Ruth remarked as we got out of the car. "The VFW put that in a few years ago."

I squinted at half a dozen wooden park benches that dotted the green. How wonderful it must be to sit there on warm summer evenings and listen to the pristine water spill over the granite blocks.

As we climbed the Town Hall steps, a black pickup skidded to a halt in the middle of the street. It was that same hunk of junk that had pulled up behind me at the four corners several days ago, horn a-blaring. The carrot-top driver gaped at Ruth and me until we disappeared inside the building. She noticed. I noticed. Neither of us commented.

In the Clerk's Office, two pear-shaped ladies were seated at cluttered desks behind the counter. Not wanting any disturbances from self-appointed routines, both avoided any acknowledgment of our presence. When we did not go away, the one with a very bad dye job piled into a lopsided braid bun atop her head grudgingly got to her feet. Taking her ever-loving sweet time, she ambled over to us. "May I help you."

"Yes, please," I said, pleasantly. "I'd like to see the record of deaths for the years 1959 and 1969."

"Well," the exasperated clerk clucked. "I will have to go fetch 'em."

"Geez, I…"

Ruth grabbed my arm, cutting me off. "Let the clerk go fetch 'em."

The clerk eyed Ruth, then me. She heaved a breath then took off.

I whispered to Ruth. "I really don't want to put anybody out."

"Don't worry about it," Ruth whispered back.

I imagined the clerk plodding down rickety stairs to a moldy cellar; even worse, crawling up into a dark, musty attic. What a slime-ball I was to force her into rummaging through piles of strewn-about documents, causing sweat to bead on her wrinkled brow. I almost called to the clerk to forget it, but then... Not twenty feet down the hallway, the clerk opened a door and disappeared. Nonchalantly, I edged my way down the hallway. I peeked around the corner. A vault.

"Will you look at that," Ruth whispered in my ear.

I jumped - I didn't know she had followed me.

"Files," she whispered.

I stared at neat stacks delineated by month and year. Crossing my arms, I grumbled out the corner of my mouth, "Why that old battle-ax."

Ruth chuckled. "Quite an effort, huh?"

Moments later, without the slightest embarrassment, the clerk waddled past Ruth and me then dropped the files on the counter. I watched the poor overworked clerk waddle back to her desk and collapse in her chair.

"Her work for the day is now complete," Ruth mumbled.

"Too bad if somebody else needs anything from here on out," I said.

"Not gonna to happen," Ruth said in a singsong voice. She leaned over the counter and distracted the clerks with the latest juicy gossip while I looked over the files. However, their insignificant prattle distracted me to no end, so at length I coughed up the money for Tommy Gray's Death Certificate. Upon further deliberation, I coughed up money for Gerald Gray's, too. I'd study them later - in a quieter place, where it was possible to concentrate.

Turning to leave the Clerk's Office, Ruth and I came face to face with the carrot-top hooligan from the black pickup - all hundred pounds of him, that is, if you factor in the wooden toothpick dangling out the corner of his mouth. We hadn't heard him slink into the building. He was leaning against the doorjamb. Faded liquid blue eyes accentuated his pasty anemic skin, ravaged with pockmarks all the way down his neck. His crossed feet just about blocked our exit. Obviously, he thought of himself as quite an important individual and therefore made no attempt to move.

Ruth leered at him as she and I squeezed by him. "How's it going, Rusty?" she muttered.

Not for one second did he take his bloodshot eyes off me. Animosity was unmistakably there. I was glad Ruth was with me when I made eye contact with him and non-verbally sent him the message that he did not impress me in the least.

A smirk stole across his face, baring crooked tartar-encrusted teeth. One tooth on the top left was missing and the one next to that one was chipped. The rest of his teeth teetered from receded swollen gums.

As Ruth and I walked down the steps of the Town Hall, she whispered, "Remember him?"

I shook my head no. "Haven't the foggiest idea who he is." I replied. I pretended to laugh it off even though thoughts of the emaciated creature made me feel like throwing up. But there was a definite menace about him, which I was at a loss to explain.

"Rusty Kane thinks he's a real hot shot," Ruth said.

I hitched my chin. "Without a doubt."

"He's one of those guys in your drawing of Pierce's Grocery. He hangs with Rick Morton. That makes him kind of special, you know."

"So, what's his beef with me?" I asked. "And Rick Morton... I only vaguely remember both of them."

Ruth shrugged, "Just ignore them. Rick is a bully - always will be - and Rusty's just a little twerp."

"With a big case of BO," I added, my fingers squeezing my nose.

Ruth burst out laughing. "You smelled that, huh?

"Doesn't he ever take a bath?" I asked. "And talk about dragon breath! Whew!"

Ruth and I diffused the air in front of our noses. Then we giggled like schoolgirls.

"Those two have it in their heads that they rule the roost around here," Ruth said.

"Some things never change," I said. "No doubt both flunked out of high school - if they even made it that far. And probably work at dead-end jobs."

"Actually, they don't work at all," Ruth said. "Nobody wants to hire those two losers anymore. They're nothing but trouble. So now, they just hang out all day long."

"Probably figured out a way of collecting disability," I said.

"Folks around here go about their business and try to avoid confrontations with the likes of them," Ruth said.

I shook my head. "Pegged them right then, didn't I?"

Ruth nodded. "Uh-huh." As she jumped back into the driver's seat, it crossed my mind that I might never get my keys back.

As we took off down the street, Rusty Kane was standing like a gunslinger in the Town Hall doorway, keeping a close eye on us. Big deal.

Back at Ruth's, we studied the two death certificates. "How about that? Tommy was born in Memorial Hospital," I said.

"That surprises you?" Ruth asked.

"Well, yeah," I said. "I was born at home." I glanced at her. "You were too, right?"

"Like most others of our generation," she said.

"Wouldn't you expect that to be the case for Tommy?" I said.

"Yeah," Ruth said, thoughtfully. "Especially since Echo Lake was so far out of the way back then. The closest hospital was in Worcester - Memorial Hospital."

I skimmed Gerald Gray's Death Certificate. "Says here Gerald Gray was born in Boston. His wife, Laura, was born in Spain. Maiden name's Medeiros."

"I thought she was of Mediterranean ancestry," Ruth said.

"Her dark hair and eyes and olive skin kind of gives it away," I said.

"Any information regarding Gerald's ancestry?" Ruth asked.

"No, but Cause of Death was accidental drowning," I said.

"Same for Tommy," Ruth said.

"Is Laura Gray still living?" I asked.

"Uh-huh."

I dropped my chin into the palms of my hands. "None of this helps at all." I glanced at Ruth. She looked a bit spacey. "What's the matter?"

"Oh, I was just thinking," she said, whimsically. "That picture of the grave you showed me this morning… It made me think… If Wally and I had a child, he or she might have been around ten years old now - Tommy's age when he drowned. I can't imagine losing any child of mine, especially so young."

I nodded. "I hope I never live to see anything happen to my Julie."

RICK MORTON and RUSTY KANE

It rained again that evening. There was a rumble or two of thunder, but nothing like the night before. I slept better, too.

The following morning, which was Friday, the forecast called for clear skies for the next several days and a waxing moon. So I called Mike Anderson. He seemed tremendously pleased that I did. When I told him to keep an eye out for Wally, Ruth, and me at his place right after supper, he said he looked forward to watching the sunset - that it had been a long time. I got the impression Mike Anderson was a very lonely man.

That evening, the leisurely stroll to the beach was truly pleasurable. The moon in its third phase was rising. Clouds were fleecy. The air was warm. In addition, Ruth and Wally's company on the deserted country road felt real nice to me. Come to think of it, I had always traveled this road alone. We stepped over the rusted chain then made our way down the lane past the place where the shack once stood. As we entered the clearing, Ruth squealed with delight. "Will you look at that! Mike built a campfire! Isn't that the neatest thing?"

"Neatest thing," echoed back at us from across the lake.

Wally put his finger on his lips. "Pipe down, Ruthie."

She lowered her voice. "Oh, but a campfire is so friendly. When I was a kid and summer nights got too sticky to hang out in the house, Mom, Dad, and me, we used to sit in front of a cinder block campfire that Dad built in the backyard. It helped keep mosquitoes away, too. And remember catching fireflies? And you know, somebody was always dropping by and we talked way past midnight. Even then, the house wasn't cooled off enough for us to sleep."

Yesterday, Tommy Gray Drowned

Wally inspected the fireplace, the way carpenters do. A cast iron pot containing steaming coffee was suspended from a metal bar, which stretched between crossbars on either side of the fireplace. "Nice job, Mike. Smelled the coffee brewing way up the road."

"Thanks," Mike answered, all out of breath and slightly flustered. Neatly shaven and dressed in black pants and a burgundy polo shirt, he was much too hot for his own good. He spotted my sketchpad and chalks stuffed under my arm. "Any new drawings?"

I shook my head, tingling all over. But then, I caught myself. Heavens to Betsy, what's wrong with me? My captivation for this guy was way out of control. I knew better than that. I tore my eyes off him and scanned the wooden lawn chairs encircling the fireplace, all of which were perched upon freshly raked sand. Mike must have worked straight out since my call that morning.

"Earned yourself a merit badge for doing this sort of thing back when you was a kid, 'eh, Mike?" Wally said.

"Nah," Mike replied. "Never was a Boy Scout. Getting to meetings was a hassle for my ol' man; and back then, mothers didn't have cars to schlep kids around the way they do now."

I zeroed in on Mike. I was not the only kid who had a lot of time on her - or his - hands. If he and Tommy had better things to do, that newspaper fiasco might not have happened at all. Maybe Tommy Gray would still be alive.

Just then, a boy frolicked towards us from the direction of the unfinished house. A plastic bag of marshmallows was circling over his head. Brutus was leaping at the bag, yipping. It was quite apparent that centrifugal force was mutilating the marshmallows into one big snowball.

"Dad!" the boy hollered. "We don't have enough marshmallows!"

"Enough marshmallows!" Echo Lake reiterated.

Mike yelled back, "That's more than plenty." He winked at me and lowered his voice. "That is, if we can pry those marshmallows apart!"

My face flushed - I could feel it. I blamed it on the campfire; although I was not all that close to the flames. I focused on the boy. As he got closer, I gasped. Chills slithered across my flesh as if thousands of itsy-bitsy spiderlings were crawling all over my body. Before my eyes was the ghost of Tommy Gray. There was no mistaking that round face. That body structure. Those hazel eyes. The boy's hair was ever so slightly darker, but it was Tommy Gray's, right down to the way it flopped in his face. Even the frolicking gait belonged to Tommy Gray.

"Meet my son Tom," Mike spouted with great pride. That winning smile flashed at me, but this time it lacked effect. "Tom! Say hi to Elizabeth Blair!" He seized the boy then roughed him up with fatherly affection.

"Stop, Dad!" The boy squealed and squirmed until breaking free. He planted himself squarely in front of me and jammed his hands into his hips. Those round hazel eyes of long ago peered up at me. "Dad says you grew up here. Why'd you leave?" His voice could have passed for Tommy Gray's. "Don't cha like it here?"

Mike hooted. "Straight forward! Just like his old man!"

I fingered my sketchpad, feeling as if I had to justify myself. "I like it here just fine. My parents decided to move away, that's all. I was just a kid, so I had no other choice than to go with them. And then I went to nursing school in Boston and met Peter… Well, I just ended up living there, that's all."

The boy who bore my little friend's first name pursed his lips. Tommy Gray traced his face and body as the boy squinted at his father. They glanced my way. Their eyes made me feel as though I had no right to leave Echo Lake - ever!

"Well, I like it here just fine!" Tom said with a decisive hitch of the chin. "And so does my Dad! Right, Dad?"

"Right you are, my boy. But people move all the time; that doesn't always mean they don't like a place."

"Well, I can't wait 'ntil I grow up," Tom spouted. "I'm comin' back here and never leavin' again! You better believe it!"

Yesterday, Tommy Gray Drowned

Apparently, Mike misread my uneasiness that was rooted in the revival of Tommy Gray, not the marital status of the man who made my hormones flare up. Hastily he explained, "Tom's mother and I split up. She lives in Worcester with her mother. He spends weekends with me. Sunday nights, he goes back to his mom and school during the week."

"Yeah, and I hate it," Tom whined. His voice shredded my insides. "Worcester is so boring and I hate that school. Lemme stay here, Dad. Please? All my friends are here. So is Brutus."

Emotion wreaked havoc on Mike. Putting his arm around his son, he muttered, "I know, Tom. I know."

Tom kicked the ground. "It's not fair!"

"No, it isn't," Mike agreed. A smile lightened his demeanor. "But, hey, you and I have the whole weekend! Plus it's Friday night! You know what that means…"

"I get to stay up past my bedtime!" Tom exclaimed.

Well, we all laughed. Hey, it's Friday night. Just like Mike said. And it felt terrific to flout our self-imposed adult bedtimes.

Ruth spoke up. "So how long have you and Becky been married, Mike?"

I shot a look at Ruth. Becky? As in Tommy Gray's sister? The way Ruth avoided my eyes I knew my assumption was correct.

"A little over ten years now," Mike said, looking quite dejected.

Tom piped up, "I'm gonna be ten next month!"

As I marveled at Tom Anderson's hazel eyes, it came to me that Tommy Gray turned ten years old just before he drowned - and suddenly I knew it was not my imagination: my fourth grade classmate did drag me back here - just like Emma said. But why? Something coinciding with this ten-year mark? What? If only my fat head could put aside Mike and his son - and for that matter, all the other distractions Echo Lake was throwing at me - maybe then I could figure out all the weirdness.

"Here, have a seat," Mike said. "Everyone! Please! Sit!"

When I just stood there, Ruth took my arm and tugged me to a chair in front of the fireplace.

I sat down, propping my sketchpad and chalks against the side of the chair.

Ruth sat down next to me; Wally on the other side of her. They put their feet up on a log, which Mike had placed there for that very purpose: to warm our feet against the fire. "It's so wonderful sitting by a crackling fire, sipping coffee and enjoying the fading light," Ruth said.

I put my feet up on the log. "Yeah, I said. "Yeah, it is."

Mike dipped a ladle into the iron pot. Careful not to get any grounds into the ladle, he scooped out enough coffee to fill a stoneware mug. He handed it to me and then set up a tray, laden with plastic containers filled with sugar and cream and topped with multi-colored lids. He scooped out mugs of coffee for Ruth and then for Wally. Lastly, some for himself. He settled onto the chair on the other side of Wally.

Meanwhile, Tom wandered off to cut twigs for toasting the fused marshmallows. When we spotted him hacking branches with a boy-scout knife, Mike chuckled, "Those marshmallows are going to have to get chiseled apart."

At water's edge, Brutus yipped. He was pawing at a decaying tree stump. "A field mouse must be holed up underneath there," Wally said.

"So, Mike," Ruth said, "I didn't know you and Becky were separated."

I squinted at her. She knew full well that Mike and his wife were separated. And she knew full well how long Mike and his wife had been married. Ruth was not one to miss trivialities like that. So what was the point of her questions?

Mike ran his hand through his hair. "Guess Becky had enough of me. Don't blame her much. Look at the place. Ten years I've been working on that house. I just don't get back to it. And I didn't pay enough attention to her either. She says all I do is mope around and sit here at this beach all day long. It drives her crazy." He looked so forlorn, so distracted.

Suddenly, I could tell he was experiencing those same unexplained sensations I was. Tommy Gray was trying to get through to Mike Anderson, too.

Tom came racing back, ashen-faced. "Dad! Dad!" He snagged his father by the arm. "Someone's coming! In the woods! Over there!"

As Mike pulled Tom close to his side, an air of anxious expectancy settled over all of us. Brutus lifted his snout to the breeze, which emanated from the path between the lake and the backwash. Picking up an unfamiliar scent, the Dobie let out an ungodly howl and then charged toward the path. "Brutus, drop," Mike hollered.

The Doberman immediately obeyed. Flattened on the ground, he glanced over his shoulder at Mike, anticipating the next command. He was primed to spring; every muscle coiled tightly. His eyes and cropped ears reverted to the path.

Uneasy seconds passed.

Rick Morton and Rusty Kane strutted into the clearing.

Mike sprang to his feet and pulled Tom behind him. I could see that Mike was on edge, but he wasn't the sort to turn tail and run. Neither was Wally who got to his feet and stepped in front of Ruth and me - a kind of barricade of sorts. He appeared to be ready for whatever was about to happen.

Ruth whispered sideways to me. "What are Rick and Rusty doing here?"

"Beats me," I whispered back.

"Up to no good, I bet," she said.

Rick Morton cast demonic eyes at Brutus and bared his teeth. The red-eyed Dobie followed suit.

Rusty Kane sniggered. Brutus had all he could do to contain instincts that spurred him to strike.

Funny how Rick and Rusty swung wide berths around Brutus. The cowards knew better than to tangle with that Dobie.

"Brutus, heel," Mike commanded.

The Dobie returned to his master's side then struck a pose. All the while, his eyes targeted Rick and Rusty. His fangs glistened in the dim light.

Everything Ruth had told me about Rick Morton was true. He still lived in a fifty's fantasyland. Blue jeans, rolled up at the cuffs, showed off dingy white socks and worn out black penny loafers. A pack of cigarettes was rolled up in the sleeve of his sweat-stained tee shirt. An outdated pompadour of glued thinning hair topped off an aging puss. His tongue played ping-pong with a toothpick, back and forth from one corner of his mouth to the other. He had a hog-farm stench about him.

Rusty was Rick's clone - although a sallower and smellier version. The nasty redhead continually spat on the ground, eagerly awaiting the trouble he knew was sure to come. He was wearing the same clothes he had on yesterday at Town Hall. Rick and Rusty's parents had obviously failed to teach their sons the importance of washing themselves and their clothes.

"What's up, Rick?" Wally asked. If concerned, he sure knew how to squelch it. His exterior was as cool as a cucumber. Yet he did not step away from Ruth or me.

"Aw, nuttin'," Rick grunted.

Put on all the air of intimidation you want Rick, I thought, but it's all a facade. Wally is more than capable of taking you and your wannabe down with one hand tied behind his back. So was Mike.

Rick gave me the once over while gnawing mercilessly on the toothpick. Gee, where did I see that before? My brain began to churn. Something wasn't right. That sleaze-bag was not at all happy about my presence. Why? And what was he going to do about it?

Rick spat out the toothpick then snorted and hooked his thumb over his shoulder. "Me and Carrot-top here is out for an evenin' stroll. H'come yous guys're hangin' here at this hour?"

"Watching the sunset," Mike said, not letting down his guard for one second. "Coffee, Rick?" He got to his feet then nudged Tom toward Ruth. Her arms enveloped the boy as she stood up.

"Nah..." Rick grunted. "Got hard stuff?"

"Not a drop," Mike said flatly.

Rick curled his lips and squinted at Rusty. He grumbled something under his breath. They rolled their eyes. They were getting irritated, losing their patience. Rick sauntered over behind me, unrolling the pack of cancer sticks from his sleeve. Everybody's attention was riveted on him - everybody except me. I sat there, feeling like a lump on a log, cursing myself for not doing something. Tension built as Rick rapped the pack on the back of my chair.

Rusty aped everything Rick did. Rick lit up a butt and sucked in nearly a third of it while stepping around to the other side of me. Rusty did the same. Rick exhaled a gray cloud that enveloped his head, glowering at me. So did Rusty. Their yellow teeth gripped glowing stubs as Rick wheezed an inept endeavor at humor. "So, you're the Spencer kid, ain't cha? Still peddling papahs?" He glanced at Rusty, his lip jiggling with half-baked humor.

Rusty sniggered, "Still peddling papahs?"

I rolled my eyes, trying to ignore them.

Rick and Rusty, on the other hand, found the question quite hilarious. Like two puppets on strings, their weight shifted back and forth while their shoulders jounced up and down. But when Rick saw no signs that I was rattled his jaw muscles twisted into knots. His eyes narrowed. Hate festered. He spat his cigarette on the ground then his foot ground it into the sand. Finally, he snapped, "What the hell ya doin' round here?"

"Visiting me!" Ruth spouted, full of defiance. "What business is it of yours?" From time to time, one wide hazel eye peeked out from behind her.

Rick glared at her. She glared back. He seemed shocked that she didn't back down, but he tried to cover it up. She seemed unshaken, but she was spooked, I could tell, running on adrenaline. The situation frayed my nerve endings. When Rick's dirty fists tightened, dread soured my stomach. I was sure he was going to haul off and slug her.

But then Wally stepped between them, puffing up his chest and hiking his pants. His eyes clearly relayed the message: Lay one finger on my wife, Morton, and you're a dead man.

Rick sized up Wally. Understanding the implications perfectly, he leered at me. Then his eyes zeroed in on my sketchpad that was leaning against my chair. "What's that?" He snatched up my sketchpad and tore the cover in half as he opened it.

"Hey!" I yelped, jumping up and grabbing for it.

"I'd advise you to back off, Rick," Mike stated.

Rick put his back to us.

"You are without a doubt the nastiest moron I ever ran into," I shrieked, trying to get around him. "You have no right to manhandle my stuff like that!"

With each page Rick turned, he grunted. Suddenly he stopped. His eyes slitted. He was picking apart the sketch of the graveyard littered with the beer cans. His forehead rumpled. His cigarette jettisoned out his mouth as he spun toward me. "What in Satan's hood is all this chicken scratch?"

"What does it look like?" I snapped, stretching out my arms. My fingers groped for my sketchpad.

Mike took a step toward Rick and me.

I put up my hand, stopping him.

"Nobody gotta remind Rick o' that graveyard," Rusty sneered.

"Give me my sketchpad!" I hollered.

Rick leered forward, inches from my face. "Why'd ya drawd the blasted graveyard?" His breath reeked of stale booze and nicotine.

I gritted my teeth, refusing to speak to that ignoramus one more minute. I stared him down, though, and tried not to inhale his stench. Oh how I yearned to tell him that his filthy pie hole needed an out-and-out lye soaping. And I really yearned to tell both of them that every last inch of them needed a good lye soaping. I crossed my arms and turned away. I just could not understand why on earth I - or that sketch - pissed them off so much. My seething fury suddenly mixed with intuition and the combination knew no bounds. A spotlight switched on in my head. Sketches - each one contained some sort of clue about something Tommy Gray was trying to tell me. Like a gentle

109

tropical wave, a new awareness washed over me: I was on a mission for Tommy Gray.

Rick glared at me, looking me up and down. Perceiving my change of mood, he clenched his fists. His eyebrows furled and then met in the middle of his forehead. His tobacco-stained teeth grated back and forth.

Somehow, the chalk box on the ground next to my chair caught his attention. He glared at it. One swift kick annihilated the box and sent chalks flying. Pieces of cardboard landed in the fire and swooshed into flames.

Needless to say, puppet Rusty Kane got off on the barbarity. Swaying neurotically, he spat repeatedly on the ground, just waiting for either Rick or me or others to strike the first blow. Rusty Kane got no satisfaction.

"Yellowbelly chicken-splat," Rick cursed, flinging the sketchpad at me. He spun around then stomped back to the path between the lake and the backwash. "C'mon, carrot top; time ta blow this crap-joint!"

Rusty shot a look at Rick and then at me. He snickered then bobbled off after his puppet master. Sounds of their exit hung in the air for several moments.

"What did they want, Dad?" Tom asked, stepping out from behind Ruth.

Quite unnerved, she kissed the boy on his sandy forehead then sent him to his father.

Mike gave a command that released Brutus then wrapped an arm around Tom and roughed up the boy's shaggy mop. "Who knows, son." He glanced at me. "Seems like Rick doesn't appreciate good artwork."

"Especially the sketch of the graveyard," Ruth said, glancing at me.

I raised one side of my lips while gathering up remnants of my sketchpad and chalks. I attempted to reassure myself that the goose bumps all over my body were coming from a sharp chill off the water and not because Rick and his wannabe had gotten to me. I sat down and wedged my feet against each other, which spread my legs in a way that Mother used to chew me out for.

"Rick and Rusty congregate up at the graveyard with their cohorts and drink all night long," Wally said. He dropped onto a chair and put his feet up on the log.

All of us scrutinized the Dobie tracking scents of the two thugs, registering every last iota for future reference.

"Holy smoly, Mike," Wally said. "You really gotta replace those rusted out no trespassing signs."

I squinted at Wally and then at Mike.

Mike winked at me. "I'll say. Too much traffic in and out of my property lately. Nasty ol' boys like them aren't exactly what I bought this place for."

Ruth handed me a broken chalk. She was shaking all over.

Wally pulled her down onto his lap and swaddled her in his muscular arms. He looked over her head at me and said, "The graveyard is right next to Rusty's house, you know. His parents were quite the drinkers. Both are dead from the drink. He still lives in that house. It's quite a pig sty, so I hear."

"Lots of rumors go around about the goin's-on in that graveyard," Ruth said. "They take their trollops in there and…"

Mike coughed - quite loudly. His eyes warned that there was a nine-year-old present. Hastily he diverted the boy's attention. "Hey, Tom, did you get enough twigs for the marshmallows?"

The boy instantly perked up. "I'll go get some more."

"Get them over by the house, okay?" Mike suggested. There was a fair amount of pleading in his tone. "And make it snappy. It's getting dark."

"Sure, Dad. Come on, Brutus!"

Obviously, the boy needed no reminders not to go near the path that led to the backwash. I got the feeling that a long time was going pass before he set foot there again all by himself.

When Tom was out of earshot, Mike sat down and in a low voice, said, "I remember Tommy mentioning that graveyard just a few weeks before he… Shoot, what was it he told me? A ruckus of some sort… Yeah, that's it. A ruckus was coming from the graveyard and Tommy couldn't sleep. Too many echoes. He told me he snuck out of the shack. The full moon made it easy for him to see the way along the trail between the backwash and the lake and up the hillside behind the graveyard."

I looked up at the moon. Its brilliance made the clouds fleecy. A couple of stars were beginning to twinkle. I couldn't decide if I felt safe or not.

"A bunch of guys," Mike continued, "one of 'em, Rick, was making some girl scream pretty bad. Tommy couldn't see who she was, but he thought it might be Linda Benson. He saw a fist fly up in the air. Down it came. And the screaming stopped. He heard laughing, so he tried to crawl up the hill for a better look. But he lost his footing and tumbled back down. Well, he high-tailed it out of there, but Rick must have put two and two together, because the next day he cornered Tommy and threatened to skin him alive if he ever opened his yap."

Ruth squinted at the sketchpad propped against my chair. "The graveyard..." she said, picking up the sketchpad. She opened it and studied the graveyard littered with beer cans. She turned to the page depicting Rick and a bunch of other kids in front of Pierce's Grocery Store. "You know what? That's just about the time Rick and Linda called it quits. We all thought she ran off. I wonder..."

My insides somersaulted. Was Linda Benson the girl who screamed? Did Rick and his hoodlum pals do the unthinkable?

Within my brain, an unmistakable voice drifted like a leaf upon an Indian-summer breeze: Y-e-s...

CRAZY

Warping manifestations of Tommy Gray and Linda Benson traversed my psyche most of the night. Trapped in tormented semi-consciousness, I tossed and turned, trying to calm myself down and go to sleep. The steady tick, tick, tick of the hallway clock heightened with each passing minute, becoming discordant clangs that dislodged any remnant of peace within me. At last, dreams overtook the night, but they were like an unexpected squall at sea:

A girl screams. Hyenic laughter.

It's so dark. I…I can't see.

A pustulating giant looms up before my eyes, filling my entire vision, robbing me of breath. Eye to eye, its pupils - gargantuan, vertical, elliptical - throbbed black evil.

Gerald Gray… No… Who? Rick! It's Rick Morton!

I spin away. I am on the dip in the path between the lake and the backwash.

Tommy is bathed in shadowed moonlight. Hovering close to him is a maiden, hair of gold, eyes of the sea.

Linda?

Tommy slowly nods. So does Linda.

Why Tommy? Why Linda? Why such sadness?

Wait… Are you beckoning to me?

Tommy slowly nods. So does Linda.

I start towards them.

They float away, up the embankment.

Wait! I run. Where are you going? I run faster. Faster. Ow! My ankle! I stumble backwards, down through the trees. Help! My hand reaches out, grabbing for anything to stop my fall.

Yesterday, Tommy Gray Drowned

Tommy's hand extends towards me.
I stretch.
Our fingers spread, straining to touch. Closer.
I can't...reach you... My cries echo throughout the night.
Tommy! Where are you?

The next morning, that mind-blowing dream gnawed at my insides. How did it end? I think I tumbled over and over...and fell into Echo Lake... There was no air. I couldn't breathe.

I trembled. "Geez, these dreams are driving me nuts!"

Nauseated by stomach acid, I showered, but the tepid drizzle felt like icy needles puncturing my skin. I towel dried; all the while, obscure peril swelled within me. Ill at ease, I fussed with my dirty-blond mop - in itself a torment throughout my existence. Then to top it all off, the pump on the hair spray bottle decided to quit. "Shoot."

In the midst of my tantrum, Cousin Ruth came to my rescue, shoving a bottle of hair spray through the bathroom door. "Thanks," I said, thinking she was truly a blessing in my life. I spritzed - well, only a time or two... "I can't believe this. Hers ran out!"

While pouring the dregs of my bottle into hers, I grumbled, "A trip to Pierce's Grocery Store is definitely in the works. Actually, it's an absolute necessity or I'll be wandering the Town of Echo Lake, looking very much like that ogre in my nightmare."

Deprived of rest, I stuffed my sketchpad under my arm and stepped out of the door into an absolutely glorious day. My stagnant lungs sucked in the freshness, making me feel as if I hadn't taken a breath all night long. My mind began to clear, and my upset stomach became a memory.

I opened my car door then wedged my sketchpad behind the passenger seat. Waving goodbye to Ruth, I slid into the driver's seat. I backed out of the driveway then stopped in the middle of the street to put down the ragtop. I lifted my face to the sun. Warmth drenched my face. I smiled at the tree-lined road ahead. It was getting greener with every passing day. I put the car in gear. Brisk air flowed around me, exhilarating my encumbered spirits. I came alive. Songbirds provided plenty of music so I didn't bother to switch on the radio. I took my time driving into the village; that's the nice thing about the country: lots of time and not much traffic. Without concern for holding up anyone, I stopped whenever I felt like it and searched out things remembered or to rediscover those forgotten. Unfortunately, at one point, a station wagon of 70s vintage came along. I pulled off onto what little shoulder there was.

The driver passed - slowly. There was no escaping her piercing eyes. I knew right away that I - and my car with no roof - had just been placed at the top of the gossip list this fine day. Well, no matter. The majestic weather made me feel as if I could take on the world.

I sighed. "Guess it's good a time as any to go by the old homestead." Up until now my entire being avoided even the thought of going there.

Shortly after passing Pierce's Grocery Store, I slowed to a snail's pace. As I passed the house where I spent the majority of my childhood, emotions stole over me. In my heart, I always knew someone else lived there, but yet… I felt like calling out: Hey, people! What would you think if I stopped and told you I grew up in your house? Would you let me in to look around? Suddenly, the past darkened my soul, making me asked myself: Geez, why would I want to do that? I pursed my lips and glared at the house. No way am I ever going in there. As pangs of resentment dissipated, I mumbled, "Good luck people. Hope you're happier than I was."

Just beyond the house, I turned around in the gravel driveway of a split-level house that wasn't there when I was a kid. Back then, only skunk cabbage and jack-in-the-pulpit reigned the swamp, which had subsequently been drained in order to use as a building lot. When I was ten, I got poison sumac in that swamp. Mother put that purple stuff on my rash, warning me not to itch, because I would get that purple stuff on my fingers and then when I put my fingers in my mouth, I would poison myself.

115

Yesterday, Tommy Gray Drowned

Sometimes I thought she hoped I would; maybe she hated me; maybe she wanted me gone; maybe she wanted me to fall off a cliff and die. Secure in self-righteous indignation and nice warm anger, I stepped on the gas.

A short distance from the old homestead, I stopped, shut off the engine, and sulked. Only a redwing blackbird, clinging to the puffy remnants of last year's cattails in the swamp to my right, disturbed my solitude. His wings fluttered with each note that praised the radiant morning. Aargh.

I squinted at the cape-style dwelling. It looked to be in fairly decent shape. I cocked my head sideways. Funny. It seemed so much larger when I was a kid. The current owner kept the same colors - pale yellow with charcoal shutters. Only minor changes were made over the years, such as the back porch, which was smaller.

Mentally, I walked up the back porch steps. I opened the screen door. Hinges squawked. In the kitchen, my eyes tripped over the butts overflowing the nicotine-stained ashtray setting on the counter. One butt had fallen onto the countertop, permanently branding the Formica. I stepped away from the stink of nicotine and headed into the living room. Newspapers scattered the hardwood floor in front of the easy chair where Father usually fell asleep after supper. I went up to the second floor, stairs creaking all the way. I stood on the landing, gazing into the nine-by-eleven space once assigned to me. The intolerably long lonely hours I had spent in that hollow room weighed down my soul. I could still hear the night whistling through the solitary white pine outside the window and a whip-poor-will tattling in the distance. I never could figure out what Will did so bad that he deserved a whipping - bad enough for Will to take flight into the darkness to tell the world: whip-poor-will?

I had to remind myself that the white pine tree and the whip-poor-will were not there anymore - just like me - but noises of the house that used to be called home vexed me. Father, an apparition in my youth, snored incessantly in the bedroom adjoining mine. My insomnia intensified as Mother screeched out in her sleep at some ignoramus who had gotten on her nerves. How dare he or she not agree with her way of thinking? At times, Mother bolted upright, fists threatening to drive home the point that her word was law, not to be questioned. Her stentorian lungs confounded the strongest debater. She was right. Everybody else was wrong.

Mother never let anyone close to her, not even me, her only daughter. Detached domination - that was her forte. Iron will controlled Father, Brother, and me. The only friends we had were those who met with her approval. Needless to say, her standards were rarely met.

We never did much as a family; an occasional Sunday drive made better without Mother's ruling presence. So it was I resided in my room most of the time, Brother in his, while Father dozed in the living room recliner night after night, the *Evening News* strewn at his feet. Meanwhile, in the television room, Mother immersed herself watching the make-believe authority of Perry Mason.

The pain of that house still made me feel dead. What did it all amount to in the end? Father was dead now. Mother was off in Arizona married to some guy I never even met. I felt so isolated and alone, sitting there in my car, disoriented. I wished I hadn't come back to Echo Lake.

I rubbed my forehead. "Well, at least my paper route got me out of that house." A slow smile lifted my face. Yes, my paper route got me away from the bitter isolation called home. And it occurred to me: "My greatest freedom was my paper route."

Mother carried it in her head that such an enterprise would bring about vast riches. Well, that didn't happen. But to this day, I couldn't help but wonder how Mother let me go off, day after day, all by myself to deliver newspapers door to door. The dangers were just as real back then as they were now. The only difference was now the media was on top of every little thing. But how could Mother send her only girl-child out into scaring heat of late July? Out into savage lightning filled downpours? Out into toe-numbing bitterness of January? Funny thing: once I found an orange, frozen solid from the bitter cold.

Yesterday, Tommy Gray Drowned

It wasn't too far from the shack Tommy Gray lived in. Kicking that orange ice ball all the way home was the only thing that kept my pitiful body warm that sub-zero afternoon.

Closing my eyes, I turned away from the yellow house, a vain attempt at blocking out the past. Upon opening my eyes again, the house next door loomed before me. My veins iced. Warren Squire's place.

Several slats were broken on the gate, which remained half-opened. The dilapidated picket fence hadn't seen whitewash in ages. The olive green paint on the double-decker house was blistered and peeling. The wrap-around farmer porches was sagging. Screens were torn and flapping in the wind. And there...there was the infamous glider...

Images of Warren Squire, six-feet tall and two hundred and fifty pounds, rocking back and forth on that glider accosted me. Back and forth... Back and forth... The metal tracks squawked; even back then they were worn razor-sharp. I wondered if plastic still covered the same compacted seat cushions. In summer's swelter, cracked and brittle plastic stuck to the back of my legs and scored my flesh as Squire's long, heavy arm draped my shoulder. His thick hand crept across my chest where there were only buds of maturity...down...across my belly...into my underpants... Filthy fingers touched, groped, probed... Nobody saw. Not even Squire's wife, because she was confined to a far-off hospital. Mother and Father were off grocery shopping somewhere where nobody knew them. Brother? Well, of course, he went with them.

"Come child," enticed the snake, luring innocence into his pit darkened by mildewed tapestry. Degeneracy surged on and on... Ripping... Pain. Spinning shadows, round and around. His voice, "So nice. Our own special secret. No one must ever know. Do not betray me. I am your friend - your only friend."

Sitting there in my car, I wanted to puke. This was not a dream – or even a nightmare. This was reality. What Squire did to me came flooding back to my consciousness. Now I knew why I drew the sketch of his front porch. But when did I draw it? During the nightmare I had back in Brighton?

I seized my sketchpad from behind the passenger seat, which resulted in the complete demise of the cover Rick had torn at the lake. I was left, gawking at a piece of the cover in my hand while the rest of the sketchpad fell onto the passenger seat. I tossed the cover into the backseat then grabbed the sketchpad. Opening it to Squire's house, my insides churned. I glared at the details. A solid four-foot wall concealed the lower halves of the porches. Nobody saw the interior of the lower halves. Nobody ever saw Squire's hands touch, grope, violate. Grimy storm windows replaced screens every winter, fogging, then icing, until frigid temperatures put a transitory halt to debauchery.

Why did Squire do such despicable things? Did the loneliness created by the illness of his wife drive him to kids? How did he have the audacity to look Mother and Father square in the eyes, knowing full well the lewdness he perpetrated upon their daughter? The vile creature living inside him surely reveled in their ignorance. And how come Mother - all-knowing Mother – didn't get wind of it? Wasn't it up to her and Father to put a stop to it? Did either of them know and look the other way? Was Mother's power just a facade? Like Ray Briggs, was I a victim because of isolation and vulnerability? And Brother? Brother... Ah, yes, brother...

Jealousy flared within me like the fire that lightning kindles in a forest ravaged by drought. After Warren was through with me, he rocked on that glider with Brother - together - close - much too close - their bodies touching. Squire's muscular arm draped over Brother who drooled because he didn't have sense enough to keep his lips together and swallow once in a while. Yes, I knew exactly what Warren Squire was doing, because he did it to me. And then, Warren Squire didn't want me anymore. Warren Squire cast me aside for Brother...then for Ray Briggs...Wally...someone else...

Rejected and hurt, I never went near Squire after that. Never said much to Brother either. I retreated into myself, for nobody could hurt me there. I pretended not to give a hoot about anything. Totally alone - that was me. Nobody cared about me. Everyone deserted me: Squire; dominating Mother; withdrawn

Yesterday, Tommy Gray Drowned

Father; slobbering Brother; Peter... Even my friend Tommy Gray.

"Tommy? That's it!" I bolted upright in the driver's seat. "Tommy made me sketch Squire's front porch! Forcing me to face my past! He wants me to discover myself, to understand what makes me tick!"

I squinted at the sketch, thinking how my childhood dictated my actions as an adult. After Peter left for Vietnam in the sixties, I lived in an emotional drought, isolated by thoughts of rejection, desertion, seduced and abandoned. Now that Peter was gone again, paranoia wracked my heart and brain: this time he's not coming back. My only choice it seemed was to retreat into that empty, meaningless world again, because I just could not bear the emptiness Peter left behind.

"Nobody ever comes back," I moaned.

Mother and Father deserted me. They took Brother and not me. Geez, I wasn't even twenty years old. Mother claimed they had to move to Arizona, because Father got lung cancer. I just know he got it from Mother's second-hand smoke. You'd think Mother would have come back after Father passed on, but she didn't. She had Father cremated. There was no funeral. There was no grave to visit. Then she remarried - just like that. So, in a sense, Mother also died, which left me with no family, good or bad. And now Peter was gone - again.

"Imagine that," I whispered. "I have lived nearly all my adulthood in self-imposed social isolation. I've carted it around with me for decades."

I slumped, but tears didn't come. I just stared at the house of my childhood and then at Warren Squire's porch. Then a thought came to me: How could I blame Mother or Father - or anyone else for that matter - when I myself kept so silent?

Warmth fanned my ear: Those days are gone, never again to return as long as 'Lizbeth wills it so.

"Tommy?" I scanned my surroundings. This couldn't be happening. People got locked up for hearing voices. But I had no explanation for hearing Tommy Gray's voice. Definitely impossible. But yet it was happening anyway.

"'Lizbeth builds barriers that will not stop hurt."

I didn't know what to do. I couldn't be crazy, but I was frantic to explain his voice.

The rumble of tires on pavement caught my attention. A car edged past mine and then pulled into the driveway of the homestead. A middle-aged biddy got out and stood there, gawking at me.

Panic seized me. I sat up and started the car.

Her contemptuous stance continued as I drove by.

I didn't look at her. I kept driving.

Yesterday, Tommy Gray Drowned

OVER THE EDGE

After pulling up in front of Pierce's Grocery Store, I sat there and tried to collect myself. Yes, I heard Tommy's voice. No, that's impossible.

Excruciating pain ruptured inside my head. Yes, possible.

I felt sticky and clammy, and for a second there, thought I smelled like Rick Morton and Rusty Kane. "Gross." I took several, deep, cleansing breaths then got out of the car. I leaned against the door. Tommy's voice had to be real.

My strength slowly returned.

I headed into the store. The bell tinkled overhead.

"Well, by Jove, if it ain't Li'l 'Lizbeth, the papah girl," Don yelped. "I heard ya was still hangin' 'round these here parts. What cha been up to?"

I shivered. "Uhm…catching up on old times…with Ruth."

The good-natured roly-poly with hair white as newly-fallen snow seemed genuinely interested in everything I had to say. For all it mattered to him, I could have been talking about the chemical make-up of the latest exploding super nova.

"Well ain't that nice," he said. "Ruth and Wally are terrific folks. Don't get better than them two."

The pall lifted off me, and I felt a whole lot better. Right there and then, I came to the conclusion that I did not make good company for myself. I needed to keep people like feisty old Don around me to keep me on an even keel.

"I'm enjoying visiting with them very much," I said. "So, where do you keep the hair spray? The pump on mine quit this morning and Ruth's bottle is bone dry."

"Know what kind?" he asked, rushing out from behind the counter.

"Oh, shoot," I said, tapping my right index finger against the side of my face. "I have no clue. But mine is in a blue plastic bottle, if that helps." I felt embarrassed. Women should know such things.

"Any of these here ones?" Don said, holding up a couple of containers embellished with varying tones of blue.

"The one on the left," I said, pointing. I squeezed my jaw between my index finger and thumb. "At least I think that's the one."

He put the other bottle back then sauntered over to me. "Here ya go, Li'l 'Lizbeth."

I reached in my pocketbook for money.

"No charge," he said, waving me off.

"But, Don, I..."

He cut me off, "No ifs, ands, or buts about it." His head shook decisively; his palm veered side-to-side. "Jes' braing back t'other one when yer back in the neighborhood. My distrib' makes good on thaings like that. Anythin' else?"

Feeling obligated to buy something, I spied homemade pies on the shelf next to the deli. They drew my attention like magnets. I picked up one of the pies and before I even got my nose close to it, the freshness bowled me over. "Mmmm, this smells absolutely scrumptious! I didn't know you were a baker."

Don laughed and patted his belly. "I should be, what with a belt size as this. Nope, it's Miss Becky Anderson what's the baker 'round these parts."

"Becky Anderson?"

"Ayup. That lil' lady's some kinda cook. One what ya got there's strawberry rhubarb. Outta this world."

"I'm a pushover for strawberry rhubarb," I said.

"Egads, plop 'niller ice cream on a slice of it and lordy, lordy!" Don said. His tongue rolled around his lips while his hand circled his belly.

I giggled then hungrily appraised that pie. I should buy it right there and then and divvy it up between Don and me this very minute. I envisioned the two of us, our chins dripping with sweet pink syrup. How decadent. How very, very grand. I placed the pie next to the cash register. "One strawberry rhubarb pie it is!" I declared. "And I'll go get a half gallon of vanilla ice cream from the freezer and we'll share it. How about it, Don?"

"Gotta take a rain check on that," Don said. "But you know'd, Ruth and Wally are fans of Miss Becky's pies."

Well, I really had my mind made up on sharing that pie with him, but if it pleased Ruth and Wally... I placed the carton of ice cream on the counter and watched Don slide the pie into a brown paper bag sideways. I twisted my fingers while watching him ring up the pie and ice cream. I scratched my head while watching him slide the carton of ice cream into an insulated bag. I cleared my throat then ventured, "Becky is Mike's wife..."

"You betcha," Don said. "Lives up there in Wor'ster with her Mama now. Comes all the way out here 'n' delivers fresh pies ta me twiced a week. Gettin' where she's gotta come more often - they sells out so fast. Tsk, tsk, tsk, shur wisht those two young-uns would patch thaings up."

I fished around my pocketbook for money. "Mike does seem terribly lonesome," I mused. "I still picture Becky as a five-year-old. Cute kid."

Don nodded. "A real looker now."

I gave him a sidelong glance. "A looker..." Threads of jealousy rippled through me.

"Ayup, she's a dandy." He slid the packages over to me. His eyes met mine. His brows came together.

I looked down at my pocketbook. The corner of a twenty-dollar bill revealed itself. I hooked onto it. My hand trembled as I handed the bill to him. He took it from me then stepped over to the register and pushed down some keys. "So whatever happened to Warren Squire?" My hand fled to my lips. I bug eyed Don. Why in the world did I ask that?

The drawer sprang open. Ding.

Don rolled his eyes. His head waved side to side. "The ol' buzzard still lives in the same place. Wife's been gone for many a year now." He slammed the drawer shut and grunted. "Squire's on his deathbed, so's I hear. Prostate cancer's eatin' 'im alive. Sorta fittin', aye-yup."

Meekly, I gathered up my packages. "Uhm…why is that?"

Don grunted again. "Ol' buzzard's a disgrace to humanity. Played around wit' young-uns round these parts fer years. Caught him once myself out back with the Taylor boy. Run Squire off, I did. 'N so's I went complainin' ta ol' Chief Briggs 'bout it - more'n once, I tell ya. Got me nowhere."

"Incredible," I muttered. Squire's shenanigans didn't stop with me or Brother - or Wally and Ray Briggs. Geez, how many of us were there? And to think, the morally bankrupt inhabitants of this cesspool of a town let that pedophile get away with it.

"If only my foot could lands three or four well-aimed kicks right where it hurts Squire the most," Don grumbled.

I couldn't help but think: Don seeking justice by violence?

Without warning, shame sloshed over me; my own silence played a part in allowing the degeneracy to continue. Well, God won't let Squire off the hook. I pursed my lips, visualizing that disgusting perpetrator of innocence lying at death's door inside that decrepit house with the gate hanging off its hinges. All alone with his misery, no one to comfort him, Warren Squire was living on borrowed time. Soon he was going to pay his debt to the devil. My satisfaction contained not the least bit of shame as I smiled to myself. Warren Squire was suffering - dying with prostate cancer - good enough for him!

Just then, the door exploded open and bashed into the wall, scattering my thoughts into dust. The bell over the door convulsed as Rick Morton stomped toward me. "What in hell are you still doin' 'round here?" he barked. The stub of a cigarette waggled out one corner of his mouth.

Rusty Kane trailed Morton, frothing like a dog itching for a bone. The stub of a cigarette also waggled out one corner of his mouth.

Morton spat his cigarette butt on the floor.

Kane followed suit.

126

"Well?" Rick growled, shoving me on the shoulder with the butt of his hand.

I held my temper while maintaining my balance. Best to keep my big yap shut. My insides, however, were up to an out and out brawl: What business was it of theirs what I did or where I went? On top of that, wasn't it about time they extinguished those cigarettes scorching Don's spotless floor?

Rusty smirked, his head bobbing over Rick's shoulder. His eyes seemed to grow wider by the second as he continually licked his colorless lips, which were quivering with anticipation. The redhead was primed for a showdown.

I stood my ground, but failed to heed my own advice. Yeah, I opened my big yap: "You jerks certainly get off frightening people, don't you?"

Rick did not take his eyes off me for a second, even with the odor of charred wood seeping into the air.

I looked down at the live butt. Rick noticed me doing that, because his worn-out penny loafer stomped on the butt then pulverized it until all that remained were powdered tobacco weed and a burn spot.

Of course, Rusty copycatted every move Rick made. More powdered tobacco weed and another burn spot.

Rick shoved me backwards, this time with the knuckles of his left hand. "Gonna make this short and sweet." Another shove. "It's high time ya hightailed it out of this town…" Another shove. "…for your own…" Another shove… "…good."

I sprawled across the counter. Over my head, Don shook a finger at Morton. "Now, Rick, leave Li'l 'Lizbeth be! Ya hear me? Ya got no business…"

"Shut up, ol' man!" Rick's lizard eyes shot poison darts at Don and then at me. "This is 'tween me 'n' her. I'm sick 'n tired of seein' that rod o' hers and her high-falootin' muzzle." His finger spiked my collarbone again and again. "Time ta hit the road back ta where ya comes from, whore; got it?"

Well, I was all for skedaddling; however, for some reason, I boldly stood my ground…uhm…I mean, countertop. I

127

concealed every emotion, not moving a muscle, maybe not even breathing. Although his ice pick of a finger hurt like the dickens. I felt like I was standing ground in the face of an onrushing Acela Express train, somehow trusting it was going to stop before it mowed me down.

Rick continued to glare at me, waiting for me to say something. When I didn't, he withdrew his finger.

Wish I could say it was courage that got me through that. As it was, bile was choking the devil out of me.

His face reddened. The vein in the middle of his forehead pulsated. Anger built like a volcano threatening to erupt. His mouth contorted. He up and downed me.

Rusty was lathering like a rabid wolf.

Suddenly Rick's eyes widened.

Oh, oh, he spotted the packages in my hands.

One mighty swat of his right hand sent strawberry rhubarb pie splattering everything. The container of ice cream sailed through the air and split open upon impacting the floor. As it spun out of control, skipping across the floor, Rusty jumped out of the way. When it smacked into the side of the cold drink case, a deranged grin blackened his pasty face.

"Get out of here, Rick Morton!" Don hollered while running out from behind the deli. "Get out now! The both of ya! Or so help me I'll ring up Chief Parker!" Don stood there, hands on hips, chin drawn up, staring down the latent punks. "No more shenanigans! Ya hear me?"

"I'm okay, Don!" I shrieked. Quickly, I issued a fervent prayer: Please, God, don't let this sweet man get hurt! Realizing I had to draw Morton's attention away from Don, I jeered, "What's the matter, Rick? Not enough guts to take on Mike or Wally last night? Oh, I get it: picking on a woman is more your style."

His jaw dropped as he leered at me. I had struck a nerve! He squinted at Don. A sickening eternity passed. His eyes fixed on mine. I felt my soul being branded with the white-hot venom of hate. A lecherous grin slunk across his face.

My insides instantly chilled - much like a searing horseshoe that the blacksmith plunges into water.

Rick curled up his lip. He turned and stomped to the cold drink case. Kicking the melting block of ice cream out of his way, he then opened the cold drink case. He snagged a drink, tossed it to Rusty, and then snagged one for himself. He pointed at Rusty, snapped his fingers, and then strutted out the door.

Rusty dogged after Rick. Just before going out the door, he jeered over his shoulder at me.

The bell above the door squawked for several moments. Then silence.

"Idiots," I sneered, prying myself off the counter.

Don took hold of my arm and patted my forearm. "Day's gonna come when those ruffians are gonna nose up ta the wrong feller."

I straightened my clothes. "That *feller* just might be *me*."

Robin's egg eyes widened, boring into mine as concern riddled Don's face.

I gave him a squeeze, holding on for a moment. I swore to myself that this was the last time this kind-hearted man was going to get involved in whatever beef Rick had with me.

"Here, lemme get cha 'nother pie, Li'l 'Lizbeth!"

I watched Don scoot off, not having the wherewithal to protest. I eyed the carton of ice cream then picked it up and turned it over. The carton was scraped up, but for the most part the contents were still protected and mostly frozen. I could shave off any foreign matter there was with a butter knife when I got back to Ruth's. Before Don caught wind of the damage, I stuffed the carton of ice cream into another bag. I slipped a twenty under the corner of the cash register then snagged a wad of napkins off the deli case. I scooped up as much of the disintegrated pie as I could and chucked the mess into the trash. It wasn't long before Don caught me red-handed. "Here, now, don't cha go fussin'. I got all day ta clean up. What's more, the shop needs a good cleanin'."

Paying him no mind, I scraped up as much as I could before I felt as if I was in his way. Wondering what could be done about the burn marks on the floor, I gave him a warm hug. "Sorry about all this, Don. I owe you big time for…"

"Don't wanna hear 'nother word 'bout it, Li'l 'Lizbeth." He waved me off. "Next time ya come 'round, we hafta keep an eye out for those fellers. Hide ya in the backroom m'self if'n I even smells 'em."

"That'll be the day I hide from anyone," I scoffed. "Especially those two nincompoops." I picked up my packages. "See you in a few, Don."

Walking out to my car, I recalled how dreadful I felt when I arrived here earlier. I felt no better now - although in a much different way. I had sort of put Warren Squire into perspective, but Rick Morton and Rusty Kane were another matter. "When are those two going to give up and leave me…" I stopped short, gawking at glob of slimy spit slithering down the hood of my car. Behind it, a glistening trail. "Someday, those two are going to push me over the edge."

MUSH

When Ruth saw me pull up in her driveway, she bolted out of the house, Kleenex in hand. Out of breath and beside herself with worry, I could tell she had been crying. "Don called me and told me to keep an eye out for you! What's stinking up Rick and Rusty's butts?"

"Haven't the faintest," I said, unbuckling my seat belt, "but Rick told me to… Well, let me quote him: 'Time ta hit the road back ta where ya comes from, whore; got it?'"

"Aw, come on, Bethie, you're not leaving!" Ruth stomped her foot and crossed her arms. Verging on tears again, she whined, "I'm just getting to know you! And the nerve of that bully calling you a name like that!"

"Don't worry about it, Ruthie. I have no intention on leaving - not until I am *real* good and ready." I handed the rhubarb pie and vanilla ice cream to her then put up the top and got out of the car. I slammed the door then stomped to the trunk where I took out paper towels and window cleaner. Cleaning off dried sputum of my windshield, I grumbled, "For the life of me, I don't understand what I ever did to deserve this."

A bit later, we sipped hot tea on the back porch. Ruth offered me a sandwich. I declined.

"All you've had to eat today is a cinnamon bun," she nagged.

"Coffee, too," I said, showing her the mug in my hand. "And this tea."

"That is not enough," she countered.

Discounting her observation, I muttered, "Why is my presence in Echo Lake aggravating those two so much?"

Yesterday, Tommy Gray Drowned

Ruth stopped short and squinted at me toying with a lemon rind. She raised her palms to shoulder level, heaved a breath then shook her head.

The black hole I was sinking into was becoming much too deep. "I need some air," I puffed, getting to my feet.

"But it's starting to rain, Bethie."

"Don't worry about it, Ruth. Be back in a few."

"Well here, take my umbrella."

"Nah, mine's in the trunk."

I could feel her standing inside the screen door, her teary eyes on me as I headed down the driveway then turned onto the deserted country road. My umbrella remained in the trunk.

My mind was mush. Any semblance of rational thought did not exist. A couple of rabbits scooted across the road; I barely noticed them.

Rain dripped like tears from the rusted links that barred the lane where Tommy Gray once traveled. I lifted my face to the heavens and felt as though he was showering his friendship upon me. I imagined him, on an astral plane, bathed in misty yellow light, rippling. He was still ten-years-old. We were standing on an incline, a slope, him at the top, me down here. He was gazing at me in his weird sort of way. I felt as if he was telling me something. Why didn't I get it?

My fingertips grazed my chin. My tongue searched out the moisture kissing my lips. My hand glided down my neck then brushed against my upper chest and stopped at a sore spot. I winced at the bruise ripening into black and blue - and it zapped me back to reality. "You are a total jerk, Rick Morton." I swiped away moisture trickling off my nose as if it were him.

I plucked my sopping tee shirt off my chest. "Well, at least I didn't retreat into my shell like a foolish turtle." The second I let go of my shirt, it reattached itself to my chest. "Wasn't long ago I'd've been out of this town in a shot. What a switch." I squinted at my tee shirt clinging to me in a less than flattering way.

A voice inside me whispered: You're soaked to the skin. Go back to Ruth's.

"I'm not ready."

The trees drooped with the weight of the rain. They appeared to be druids arching over me. Branches transformed into swaying arms that threatened to snatch me up. The timbre of the rain became a voice, bleating, terrorizing my soul: Time ta hit the road back ta where ya comes from, whore; got it? Got it? Got it?

I shouted away my trepidation. "I'm not ready to go back!"

"Go back!" came the echo of the lake. "Go back..."

I stomped down the barren country road.

There had to be some connection between Rick and Rusty and me. What was it? I just couldn't figure it out. Perhaps I was trying too hard. Maybe I should leave it alone; let the answer come on its own.

Mike Anderson's house came into view. I half-expected to feel safer; instead, its cloaked-in-tarpaper-blackness portended unfinished business. No cars in the yard. Brutus was yelping in the bay window and it gave me heebie-jeebies. I called out to him, "You want to go with me, don't cha, fella?"

Even though my voice did not reach his ears beyond the glass, he jumped down as if capable of reading my lips. I heard his claws digging at the front door and then he was back at the window again. He seemed to be begging me to set him free.

"I don't have a key!" I cried, displaying my empty palms as if to prove it to him. "You know I'd love your company."

Echo Lake called, "Your company... Company..."

I was almost crying now, because I realized how much I loved that mutt and hated not taking him with me. "Besides, it's raining and you'll get soaked like me. I don't want you to catch a..."

"Don't slow down now, carrot-top!"

I gawked over my shoulder. The black pickup! Rick Morton and Rusty Kane! My insides revolted: How many times did I have to face off with them?

"Step on it, will ya?" Rick hollered. "I cain't latch onto the whore!"

I made a dash for Mike's house - and Brutus. I ran for all I was worth.

"Gotcha!" Rick smelled like an alcoholic sewer as he swooped down upon me.

As we wrestled in the muck, I squirmed to get away. "Get off me!"

"Cut the crap!" he yelled, struggling to pin me to the ground. His soggy hold on my left arm slipped to my wrist.

A blur of echoes off the lake mixed with the drizzle.

"Let...me...go!" I snarled. I yanked my arm free then shoved him away and scrambled to my feet.

He came at me, inebriated fire in his eyes and a constant stream of curses vomited out his mouth. His grim-encrusted fingers formed claws.

I took a swing at him, a right upper cut. It caught his chin. He staggered backward. "Leave me alone!" I shrieked. I clenched my teeth and kicked him in the shin.

"Eeoow!" he shrieked.

Brutus howled beyond the window. Talons screeched down the glass.

I should have run right then and there, but this was my fourth confrontation with these bullies. Somehow, it wasn't as terrifying as the other times - even though it should have been. Confrontations were getting to be a habit - that's why I just stood there, soaking up the image of Rick Morton hopping about on one leg. Surely, he had enough. Surely, he'd leave me alone from now on.

Demonic eyeballs, clouded with pain, marked me. His pain transformed into searing daggers of hate that perforated my soul.

The hair on my neck bristled. Oh-oh...

"Aargh!" he bawled, hurling himself at me.

I turned to run, but his weight knocked me off kilter. Like a linebacker he brought me down. Air surged out of me. Then the side of my face took the brunt force of his full hand. I spun like a top. He snagged my hair and I came to an abrupt stop. His free hand crushed against my lips. My teeth gored the inside of my mouth and I tasted something metallic. Blood - my blood!

Brutus howled. Talons screeched up and down the windowpane.

Rick grunted and cursed the weather while dragging me towards the decrepit pickup.

I dug my heels into the muck and then into slippery pavement. Somehow I managed to chomp my teeth into his hand.

He cussed as his grip loosened.

I wrenched free and tumbled backward. Smacking into a rock, I felt my right kneecap move to the left and then a sharp pain shot up into my inner thigh. I spat out blood while clambering to get to my feet, spinning around then stumbling off.

A closed fist clobbered the nape of my neck. I felt as though I was struck by a wrecking ball. My head boggled back and forth while the rest of my body hurtled through the air like a ragdoll. I landed face down in the ditch, breath vomiting out of me. Something cracked my skull then white agony flashed throughout my brain.

An arm hooked my neck, jerking me backwards.

I couldn't breathe! Choking… Blackness…

Yesterday, Tommy Gray Drowned

BOUND

Drizzle washed the darkness away. I sensed hands gripping my arms, my legs. I was being lifted. I smelled cigarette smoke. Reflexes spurred me to fight, but an inner voice cautioned against it: Such action could prove futile and potentially fatal. Time was needed to regain strength, to figure out location, to plan an escape. Except... My head... It throbbed like the dickens. So did my right knee. I won't be spending an evening ballroom dancing any time soon - even if Peter was home.

Ka-plunk. I landed on something hard - the truck bed? Air gushed out of me. Thinking straight verged on the impossible. Better feign unconsciousness - actually, I blacked out.

I came to, looking up into drizzle and a mixture of oaks, maples, and pines passing above me. Where was I? I was bouncing along. Where was I going?

A filthy rag cut into the corners of my mouth and the taste of motor oil and dirty hands was stimulating excessive drool. Unable to spit it out, I refused to swallow. Ashes peppered my face. I tried to move my hands to defect the ashes, but discovered my hands were bound in front of me with a single length of frayed bailing twine. A dated deer rifle lay across my belly. Heavy moisture dribbled from my nose, across my cheek, and passed below my earlobe. Was that moisture coming from my nose? Was it blood? From where Rick hit me?

I became aware of my ankles. They were bound - probably with twine. And I became aware of the sound of surging water, getting closer and closer. It sounded heavier than rain.

Yesterday, Tommy Gray Drowned

Rick and Rusty grunted and groaned. They sure must have had all they could handle to haul me off the truck bed, because they were having one heck of a time carrying me through the woods. I wasn't overweight, but still they nearly dropped me several times. But that didn't faze them or deter their constant cussing and bickering. They never shut up. Good for me; the boneheads had no clue I had come to.

"Look what ya gone and done, Rick!" Rusty squawked. "We're in for it now! Fer shur! Fuzz're gonna swarm all over me 'n' you! Like flies on road-kill! All over us! Jus' wait 'n see!"

"Shut yer yap!" Rick bellowed, his voice surpassing what sounded to be a waterfall. "I told the whore ta scram! Did she get her butt outta Echo Lake? No! Now, she's gotta pay! Big time!"

They dumped me onto a hard surface and once again the wind was knocked out of me. As my lungs involuntarily sucked in air, I closed my eyes - just in time - I knew Rick was zeroing in on me. As I cloaked all signs of consciousness, I felt the deer rifle slide off my belly. I didn't hear the rifle hit the ground, so I knew Rick caught it. Next thing I knew, he was jabbing the butt end of it into my arm and then into my thigh. He was watching, waiting for me to react.

An eternity passed.

He spat on the ground then sucked air between his teeth. "Lucky fer us she was out walkin' like that."

By the level of his voice, I knew he had his back to me. So I peeked out one eye. An incredibly powerful waterfall roared a few feet beyond Rick and Rusty. Placid was not its nature at all. It was raw power - like standing to close to loudspeakers at a Stone's concert. This was the waterfall that dumps into Echo Lake from Fern Cove.

Rusty spat his cigarette butt on the ground. "Sittin' duck, that's her."

Rick sniggered. "Hey, good times." He sucked in air through his teeth again.

"Gotta admit, Rick, she shur got nads standin' up ta me an' you like she done."

"Well, yeah!" Rick held up his hand. "Look at da teeth holes!"

Rusty dogged Rick, "But the cops, Rick... The cops are..."

"Shaddup yer yap, I says!" Rick barked.

Cold mist sheeted my body, which were already drenched from the driving rain. I began to shiver uncontrollably. Unable to stop it, I swore never to wear another tee shirt ever again. The foolish thing wicked up every iota of chill out of that granite ledge, which gored into my back. I clamped my jaw down in an effort to stop my teeth from chattering. My neck and shoulders were cramping. I shifted my weight, hoping that the abductors might fail to notice. I gritted my teeth against the pain in my knee.

Rusty swayed to and fro; his hands kneaded each other. His right shoulder twitched as his panicky eyes darted about, fixing on nothing. "Ya shur she knows, Rick?"

Rick snorted. "Don't give a hairy rat's butt one way 'r t'other. The whore's pokin' her nose around much too much in things what ain't none o' her business. Humph! Goin' down Town Hall like that 'n' drawin' them picchas 'n all."

Neuroses wracked Rusty's bony frame. His tongue licked his lips nonstop. "Sooner or later, she's gonna put two and two tagether, Rick."

"She has already," Rick said, lighting a cigarette. He blew out a lung full of smoke that swirled back into his face.

"One way or t'other, Rick, it's like that Gray kid said: 'We're up a creek without a paddle.' I mean, the piccha o' the graveyard's downright freaky. Looks jes' like that night when..."

Rick growled, "Shut yer friggin' yap."

"But Rick. The beer cans!"

Rick sniggered. "Whoo-ie! Talk about wasted."

"And oh! Oh!" Rusty stammered. "Did ya see the grave, Rick? Did ya see it? S'pose they'll reckon Linda's down there, Rick?"

My eyes shot open. Linda? Down where? She's buried in the graveyard?

Rick snorted. "Nah. Afta all these years? Idiots in dis here town ain't got brains 'nough ta figure nuttin' out, never mind a thing like this. Afta all these years? Uh-huh."

Rusty shook like a leaf. He lit up a cigarette then scuffed his feet across the granite. "Lucky fer us that old geezer got planted that day, huh, Rick?"

"Shur came in mighty handy fer gettin' rid o' Linda," Rick boasted, flicking away cigarette ashes.

Rusty winced. "We went nuts, huh, Rick?"

"Got that right, Carrot-top."

"We shouldn't o' outta done what we done, Rick. An'...an' you...you shouldn't outta o' hit Linda so hard. Ya shouldn't o' kilt her, Rick. Ya shouldn't o'..."

Rick pitched his cigarette into the falls and then one-handedly, grabbed hold of Rusty by the neck. "Listen, crow bait..." Rick's eyes blazed and his nostrils flared as he lifted the redhead off the ground. "Shaddup! Hear me?"

Rusty's eyes bugged out. His face turned a pasty shade of bluish purple.

Rick waved the deer rifle in his left hand at arm's length. "Any more bellyachin' outta ya 'n yer da firs' piece o' dog meat over dese here falls!"

They were going to dump me into that waterfall? Because they think I've sniffed out their secret? For crying out loud, I had no idea they killed Linda Benson - not until now. They spilled the beans on themselves!

"Okay, okay," Rusty choked out. "Don't git so techy!"

Rick hurled the redhead against the granite wall a short distance from me. He snickered while watching the redhead slither down the wall. Memories of spit slithering down the hood of my car accosted me.

Rusty hacked for breath while tottering to his feet. "So, what're we waitin' for, Rick? Let's git it over wid 'n git outta here afore someone gits wise."

Rick snorted. "Ain't nobody gonna bug us back here." He leaned the deer rifle against the granite wall. "Git the beer."

As Rusty disappeared in a narrow opening between a granite wall and waterfall, my predicament overpowered me. I had to get out of here or I was going to find myself smashing into boulders thirty feet below the ledge. But how? My knee was killing me. My mind was raging confusion.

I squeezed my eyes shut, trying to block out the image of myself dying like that. When that did not work, I pursed my lips then wedged open my eyes. Rick's face was twisted up and his finger was burrowing into his nose. Disgusting…

I scanned the area. Those two were so dumb that I should be able to trick them - somehow.

First of all, I had to free myself. My tongue ejected the filthy, oozing gag that was stretched and saturated with drool and my blood. As the taste of oil and dirty hands lingered in my mouth, I realized that not keeping the gag in my mouth was a big mistake. If Rick found out, he'd chuck it back in my mouth and tighten it up again - tighter than before. He'd also know I had come to. He might decide to get rid of me right then and there. Too risky. I snapped up the rag and clenched it between my teeth. To heck with the taste. I had to stay one-step ahead of Rick and Rusty. My survival depended on it.

I wriggled my feet. Oh, my knee… That's when I noticed the frayed twine had slackened just enough to slip off my wet ankles. I gritted my teeth against knee pain and freed my legs. But now what? I wriggled my toes, maneuvering the rope to make it appear as if my ankles were still bound. Then I concentrated on my wrists. The twine was too tight. No matter what I did, nothing loosened it. My fingernails were turning blue from the cold and lack of circulation; still, I dug them into the fibers of the twine. Separating the fibers was difficult then severing each one seemed to take an eternity. As each broke, I smiled and then dug at another one. Then another. And another. I had a long way to go. Was there time enough to cut all those fibers and break free? What then? If I didn't figure out something, I'd be back to square one - that being, getting dumped into that waterfall.

My heart sank when Rusty reappeared. He was carrying a couple of six-packs on his shoulder. A bag of chips rode on top.

Yesterday, Tommy Gray Drowned

"How long we gonna wait, Rick?" As Rusty set down the load, the bag of chips slid off and crashed onto the ledge. The bag split open and chips shattered into pieces all over the ledge.

Rick jammed his hands into his hips, scowling at the mess. He shook his head as he reached for one of the six-packs and tore into it. He shot a can at Rusty then snagged one for himself and popped the top. He chugged down half the brew then came up for air and belched. "Dark's soon enough. No one's gonna track us down back here, what wid da rain 'n' all. That whore's gonna be dead as a doornail 'fore anybody finds her floatin' in Echo Lake. Yep, mornin's soon enough fer 'em ta reel in her sorry butt."

I yanked on the twine. My fingernails had severed many fibers, but not enough. I tried to convince myself that by the time it got dark, I'd be free. Those two idiots would be completely inebriated by then, so maybe I could catch them off guard. I envisioned them coming to get me. When they picked me up, I'd pretend to be only semi-conscious - and drag my feet. Yeah, that's what I'd do - make it look as if my injuries were in themselves life-threatening. Those jerks were going to have to haul me to that waterfall - Rick on one arm and Rusty on the other. Perhaps I should blather. That would really make me look out of it. Then, at the right moment, surprise! I would shove both of those murderers away from me - hopefully, right into that waterfall. They were going to get a taste of their own medicine. In the meantime I'd make a mad dash out of there as fast as my forty-year-old legs could carry me. I could do it. Yes, I knew I could. They'd never catch me.

More fibers gave way as I formulated contingent escape plans. The ledge had two exits. One way was to the right of me, into the woods. But that was on the other side of the two belligerent boozers. Out of the question. Not only did I have to get past them, but also, once I got into the woods, I had no idea which way to go. And knowing my luck, I would probably trip over something and fall flat on my face. The other escape was behind me, to the left of the waterfall - the way they brought me here. What if the surroundings changed since I was a kid? I should have paid more attention when they were carrying me hear.

I did know this waterfall was not too far from Mike Anderson's place - maybe a mile, if that far - at least I hoped so. What if it's farther? These old legs of mine might not make it. What if I trip? What if... Curse my insecurities!

To my horror, Rick started swaggering towards me. I stopped working to free my wrists and clamped my eyes shut. Desperately, I feigned unconsciousness, trying to breathe normal. Still, my heart pounded so bad I thought for sure it was going to give me away. His foot swung over me - I knew it without even looking. He was standing over me, spread-eagled. Panic surged within me. Don't move, I told myself. Don't move one single muscle.

I heard him slurping beer. Then he drawled, "Know what, Rusty, ol' boy? I'd like ta rub da bone wit' this here whore."

"Betcha dollar ta donuts she's mighty fine, Rick."

Rick gulped down beer. He burped. Metal squawked and I knew his hand was crushing the beer can. Then came the sound of metal striking the granite wall to my left. It ricocheted off the wall then skipped out the other side of the ledge and into the woods. Next thing I knew, Rick was down on one knee next to me. Panic surged within me. Don't move. Don't move one single muscle. Beer breath blasted my face. He was fingering my hair. Saturated strands plopped onto my forehead. I battled the terrorized revulsion spinning my brain round and around. His fingers slithered down my cheek and neck, grazing the sore spot on my upper chest.

I silently cursed the bonds restraining my hands.

He groped one of my breasts then discovered a nipple, hardened by the cold and outlined on the accursed clinging tee shirt.

If only my hands were free... I'd belt that heaving, alcoholic pervert straight into next week.

His fingers wormed across my belly, down across my thigh, and up between my legs.

Yesterday, Tommy Gray Drowned

My breath became increasingly shallow. How much longer could I go on pretending to be dead to the world?

"But," Rick hissed, tapping me on the side of my head and then standing upright. "Any half-wit knows da pigs catch on mighty quick dese days. No autopsy's gonna dig my juices outta dis whore." He sniggered as he lifted his leg over me then stepped away. "I gotta take a piss."

Seconds later, urine pelted on the granite wall near my head. Specks of it peppered my face, assaulting every last sense left in my hypothermic body. My senses railed with the thought of amber liquid funneling only inches away. Queasiness overpowered me. I found it impossible to stop the looming images of that filthy pervert sprawled on top of me, getting it off; images of Warren Squire mixed with Rick's pocked face, both rubbing against mine, laughing, fiendishly delighting in my powerlessness. Too heavy! I couldn't breathe! My brain spun round and around. My gut seemed to implode: Open your eyes! If you don't, you will pass out!

I cracked open one eye. Rick was turning toward the waterfall, zipping up his fly. He vigorously adjusted his male anatomy while tottering back to the edge of the falls.

Relief zinged through me. But then, I could not stop the pounding in my chest. I feared I might have a heart attack - I mean, even at my age.

Rick snapped his fingers then Rusty tossed him another can of beer. Rick guzzled down the contents then fired the empty can into the cascading surge. Their squabble began anew. However, the roar of water drowned out their words as they squatted on the ledge and swilled down more beer. They flicked empty cans and cigarette butts into the waterfall impatiently waiting to pitch me in it when darkness fell. The impact on the rocks below was going to cover up the true cause of my death. No one was ever going to detect the bruise on the back of my head or my bloody nose inflicted by Rick. Things looked dismal. So this was how my life was going to end - helplessly caught up in a swirling maelstrom, smashed against rocks thirty feet below this ledge. The current was going to sweep what's left of me into

Echo Lake where the murky depths were waiting to swallow up my soul - just like Tommy Gray. Yes, this was it. This was how I was going to die.

Yesterday, Tommy Gray Drowned

LAST STRAW

Odor of urine penetrated my nostrils. Of all the indignities heaped upon me by Rick Morton, that odor was the last straw. I made up my mind right then and there: That piss ant and his wannabe were not going to succeed in killing me!

Never so angry, never so determined, I spat out the filthy rag and kicked the twine off my ankles. Then I put pressure on the last fragments of twine ensnaring my wrists. Free at last!

Wriggling toward the left exit, I put distance between them and me. Come hell or high water, I was going to get out of there! And then! Yes, then! There's going to be one nasty showdown between them two and me!

A muffled snort.

I pulled up short. "Brutus!" I could see it in his eyes that he controlled whatever the next few moments had in store. He looked away from me. My eyes followed his, over my shoulder. Upon zeroing in on the kidnappers slouched at the edge of the waterfall, his eyes blazed and his muzzle tightened, baring glistening fangs. From the canyons of his throat came a menacing growl - the same kind that was once intended for me.

Warm pressure on my shoulder made me look. A hand! I knew that hand. My eyes followed the arm attached to that hand - up - up. "Mike!" I reached out for him as he squatted in front of me. His arms wrapped around me like a sweet-smelling blanket. I burrowed my soggy face into his muscular chest. I was so frozen that my teeth clattered no matter how I tried to stop them.

"Rusty sees us," Mike said.

Yesterday, Tommy Gray Drowned

I looked over my shoulder. Rusty's mouth gaped open. He nudged Rick, stuttering indistinct words. His finger pointed at Mike, Brutus, and me.

Rick snapped his head around. "What the…" He hurled himself at the deer rifle. Raising the barrel, he wobbled toward us, a crazed grizzly.

"Sic 'im, Brutus," Mike commanded.

The Doberman went right to work, knocking Rick off balance. All too quickly, Rick recovered, flipping the rifle then using the butt of it to ward off the charging Doberman. His swing was premature, so it missed Brutus. As the Doberman leapt upon him, the rifle soared into the air. It smacked into the granite wall several feet from Mike and me. Blam!

The bullet hit Rusty. He clutched his shoulder, screeching like a barn owl and hopping about. Suddenly, he caught sight of the rifle. He stopped short, gaping at it. He gaped at Mike. He gaped at me. He gaped at the rifle.

"Don't do it," Mike warned.

Nerve-racking seconds passed.

Rusty broke for the rifle.

Mike vaulted away from me and got to the rifle first. He kicked it into the waterfall then came about, facing the Rusty.

The redhead froze in his tracks. His liquid eyes bugged out his pasty face. Suddenly, he twisted around and fled out into the woods opposite me.

Meanwhile, Rick was sprawled upon the ground, holding Brutus by the neck, at arm's length. His fingers bored into the coppery mane, which dragged open the Doberman's mouth, exposing fiery gums and glistening fangs. One deadly bite meant severing the man's jugular vein.

It was a standoff.

Brutus managed to shake himself loose. He backed away to regroup.

Rick stumbled to his feet, teeth clenched.

My hand muffled my alarm.

Brutus bristled. He mounted the third attack.

Rick deflected the Dobie.

148

Both lost their footing.

Brutus slid onto his side, toward the waterfall.

"No!" I screamed, trying to get up.

Mike snagged my wrist. "Brutus can take care of himself!"

I tried to shake free. "But he's heading for the waterfall!"

Mike forced me to look into his eyes. "So you're going to go with him?"

"I…I…" I shook my head and wrenched on my arm.

He pinned me on ice-cold granite. "You're not going over those falls!"

Helplessly, I lay there, watching Brutus writhing toward the edge, writhing toward that waterfall. The thought of losing him was worse than the pain in my throbbing knee.

The Dobie up righted himself. Though he dug his claws into the granite, he continued to slide. As his hindquarters dropped over the edge, his claws got a foothold on the rocky lip. He dangled there, the downward spiraling current nipping at his hindquarters.

"I gotta help him!" I screeched, squirming to get away from Mike. "Let me go!"

"Never!"

My brows came together. Never? I gawked at Mike.

His eyes were intent, unflinching.

I pulled my eyes away then looked back at Brutus. Clamped onto the rocky lip, the Dobie lifted his snout towards the heavens. His head seemed to brace against an unseen entity, which stopped him from going over the edge.

Not far from Brutus, Rick had stumbled backward; but inches from the edge, he managed to steady himself. Then his hand reached into the back pocket of his jeans. Out came a switchblade. He snapped it open, clenched his teeth, and staggered towards the vulnerable Doberman.

Mike was on his feet. "Don't you dare!" He hurled himself at Rick.

I doddered to my feet, wincing from the pain in my knee. I had to help! Struggling to catch my breath and my balance, I scanned the ledge. The carton of beer! I could hurl beer cans at that bully! I limped to the carton and snatched it up. Empty! I turned it upside down. There had to be one stinking can in there! Nope, not one. Every last can had been drunk and then tossed into the waterfall. I squinted over my shoulder just as Rick deflected Mike back in my direction.

Rick's left foot skidded across a patch of wet moss and then went out from under him. His right foot swung high into the air as he catapulted backwards, arms flailing. The raging maelstrom seized his arm - only inches away from Brutus now slowly but surely hauling himself to safety. Rick yanked on his arm a couple of times then pitched around to see what had a hold on him. Surprise eclipsed his face, then rabid anger. As he faced his watery captor, the switchblade flew out of his other hand and bounced across the ledge. No matter his strength, no matter how much he battled, nothing stopped him from being consumed by the waterfall similar to the way prey is consumed by a boa.

Now that should have been the last of Rick Morton and his shenanigans, but it wasn't. I couldn't believe it when Brutus took it into his head to charge right after Rick - even if it meant leaping right into that waterfall. "No," I screamed.

"At ease, Brutus!" Mike commanded. "Heel!"

Whatever happened next was a blur to me - that is until I felt a slimy tongue lick my ear. I found myself lying on the ground – and another slimy tongue licking me. I raised my hand to fend it off then lurched upright. "Brutus!" I grasped his head. "Brutus! Good boy! Oh, what a good boy!" I hugged him and kissed him - pretty much the way I did to Peter when he came back from Vietnam the first time. "You crazy mutt."

That's when my eyes fell upon the switchblade. The waterfall had taken Rick, but... "Where's Rusty?"

"The little twerp high-tailed it out the other side," Mike said, picking up the switchblade with two fingers. "Without Rick, Rusty doesn't amount to... Well... Much." Mike used the granite wall to retract the blade. "Cops will nab him in no time." He slid the switchblade into his back pocket then helped me to my feet. "Come on; let's get you to my house. I have to call Chief Parker."

My frozen legs buckled. "Oh, my knee…" I gritted my teeth.

Mike propped me up. "You need to get to a hospital."

"No. No hospital," I said, clinging to him. "I'm okay."

"But look at you," Mike argued. "You might have torn ligament in your knee; and you got blood all over you."

I clung to him, probably more than I should have. "Let's just get out of here. I'm an ice cube."

He looked at me kind of strange.

"You're the only thing keeping me warm," I said.

He smiled that perfect toothy grin of his.

Instantly I wasn't quite so cold.

He went to pick me up in his sinewy arms.

I elbowed him. "I can walk."

"You sure?"

I smiled up at him. "Just let me hold onto you for a while."

Yesterday, Tommy Gray Drowned

BEAT THAT

The roar of the waterfall faded as Mike, Brutus and I headed out to the deserted country road. Out from under the trees, I looked up the canopy of stars and the nearly full moon trailing across the lake. On the opposite shore, window lights flickered among the trees. Our footsteps on the pavement sliced the silence. I limped along, clinging to Mike. "Thank goodness the rain is over," I said. "How did you find me back there, anyway?"

"Ruthie called me at the Water Works, but as luck would have it, I had already left for the day," Mike said.

I rolled my eyes. "Let me guess: she went looking for me," I said.

"You got it," Mike said.

"That's Ruth for you," I said.

"When she couldn't find you," Mike said, "she called Don Pierce and asked him to keep a lookout for me. About that same time, I was driving past the store on the way to Fox Creek to run an errand. Well, that old dude came barreling out of that store and ran right smack in front of my car!"

"Oh, my God!"

"Yeah, I almost hit him," Mike said. "He filled me in about Rick and Rusty messing with you earlier and also that Ruth told him you didn't come back from a walk."

"Pretty dumb thing for me to do," I said sheepishly.

Mike was silent. Our footsteps crunched on some twigs.

"Hey, listen," I said defensively, "How was I supposed to know that those two were out to get me that bad?"

Mike pulled up short, letting go of me.

I stopped and looked back at him. Brutus did, too.

153

He shook his finger at me. "Women should not go roaming around back roads like that - under any circumstances!"

"I did when I was a kid," I countered, limping off in the direction of Mike's house.

"You shouldn't have done it back then either!"

I heard his footsteps hurrying up to me. Pretty soon, I was clinging to him again, still limping, but not as painful. Brutus was right there by our side.

I changed the subject. I didn't like Mike mad - or whatever he was - at me. "I suppose Ruth was at wit's end when you got to her place."

"Crying and carrying on," Mike said. "When she told me you headed off in the direction of my house, I hoped against hope you somehow got in and was safe and sound with Brutus. But she said she had been there and you weren't there and Brutus was also in a frightful state. He was all lathered up when I got there - the worst I ever saw. No denying it, something serious was up."

"Brutus saw it all from your front window," I said.

"It's cracked, you know," Mike said.

"Cracked?"

"Yup," Mike said. "Claw marks gouging all the way to the top. I'm going to have to replace that window - framework and all."

"No kidding," I said. I shook my finger at Brutus. "Bad boy."

His little pointy ears flattened against his head.

I laughed. Mike laughed. And it looked as though Brutus laughed, too, as his long pink tongue flopped out of his mouth.

"You could care less, right boy?" I said.

Mike beamed at his Dobie. "I tried to calm him down. He did, but only a little - not enough to let him go it alone. So, I tethered him and..."

"You leashed Brutus?"

"Haven't done that since he was a pup."

"Poor Brutus," I said.

"Well, let me tell you," Mike said. "That dog tugged that rawhide so hard, I had to run to keep up with him. He tracked you down in a heartbeat. But I have to say: when I found that black hunk-o'-junk hidden in the bushes, I knew in a flash Rick brought you behind those falls. I gave Brutus a caution command, and he finally listened to me and…"

I cut Mike off, "I know the rest."

We were silent as his house came into view. Brutus raced for the front door. It was half open, so he charged inside.

When Mike and I arrived at the door, Mike shouldered it open the rest of the way. Then I tripped over the threshold. He caught me then swung me up into his arms and carried me to the sofa beneath the gouged and slimy window. He knelt on one knee then set me down. As he lingered over me, I willingly drifted within his presence. My body trembled, anticipating his touch, his kiss, craving tenderness. Abruptly he stood up and whipped an afghan off the armchair. Quickly he draped it over me then took off for the kitchen, running his hand through his hair.

I felt like the lights had gone out - almost as bad as when Peter left me…twice…

I heard Mike talking on the kitchen wall phone. Moments later, he returned with an ice pack. "Here, this should help that bruise on the back of your head."

As I placed the icepack against the bruise, I spied Brutus by the armchair, standing vigil over Mike and me. "Making sure your master gives me his undivided attention, huh, boy?" I glanced at Mike and gave a nervous chuckle.

He hitched of his chin and gave me a thin smile.

I looked at Brutus and snapped my fingers. "Come here, you silly dog."

Brutus pranced over to me and dropped his snout on my lap. I roughed up his ears. "What a good boy." I stroked his silky black and copper fur.

"I gave Ruthie a call," Mike said. "She and Wally will be right over. I called Chief Parker, too, and volunteered to take Brutus out to run down Rusty Kane, but Chief says that's not necessary, he'll take care of all that. He'll be here as soon as he can."

I sensed Mike did not really want to go hunting down Rusty. I didn't welcome the idea either.

It seemed only minutes later Cousin Ruth charged through the front door without knocking. "Bethie! Are you all right?" She gasped. "Look at you! Your face is a mess! Where'd that blood come from? Let me see!" She went to touch me, but then drew back. Her eyes never left me as she commanded, "Get me a damp face cloth, Mike! What did that maniac do to you, Bethie?" She didn't give me a chance to answer. "Hurry, Mike! I need to..."

"Ruth!" I grabbed hold of her hands. "Ruth! I'm okay!"

"Take it easy, Ruthie," Wally said, coming in from parking the car. "Listen to what she has to say."

"You guys are not going to believe this," I said. "Rick and Rusty and a bunch of other guys killed Linda Benson."

"No!" Ruth exclaimed, her eyes big as marbles.

"Yeah." I nodded affirmation. "And they buried her on top of some guy who was buried earlier that very same day."

"Where?" Wally asked.

"In the graveyard."

Ruth pulled away from me. "Down the road from my house?"

"Yeah."

She gaped at Wally. Utter disbelief blanketed his face. They both gawked at Mike. All three zeroed in on me.

"I-I don't get it," Ruth stammered.

I took a deep breath then explained, "Rick and Rusty and a bunch of other guys were goofing off in that graveyard one night and...well...Rick ended up hitting Linda hard - real hard - hard enough to kill her. Then he and Rusty - maybe some of the others, too - buried her right on top of some guy who was buried earlier that same day."

"Who's the guy?" Mike asked.

"Don't know," I said.

Ruth turned circles. "So Linda didn't run off at all." She stopped, her eyes burrowing into mine. "What on earth possessed them to do such a thing?"

"Rusty said they were all drunk and things got out of hand," I said. "Rick hit Linda. He hit her real hard. He killed her, Ruth. He killed her."

Silence fell over the room.

Mike ran his hand through his hair. "So that's what Tommy saw." He started to pace.

"Suppose Rick had something to do with Tommy's death?" I wondered aloud.

Wally winced. "Maybe the kid didn't drown after all."

Ruth wrung her hands. "If we... If this whole town is wrong about Linda running off... Well, we can all be wrong about Tommy, too."

Deep retrospection enveloped the room.

Mike stopped pacing. He folded his muscular arms across his broad chest. "But I was the only one there the day Tommy drowned."

"You sure?" Wally asked.

Mike scratched the back of his neck. "God, I don't know."

Rotating blue lights and headlights illuminated the place. All eyes shot to the front window and Brutus vaulted over me then stood on the back of the sofa, barking wildly.

"Brutus heel," Mike commanded.

The Dobie jumped over me, down onto the floor, and took up a stance beside his master. He remained there all the way to the front door.

When the door opened, two men - one wearing a black leather bomber jacket and street clothes, the other in a cop uniform - entered. Both removed their hats.

Mike allowed Brutus to sniff the men. Then the one in the leather jacket stepped over to me. He was a hulk of a man with weathered skin and spiked, heavily graying brown hair. "I'm Chief Parker." He hooked his thumb over his shoulder. "That's Harold."

Yesterday, Tommy Gray Drowned

After relating every detail of what transpired that day, I shivered, "There's no way Rick survived going over that waterfall." In my gut, it was more of a question than a statement.

Chief Parker shook his head. "I got my people out there right now. The body will surface sooner or later."

"How about Rusty?" Ruth asked.

The telephone in the kitchen rang. Mike went to answer it.

Harold piped up. "Kane won't evade capture for long." Harold looked like a rookie, young and lean. He certainly acted like a rookie.

"The only place Rusty knows is Echo Lake," Parker said.

Mike hollered from the kitchen, "Chief, it's for you. It's Officer Henderson."

As Chief Parker headed off to the kitchen, Wally set about building a fire in the granite fireplace, and Ruth helped me limp to the bathroom. Left alone to take a shower, I removed my filthy clothing, taking a second look at my bloodstained tee shirt. "I swear I'm going to throw out every tee shirt I own." I stuffed all the clothing into the evidence bag Ruth had somehow gotten hold of and then turned on the water. It ran hotter than I usually liked it, but I made no effort to cool it. My skin still had a chill to it. I lathered up, furiously ridding myself of this ghastly day, the grime, Rick's dirty paws. Then I rinsed off for what seem a long time and shut off the water. I reached for a towel and jammed it against my face. How good it smelled.

Changing into the lavender sweat suit Ruth had scrounged from my suitcase, I was glad I had packed it. The soft fleece pile soothed nerve endings, which from time to time, spiked my skin. How good it felt to be clean. My knee seemed better, too.

Honeysuckle perfume, I thought. The kind Julie and Emma LaRosa wore. I wished I had some of that.

I glanced at the mirror. "Is my nose broken?" I squinted close to my reflection. My fingertips explored the bridge of my nose. "Doesn't seem broken…" Even if it was, I knew that not much could be done about it short of plastic surgery. I eyeballed a welt on my cheekbone. "Maybe I should have gotten checked out at the hospital, just to be…"

I jumped back, thinking I saw a shadow. I spun around. Nobody was there. My eyes shot back at the mirror. I swore Rick Morton was standing behind me. Fear made me dizzy. Bile pumped into my throat. There didn't seem to be any relief from the memory of him, which kept coming back on me. I squeezed my eyes shut and flattened my hand on my chest to stop the pounding of my heart. Feeling my legs buckle, I opened my eyes and grabbed hold of the washbasin. Completely unnerved, I told myself: Nobody's there; nobody's there.

I took a trembling breath then grabbed a comb out of the medicine cabinet. I yanked a hand towel off the bar and limped back to the living room and the safety of others.

Chief Parker stood up. "Rusty Kane's in custody, Mrs. Blair."

"So you can relax now," Ruth said.

"That's a relief," I said, toweling dry my hair.

Harold the rookie piped up, "Kane's singing like a jaybird. He didn't even try to skip town. Just sitting in his living room, nursing a gunshot wound, watching TV. The place is a pigsty - stinks worse than the town dump on the Fourth of Ju…"

Parker cleared his throat, loudly, and eyeballed Harold - a clear signal for the rookie to can the chatter.

Harold humbled himself, lowering his eyes, and took a step back. His lips pursed as his brows scrunched.

Chief Parker brushed off irritation. "The bullet grazed Kane's shoulder. Henderson says Rusty was waiting for Rick to show - didn't have a clue Rick went over those falls."

"So what did he say about Linda Benson?" Ruth asked.

"Claims only one other guy took part in the actual murder," Parker said. "That was Jack Whitaker."

Wally cringed. "Whew. Pretty tough character."

Chief Parker rolled his eyes. "No denying that."

I shot a questioning look at Wally. He explained: "Jack Whitaker belonged to a motorcycle gang from up north. One night - must've been more than fifteen years ago - the bunch of them got to drinking and tore up a bar on Hampton Beach. Got themselves kicked out. Not far from there, he ran his bike into a bridge abutment and that was the end of him."

"So there are no other witnesses," Mike said.

My stomach turned as I ran the comb through my hair. I snagged a tangle and began to hack at it.

Ruth grabbed the comb out of my hand. "Here, give me that, Bethie. Now sit down. Relax."

I squinted at her, thinking, odd advice coming from her. She freaked out over every little thing - almost as bad as Margi LaRosa did. But then, everything happens to Margi.

"So now what?" Mike asked.

"Well, tomorrow, the coroner's office will go to the graveyard," Parker said. "Hopefully, they'll find Linda Benson's remains without too much difficulty."

Ruth leaned over me. Her eyes were big brown orbs as she tapped the comb on her bottom lip, "Hey Bethie... That picture... The grave..."

Chief Parker's brows arched. "Picture? Grave?"

"Bethie forgot to tell you about the sketches," Ruth said and then eagerly filled in the blanks ending with: "One of the gravestones in her sketches might belong to some guy who was buried there just that day. They threw Linda on top of him." By now, everyone in the room knew that fact.

Parker got to his feet. "I've seen a lot in my career, but this one takes the cake." He sent me a sidelong look. "Did you happen to catch the name on the headstone?"

I mulled it over as Ruth gnawed incessantly on the comb. I frowned at visions of Rick and Rusty bickering back and forth. "I'm sure they didn't say the guy's name."

Ruth pointed the comb at me. "Bet it's on that sketch and we never even noticed."

"Maybe," I said.

"The beer cans blew our minds so much that we never noticed any other details," Ruth said.

"Beer cans?" Parker echoed.

Ruth nodded the way animated little girls do. "Yeah. Lots of other things might be there too, for all we know." She grabbed my hand. "Let's you and me take a drive back to my house and get that sketchpad."

Before I could open my mouth, it seemed, she was calling over her shoulder, "Be right back!" And the door closed behind us.

On the way to her house, Ruth said, "While we're at it, I'll put an Ace bandage on that bum knee of yours."

"It's no big deal," I muttered.

"I'm doing it and you can't stop me!"

So after Ruth wrapped up my knee, I fetched my sketchpad out of my car. As I wormed into the front seat of her car, she jumped into the driver's seat. I buckled up. When I didn't hear her buckle up or start the car, I looked at her. She was staring at me. I blinked at her. "What?"

"Aren't you going to open that?" she asked.

I looked down at my sketchpad. The hairs on my neck bristled. I felt like unmolded gelatin. "Not until I absolutely have to."

Ruth buckled up then started the car. The ride back to Mike's was silent.

When I handed the sketchpad to Chief Parker, he looked skeptical. He flipped it open and it came as no surprise to me to hear him wince. "Mathias Artimus Johnson," he said. "Name's plain as day on the gravestone. Can you beat that one?"

Ruth gawked at me. "How in the world did we miss it?"

I bit the inside of my cheek.

After the Chief and deputy left, the four of us talked into the night. We sipped the coffee Mike made and ate the brownies Ruth picked up at her house while I went for my sketchpad - that's after she strangled my leg with an Ace bandage.

We broke it up shortly after two. Wally and Ruth went on ahead to wait in the car while I patted Brutus and told him for the hundredth time what a good dog he was. He seemed genuinely proud of himself. Then I embraced Mike. "Thanks for being there."

161

Yesterday, Tommy Gray Drowned

He clung to me longer than I expected. Closer. And tighter. It felt so good to be held by a man. I didn't break away, because I felt safe, wanted. This time it was not just his heat that I craved. My entire being hungered for his strength, his tenderness, his undeniable nearness - and I sensed he was feeling the same way. So lost and alone, we both yearned for the touch of a loved one. His full lips tempted mine. I gazed into his eyes. Suddenly I saw Peter looking back at me. My loved one was Peter. Mike's loved one was Becky.

I broke away; although I never felt such reluctance. But I did break away. I did let go of his hand. "Good night, Mike."

LINDA BENSON

Noises resonating through the woods drew my drowsy eyes to the bedroom window. Weird how I didn't get up to shut it during the brief night, especially considering my latest run-in with Rick Morton and his wannabe. I was so pooped when I finally got to Ruth's that I crashed in bed and never gave that window a second thought. I slept like the dead and now, here I was, nestled between warm sheets, the bedroom chill throttling all motivation to leave the bed.

Yet the commotion outside pestered me. I turned over and peeked at the clock radio beneath the lamp on the nightstand. Almost ten. In spite of the late morning hour, I did not feel like waking up. So I just laid there. I moved my leg, the one with the Ace bandage. Incidents of the previous day jolted me: the roar of the falls; the dankness; the cold mist. All of it filled my senses - plus the ledge digging into my back as Morton's filthy paws molested every square inch of me. What a piece of scum. His face was as vivid to me as at that moment he lost his balance and catapulted backwards toward the waterfall. His surprise when the surge seized his arm. And then a whole lot of rage. His appearance took on a satanic quality. What did he think; he was invincible? Curious how the waterfall, white with supremacy, seemed to decree that Rick Morton belonged to the ages. I quivered. How ironic that Rick Morton met his end in the same manner he intended to use to get rid of me.

My stomach convulsed with the vision of Rick brutally murdering Linda Benson and then burying her on top of some man named Johnson. The whole thing outraged me, but then a tranquil gentleness seemed to permeate the room. I glanced around and saw something that looked like fireflies. Faint bits of light. I thought floaters were toying with my eyes, so I blinked. The fireflies were still there. I rubbed my eyes. Linda Benson... Was she was those faint bits of light? Now that her fate had finally come to light, peace at last was hers. I felt relief; however my sadness over the whole unfortunate affair could not be denied.

An engine revved beyond the window; and shouting. I glared at the window. "What is all that commotion?"

Puff!

I looked back at the fireflies. They were gone.

A helicopter thumped overhead. I gawked at the ceiling. The helicopter flew over the house. Clamping my hands to the blanket, I squinted at the window. Thumping of the helicopter. An engine revving. Shouting. I gasped. "The coroner's people!" I tossed off the blankets. "They're digging up Johnson's grave!" My legs wrestled with the blankets until finally, I was able to kick them off. I got rid of that foolish Ace bandage then leapt to my feet and grabbed my blue jeans off the foot of the bed. Jouncing around on one foot and then the other, I pulled on the jeans then zipped them up. "Sweatshirt... Where's my sweatshirt?" I spied it on the floor at the foot of the bed. I snapped it up and jammed my head into the neck opening, at the same time, worming my arms into the sleeves. I snagged my comb off the bureau and ran it through my hair. Dashing out of the room, I scooped up my shoes and socks. Making the bed was the furthest thing from my mind.

Ruth had coffee waiting for me. "I knew you wanted to be there," she said.

I plopped down at the kitchen table. Between chugs of coffee, I yanked on my socks then jammed my feet into my shoes.

"I'm going with you," she said, reaching for the keys on the rack next to the door. "You're not running loose in this town another minute." She slammed my sketchpad and chalks against my chest. "Come on, Bethie! Let's go, let's go!"

"Hold your horses!" I swilled down the dregs of coffee that made me cough all the way to the graveyard.

A feeding frenzy of reporters and videographers created chaos in and around the graveyard. Ruth had to park far away from the entrance. "It would have been quicker if we had walked," she grumbled.

As Ruth and I hurried to the entrance, several reporters stuffed microphones in my face. I flagged them off. "I have nothing to say." We picked up the pace to a dead run. Reporters chased after us. The helicopter circling overhead thumped the atmosphere. That infernal engine revved. And all the shouting! It all got on my nerves.

A woman reporter holding a microphone bearing the logo of a Boston television station spotted us and stepped in our way. "What did Morton have against you, Ms. Blair?"

A male reporter caught up to us from behind, hollering, "How long did you know Linda Benson, Elizabeth?"

At the entrance to the graveyard, an insistent pinhead of a reporter popped up in front of me like a jack-in-the-box, shoving a microphone so close that I thought it might have nicked my front tooth. He knew he did it, but still, without the slightest remorse whatsoever, he squawked, "Come on, Mrs. Blair, show us your sketches! We got a right to see those sketches!"

"Right?" I shrieked, stopping in my tracks. "What about my right for you to not bash in my teeth? What about my right to privacy?" Like cannonballs, those words lobbed out my mouth. I glared at him.

A self-satisfied leer grew on the pinhead's face.

"Aargh!" I grunted, skirting around him. I came face to face with more reporters and microphones. "Get away from me!" I raged.

The helicopter rumbled overhead. The engine revved within yards of me. And the shouting... My head was about to explode!

Ruth tugged on my arm with one hand, pointing with the other. I could hardly hear her as she yelled, "There's Chief Parker! Nobody will bother us if we stand next to him! Let's go!"

Yesterday, Tommy Gray Drowned

We ducked - actually ducked! - surprising all the reporters, and scooted to Chief Parker. A few of Echo Lake's finest were with him, including Harold the rookie.

Well, the idea about not being bothered? That didn't work out all that good. Those news hounds not only pestered the daylights out of me and Ruth; now they were going after Chief Parker and his troops. It didn't take long for him to get fed up with the lot of them. "Back off!" he barked, his powerful hand gesturing. "Control yourselves or I'll clear the area of the lot of ya! And Harold! Get that 'copter out of here before I shoot it down myself!"

Then revving engine finally quit and the helicopter thumping faded. "Thank Jesus for that!" Parker said.

Two men in orange work suits had already hacked through the thicket and were just about to reach Johnson's grave. Several other men in ordinary work clothes were piling the brush off out of the way. A defensive thorn had gashed one of the guys pretty bad - scarlet trickled down his arm, although he paid it no mind. Upon reaching the tombstone, they were joined by several other men in ordinary work clothes. Together they jockeyed the tombstone off to one side. The two men in orange scraped the top layer of sod then four technicians wearing white lab coats, latex gloves, and paper boots surrounded the site with plastic sheets. Gradually, two technicians removed layers of soil. The other two sifted through the dirt, giving cursory scans to foreign matter before dropping it into plastic bags and handing it to officers to seal and label.

The tedious job went on for several grueling hours. The sky grayed and a raw wind came up out of the Southwest. I shuffled, trying to keep warm. Lots of other people were doing the same thing.

Nearby, a video camera illuminated the face of a reporter. I recognized her as the lead anchor of Channel 7 News. She began speaking, her voice level, into a microphone: "Investigators are being extremely meticulous. Using brushes and specialized tools, they are carefully preserving pieces of evidence from the murder of teenager Linda Benson who was thought to have run away from home three decades ago. Rusty Kane, now incarcerated, gave details of the crime, which led to this scene today. Technicians are now about three feet down. Let me see if I can get a closer look." Moments later, she said, "They have reached the cement vault encapsulating the casket. They are removing the lid. There is the casket. They are opening the cover and..." She gasped.

Horrified spectators gasped. The frenzy of previous hours vanished instantly. Silence came down on the graveyard like a rock.

The anchorwoman placed her hand over the camera lens and the lights went out.

Everything within me rejected the sight of Linda lying on her side, arms bent at the elbows, hands clasped in front of her face. Her knees were bent - as much as the casket allowed. She appeared to be beseeching the Lord to take her into His arms. Only teeth were left of her mouth, which had dropped open. A tarnished barrette still cinched a tuft of golden tresses. Decayed fabric - clothing - so savagely ripped off her body during the gang rape, was strewn across her torso. The bones, the beseeching hands, the blond hair was too much to fathom. "What an incredible waste," I moaned.

Well, of course it was not long before cameras flashed again - after all, reporters had to report. As a few people turned away and left the graveyard, the Channel 7 anchor was at it again: "Before me is the gruesome result of the despicable deed perpetrated by Rick Morton and several others upon seventeen-year-old Linda Benson. Her petite body was discarded like trash inside the coffin of a complete stranger."

My tears could no longer be contained as grief intermingled with fury and mounted within me. I envisioned Rick tossing those clothes on Linda, that satanic look blanketing his face - the same one I saw that day in Pierce's Grocery and again when he plummeted over the falls. I clenched my fists so tight that my nails dug into my palms. I so wanted to claw into his nefarious face until it was nothing but bloody gouges. I felt his finger jabbing into my chest, his voice taunting: Ya ain't never gonna get yer stinkin' claws into me. I winced - angry, mournful, frustrated.

Ruth clutched my hand, enwrapping it in hers, and softly wept. Her hands were so warm; mine so cold. Raindrops began to pepper us.

The anchorwoman was not deterred. She continued to color the scene for her audience - and for ratings. "Transparent clouds sail across the overcast sky as if they were angels shedding tears for Linda Benson."

Through blinding tears, I wanted to scream at that anchorwoman: It's raining, you idiot!

"Don't cry, 'Lizbeth…'"

I glanced at Ruth. "What did you say?"

She raised her eyebrows. "I didn't say anything."

Then who spoke to me? I wondered. Certainly not those reporters. They knew better. The volunteers? No. Everyone but me was focused on the grave.

"Linda is at peace now…"

"Tommy?" I breathed, scanning the graveyard. His whisper was coming from beyond here, somewhere remote; and it washed over my soul like a song. "Why can't I see you?"

"You okay, Bethie?"

A pure light veiled my entire being with a tranquility I had never experienced. My ten-year-old friend had come back to me and I took pleasure in it. Yet, as swiftly as he had returned, he left. I had no chance to make things right. And then I heard, "Help me, 'Lizbeth…'"

Blinking back tears, I moaned, "I don't know how. Tell me what you want me to do!

No reply.

Tears streamed down my face.

Ruth touched my shoulder. "What's the matter, Bethie?"

I glanced at her.

Anxiety marked her tear-stained face.

"Yeah," I whispered. I gave her a reassuring hug. "I'm okay." And then I *really* cried.

She did, too. She handed me a pink tissue - only a few were left from the thick wad she had brought with her.

Indelicately I blew my nose as wind-driven sheets of rain bore down upon us. "I feel like I'm dreaming one awful nightmare."

"Let's get out of here," Ruth said.

I shook my head. "I can't leave."

"I know, Bethie." She swayed back and forth, cold and wet, for several moments. "I'll go get the umbrella in the car. Be right back." A short time later, she sidled up to me, a multicolored umbrella over her head. She pulled in close to me so I was also shielded by the umbrella. We stood there, shivering, the gray rain pelting the umbrella, watching technicians scurry about, wrapping up the crime scene before it was complete muck.

I cleared my throat. "Tell me what Linda looked like, Ruth."

"Gosh, Bethie. It's been such a long time… Well, now, let me see… Linda had the most beautiful blue eyes I ever saw. And her blond hair shined like gold even on dark days. She had the cutest little turned-up nose - I was always jealous of that. You know, small noses don't run in our family."

We both let out a shabby giggle.

I gave her a sideways glance. "Feels kind of strange, doesn't it?"

"What?"

"Finding levity in such a morbid situation," I said.

Ruth shrugged. "Sometimes laughter is the only thing that keeps us sane."

I sighed. "Levity certainly hasn't been prevalent in my life."

Ruth glanced at the bones as if verifying an assumption. "Linda was small for her age - at least I think so."

"Maybe because she fended for herself since she was just a half-pint," I said.

"She clung to Rick," Ruth said. "And he liked that - you could tell. He might have turned out okay if he cared about her the way I thought he did. I'm at such a loss as to why he did this.

169

Yesterday, Tommy Gray Drowned

I really thought he had a thing for her. If you could have seen them together…"

Ruth and I stayed until the coroner's silver SUV carted away the remains of Linda Benson. At that juncture, I turned to Ruth and said, "I just decided: When the coroner is through, I'm going give Linda a proper funeral."

Ruth smiled at me then took hold of my arm. "Come on, Bethie. There's nothing we can do here; and we're both tired. Let's go see Don." She tugged me away from the grave. "We'll get him to make us a sandwich and a cherry coke. Neither one of us has eaten yet today."

"My legs feel like lead, Ruth."

"Mine too, Bethie."

Halfway out of the graveyard, my knees locked and I stumbled over a rusty beer can. I grabbed for Ruth and she for me. Arms around each other, we steadied ourselves.

"Glad you're here, Cous'," I said

She kicked the can into the woods. "Glad to be of service…Cous'."

We continued out of the graveyard.

"You're the sister I never had," I said.

"Feeling's mutual," she said, taking her car keys out of her pocket.

"I haven't been this devastated since Peter left me - both times."

"You must have been crushed," Ruth said. "I know I would be."

"I'll never forget that muggy August morning back in the 60's," I said. "When Peter walked out the door, he called to me over his shoulder with that silly grin of his, 'Don't worry, Bethie. Nothin's gonna happen to this bod'! I'll cherish you in my heart, my little morning eyes, forever.'"

"Thank goodness, he came back," Ruth said, sliding the key into the door lock. "He'll come back this time, too."

"It took twenty years the first time," I said.

"I didn't know that," she said, getting into the driver's seat. She leaned over and unlocked the passenger side door for me.

I opened the door. "This God-awful feeling is eating at me, Ruth: He's not coming back this time." I plopped onto the passenger seat. I felt so very old, so very tired. "What am I supposed to do, wait for him another twenty years?"

"Wish you came back to Echo Lake back in the '60s," she said, buckling her seatbelt. "Mom and Dad were still kicking around. They would have been there for you. You know that, Bethie, don't you?"

"I was afraid," I mumbled.

"Of what?" Ruth said, starting the engine.

"You know how Mother was."

"That was her, not you," Ruth said, pulling out onto the street. She sent me a quick glance. "You have to give people more credit than that. Now buckle up."

I gave her a wry look then pulled the belt over my shoulder and snapped it in place. "I didn't want to have to explain."

"Mom and Dad already knew how things were when you grew up. They wouldn't have held one blessed thing against you. Did I give you a hard time when you got back?"

"No," I said, childlike, looking out the side window.

"Well then," she said. "There you go. You don't have to go it alone, Bethie. We all got troubles. Most of the time, we can't do a blessed thing about them, but it sure is nice to have others around to take the edge off. And you don't have to spill your guts about what's eating you if you don't want to."

I sat there, ruminating about my childhood. The isolation I experienced poisoned my adulthood. Funny how this time, it was different: Peter was gone again - and I was sick of it; and I did come back to Echo Lake; and in spite of Rick Morton and Rusty Kane, I had a few good thoughts about being here.

Yesterday, Tommy Gray Drowned

WHACKED

When Don Pierce spotted Ruth and me pulling up in front of his store, he dropped everything and raced outside to greet us. He even left a customer standing at the cash register, which was not like Don at all. Somehow, he knew about everything that went on from the time I left his store until now. But then, Don Pierce knew about everything that went on in Echo Lake. I thought back: never once did I ever see him outside his store. Amazing. I often wondered how he got home at night.

"Ya cain't knowd how good ya look ta these ol' eyes, Li'l 'Lizbeth!" He wiped his hands on his crisp white apron then clasped my hand in his. "'Twas aginst m' better judgment ta let cha out o' my sight." He brushed my hand across his silky cheek. "I jes' shouldn't o' let cha go. I shuddah knowd those two hooligans wan't about ta let thaings be."

I cupped his other cheek in my free hand then kissed the stout elf on the bridge of his nose.

Embarrassed, he glanced around to see if anyone saw what I did.

"You couldn't have known what was in their minds," I said. "Hopefully the experience has toughened me up and made me a better person." I rubbed the bruise on the back of my head, unsure about any of that.

Ruth started for the store. "How about a sandwich and drink, Don?"

"Shur thaing, sure thaing!" Don dashed for the door and held it open for Ruth and me. He looked up and down the street as if making sure Rick and Rusty were nowhere in sight and then followed us into the store. At the deli, he asked, "Ya want the same's I make fer ya t'other day, Li'l 'Lizbeth?

"That would be great, Don. What are you having, Ruth?"

She waved me off. "Don knows me by heart."

He went right to work behind the deli; however, he didn't hum the way he usually did back there. Other things occupied his mind. "It's all over town 'bout what Rick done ta poor Linda," he said without looking up. "Cards stacked aginst that young-un from the outset - what with her mama runnin' off like she done. Poor chil'. Knee high to a grasshopper at the time. Too young ta be minus a mama."

I shot a questioning glance at Ruth. I didn't know what to expect. I was constantly off balance, not knowing what was going to happen next. Any sense of routine was illusory.

"Linda was born out of wedlock," Ruth said. "Nobody but her mother knew who the father was - and her mother wasn't telling. They lived with the grandmother in that old mill house across the street. Remember? The one I told you about that the town tore down? Then Linda's mother ran off with some guy she met at the bar - so I was told. I never knew the woman."

"That chil's grammaw was too ol' and sickly ta take proper care of herself, never mind that chil'," Don said.

Ruth gave a rueful nod. "Linda was about a year or so older than me - always running the roads, day and night. I thought she was nice enough, except that she was so wild and free. Everybody called her a tramp, just like her mother. That's why my mother didn't like me hanging around with her. When everyone thought Linda ran off, Mom said, 'Well, it's to be expected.' Linda threatened to run away all the time - a couple times she did, but a day or so later, she always showed up."

Don shook his head. "That's how come not a blamed sole took off a-lookin' fer her da last time she disappeart."

Just then, the bell over the store door jingled. My eyes shot to the door. Shades of Rick and Rusty brought my stomach to my throat. But it was only a petite young woman. She barely made the floorboards creak, even though she was carrying pies in a fairly large metal pie-safe. Brunette hair cascaded over her

174

shoulders while silver barrettes kept it off her face. Her fair skin was untouched by makeup.

"Well, hey there, Miss Becky," Don yelped. "Ya got me more o' dem luscious pies o' yorn? I'm out agin, ya knowd."

I felt like butting in: Well, yeah, that's because a strawberry-rhubarb pie war broke out here yesterday. However, I figured it was best to keep my mouth shut. I didn't know how Becky might take that kind of news.

"I brought you six," Becky said, lifting the pie-safe onto the counter. "How ya doin', Ruthie?"

"Hungry as all get out," Ruth jabbed, playfully. "Look at Don back there, just goofing off, while here I am starving to death."

"Tsk tsk," floated out from behind the deli.

"Where's Tom?" Ruth asked.

"With his Dad at the Water Works," Becky replied, pensively tossing her long thick tresses over her shoulders. "Tom sure misses Mike and that dog of his…"

"Hey!" Ruth chirped, "Why don't you have Don make you a sandwich and cherry coke and eat lunch with Bethie and me?"

Becky gave me a timid glance.

"Oh," Ruth said. "I'm sorry. I didn't introduce you two. This is my cousin, Elizabeth Blair. She's a Spencer. Grew up right here in Echo Lake and delivered the *Evening News*."

"It's been a long time," Becky said. Hesitantly, she extended her hand to me. Her eyes met mine.

Something told me that Becky and I were going to spend time together; we were going to be friends. I felt good about that. "Nice to see you again, Becky." I grasped her hand and shook it with genuine friendship.

She smiled then withdrew her hand. She gave Ruth a look and then Don. "Uhm…okay… I can hang out for a spell. But only a frappe - got that, Don? Chocolate."

"Comin' right up, Miss Becky!"

I insisted on paying the tab. Then I settled next to Ruth on the wooden bench near the front window. The honey-colored table before us gleamed through glassy layers of varnish. I glanced back at Don busying himself behind the deli, humming a World War II ditty that Father used to whistle when he was down in the cellar, putting around. Don winked at me, appearing to be pleased that the three of us remained in his store to eat. He probably wanted to keep an eye on us after all that happened in the past day or so. A thought whipped across my mind: Don had become a father figure to me.

"I heard what went on up at the falls last night," Becky said.

I looked at her. She was delicate of bone and features, which were dark, very much like her mother's and quite the opposite of Tommy who took after his father. Come to think of it, Gerald Gray might have been albino, or very close to it. His hair was as white as Don's, yet he was not very old when I knew him back in 1959. He was much too young for white hair. His skin matched the colorlessness of his hair, too. His steel gray eyes were as neutral as a sled dog. On the flip side, Tommy's eyes were a curious shade of hazel - probably from the blending of his father's steel eyes and his mother's ebony eyes.

"I'm so grateful that Mike and Brutus showed up when they did," I said.

"Mike's a great guy," Becky mumbled. "So you're married…"

Within her shadowy query, I sensed subtle innuendo - or perhaps suspicion? Did she know that Mike was attracted to me? Did she think I was out to get him for myself? I felt self-conscious and foolish about my attraction to him.

Ruth spoke up, "Bethie's husband is in Vietnam, looking for MIAs."

Just then, Don picked up Becky's hand and placed a wad of bills into it. That's when I caught sight of the platinum wedding band and diamond on the third finger of her left hand. She loved Mike.

"Braing more o' dem pies, soon's ya can, Miss Becky. I knowd fer shur the ones ya jes' brought's sold already." Don turned away for a second then spun around back to her. "By the by, Miss Becky. Missus Carter wants ya ta raing her up. She wants ya ta whip up a fancy cake for Li'l Kate. She's givin' a big shindig for the chil's sixteenth birthday. 'Magine that: Li'l Kate, sixteen. Whew! I shur am gittin' on. Mm, mm, mm." Don shook his head and walked away in deep thought.

Ruth did not hide her amusement. Turning to Becky, she said, "You ought to open your own bakery. There is plenty of business for you here in Echo Lake."

"What cooking school did you go to?" I asked.

Becky brightened. "Mom's kitchen, that's where. Dad was in the merchant marines - gone more than he was home...small blessing..." Her face turned gloomy for a second then brightened up again. "Mom had lots of time on her hands and so she cooked - and taught me while she was at it. We used to have such great times... Well, we still do... But not like before...uhm... before Tommy drowned. Mom lost some of her spunk after that. Well, then my father died... Too bad. Dad wasn't all that good to Mom anyway."

"Why's that?" Ruth asked, her brows fusing.

"Mom was like a schoolgirl whenever Dad was coming home from sea. For days before, she cooked and cleaned until that old shack we lived in sparkled - as much as a place like that could... And she practiced fixing herself up in lots of different ways. She wanted to be just perfect for him."

Becky's voice became ominous. "When Dad first came home, everything was so wonderful: trinkets; a hug or two... But after a few days, all that changed. He got to drinking and we kids always got in his way. Most of the time, Mom stepped in between us and him. That made him furious. And boy, did she get whacked."

I winced. "How dreadful."

"Nobody ever tried to put a stop to it?" Ruth asked.

Becky shook her head. "Not back then."

"Yeah, right, that was family business," Ruth said, shaking her head. "People kept their noses out of a man's domain back then."

"Besides, I don't think anyone knew that kind of thing went on in that old shack," Becky said. "We were so far out - away from everyone. That's the way Dad liked it."

"So nobody ever heard or saw a thing," I said.

"Mom was good at hiding it - that's if she did go out," Becky said. "She was an expert at makeup. But most of the time, she stayed to herself, so when things did happen, nobody missed her. She went visiting only after Dad went off to sea. He didn't take to her socializing at all."

Becky pursed her lips, waving her head side to side. "Mom told me once that the old Doc Morgan caught onto the abuse, so when she got pregnant and Dad came home, Doc Morgan made up excuses to put her in the hospital."

"It was the only way to protect her and the baby," I said. "That's how they did things back then."

"So that's why Tommy was born in the hospital," Ruth said.

"Me, too," Becky said.

"So your father never got to you and Tommy?" I asked. I was badgering Becky, but didn't know why.

Almost inaudibly, Becky said, "Well... Sometimes..." She fiddled with her fingernails.

I pressed on, "What do you mean? He pushed you and Tommy around, too?" Anger swelled my brain, though that anger did not seem my own.

"Tommy more than me." Becky cast a furtive glance at me - that very same glance her brother sent me the day of the newspaper fiasco. Her eyes shimmered with moisture.

I clenched my teeth and squinted at Ruth. She felt like I did, I could tell.

Without further prodding, Becky bared a horror never before laid bare: "Dad got crocked one day and tripped over my baby doll. He didn't fall, but boy, was he mad. Well, he hollered at me. His spit flew all over the place - I remember that. He backed me into a corner and went to grab me, but Tommy got between him and me and pushed me out of the way. Dad latched onto Tommy's arm. It all happened so fast..." Her eyes squeezed shut as Becky sat there trembling. Her hands gripped her head. "I heard a snap. Tommy screamed. Oh, it was just awful. He fell on the floor and tried not to cry. Dad got so mad when any of us cried - plus Tommy was supposed to be a man - just like Dad - and so he called Tommy a sissy. But Tommy couldn't help it. Tommy was in terrible pain. Well, Dad… He… He kicked Tommy right in the belly with those big heavy shoes - you know, the kind the merchant marines wear so if something heavy falls on their feet their toes don't get squashed. Well, all the wind came out of Tommy, and he laid there all rolled up in a ball - so awful still, so quiet. I was so frightened when he didn't wake up. Thinking back on it now, I'm sure Tommy passed out."

I struggled to contain the rage within me. "Where was your mother all this time?"

"Outside, gathering branches to put in the woodstove," Becky said, sadly, then quickly added, "But when she heard the commotion, she came running. She dropped the branches on the floor and then shoved my father away from Tommy. But then Dad fell and hit his head on the woodstove. I think the impact knocked some of the booze out of him, because he staggered to his feet and when he saw what he did to Tommy, he said, 'Now look what I've gone and done.' His voice was all slushy from the drink - sloppy, you know."

Without warning, my ten-year-old classmate, arm in a sling, blasted across the screen in my mind. It sickened me, because I didn't remember that. It sickened me thinking about Tommy laying on the floor, his poor mother comforting him, and his broken arm… I forgot about his broken arm. How could I have been so heartless? "His broken arm…" I said. "That happened just after he started fourth grade, didn't it?"

Becky hung her head, nodding. "Day after Thanksgiving. I'll never forget that day as long as I live."

The anguish I felt for my classmate mutated into fury that knew no bounds. If I could have gotten my hands on Gerald Gray, I would have killed him myself, right there and then.

"How long did that garbage go on?" Ruth demanded. Outrage replaced her ordinarily cheerful nature.

Yesterday, Tommy Gray Drowned

"Ever since I could remember," Becky murmured.

I gritted my teeth and turned away, straddling the wooden bench. I clenched my fists and pounded my knuckles into the seat.

Ruth grabbed my hands and made me stop.

Becky peered at us. "But that day was the worst. Dad left for sea again - real soon."

"He didn't have guts enough to stick around and have to look at what he did to Tommy," I said.

"Didn't the doctors and nurses at the hospital question the injuries?" Ruth asked.

"Tommy didn't go to the hospital," Becky said. "Doc Morgan came to the house to set Tommy's arm. Even worse, Mom and Tommy kept it a secret about Dad kicking him in the stomach."

"I suppose Doc Morgan kept his mouth shut," I said.

Becky twisted up the side of her face.

"But how could anyone not notice?" Ruth demanded.

"Doc Morgan was awful old," Becky mumbled.

"Oh for heaven's sake," Ruth huffed, turning her back to the table and crossing her arms.

Becky cleared her throat then explained: "While Doc Morgan set Tommy's arm, Mom conjured up a mixture of eucalyptus, peppermint oil, and herbs to paste on Tommy's ribs. I helped tear up strips of sheets to wrap around him. Poor Tommy... He was in so much pain... And I couldn't help him. Mom gave him a mixture of whiskey, lemon, and honey. In no time, he fell asleep. But several times during the night, I heard him moaning. Mom got up and went into the kitchen to make more of that whiskey concoction. The smell of peppermint, eucalyptus, whiskey, all kinds of stuff filled the whole house. It wasn't long before Tommy was quiet again." Becky took a deep breath. As she did, her bottom lip trembled. "To this day, the smell of those things turns my stomach." Suddenly Becky collapsed on the table and sobbed inconsolably. "It's all my fault! I shouldn't have left my baby doll there in the middle of the floor! It's all my fault!"

I grasped her hand. "Shh... Don't blame yourself."

Ruth squinted over her shoulder at Becky and then at me. I shook my head.

Ruth turned back to the table. "How could it possibly be your fault?"

"She's right," I said. "You were just a little girl."

Becky peered at me with that same look her brother had given me so many years ago. She peered at Ruth. She chewed the side of her mouth. A moment later, she said, "After Tommy drowned, Dad stopped hitting Mom. The times he drank, he disappeared - sometimes for days at a time. And Mom didn't seem to care where he was. I just know Tommy's death ate at Dad. Then ten years later - just about to the day Tommy drowned, they pulled Dad out of that water, close to the same spot where he found Tommy. No one knows what happened, except that Dad was drinking that day and he was alone. Somehow, he fell out of the boat and..."

Yesterday, Tommy Gray Drowned

ON TRACK

"The condition of that graveyard really bugs me," I groused, at supper, that evening. "It was always groomed to perfection. Now look at it."

Wally rolled his eyes. "Sure was nice to see tiny American flags fluttering over the graves of veterans on Memorial Day."

"Flowers decorated every last one," I said, taking the bowl of mashed potatoes from Ruth.

"And we school kids marched all the way out there to sing patriotic songs," Ruth said, pouring gravy over her mashed potatoes.

"The American Legion, the VFW, and the DAR followed right behind us," Wally said, waiting for me to pass the bowl of potatoes to him.

"There was always some long-winded old vet who droned on and on about something none of us could hear," Ruth said.

"Pass the potatoes and gravy, please," Wally said.

As I handed him the potatoes, I said. "Hey, don't forget the twenty-one gun salute." I clasped my ears to memories of retorts blasting back from Echo Lake.

Ruth handed him the gravy then leaned on one elbow. Her fork toyed with the green beans in her plate. "It's been a long time."

"Still can't believe the VFW bought our four-room schoolhouse and turned it into a social club," I said.

"Does seem sacrilegious somehow, having drinking going on in the place where we all learned our ABCs," Wally said. He chucked a fork full of mash potatoes and gravy into his mouth.

"Shoot, we even walked home for lunch," Ruth said, offering Wally the platter of baked chicken.

Wally swallowed quickly while taking the platter. "Regional schools put a stop to that. Now kids get bussed out of town every day."

Ruth heaved a sigh. "Too bad we don't have our neighborhood school anymore. Kids these days don't know what that's like."

Ruth and Wally's experience in that four-room schoolhouse was a lot different from mine. They were part of the social network in Echo Lake, and their parents took part in town activities. Mine didn't. That, plus things like my name, my paper route, and the part of town I came from, helped to foster a social rejection within me, which I allowed to rule my later years. Still I truly enjoyed marching to the graveyard on Memorial Day. The other kids could not keep me out; I felt as if I belonged. "It looks so small," I mused, staring at my fork of mashed potatoes, gravy dripping into my plate. "It wasn't like that when I was a kid."

Ruth jabbed my arm. "Your fork?"

"The graveyard, wise guy," I said. I stuck my tongue out at her.

Ruth snickered. "Of course, it looked bigger. Everything looks bigger when you're a kid."

I scrunched up my nose at her as I stuffed the forkful of mashed potatoes and gravy into my mouth.

"Hey, you two," Wally scolded. "Cut your scrappin' or I'll rap your heads together."

"Where have I heard that before?" I smirked, putting down my fork. I wadded up my napkin and shot it at Ruth. "How in the world did all of us fit into such a small place?"

Ruth returned fire. "The graveyard?"

I ducked.

Wally threw his hands in the air. "I give up."

Ruth giggled. "Principal Cole used to be in charge of Memorial Day."

"'Decoration' Day," I said, picking up my fork. I pointed it at Ruth. "That's what Principal Cole called it."

"One time or another," Wally said, "just about every person in Echo Lake went through ol' lady Cole's school. She was a feisty old bird even back when I went there."

Ruth laughed. "And she's still walking this earth."

"To this day that ol' windbag still makes our knees quake," Wally said. "Her word is law! She doesn't take guff from any of us. When she says things are gonna be done a certain way, that's exactly how they get done - no ifs, ands, or buts about it."

Ruth slammed her hand on the table. "Hey, you know what? We should pitch in and restore that graveyard!"

"The idea does have merit," Wally said. His brows lifted as he glanced in my direction.

"Uhm…sure," I stammered. "I think so."

Wally scratched his head. "Town Fathers might balk. They're pretty tight-fisted when it comes to doling out funds."

"So what," Ruth said, waving him off. "Let's do it anyways."

"I'm willing to share in the cost," I said.

"We'll take turns every year to keep up the place," Ruth said. "It takes more elbow grease than anything else." She jumped up and began to clear the table. "Come on, you guys! Let's go to Worcester for supplies!"

As she went for his plate, Wally grabbed it, squawking, "Hey, I'm not done yet!"

Ruth stepped back and jammed her right hand into her hip. "Aw, come on, Wally," she huffed. "Get a move on. By the time we get to that building outlet where you get the biggest discount, it'll be closed."

He tore up a roll and hastily scraped up the gravy in his dish. He stuffed the roll in his mouth, sputtering, "Mmm, yeah, you're right." He handed his dish to Ruth then shoved himself away from the table. "When I get back, I'll put together a proposal to submit to the selectmen."

"Can't hurt to try," Ruth said, hurrying to the sink.

"You two go ahead," I said, picking up my dish. "I just want to veg. Leave the table be. I'll take care of cleaning up."

185

Yesterday, Tommy Gray Drowned

They didn't seem to mind. I sensed they wanted some private time. It must be hard having me around all the time. Maybe I should go home. No, all I would do is mope around, missing Peter. I was too busy here to think about him all the time. Besides, something within me insisted I was needed here more than in Brighton.

After Ruth and Wally left, the house felt so incredibly empty. Fighting off the feeling, I discovered how much I had come to depend upon their company. "They'll be back," I kept telling myself, while attacking the stack of dirty dishes in the sink. "After all, this is their house." My voice disturbing the silence insinuated that indeed I had overstayed my welcome. "But I don't want to leave," I whined. "I feel safe here - in spite of that Rick and Rusty. And Warren Squire… And the ghost of Tommy Gray messing with my mind."

I just couldn't trust myself alone in my own house. Not without Peter. What if I close myself up like a recluse like before when he didn't come home from Nam the first time? "Well, you know what Peter? Mike seems to need me." My hand fled to my mouth as guilt pricked my heart the way a thorn protects a rose. Mike had a wife. His loved one is Becky. Becky's loved one is Mike. My loved one was Peter - my husband - in Nam.

I turned on the stainless steel tap full blast, and of course, that caused gravy to leap off a plate right onto my blouse. "Great. Just great." I grabbed the dishcloth and stuck it under the spewing tap. "Ye-e-ow!" I yanked my hands out of the scalding water.

On the verge of tears, I leaned against the sink and stared at the cloth being taken by the steamy water down into the garbage disposal. I bit the inside of my mouth then heaved a cleansing breath and cooled down the water. Warily I rescued the dishcloth with two fingers. I rinsed it out then made a feeble attempt at cleaning the gravy off my blouse. The stain spread. "It's worse than if I left it alone in the first place. Oh, I give up." I rinsed the dishcloth again then wrung it out as if it were my missing husband's neck. "On top of everything else, Peter doesn't even know I burned my hand." Submerged in self pity, I plodded off to the dining room. Mindlessly, I scrubbed the table.

On the way back to the kitchen, I picked up a stray wineglass from the hutch. Unfortunately, my hand failed to clear the door casing. Thank goodness the glass didn't break. Not so much as a chip; although, I fully expected to see a black and blue knuckle real soon.

I dropped open the dishwasher door then loaded the dirty dishes. My anguish turned into soft reflection of that last morning when Peter and I sailed out of Plymouth Harbor. What a glorious sunrise we had witnessed while standing at the helm of the forty-foot sailboat we chartered out of Boston. A fresh wind luffed the sails ever so slightly and flirted with my hair. The red orb teased the horizon as cormorants and other seabirds plummeted into the surf for their first meal of the day.

My mind drifted to our new home in Brighton. Velvet nights. Mornings, wrapped his arms, gazing from the balcony overlooking the Charles River where day sailors plied the shimmering waters. In the background the mighty Prudential Tower, so much a part of our personal history, refracted the sun's rays.

My heart skipped a beat as I conjured up images of Peter the day he returned to me from Vietnam - the first time. The way he stood there in the doorway. That silly grin of his. I loved him; and yet I hated him for leaving me alone for such a long time. His lips brushed my ear. His warm breath. "Bethie…"

Oh, I loved Peter beyond words for coming back to me back then. But was he going to come back to me this time?

I plunked down on the sofa and called home. No messages on the machine. I called Julie. She had not heard from Peter either.

I grabbed the remote and turned on the TV, hoping against hope that the evening news might report on the mission to Vietnam. Three minutes of national news coverage centered on the politicians who exploited the limelight while Peter and the other tagalongs did all the dirty work. Fear that something was dreadfully wrong spread over me like crab grass. Though cleverly orchestrated, a stray camera caught Peter getting into a military truck.

My hand stifled a gasp, but doing so did not stop the moisture from welling in my eyes, doing so did not stop my heart from crying out for him to please come home.

A faceless journalist was describing the group leaving for a reported crash site in the jungle several miles off the Ho Chi Min trail. When that journalist said that what I had just seen was made from tapes filmed several days before, I was shattered. Then I found out that no new developments had come from there since that filming. Casting aside heartbreak, I began to fume. "What a rip-off."

Frustrated by the minuscule news report, I aimed the remote at the TV then clicked it off. The remote landed in the corner of the couch as I got to my feet. I rotated my head in an effort to relieve the tension in my neck.

Stomping off to the dining room, I muttered, "That man has absolutely no clue what's going on with me." I snagged a pot off the stove. "How utterly selfish. He is supposed to love me. I'm more important than that dumb mission."

"Hey! Anyone home?"

I reeled. "Tommy?"

The pot flew out of my hand. It crashed onto the tile floor then skidded across it and smashed into the refrigerator.

A happy voice called, "Yup!"

I dashed to the screen door. There stood… "T-Tom…" I looked up. "Mike." I shrunk against the doorframe. I was going nuts. That kid sounded too like his deceased uncle.

"You all right, 'Lizbeth?" Mike asked. "You look like you've seen a ghost."

Words just did not come to me. I turned, without looking at either of them, and pushed open the screen door. I gave a lame gesture that invited them in.

Brutus stampeded past me.

Without the slightest hesitation, Tom demanded, "What was all that racket?"

I cleared my throat. Finally my voice appeared, but it was raspy and unfamiliar. "Nothing. Dropped a pot, that's all."

"Tom and I decided to pop over and hang out for a while," Mike said.

"Where's Ruthie and Wally?" Tom asked, but didn't wait for an answer. My eyes followed him heading straight for the living room - shades of Tommy Gray. Brutus, having given the kitchen a cursory inspection, trailed Tom into the living room.

Somehow, I managed to tell Mike about Ruth and Wally going to Worcester and their reason for doing so.

"What a terrific idea," Mike said. "Count me in."

By the time Mike and I got to the living room, Brutus was off checking out the rest of the house and Tom had already found the remote where I had thrown it. The TV was on a cartoon channel - a little too loud. "Turn it down, Tom," Mike said. "You know, son, you really should ask first. You just don't…"

I cut him off, "Oh let him be. Want some popcorn, Tom?"

"Uh-huh," the boy muttered, mesmerized by the illuminated tube. He didn't even notice Brutus come back, panting with delight and flopping down beside him.

"Come on, Mike," I said. "While the popcorn's popping, I'll make us some iced tea."

"Tom and Brutus take over every place they go," Mike said, trailing me into the kitchen.

Their being there lifted the oppressive silence and took me away from my head. Yet, when I made eye contact with Mike, sparks didn't fly like before. I tossed a box of microwave popcorn at him. "Here. Make yourself at home." As he set about opening the box, I stacked the remaining dinner dishes in the dishwasher.

"Saw you on TV," he said.

"TV?"

"You and Ruthie… At the graveyard?"

"Oh yeah," I said. "I missed the local news." Once again, I began beating my gums about that stupid report.

Yesterday, Tommy Gray Drowned

Mike placed a bag of popcorn into the microwave. "Settling down after all that mess with Rick and Rusty is just about impossible," he grumbled, staring into the microwave. "Reporters have been banging on my door ever since."

I got out three glasses; two for ice tea; one for chocolate milk. "Can you believe all that's happened since I came back to Echo Lake?"

Popcorn exploded faster and faster.

"Seems like every time I turn around, something else crops up. And..." About to say that my husband had also dropped off the face of the earth, I felt Mike's hands on my shoulders. I felt his breath; his lips toying with strands of my hair.

"Things will settle down now," he said.

Explosions of popcorn were becoming sporadic.

Gently, he turned me around. His cobalt eyes gazed into mine.

For an electrifying moment, I wanted him to kiss me, to hold me, to take me to another place - somewhere safe, worry free - a place where only Peter had ever taken me. I was lonely. And so was Mike.

Suddenly aware that our attraction for one another was based on separation from our beloved spouses, I pulled away. I opened the refrigerator. "Ruth and I had lunch today..." I took a deep breath. "...with Becky."

I heard Mike wince. I knew his indiscretion confronted him.

I took the pitcher of ice tea and the carton of chocolate milk out of the refrigerator then went about filling the glasses.

Mike took three bowls out of the cabinet then the popcorn out of the microwave. He went to dishing the popcorn into the three bowls.

The silence between us was driving me nuts. I had to say something, so cleared my throat and said, "Dreadful thing what Gerald Gray did, isn't it?"

"What's that?" Mike asked.

"Well, you know," I said. "How Gerald pushed around his family whenever he came home from the merchant marines."

"No," Mike said. "I didn't know."

I turned to him. He stood there, totally confused. How in the world could he not know? "Y-you don't know?"

"What're you talking about, 'Lizbeth?"

"You mean...Tommy never told you? Becky...never...?"

"Told me what?" Mike demanded.

Oh, no, I thought. Me and my big mouth. Now I have to tell him. There's no way out of it. No, I can't do it. I looked at him. He was waiting for an explanation. I felt so slimy. "Remember that broken arm Tommy had?" I asked.

His brows knitted. "Yeah?"

"Gerald did it."

"What?"

I stepped back. "Tommy took the brunt of Gerald's drunkenness the day after Thanksgiving. Tommy stepped in between Gerald and Becky."

Mike squinted as if he didn't believe a word of it. He ran his hands through his hair then feverishly paced. "For crying out loud, why didn't Becky tell me? Why didn't her mother..." Mike stopped in his tracks. "Why didn't Tommy tell me?"

"Maybe they tried," I suggested.

Mike spun around and faced me. His hands jammed into his hips. "What do you mean by that?"

"When Tommy didn't like someone or something, he let you know about it," I said. "You told me that, right? What did he tell you about his broken arm?"

"He said it was killing him..." Mike hesitated. "Yeah, now it makes sense. His old man left just after that. Tommy wasn't his old self. Something was different. He complained about a bellyache all the time and I called him a sissy. He got real mad and avoided me for days."

"That newspaper stunt was entirely out of the ordinary for him," I said.

"I couldn't talk him into doing a thing like that before," Mike said. "His mother went ballistic. I never heard anyone belt out like she did."

I chuckled. "Hey, you should've heard it from my angle."

"I'll bet," Mike said. He chuckled.

I felt relieved. I hated the thought of Mike being angry with me.

Suddenly, his face darkened. "His old man came back just days before Tommy drowned. Yeah. And Tommy got real quiet. Maybe that's why I remember how silly he was with the mayonnaise. That's the first time in days he lightened up. His mother ragged all over him for putting that mayonnaise on his poison sumac, but she wasn't really mad at him - you could tell. Those dark eyes of hers twinkled."

"Tommy looked at her the same way," I said. "I saw that when she told him to help me pick up my newspapers."

"They had a real neat relationship," Mike said. "Like they had their own special secret or something."

"You know what, Mike? I think I'd like to talk to her sometime."

"I just can't understand why she never told me about Gerald," Mike said. "In all these years?" He shook his head in disbelief. "And as much as Becky and I talked about Tommy, she never brought up one word about any abuse."

"Adding to your pain was the last thing she wanted to do," I said. "Besides, she blames herself for what happened the day Tommy drowned. Becky loves you, Mike, a lot more than you think. She told me so - Ruth, too. Your wife really misses you and wants to be with you."

"Well then, why doesn't she just come home?" he asked, half-irritated, half-sad. He ran his hand through his hair then started pacing again. "I just don't know what Becky wants from me."

"She wants you to be happy, Mike. That's all. She says you're so moody all the time. Nothing gets done around your house anymore. In the beginning, you two had such great plans, but all that fizzled. Now all you do is sit on the beach with Brutus and stare out over the lake - for hours on end. Becky hates seeing you like that. She gets depressed watching you. But you know what, Mike? She's been hurting, too. She didn't know how to stop Tommy's pain and now she doesn't know how to stop yours."

Mike stared at me, trying to make sense of what I just said.

Sensing his bewilderment, I said, "I told Becky that I know for a fact that you love her very much. You're a very lonely man - I'm right, huh Mike? You miss her; you miss your family being together, beyond words, don't you?"

He said nothing. He just stared at me. Once again, he ran a hand through his hair.

"I bet that's one of the things Becky loves the most about you," I said.

"What?"

"The way your run your hand through your hair like that."

He flushed. After a few pensive moments, he whispered, "I went into a tailspin when Tommy drowned. I thought I was over it, but... I made everything miserable for myself and for anyone who came in contact with me."

"Listen to me, Mike. You two love each other - anyone can see that - even me - and I haven't known you all that long." I took his arm and tugged him to the doorway of the living room. I pointed. "And you two made that beautiful boy in the image of Tommy."

Mike peered at his son. A father's smile began to glow.

The boy had taken off his shoes and socks and thrown them in a heap in front of the TV. He was sound asleep with an arm stretched over his beloved black and copper Dobie.

Quite contented with his sweltering predicament, Brutus merely panted. He made no attempt to move to cooler quarters.

"Tom has so many of his Uncle Tommy's characteristics," I whispered. "Even his voice."

"The only difference is that Tom is a lot feistier than his Uncle Tommy," Mike said.

"Tom gets that from his father," I said.

Yesterday, Tommy Gray Drowned

"I'm the first to admit that, 'Lizbeth. I sure was a handful. But the day Tommy drowned, I changed and I haven't been the same since."

"Me, too," I said. "I can't let go of Tommy. I see his face in the water no matter where I am. For the life of me, I still cannot comprehend why Echo Lake killed him. That day, it became a silent monster in my eyes. It was waiting to get some unsuspecting slob without any warning at all. I get so creeped out just thinking about it."

Mike leaned against the doorjamb, gazing intently at me. He was waiting for me to continue.

I swallowed hard then said, "I delivered papers until I turned fourteen, remember?"

He nodded.

"Every day I passed that cemetery where Tommy is buried, I swear I heard his voice. I don't know how many times, he called to me. He was alone. He wanted company. So I trudged up to that grassy knoll and sat Indian-style at the edge of his grave. I never spoke a single word, but I felt an insatiable need to communicate in some way. And I'm sure we did communicate, because I left carrying a feeling like none other. If ever a soul other than my own breathed within me, surely it did then - it does now - and that soul belongs to Tommy Gray."

"That same feeling comes over me when I sit at the lake," Mike admitted. "It's like he wants me to know something. Or perhaps, he just misses being there with me. You suppose?"

I shrugged. "One thing I do know: your son Tom is going to be ten years old soon. That's how old Tommy was when he drowned. Maybe, deep down inside you and me, that ten-year connection is bugging us."

Mike thought about that. From the look on his face, I think it made sense to him. He looked back into the living room. "My son is such a blessing and yet... I love him so much... But sometimes it's hard for me to look at him. He's a constant reminder of Tommy and how I stood by and let him drown."

"I'm convinced that Tommy made me come back to Echo Lake," I said. "You saw those sketches. Every one of them means something - I just know it. But I can't seem to figure out what. Tommy's grave. Tommy in the lake. Tommy and me picking up newspapers. What does it all mean? When I try to figure it out, Tommy lets me know if I'm on the right track."

"How's that?" Mike asked, straightening then crossing his arms.

"Well, take for instance this afternoon," I said. "Ruth and I were listening to Becky. I was truly angry at Gerald's cruelty, that's a fact; but in my head…oh, my God. Fury like I never felt before." I found myself trembling and had to do something to stop it. I hurried to the counter and started to slice lemon wedges for iced tea. "And this Linda Benson thing… All this stuff… It's making me crazy!"

Mike took the lemon and knife from my hands. "Here, let me do that." As he sliced the lemon, moments passed without a word.

I squinted at him. "You think I'm whacked out, don't you?"

"Not at all," he said. "If you're whacked out, what does that make me? I'm well beyond that."

"Only thing I can say is," I said, "the sooner we figure this out, the sooner Tommy will rest."

"I have to admit," Mike said, "if he goes away now, I'm going to miss him."

The eeriest sensation came over me: the truth was not going to remain hidden in the depths of Echo Lake very much longer.

Before I could stop myself, I wrapped my arms around Mike's waist and held on tight. I put my cheek on his shoulder blade and whispered, "I'll miss him, too."

Yesterday, Tommy Gray Drowned

JOURNEY

I just stepped out of the shower Sunday morning when urgent knocking rattled the bathroom door and then, "Bethie?"

"What's up, Ruth?"

"Julie is on the phone. She's insisting on speaking to you this minute. I told her you were in the shower, but…"

I cut Ruth off, "I'll be right there."

Rampant theories set my head spinning: Julie must've heard from Peter; he's on his way home; maybe he's home already! I chucked my arms into the sleeves of my flowered bathrobe and cinched it so tight that my last two ribs hurt and breathing was nearly impossible. Oh well, I wasn't breathing anyway. Grabbing the towel with one hand, I yanked open the door with the other.

Ruth was standing there, wringing her hands, more nervous than me. I could read her mind: what if something happened to Peter? Considering resent events, luck was dicey. The news about Peter can't be good.

I bent over and wrapped the towel around my dripping hair. What if… What if… Heartbeats choked me.

By the time I put the phone to my ear, panic had taken control. I could hardly speak: "Hullo?"

"Mom? Are you sitting down?" Julie's voice contained an awful lot of enthusiasm for bad news.

"Uh-huh." I lied.

"Mom, I'm pregnant! Mom! Are you listening? Ken and I are going to have a baby! You and Daddy are going to be grandparents!"

Yesterday, Tommy Gray Drowned

"Oh…" was all I got out. I didn't know whether to laugh or cry. I felt my body sway. I was happy and yet disappointed that her call had nothing to do with Peter. I fought for control: Shame on me; I was the most selfish worm that ever crawled upon this earth; Think about Julie for a change; This was marvelous news for her. Somehow I managed to pull myself together then speak more enthusiastically, "Why, that's just wonderful, Julie! When?"

"Christmas time, Mom! Our first anniversary!"

"Julie, take it easy," I said. "A breath once in a while is a good idea." I was teasing her, of course; although inside me, self-flagellation was in full earnest: I better be a more competent grandmother than I was a mother; What a jerk I had been, shutting my only child out of my life during her growing years; How could I have been so insensitive?

Back in the sixties after Peter was drafted and left for Vietnam, I found out I was pregnant with Julie. Shortly thereafter, the Vietcong ambushed his platoon and he came up missing in action. Having received no word of him, I called his parents who lived in Virginia. It seemed as though they didn't want anything to do with me, so I never told them. Neither Peter nor his family ever knew he had a daughter. Four years later, he turned up in a remote Cambodian settlement, without any recollection of who he was or how he got there. Because he and I were not married, the United States government had no obligation to let me know.

I wallowed in self-pity for years, bitter about the past and afraid to face the future. In the meantime, our sweet Julie grew into a beautiful young woman. Then she moved out of the house - away from me. I didn't blame her none. I never really talked to her anyway. I deserved to be alone, but I missed her so much it hurt. Did I tell her so? No. We barely kept in touch, which fueled my self-imposed isolation. I had myself convinced that I had done something horribly wrong in my life to deserve having nobody to love - but for the life of me, I had no clue what that was.

Almost a year had passed when Julie met Emma LaRosa. Julie's life changed for the better and shortly thereafter, so did mine. Every life Em touched flowered - the way the wilted plant did when ET's finger touched it. Emma worked her magic on Julie and reunited us on Thanksgiving Day. I could never be Emma, but I was going to bust my butt to follow her example: selfless; warm; constant. Emma made me understand that missing someone is natural, but keep it in perspective. Move on. Time has a way of working things out. So I took her advice. From then on, every time I found myself sinking into the dark abyss of despair, I pictured Emma, her serenity, her strength. How would she act? Then I was okay. And what do you know? Peter found his way back to me. We were married a short time later. Then last Christmas, Julie and Ken got married. Finally, I had my own complete family. Except, a dumb ol' bunch of Congressmen and some other high mucky-mucks convinced Peter that he was the only one with background enough to go back to Vietnam and persuade the government there to return MIAs back to America. So off he went, back to Vietnam, leaving my feeble heart to struggle with his absence.

The first night without Peter was excruciating, an eternity, just like back in the 60s. I missed him. I loved him. He deserted me. I hated him. Emma's words kept echoing in my ear: Keep it in perspective, dear; move on; time has a way of working things out. Well, okay then. I did move on - or should I say I went on the road, back to Echo Lake. But so far, time had not worked things out. And now our daughter was going to have our first grandchild. And where was Peter? In Vietnam - just like before - and no word of his whereabouts.

Tears swamped my eyes. I was heartsick. I gritted my teeth. I had to be strong. I had to be there for Julie, Ken, and the baby.

"I'll be home sometime this afternoon," I promised - not only to Julie, but also to myself. More than anything else, I needed to put my arms around my baby girl, which included her baby.

Well, I told Ruth the happy news. Man, did that woman jump up and down! She latched onto me like a monkey and danced me across the living room and into the kitchen and back into the living room again. I laughed away my heartache as I leapt about with my silly cousin. We were two giddy schoolgirls in a dance without music.

Wally rushed in from the backyard. "Hey, what's all the fuss about?"

"Bethie's going to be a Grammy!" Ruth screeched. She broke out in song: "Bethie's gonna be a Grammy! Grammy, Grammy, Grammy!"

Wally let out a war whoop then wrapped his arms around me so tight I thought my ribs might crack. Then he latched onto Ruth and the three of us did ring-around-the-rosy. Talk about excited.

I couldn't help but think what a shame Ruth and Wally did not have children of their own. They would be the best of parents. I just knew it.

"Come on, you two," I said. "Get your things packed. We're off to Brighton. It's time you two meet Julie and Ken."

Wally stopped short. "I can't. I just got off the phone with Mike. I promised to give him a hand with a few things."

Ruth's excitement vanished, replaced by disappointment. Obviously, she wanted to go with me.

"You two go anyway," Wally insisted. "I'm gonna be busy with Mike. Plus that other job up at Fern Cove needs to get finished up, too."

Ruth hesitated, "Well…"

Wally persisted. "Makes no sense for you to hang around all by yourself, Ruthie." An hour later, he kissed her good-bye and said, "Call me every day."

"Promise," she said.

"I'll have her back on Tuesday," I said.

I took the route Ruth suggested: through Fox Creek. It was a well-organized town - twice the size of Echo Lake. Three church spires of differing denominations rose into the heavens instead of the single one in the Village of Echo Lake. The drug store still carried the same name: Riley's Pharmacy.

"Is that place still run by the same guy?" I asked.

"Yes and no," Ruth replied. "Old man Riley is semi-retired. His son Paul took over the business end of things. Paul went to college somewhere in Boston and is now a druggist, same as his dad. There's Nancy's."

I squinted at the hair salon next to the hardware store and two doors down from the Riley's Pharmacy. Thirty years ago, Nancy's Beauty Shoppe was the only place - not counting the barbershop at the end of Main Street - to get your hair cut. All the girls went there for prom do's. I would have, too, if not for moving away from Echo Lake.

"Is Nancy still hanging in there?" I asked.

"Only does a few regulars," Ruth said. "Mary runs the place for Nancy. I think you went to school with her."

"Who?"

"Mary Mason."

"The one that hung around with Anne Ford?"

"Uh-huh. Mary lives in Milford…or is it Framingham? Geez, I can't say for sure. Nancy's daughter married some guy from Connecticut and lives there now. One of Nancy's sons is a realtor here in Fox Creek. Making a pretty good living at it, too. He married Anne Ford."

"How about that," I said. "I always expected little Miss Ford to marry some out-of-town pretender and live in some exotic place. Mary Mason, too, for that matter."

Ruth laughed. "Well, Anne is still at the top of the food chain around here."

"But Mary lives in Milford," I said. "That must put a crimp in her and Anne's relationship."

"Their relationship took a nosedive during their senior year when Anne took up with Nancy's realtor son." Ruth said. "Anne wanted him for herself. Anyways, Nancy's other son lives up past Fern Cove. Wally built homes for the whole bunch of them - except Mary."

"Funny how some kids stuck around while others moved on," I said.

"Yeah," Ruth said, an underlying sadness entwining her voice. "Wish things were like they used to be when we were kids - everybody together and all."

No way did I ever want to go back. Ruth's family smiled and hugged for no good reason at all while mine never showed an ounce of affection towards one another. I never heard I love you fall from the lips of either of my parents. Once in a great while, Father got frisky with Mother, but she always pushed him away. "Behave yourself, old man," she'd say. So most nights Father went off to bed early, long before Mother. He was snoring up a storm by the time she got there. Once or twice, I thought I heard bedsprings creaking and strange undertones emanating from their bedroom - when they thought Brother and I were asleep. I was always such a night owl. Chewing it over now, if Mother and Father were doing what I thought they were doing, they certainly stifled their activity. Not at all like Peter and me. I giggled at the thought of stone-faced Mother taking pleasure in such things.

"What's so funny?"

I glanced at Ruth. She was grinning at me, her eyes eagerly searching mine.

"Oh…uhm…" I stammered, trying to come up with another humorous subject to talk about. "I was just thinking how goofy your father was. His high cheekbones always turned so rosy when he laughed. I can just hear his gravelly voice right now, weaving that story about how I scared the bajeebies out of him."

Ruth giggled. "You don't know how many times he told that story. That happened at a camp they rented one summer up at Lake Winnipesaukee."

"Can you imagine?" I said. "Snoozing on an inner tube halfway out in the lake and having a two-year-old swim up to you like that and say, 'Look! Me swim!'?"

Ruth laughed so hard that tears welled in her eyes. "Dad almost took a heart attack right then and there. Gosh, I miss him so much. Mom, too."

"I would have loved to see them again," I said.

"They would've loved to see you, too," Ruth said. "You were always one of Dad's favorites, you know. They felt so bad because they didn't get to see you more often."

"Actually, the only time I saw any of you was when I delivered your newspaper," I said.

"Your mother wasn't much for visiting," Ruth said. "Too bad. You and I lost out on so much."

My insides smoldered with the thought of Mother living in her own little world, denying me of mine. To this day, she still possessed no desire to have anything to do with me. Arizona gave her excusable distance. Sure, we talked - when I called her - but if I never called, it would make no never-mind to her. Suddenly, a horrifying thought occurred to me. I was no better than Mother was. Just like her, I had pushed my daughter aside for my own selfish ends. How hateful of me. Well, I was never going be that way ever again. I was so lucky that Julie forgave me. I won't blow it again.

"Slow it down over here," Ruth said. "I want you to see where Rick Morton lived. It's just around this bend. Right…right…there! See that?"

Centered within a private setting, a two-story wood-frame house was nestled up against a lush backdrop of white pine and birch. Two young men on ladders were in the process of attaching a light blue shutter onto the recently painted house. Other people were working in the yard, mowing and trimming and such. The sweet smell of newly mown grass wafted in the early spring air.

Ruth lowered her voice as if someone might hear. "The woman tending the flower garden? She's Rick's wife."

As if sensing our eyes, the woman looked up then turned and focused on my car. All at once, I cursed myself for buying a red convertible. It certainly did not blend into the woodwork.

The woman stood up and stretched her back. Then of all things, she motioned to us.

Ruth gasped. "She wants to talk to us."

I swallowed hard. "Shish, I don't know…"

"I think it's okay," Ruth whispered.

Yesterday, Tommy Gray Drowned

From the agreeable look on the woman's face, I got the same feeling as Ruth. I pulled off the road and hit the brakes.

The woman trotted barefoot to my car, swiping her dirty hands across the front of the blue shirt she was wearing. It was a man's button-down, much too big for her slender five-foot-five frame. The soiled knees of her faded blue jeans revealed a heavy dose of gardening. She called out, "Ruth! So nice to see you!" Her hastily cleaned hand complete with dirty fingernails extended toward my cousin. They shook hands then the woman reached across the front seat and offered her hand to me. "I'm Jenny. Rick's kind-of-ex-but-now-widow."

Dumbfounded that her voice contained not the slightest hint of grief, I shook her hand. Her grip was firm, genuine, sincere. I tightened mine. "Elizabeth Blair," I said. "Ruth's cousin." I held onto her hand an extra second. "I grew up in Echo Lake."

Although younger than me, her face laid bare an inner turmoil, plus her light brown hair seemed to be prematurely graying. Melancholy clashed with the exuberance shining in her soft brown eyes as she swished her disheveled bangs out of her face with the back of her hand. "What do you think of my lovely home?" A wide gesture enveloped the property. "I came back that very night Chief Parker called me with the news that Rick took a header into the falls below Fern Cove. Sure is nice to be home again."

My mouth dropped open. "So, uhm…you're okay with what happened?"

"No reason to be else-wise," she said. "Truth is: Rick and I weren't together for at least five years. This place was mine long before I met him. After we separated, I couldn't get him out of here. I didn't dare to do anything about it - or even divorce him. I was lucky to get away from him with my life. Rick was the kind of guy who got real mad in a real hurry, and when he did, God bless the person who got him riled up."

"You don't need to tell me that," I said. "I've lived through a couple of his fits - one which resulted in his own undoing. Just wish none of it ever happened. If I could've done anything to stop it…"

Jenny cut me off, "Listen. Don't pretend it didn't happen. I knew in my heart that sooner or later he'd get his. You were just in the wrong place at the right time."

"Whatever possesses a person to do such things?" Ruth said, sounding unnaturally subdued.

Jenny shrugged. "Rick had it pretty tough growing up. His father would just as soon spit in your eye than to speak to you. His mother was some scared woman while old man Morton drew breath. She's passed on now, too. Rick may have truly loved me - maybe that Linda Benson, too - but you know what? Rick didn't know how to love. It was bad enough when he started pushing me around, but when he pushed around my son Benjamin… Well, that was the last straw. I got us out of here in one big hurry. My son is all I have left of my first husband. I am not about to let anything happen to him. It ended up that we had to hide out in women's shelters outside of Boston. They kept moving us around to different places until Rick found better things to do. That's Benjamin, over there, putting the shutters back on the house." Jenny savored the sight. "He's such a good boy."

I followed her line of sight. I didn't see a boy; I saw a grown man.

Ruth spoke up, "Wonder when they'll find Rick's body."

Jenny shrugged. "Who knows? He'll turn up sooner or later. He's probably stuck between rocks in the basin below the waterfall - that's what Chief Parker says."

"Wally says they have to be real careful about diving anywhere around there because of the early spring runoff being so high and so fast, this year," Ruth said.

Jenny readily agreed. "I wouldn't want any diver risking his life over the likes of Rick Morton's sorry butt, that's for sure."

Realizing that Rick was still out there unaccounted for made me quiver - even if his body was snagged at the base of that waterfall. Nah, he's dead, I convinced myself. So quit worrying about it. My own eyes watched him plunge into the rapids -

sucked him down in a heartbeat. Shoot, at this very moment, the angels must still be holding that heathen under all that agitation, trying in vain to wash years of crud out of his nefarious soul.

"We better get going," Ruth said.

I nodded. "Well, it was great meeting you, Jen. Good luck to you and Benjamin."

"Stop by again when I'm not so busy," Jenny said. "We'll catch up on stuff."

I put my car in gear then applied a little pressure to the gas pedal. Pulling away from Jenny, I took one last look at the house nestled up against white pine and birch.

Ruth heaved a contented sigh. "Feels good to see Jenny and her son piecing their lives back together again."

I gulped back emotion, wishing in some far-fetched sort of way that I could trade places with Jenny. Imagine: me and Peter putting around a cozy nest like that. Looking back at the road, I took a deep breath and said, "Whatever happened to her first husband?"

Ruth hesitated.

I glanced at her then back at the road.

"He died in Nam," Ruth muttered. "Two days before the cease fire."

Her words slammed me. Then frustration burnt my soul where scars of Peter's first leaving never healed. "That war will always be a plague on our generation."

Ruth sighed. "Suppose Peter is okay?"

"The question of the century," I said.

"I don't know how you go on not knowing," Ruth said. "I'd need answers."

I slammed my hand on the steering wheel. "That's it! As soon as I get home, I'm calling the State Department!"

STORM

It was five o'clock when Ruth and I drove through the open wrought iron gate and parked in front of the hundred-year-old brick manse perched atop a cliff overlooking the Atlantic Ocean. As we got out of the car, thunder rumbled off to the west where ominous clouds percolated, fired by potent outbursts of lightning. Soon, heavy weather was going to fulfill the weatherman's prognostication.

Anticipating the storm's wrath, seagulls screeched overhead. Hordes of sea birds were heading for the safety of nesting islands off the coast.

At the front door, the main resident of the manse, Ralph the cat, greeted us. Ruth bent down and stroked his back. The gray tiger arched his back, higher and higher as again and again, he circled back for more. Unable to resist him, Ruth picked him up and burrowed her face into his luxuriant fur. Ralph loved every moment.

Suddenly the front door flew open and there was Julie. "Mom!" she shrieked. "Uhm, I mean Grammy!" She started jumping around in frenzied excitement.

Not at all accustomed to such activity, Ralph bristled into one humongous fur ball and leaped out of Ruth's arms. He charged through the open door then up the winding stairs to some quieter hideout.

Julie gave me an exuberant bear hug. As we rocked back and forth, I didn't want to let go of her; holding my child made me feel whole again. She smelled so good, like honeysuckle on a whimsical summer breeze. Strands of her blond hair feathered my cheek.

Yesterday, Tommy Gray Drowned

She gave Ruth the same enthusiastic welcome. "So, Ruth. I hear you're not any more successful at keeping my mother out of trouble than the rest of us."

Ruth poked me on the shoulder. "Well, to put it mildly, Julie; we all must, at all times, keep a level eye on this woman."

Large smatterings of rain began to pelt us. Julie backed into the house, motioning to Ruth and I. "Come in, come in," she said. "Everybody's in the dining room."

"Look at this place!" Ruth exclaimed as we followed Julie down the hallway. "It's awesome."

I got a big kick out of her wide-eyed wonderment.

Julie giggled. "Thanks. I'll show you around later."

When Ken spotted us entering the dining room, he staggered to his feet. He floundered while kissing me. I felt spittle of the single malt scotch that laced his breath. Backing away from me, he hoisted his half-empty glass and asked, "Wanna drink?"

"Uhm, no, thanks," I stammered, waving him off. "Maybe Ruth might…"

"I'm all set," Ruth injected.

I could tell she was not at all comfortable with his inebriation. I felt bad. I had bragged so much about Ken. I took hold of her arm and gave a tug. "Come on, Ruth. I want you to meet Emma."

From the head of the massive mahogany table, the matriarch of the LaRosa family reached out her hand. I took it then bent to give her a kiss on the cheek. As I introduced Ruth, Emma's daughter Margi dashed up to us in her normal flamboyant way and nearly knocked me into her mother. "Oh my God, Elizabeth! I saw you on the news!" She seemed close to hyperventilation. "What on earth did you get yourself into this time? Are you okay? Let me look at you! Here, gimme a hug!" She wrapped her arms around me and squeezed - I think she may have cracked my spine…just joking. She took a step back, shaking her finger at me while the fingers of her other hand dug into her waist. "Don't you dare go back there! You hear me?"

Over Margi's shoulder, I caught sight of Janice, Emma's daughter-in-law, propped in the corner next to the French doors that opened into a stormy backyard. Her unselfish actions on the day of a Brighton Savings Bank robbery had saved my life and Emma's too. She smiled demurely at me. At her side was her husband, Adam LaRosa. I let go of Margi then soaked up the sight of Janice, now six months pregnant with twins. Adam gave her a steadying arm as she waddled to me.

"My humble little heroine," I whispered, wrapping my arms around her.

She clasped my other hand then Adam and I helped her to the table. "Have you heard from Peter?" she asked, while easing her blossoming form onto a chair.

I sat down beside her; Adam on the other side of her. I heaved a sigh. "Nothing," I said.

"She keeps calling the number Peter gave her before he left," Ruth said, sitting down beside me. "All she gets is the voice mail of a Mr. Tanner."

"Hate when that happens," Ken slurred. He slugged down the last of his scotch. "Voice mail. Answering machines. Bhah! Jus' high tech means of screenin' calls. Ignorant, if you ask me."

The room went silent.

I glanced at Julie. She was fidgeting. Abruptly, she took off for the kitchen. I cleared my throat, loudly to divert attention. "I left a message for Mr. Tanner."

"What else can you do?" Ruth said.

"Nothin'," Ken snapped. "Dealt with that crap plenty of times after the plane crash." Haggard and preoccupied, he lumbered across the room to the cluttered wet bar next to the fireplace. "Frustrating." He poured himself another scotch.

"Ken," Julie called from the kitchen.

"Huh?" His glazed eyes shot towards the sound of her voice. He grunted, "Humph." He swilled down the drink then grimaced. He slammed the glass onto the bar and headed off to the kitchen. His gait was precarious - to say the least.

A short time later, Ken and Julie returned. She looked quite distressed while helping him push a serving cart laden with food up to the table.

Emma had taught my Julie quite a bit about cooking. More than likely, the old woman had an active hand in today's preparations.

Ken usually did his share of the cooking and enjoyed doing so, but I doubted that this was the case this day. However, his excessive drinking concerned me. It was not like him at all. What's more, he only picked at his food.

After supper, Ruth and I helped to clear the table. "What a spacious kitchen," Ruth said, ogling her surroundings while setting dishes on the counter. Her fingers began to explore every inch of the kitchen. "How many rooms does this house have?"

I shrugged. "It goes on and on."

Margi piped up, "Hey, Jules! Go ahead and show Ruth around. Take your mother. Ken and I'll handle the cleanup."

I seriously doubted how much help he was going to be, but I sloughed it off and decided to tag along with Julie and Ruth. The manse where my daughter lived still awed me. Besides, snooping had lately become a pastime of mine.

Upon entering the master bedroom in the back corner of the house, Julie switched on the lights. Halos of dusty rose surrounded the table lamps and cast shadows across the lush ivory carpet that muffled our presence. "Geez," Ruth said. "You really lucked out the day you met Ken."

I could tell Julie was blushing by the tone of her voice. "Ken and his first wife restored the manse."

I spoke up, "But Julie redid this bedroom. Didn't she do a great job?"

"Uh-huh!" Ruth said.

Floor-to-ceiling windows, framed with creamy sheers, overlooked a black and blue ocean capped by a low cloud ceiling that choked out Minot's Light. Unexpectedly, the gale outside threw open the French doors. A howling swirl tore across the room. Julie and I rushed over to close the doors. The curtains flogged us until we managed to latch the doors.

The three of us wandered through two more bedrooms then Ken's study and several bathrooms. We ended up in the foyer at the spiral staircase.

Ralph had regained his composure and was drifting down the stairs, nonchalantly rubbing against each spindle. Julie picked him up. "Ralph is the only one who comes and goes upstairs," she said. "I go up there every once in a while - but only to dust. Ken lost his first wife and daughter in a plane crash several years ago and refuses to set foot in those bedrooms or change one single thing. We live on the first floor. He lets me do whatever I want down here."

"You're certainly not cramped for space," Ruth said while plucking the purring cat from Julie's arms. "Just this floor has more room than my entire house - including my garage!"

As Ralph cuddled up in Ruth's arms, I chuckled. "You made a friend for life, you know."

Ruth gazed at Ralph, cooing, "You sure love attention, don't you?"

"How come you don't have a cat, Ruth?" I asked.

Ruth shrugged. "I always heard that it wasn't healthy to have a cat around when…" It was obvious that she still wanted to have a baby.

"Ken's daughter used to play with Ralph all the time," Julie said. "Ralph still misses her."

"Ken must be looking forward to having another child," I said.

"I guess… But it seems like my pregnancy is stirring up things that have been bottled up inside him."

"Like what, sweetheart?" I asked. I bit my tongue against adding: Is that the reason he's drinking more than I ever saw him drink?

Julie sighed. "Oh, I don't know. He gets so restless. And you know him, Mom. He's never been like that."

"Well, don't worry about it," I said. I tried to reassure her with humor. "I hear men get morning sickness, too."

Back in the dining room, we sipped coffee and watched the rain sheet across the illuminated patio beyond the French doors. Crooked fingers of lightning stretched down from the sky, illuminating the backyard, the cliffs, and the turbulent sea. Thunder clapped, lights flickered - and Ken paced. He stopped abruptly and yanked the curtains closed. He switched off the patio lights. His hands rubbed his arms as if he was cold. He eyed the fireplace. His fists bunched and then dropped to his side as he darted for the fireplace. In a heartbeat, fire swooshed across the gas log, setting faces aglow.

His restlessness was driving Julie crazy, and I wished he would settle down for her sake. I was glad when he disappeared into other parts of the house. But then, I found myself the center of attention.

"So, Elizabeth," Emma said, "have you figured out those drawings yet?"

"Not all of them," I said.

"One of them revealed that awful murder," Ruth boasted.

"I don't understand," Janice said, her hand circling her distended belly.

"You didn't see Elizabeth on the news?" Margi asked.

"You know I'm not much for TV," Janice said.

"The sketches are back in Brighton," I said, "or I'd show them to..."

Ruth cut me off, giving gruesome details of Rick Morton killing Linda Benson and then burying her body on top of Johnson's casket. I was relieved that I did not have to repeat all of it.

"What about that odd drawing of the boy in the water?" Emma asked. "I remember that one quite well."

I shrugged.

"Things weren't right in Tommy's life," Ruth said. "Maybe that's why he's half in the water and half out."

"What things?" Emma asked.

"His father pushed Tommy around quite a bit," Ruth said. "Plus Rick threatened to kill Tommy, because he assumed Tommy saw him murder Linda Benson. Sad thing is: Tommy didn't get a good look at what actually happened. He couldn't have known Linda was dead, because he ran off seconds before that happened."

I nodded. "He told Mike about it, but never mentioned they killed her."

"Mike swears Tommy didn't know," Ruth added, "but that wasn't what Rick thought."

"So here I come along, thirty years later, and draw those sketches," I said.

Ruth chuckled. "I must say, you really stirred up a hornet's nest! Sleepy little Echo Lake will never be the same!"

"Sometimes, we wish to go back to the past, thinking that everything was better back then," Emma reflected. Her demeanor resembled a wise old sage. "Quite often, things were not at all as they seemed."

Ken came back carrying candles and flashlights. Good thing, because moments later, a loud crack of thunder shook the house; the living room flashed white; off went the electricity. Within seconds, a flashlight beam sliced the darkness and Ken was trying to open a matchbox. Julie and I got up to help him. After we lit the candles, he retreated to the bar and poured himself another drink. The candlelight picked up his ghostly eyes rolling round and around in their sockets. He scanned the room as if hearing somebody calling his name. Scotch in hand, he hurried off into other parts of the manse.

"I don't know what has gotten into him tonight," Julie lamented.

"He's jittery about the baby, sweetheart," Emma said. "And having all of us around here, so excited and all, probably makes things worse."

"He'll be okay, kid," Margi said. "Just give it time." She hitched her thumb over her shoulder at Emma. "And you know what Ma says all the time: Time has a way of working things out."

Time, I mused. With time, Julie and Ken will work things out. At least they're together - not like Peter and me. I'm always trying to keep things going all by myself. It's so hard. Well, when Peter gets home this time, I am going to give him a stiff talking to. He just cannot keep going off and leaving me and his family like this.

A while later we saw Emma, Margi, Janice, and Adam off. Ruth and I came back into the living room while Julie went in search of Ken. She came back quite upset. "He's passed out on the floor in the study."

"Here," I said, patting the sofa next to me. "Come sit with me."

She wrung her hands, on the verge of hysteria. "What if he doesn't want the baby, Mom?"

I gave a little chuckle. "Ken wants the baby. He's just having a hard time about something. Just hang in there and be patient."

She sagged on the sofa, beside me. "What am I going to do, Mom?"

"You both need to get out of this house," I said. "How about if Ruth and I pick you up Monday morning at ten? We'll make a day of it."

An hour or so passed. Power was still out - so was Ken. Julie calmed down and from time to time, was drifting off to sleep. So I put her to bed then Ruth and I made a break for Brighton. Lights flickered on just as we crossed the city line. Electricity wasn't restored in Cohasset until dawn.

FACELESS

Monday morning. "Still no return call from Mr. Tanner?" Ruth asked.

I shook my head.

"It's totally mind-boggling," she fumed. "To think that your husband put his life on hold and in harm's way for his country's business, not only once, but twice, and yet some sort of faceless bureaucrat named *Mr. Tanner* hasn't the decency to return a measly phone call."

I sighed. "If only I knew what was going on. Is it too much to ask if Peter's okay?"

The gross injustice gnawed at my insides until finally, at nine thirty-seven, I got fed up and left a very unkind message for Mr. Tanner. No more than ten minutes later, the phone rang and a nasally female voice announced, "Please hold for Mr. Tanner, ma'am."

Moments later a diplomatic voice, so gooey a butter knife couldn't slice through it, came on the line: "William Tanner here. How are you today, Ms. Blair?" Surely, he didn't expect an answer to such a superficial question, did he? "Ms. Blair? Are you there?"

"Where's my husband?" I asked, blunt and to the point.

"At this precise moment, I cannot say," Tanner replied. "But the mission's going well, so I am told, and…"

"What do you mean, you cannot say?" I demanded. "It's your business to say!"

"Ms. Blair…"

"It's *Mrs.* Blair," I snapped.

Yesterday, Tommy Gray Drowned

"Pardon me, Mrs. Blair. The issues here are complex, so it is of extreme importance to maintain a high degree of secrecy - as well as security - in order for successful negotiations to transpire." The tone of his voice revealed that Tanner was tremendously proud of himself for evading my question so artfully. In the past, I might have accepted this and slunk into a dark corner somewhere like a good little girl, but too much water had gone over the dam. I was a different person now.

"Look, Mr. Tanner," I said, fighting to maintain control. "The innocence I once had toward my government ended a long time ago." I knew that shouting might label me a lunatic and bawling would make me a crybaby. "Information was withheld from me back in the 60s because Peter and I were not married, but we *are* married now."

"Please, Mrs. Bl..."

I cut him off, "Which means, Mr. Tanner, I - and my daughter - deserve better than this honey-coated line of trash you are giving me. I am more than capable of separating fact from fiction."

"Our government has been harshly criticized in the past, Mrs. Blair. Undeservedly so, I might add."

"Here we go again," I said, rolling my eyes. Frustration swelled inside me - so fast, in fact, that momentarily, my voice failed me. Perhaps that was a good thing. Tanner might not have liked being called a joke. But who did he think he was talking to?

"Let me reassure you, Mrs. Blair. Your husband and his entourage have the best security possible."

"You don't have a clue where any of them are, do you?" I sounded cocksure; although I was only guessing. "Suppose I let the media in on this? Bet they'll have a field day, wouldn't you say?"

Tanner succumbed to the pressure. "Everything humanly possible is being done to locate your husband. Based on sketchy information..."

My heart screamed out in terror: Peter *is* missing! Oh no! Not again! My head exploded, derailing my train of thought. Weakness crept over me. My knees buckled. On the brink of dropping the phone and collapsing onto the floor, a spark ignited my soul then erupted into an inferno. I became a mad woman. My anger and pain detonated. "Had *I* been the wife I should have been, *never, never* would I have let my husband go back to that dreadful country in the first place! But if you think for one blessed minute that I am going to spend the *next twenty years* of my life awaiting his return, *you* are sadly mistaken. I lived through that nightmare once, and once is *one time too many for anyone*! So, Mr. Tanner, or whatever your name *really* is, I want answers! *Now!* And if I don't get them, I promise to *God Almighty* that the world will find out that you self-serving bureaucrats are covering up some sort of dirty deal - just like back in the 60s."

Tanner did not know what hit him. "Give us a little time, Mrs. Blair. Please."

"How much time?" I charged.

"A day or so, Mrs. Blair, that's all. I will personally keep you apprised of the situation. Daily."

My hands were tied, but I refused to let him off the hook. Still, what else could I do, but cave to his request? Hanging up the phone, I leaned against the wall and closed my eyes. Despair mounted within me. I had to conquer the urge to close myself off from the world until Peter returned. I had to believe my husband was coming back to me, but...

"You all right, Bethie?"

My chest heaved as I drew in a very deep breath. I turned to Ruth. Dismay riddled her face. I had forgotten that she was in the house. She had heard the entire conversation. She had no choice but to hear it. If I wasn't yelling, I was pretty close to it. I squeezed her hand and said, "Yeah." I went into the bathroom and put a damp washcloth on my burning face. My eyes gazed back at me from the mirror. What precious little time Peter and I had spent together. Our dreams had not even begun to be realized. Like dying embers blown by the wind, our life together had once again been snuffed out, leaving a hollow chill where his love used to warm. What was I supposed to tell Julie? I hurled the face cloth at the mirror. "Dammit!"

Yesterday, Tommy Gray Drowned

Despite the unthinkable news, I was determined to carry on with plans. I had to keep going for Julie's sake - and the baby's. Not only that, Ruth was there. I couldn't wimp out on her - and I knew full well she wouldn't let me anyway. So we picked up Julie and went to the mall that had just opened last week near the Rhode Island border. Margi tagged along. I skillfully delayed in revealing that Peter was once again missing in Vietnam. Our day was not going to be spoiled. Peter would have wanted it that way.

I helped Julie to pick out maternity clothes, which she really didn't need for quite some time. When she saw the perfect crib and matching bureaus, I could not stop myself from purchasing the entire set. Oh well, I thought, I was going to be the grandmother sent from heaven - just wait and see. My grandbaby was going to be spoiled rotten.

Of course, the crib set required a comforter, matching sheets and bumper. There just happened to be a complete outfit that filled the bill ever so perfectly. The colorful teddy bears and butterflies cavorting all over it called out to me, "Buy me! Buy me!" So I did.

Later that afternoon, we headed for Emma's. At her age, good and bad days were a toss-up. Today was a good day. Her usual spread of Italian delicacies, which she made from ancient family recipes, awaited us.

When Julie gushed on and on about all the cool things I bought for the baby, a twinkle lit up Emma's eye. "Now Elizabeth," she taunted, "You cannot go and buy everything for that sweet *bambino*. The rest of us will not have one blessed thing left to give him - or her."

I hung my head and swayed side to side. I sent her a sheepish look while jiggling my shoulders. Never in my life had I ever appreciated the meaning of friends and family more than I did right then. No way could I ever retreat into lonely isolation again - even if Peter never came back to me. But he was coming back. To my surprise, I had no doubt of it.

So because Emma, Margi, and Ruth were there, I came to the conclusion that this was the best time as any to tell Julie about her father. If my daughter took it badly, my friends and family could help her - and me. I cleared my throat and said, "Julie, I have something to tell you."

She glanced at me. Gaiety suddenly vanished from her face. "What's going on, Mom?" Her doe eyes searched my face. She always knew - before I even opened my mouth - when I had bad news to tell her.

"I talked to Mr. Tanner this morning," I said. "He told me that nobody knows where the Congressmen are…or…"

Margi and Ruth gasped.

Emma covered her mouth with her hands.

Julie squeaked, "Dad?" Terror swamped her as color drained from her face. "Dad is missing? Again? No! This can't be happening!"

I grabbed her hand and patted it. Ruth took hold of Julie's other hand.

"He's going to be all right, sweetheart," Emma said. "I can feel it in my bones."

"Tanner is going to call me every day," I said. "He swore that to me. If he doesn't, I told him I'll find me a good reporter and…well, Tanner didn't appreciate that much."

"Good for you, Elizabeth!" Margi barked. "That's what ya gotta do! Hang tough!"

"Sometimes that's easier said than done," I said.

"Something's up and Tanner's not talking," Ruth said. "Nobody is. Haven't you noticed? The last few nights on the evening news, there's been absolutely no updated report whatsoever on the mission."

"What're we going to do, Mom?" Julie whimpered. Tears trickled down her cheek.

I struggled for strength, but my insides were turning to mush. I wiped away her tears then wound a lock of her silky blond hair around her ear. "Well, first of all, young lady, I don't want you worrying. You have to take care of yourself and that little one. Let me do the worrying for the both of us, okay?"

"Your mother is right, dear," Emma said. ""Let her take care of it. She knows what to do."

I shot a look at my old friend. She had a lot more faith in me than I did. I only wished I did know what to do. I set my jaw. Now was not the time for my dumb insecurities. I would figure out something…somehow…

That evening when Ruth and I arrived back at my place, the message light flashed on the answering machine. One call. It was not Tanner.

Wally's singsong voice filled the room: "It's after nine-thirty, you two! Haven't heard from you all day!"

Ruth picked up the phone and called home. I took a shower. She was still on the phone when I finished showering. When she finally hung up, I jabbed, "Wally really misses his sweet baby Ruth."

"This is the first time we've been apart since the day we got married," she said. Melancholy laced her voice. "I didn't know I'd miss him so much and it's only been two days. How you can stand being apart from Peter so much is beyond me. You certainly are a lot stronger than me."

Her comment caught me off guard. I wanted to tell her how wrong she was. I wanted to tell her about the shabby way I treated Julie in the past, because Peter's absence entrenched my entire being in self-pity. I wanted to tell her how petrified I really was. Instead, I softly countered, "I'm not as strong as you think. Life has forced me to be this way."

"You are the strongest person I ever met," Ruth argued. "Look at how you stood up to Rick and Rusty. And those sketches of yours; you're not the least bit afraid of whatever those mean. If I ever did anything like that, I'd freak out for sure. And whenever I heard you talk to Tanner that way… Wow. You really gave that guy what for."

Her wide-eyed assessment made me chuckle. Then again, thinking about it, I began to see her point. "As Wally often says, 'Sure as shootin'!' I guess I really did. How's he doing anyway?"

"He's helping Mike with something or other." She hesitated. When she continued her voice became morose. "He says Chief Parker stopped by Mike's. The preliminary report of Linda's autopsy is out." Ruth hesitated again, studying her fingernails. "It says that more than likely Linda was alive when Rick and the others dumped her on top of Johnson."

I gasped. "Alive? How in the world do they know that?"

"I'm not sure, exactly..." Ruth rolled her eyes to the ceiling as moisture welled and then overflowed. "Except that Chief Parker says that the way her hands and fingers were bent, sort of clawing...and her mouth..." Ruth's voice trailed off. She trudged to the kitchen table. I followed. She sank into a chair. Her elbows propped her hands against her chin.

I went over and sat down on the chair next to her. I watched her fingers rotating her temples. She was in a terrible state. Her breath was labored. I didn't know what to expect.

Ruth heaved a tremulous breath. "Linda's mouth was agape - wide open. She was screaming down there under all that earth...and nobody heard her..." Ruth started to weep. "And... And the report also says...first indications are that...she was..." Ruth collapsed on the table and sobbed inconsolably.

"Linda was pregnant," I said.

Ruth looked up at me. Her red swollen eyes searched mine for some sense in all this.

My heart ached. No words of comfort were forthcoming for my cousin - or for me. I put my arm around her. She shuddered. "How can anybody do such a dreadful thing to another human being? And a little tiny baby? A baby! I would do anything to have a baby. And here...a baby that never was... That baby never even stood a ghost of a chance."

I put my head against hers and whispered, "Our only prayer can be that Linda and her precious little one are in heaven now."

Ruth swiped the back of her hand across her cheek. "There certainly was no paradise here on earth for those two."

I got up and retrieved the box of tissues on the refrigerator. "Yeah, her mother deserted Linda, leaving her with no clue who her father was." I set the box between us.

"And her grandmother was so sickly," Ruth said as we both drew out tissues. We dabbed our cheeks then blew our noses.

"Poor girl," I said, crushing my tissue in my hand. "She was starved for affection, that's for sure."

"What a crying shame that the esteemed residents of Echo Lake did absolutely nothing for Linda except to label her a tramp," Ruth grumbled.

"Come on," I said. "Let's make some tea and then curl up on the sofa." I filled two mugs with water and put them in the microwave.

Meanwhile, Ruth unwrapped two tea bags. "Why didn't my Mom recognize Linda's situation?" she said. "Gosh, the image of Linda as a child is still locked in my mind. A scavenger looking for love. I can't believe she found even a tiny semblance of love in Rick Morton, the man who ended up killing her."

The microwave dinged. I took out the mugs and handed one to Ruth. We pensively dunked the tea bags into the mugs.

"I see pieces of that unconnected waif in myself," I said.

Ruth gave me a sidelong glance. "What do you mean by that?"

"Even though my parents were there physically, they were not there for me emotionally," I said. "I didn't die in body like Linda. I died in spirit. Then Peter came along and made me feel alive for once in my life. Then he left. And worse, he came up missing in action. There wasn't even a body to end the uncertainty. No grave to visit - just like when my father died. I became emotionally dead to the world. And to Julie."

"Well, Peter is not your only family now," Ruth said. "You got all the rest of us and we're keeping you!"

It was just before dawn. I stood in the doorway to my bedroom. The last twenty-four hours had been another emotional rollercoaster ride. I gazed at the bed where I had spent the most blissful moments of my life captured in Peter's arms. The bed looked so big. So empty. So cold.

I felt like an intruder stealing across the room to Peter's side of the bed. I slid my fingers across the mint green satin comforter. I drew it back, uncovering his pillow, drawing it back as if I was undressing my lover. I drew back the blanket and top sheet.

I crumpled onto the bed.

Dreams swept me away, into the rapture of his arms.

He touched me. His lips warmed mine. And Peter and I were one.

Yesterday, Tommy Gray Drowned

AWKWARD

Tuesday afternoon, Ruth and I stopped for groceries in Framingham before driving on to Echo Lake. My cousin wanted to make her husband and me a special homecoming supper. Plans changed, however, when we arrived at her house. As we set the groceries on the kitchen counter, Ruth noticed a new magnet, shaped and decorated like a luscious strawberry, attached to the refrigerator door. A scribbled message was beneath it:

> Hi Ruthie!
> So glad my precious cherub is home!!!
> Missed you more than you will ever know. Don't
> bother with supper. Mike wants us at his place
> at 4. See you there!
> Can't wait to see you!
>> Love ya!
>> Wally.

Ruth frowned. "Four o'clock doesn't give Mike much time to make supper. He gets off his job at the Water Works at three-thirty."

I shrugged. "Maybe he took the day off."

"Could be he's coming home early," Ruth said.

"Maybe," I said as we went back out to the car for the rest of the groceries and suitcases.

"I think I'll make something to bring along," Ruth said. "Just in case."

"Can't hurt," I said, giving it no more thought.

When we got to Mike's, four cars were parked in his driveway: Mike's; Wally's; Becky's; one I didn't know. I figured Becky was dropping off Tom for a visit.

Yesterday, Tommy Gray Drowned

The second we got out of my car, Ruth shifted my attention to the house. "Will you look at that!" she exclaimed, jamming her hands into her hips. "They hauled all the junk and old building materials to the dump."

"The place looks great," I said as Wally trotted toward us. I cast a questioning glance at him. "Is that what you two were up to while we were gone?"

"You betcha," he boasted. His eyes sparkled as he grabbed hold of Ruth and lifted her off the ground, spinning her around. "So glad you're back!" When he finally set her on the ground, he gave her a great big kiss. He kept hold of her hand as he dragged her off toward the house. "Wait till you see everything Mike and I did!"

I grabbed the tossed salad that Ruth and I had put together then took off after them.

Wally pointed out the much-needed roof and the first siding the house had ever seen. I smiled and said. "White clapboards and Sherwood green trim."

Mike and Tom came sprinting around the back corner. They nearly mowed down the lot of us. "See, Dad?" Tom panted. "Told you I heard a car door slam."

Mike bent forward, huffing and puffing, his hands braced upon his knees. "Right as usual, m'boy. Hey you guys, what do you think of the place now?"

"Oh, it's absolutely gorgeous!" Ruth declared. She stood on her tiptoes and gave Mike a peck on the cheek. "You guys must have worked your tushies off every minute Bethie and I were away."

Mike winked at Wally. "You might say we kept ourselves out of trouble."

"We took off work yesterday just to finish up and surprise you two," Wally said.

"Come on," Mike said, giving us a wide beckoning gesture. "The barbecue's all fired up and ready to go."

"I smelled burning charcoal way out front," Ruth said.

In the backyard, Tom ran up to an older lady who was reclining on a lounge chair, enjoying the late afternoon sunshine. "Grammy! Grammy!" he squealed. "Ruth and 'Lizbeth are here!"

Her dark eyes opened with a start. As she turned toward us, her salt and pepper hair glittered in the sunlight. "Yes, yes, child. I see, Tom." She brushed flaxen strands off the boy's forehead then patted his cheek. Rising from the lounge chair, she seemed reluctant to end her meditation.

"You remember Tommy's mother, Laura Gray, don't you, 'Lizbeth?" Mike gestured to the woman while flashing his perfect ear-to-ear smile at me - flashing his magnificent cobalt eyes at me. My heart skipped a beat as heat surges flushed my cheeks. I quickly looked away. Shoot, I didn't have a handle on this infatuation after all. "You said you wanted to see Laura again, right?"

"Uhm, sure," I stammered while placing the tossed salad on the picnic table. I extended my hand to Mrs. Gray. How many times did I imagine this woman towering over me, bellowing for her son, her eyes coal-black? Well, standing before me now, she was nowhere as tall, nowhere as heavy-set. Likewise, her eyes were a soft chocolate, benevolent - like when Tommy showed up that blustery day and they exchanged glances. "It's been a long time, Mrs. Gray."

"Laura," she said. Her lips wrinkled with a hint of Tommy's demure half-smile. "Call me Laura, dear."

The sliding glass door slid open and Becky stepped out onto the deck. I gawked at her and then the tray she was carrying. It was loaded with dishes, napkins, and silverware. Well, I guess she's not just dropping off the kid. A twinge of resentment pricked my gut as she stepped down onto the lawn and walked toward us. She was glowing. She looked like a teenager in those white jeans and powder-blue blouse splashed with hot pink hibiscus flowers. I calculated her age: eight years younger than Mike; five years younger than me. That's all. Only five years. But look at her. Humph. I wished I had dressed nicer. More youthful. Five years younger-looking - as if that were possible.

Yesterday, Tommy Gray Drowned

I felt Ruth's eyes all over me. Her jaw was agape and those famous family eyebrows were undoubtedly arched. I avoided her stare, concentrating on achieving a poker face and then maintaining it. Hopefully, nobody sensed my errant feelings.

"Terrific!" Becky exclaimed. "Everyone is here!" She placed her cargo on the wooden picnic table. "Oh look at that salad!"

"Mom, can I have some potato chips?" Tom whined. He knew full well what the answer was going to be, but he tried anyway.

"Not before supper," Becky replied with all the patience of her mother.

His little round face turned down. Faker, I thought.

Becky tossed a green and white checkered tablecloth at him. "Here, Tom. Help me set the table."

The tablecloth landed on his head. As he yanked it off, his face brightened. He bunched it up and threw it back at her. She handed him two corners then they snapped it open and spread it across the eight-foot wooden trestle table.

"Now Tom," Becky said. "You put the dishes, napkins, and silverware on the table while I go get the rest of the food in the house."

I watched Ruth and Laura follow Becky into the white house with green trim. The three chattered back and forth. Ruth was so much like her mother; both got along so well with everyone. Friendliness was second nature to them. I always found it difficult to warm up to people that quickly. I resented myself for being that way. I couldn't help but think that Ruth and Wally were two peas in a pod, because he had already jumped in and taken over the grill without being asked, just chattering on and on with Mike. Wally had a real knack for barbecuing. Everything always came out perfect. Peter was that way, too.

I scrunched up the side of my face and looked at Mike arranging the wooden chairs he had fashioned himself. Each seat had to be strategically placed to ensure the best view of the sunset. The loneliness I had seen in him had vanished. He carried himself prouder, bouncier, as if a tremendous burden had been lifted off him. I wished I felt that way.

Mike gestured to me. "Come on over and set a spell."

I felt awkward, out of place, tramping over to the chairs. I didn't sit down. I just stood there as aromas of steak, hamburgers, hot dogs, rolls - you name it - inundated the evening air.

"The place sure looks great, huh?" Mike said.

"So do you," I said. "Working around here certainly agrees with you."

"Feels good to be productive for a change," he said. "That plus the fact that Becky and Tom moved back." His happiness glistened. Was that moisture welling in his eyes? He turned to me. "Thanks for shaking me out of my funk."

I gave him a confused look.

"That talk you and I had at Wally's last Saturday night," he explained. "You're absolutely right. Becky and I do love one another. And I've been a real jerk for thinking I'm the only one hung up about Tommy Gray. I sat up half that night chewing it all over. You reminded me of so many good things in my life. Becky. Tom. How empty my life was without them. How lucky I was to have Tommy Gray in my life - even if it was only for a short time. I have been such a fool. Later on that night, I walked down to the beach and sat in the dark with Brutus. I thought about Tommy and his old man. And Linda Benson. Rick and Rusty. So many wasted lives." Mike's head bobbed side to side as he scanned Echo Lake so peacefully reflecting the late afternoon. He turned and gazed into my eyes.

I looked down and picked at my fingernails, but all I could see were those eyes of his.

"Just before dawn, it came to me. The cycle of unhappiness must stop - if only in my life. Whatever it takes, I had to get Becky and Tom to come back to me."

My thoughts blackened: now that Becky was back, Mike became completely off limits to me. I looked at him out the corner of one eye. A small piece of me wanted this gorgeous hunk available - just in case Peter didn't come back. Mortification seared me. How could I think such a rotten thing? Of course, Peter was coming back. What's wrong with me? Suddenly, I realized Mike was still talking.

"First thing Sunday morning," he said, "I called Wally and asked him to help me to put clapboard siding on the house. We ran you and Ruthie off to Brighton and then got to work. One thing led to another and *voila!* What do you think?" His arms opened into a wide, triumphant gesture.

"I couldn't imagine better colors," I said.

"And you know what?" Becky interrupted.

I nearly jumped out of my skin. I did not hear her come up behind me. Quickly, I dissected everything I had said. Was there the slightest hint that I possessed an interest in her husband?

"Mike is turning the room off the kitchen into a bakery," Becky crowed while placing the tray she was carrying on the picnic table. She came over and stood beside me. "I'm opening my own business - Becky's Cookin'. How's that sound?"

"Terrific," I said, putting my arm around her slender shoulders. I gave an awkward squeeze. "Maybe you can help Emma and Julie teach me the finer points of how to not burn water."

Becky giggled.

Mike winked at her.

She went over to him. Her arms encircled his waist. They snuggled like newlyweds, totally smitten with one another. She looked like a child's ragdoll in his arms. They had found their way back to each other. And I was jealous.

I turned away to hide my emotions. Oh, how I wished Mike and Becky were Peter and me. That thought surprised me, a happy surprise, because I realized it truly wasn't Mike I wanted.

Tom busted out of the house - crash, boom, bang! Brutus charged right behind the boy and smacked into him when he stopped short on the top step. Tom had spotted his parents embracing and now his face was all lit up. Leaping to the ground, he raced to his parents - Brutus nipping at his heels. His chubby arms strained to wrap around Mike and Becky. Brutus danced around them on his hind legs.

What a miracle, I thought. A family reunited. Well, thank goodness, this dumb temptation of mine didn't go any further than it did.

Wally piped up, "Okay, you two lovebirds; cut that out and let's eat." As he placed a dish of sizzling delights on the table, Ruth and Laura piled on more trays of food.

Against a backdrop of gold, blue, and pink, we feasted. The unity that none of us could have possibly predicted just a week before made the meal complete. I sat beside my cousin Ruth, whom I had forgotten existed, and her husband. I had made a friend of an old enemy who was sitting across from me with his wife. I was getting to know Laura and Becky, who used to be nothing but misplaced images floating in memory. And even little Tom managed to fill some of the void left by my absent classmate, Tommy Gray. My life was coming together. I was even going to be a grandmother. The only thing missing was Peter.

"That's a terrible thing - that business of Rick murdering that girl," Laura said, handing me a huge plate of barbecued meat. "I'll bet you didn't know what you were getting yourself into when you came back to Echo Lake. Is this your first time back?"

I nodded while stabbing a piece of chicken. "I'm glad I came, in spite of Rick."

"Mmm, yes," Laura said. "Becky told me that you drew some very unsettling pictures of my Tommy. Wish I could help you out with things."

I smiled at her. "You already have."

"How's that?"

"Well, now that I've heard your voice again, maybe I won't keep picturing you hollering anymore."

"Oh, dear, did I holler at you?" Taken aback, Laura searched her memory. Her brows came together. She shook her head. "I don't recall hollering at you."

"No, no," I said. "Not at me. You were hollering at Tommy - the day he took my newspapers."

"Oh, yes," she replied softly. "That happened just before he...uh...he..." She inhaled a shaky breath. "Today is his birthday, you know." Her voice was barely a whisper. "Tommy would have been forty years old."

My breath seemed to cease. The silence was excruciating. Not even the breeze rustled the trees.

"Imagine that," Mike murmured. "Wonder what he might look like today? I always pictured him ten years old."

"My birthday's coming," Tom chirped. "And I'm gonna be ten years old. Just like Uncle Tommy."

Uneasy laughter relieved the reticence. Thank God for a child's innocence. Thank God we were all going to make sure Echo Lake won't ever snuff out his life the way it did his uncle's.

Mike mussed up his son's hair then put him in a headlock.

Tom flailed his fists, quite often missing his father. "Dad, stop!"

They continued to roughhouse for several moments. Then Mike gave Tom a nugie.

I turned to Laura. "Been meaning to ask you: what's that purple stuff you dab on poison sumac? Mike and I were talking about it just the other day. I can't remember ever hearing the name of it."

Laura chuckled. "That purple stuff - as you aptly call it - is crystal violet."

"Hope you know, it didn't stop the itching one bit," Mike huffed, releasing his grip on his squirming son.

"Actually, dear, it is not meant for that purpose. Crystal violet stops infection caused from scratching. Years ago, we mothers told our children it stopped the itching, hoping our white lie might have a placebo effect."

"Well, that didn't happen," Mike said, getting to his feet, "Come on, Tom. Now that we know the name of that purple stuff, let's go see what we can dig up about it on the Internet." He bent at the knees. Tom jumped on his back. Away they galloped - Brutus on their heels.

Becky shook her head. "Those guys and their silly computer. Mike is teaching everything he knows about it to Tom."

Wally spoke up, "Mike and I used that computer to put together the restoration proposal for the graveyard. Hand carried it myself to each and every selectman. Hopefully, we can get started pretty quick."

"I'm anxious to see it's up to par for Memorial Day," I said.

"I'm gonna contact Principal Cole," Wally said. "Maybe she'll help organize a parade - school kids, vets, the works."

"Gerald's buried beside Tommy," I blurted out. As all eyes darted at me, I wondered where the heck did that come from?

"You went there?" Laura asked, her expression puzzled, yet pained.

I nodded.

"How come?" Becky asked.

I shrugged. Embarrassment warmed me. I hated myself for mentioning Gerald and spoiling the evening. "Look, I really didn't mean to upset any of you."

"Don't worry about it, dear." Laura spoke hastily. "I've never let it go either."

Let it go? How did she know that I didn't let it go?

She continued, "And let me tell you, Gerald carried a terrific burden. If I wasn't with him the day my son drowned, I surely would have suspected that drunken fool drowned Tommy. So many times Gerald babbled on and on about killing Tommy. And then of all things, Gerald drowned, too. Almost ten years to the day after Tommy."

"How did he drown that day?" There I go again, asking a question that was none of my business.

"No one knows how Gerald ended up in the water," Laura said. "But I was the last one to see him alive." She faltered. "He was in a pitiful state that day. The ten-year anniversary of Tommy's death hit him pretty hard. He drank for days on end, ranting and raving that he killed Tommy. He slobbered on and on about how he could not find Tommy in the water that day. In his alcoholic stupor, he seemed to speak to Tommy. 'I'm sorry, I'm sorry,' he kept saying. 'I never meant to hurt you.' Well, that day was so nice and sunny - just like that Sunday Tommy drowned. Not a cloud in the sky. There is no reason for either of them to drown…" Her voice trailed off as she looked up to the heavens, holding back angst, struggling to compose herself.

Becky rubbed her mother's back. "It's all right, Mom. There's nothing you could do."

Laura forged on, "I thought Gerald was in the bedroom, passed out just like so many times before. After a while when I didn't hear him snoring, I peeked in. He wasn't there. I searched the shack inside and out. He was nowhere to be found. Well then I knew. In the pit my stomach, I knew. I took off for the beach; and sure enough, that old wooden boat was out in the lake, drifting off with the current; the oars close behind. Gerald was in that water; and God forgive me, I took my time getting back to the house to call Chief Briggs. I didn't hurry. And I didn't go down there when they hauled Gerald out of the water either."

Ironic, I mused. For someone who at one time had so much love for her husband, Laura Gray didn't mourn his loss. I suppose, I didn't blame her any - if I were married to such a brute and he beat me and my kids, I wouldn't mourn for him either. Sooner or later, love for such a man had to end.

"Grammy, Grammy!" Tom burst out of the house. The sheets of paper in his hand billowed over his head. "We found that purple stuff on the computer!"

"There it is, folks," Mike said, trailing his son. He was quite delighted with his success. "Pass those papers around there, Tom, so everyone can see that crystal violet is called gentian violet and stops infections from bacteria, mold, and fungi. Simple as that."

Tom did as he was told and then sidled up to Mike, gazing up at him with a forlorn look. "Can we go fishing now, Dad? Fish are jumpin' like crazy. See that?" His stubby index finger pointed towards Echo Lake where seconds before a sizable bass broke the surface, leaving ever-expanding circles rumpling the water.

"That would not be polite, son. We got company."

The boy crossed his arms and put his back to his father. His face drew up into a vinegary pucker as he scuffed his shoe across the ground.

"For heaven's sake, Mike," Laura said. "Take my grandson fishing."

The rest of us chimed in, "Yeah, Mike, take him fishing."

Tom faced his father. His hazel eyes peered at him hopefully. He looked so much like Tommy Gray did that day he said to me, "I'm sorry, 'Lizbeth."

Mike threw his hands into the air. "Okay, okay! Go get the gear, Tom."

The boy squealed with delight, hopping up and down. He dashed off. Brutus yelped then took off after the boy. And all that bedlam reverberated across the lake.

"You going?" Mike asked, elbowing Wally.

Half asleep, Wally yawned. "Nah, you two go ahead."

Yesterday, Tommy Gray Drowned

FOCUS

Reclining in one of Mike's homemade lawn chairs, I watched as Tom, wearing a fluorescent orange life preserver, and Mike, wearing a red and black flannel shirt, rowed out onto Echo Lake. Brutus was silhouetted against a tapestry of pink, gold, and blue, pointing the boat. Too bad I left my sketchpad and chalks at Ruth's.

Time wore on. The rowboat drifted aimlessly, poles extending out over the water. Tom waved at all of us and gave a high sign that things were right as rain.

Indistinct conversation bounded over Echo Lake. Every so often, Brutus yipped at a fish in the crystal-clear water. All of which, disturbed Wally's nap. "They'll never catch a fish if they don't stop all that confounded racket," he mumbled.

A cool breeze came with the setting sun. It sent us all scurrying for more clothing. As I pulled my fisherman's-knit sweater close to my body to ward off the chill, I looked out over the lake. The water was rippling. "Where did Mike and Tommy go?" I asked.

"Beyond those trees," Laura said, pointing with her nose while buttoning her green sweater all the way to the neck. "They caught a fish."

"Already?"

"Must've been a big one," Laura mused. "It dragged the boat as they reeled it in."

"Nice to see those two together again," Becky said, assembling dirty dishes on trays.

"You ever go fishing with Mike and Tom?" I asked.

"She's afraid of boats and doesn't swim either," Ruth jabbed.

"Oh, I can swim," Becky said. "Problem is: I don't know enough to come up for air." She giggled as she picked up a tray of dirty dishes and brought it into the house.

I schlepped a tray of catsup, mustard, and other condiments into the house. Then I settled myself on a wooden lawn chair between Wally and Laura.

Dishes clinked inside the house where Ruth and Becky prattled incessantly. No one could get a word in edgewise between those two. That's why Laura and I retreated to the back yard.

I glanced at Wally, snoozing in his chair. His feet were stretched out onto another chair. He looked so peaceful in the fading twilight. I looked back at the lake, naked without the wooden rowboat and its male passengers. A sinking feeling washed over me. I missed their voices, Brutus barking. It was getting downright choppy out there. I was getting apprehensive about that. The welt of waves felt almost sinister to me. I clutched my shoulders against the chill.

A presence built inside me. My thoughts became jumbled, growing wild, out of control, as if caught in a cyclone of cold blustery March wind.

I squinted at the lake. Alarm caterwauled throughout every fiber of my body; heartbeats choked my breath. Something was wrong. I got to my feet. My legs quaked beneath me. I tried to conceal my anxiety while nudging Wally. "Hey, how about a walk?" I nudged him again. "Let's go for a walk, Wally."

"Nah." He yawned and smacked his lips.

"Come on," I insisted, tapping on his shoulder. "Get off your duff, old man. You've napped long enough."

My insides churned. I had to get Wally up. The horrible feeling that I was going to need him rippled the hairs on the back of my neck. I yanked on his arm. "It's much too early for sleep. You'll never sleep tonight." I yanked on his arm again. "Come on, Wally."

"I'm up, I'm up!" He stumbled to his feet and then stretched like an athlete before the big competition.

I headed off toward the beach. I kept looking back to make sure he was coming.

Wally tramped along, not too far behind me, kicking his right leg out to one side then kicking his left leg out to the other side. He stretched his arms out then up over his head. Hands clasped, he leaned side to side.

Ca-plo-osh!

I froze in my tracks, my eyes tracking the source of the noise. It originated from beyond the trees near the beach.

Echoes: Ca-plo-osh! Ca-plo-osh!

Urgent barks.

A mishmash of echoes.

I gawked over my shoulder. Yes, Wally heard the commotion, too. There was a moment of frozen tension between us. Neither of us moved.

Ca-plosh! This time larger! Louder! Ca-plosh!

"Dad! Dad!"

The lake was alive with echoes: Ca-plosh! Dad! Help! Dad!

My heart pounded as I zeroed in on the location and made a mad dash for the beach. I heard Wally bellow, "Ruth! Call 911! Becky! Laura! Call 911!"

Then I saw it. "The boat's overturned!"

Brutus was clawing at the side of the capsized rowboat, trying to climb on top of it. He kept falling back into the water.

A short distance away, a head outlined in orange bobbed in the water. Small hands flailed. "Dad! Help! Dad!"

My terrorized heart seemed to scream out: Where's Mike? Mike's not there! Where's Mike? I raced down the embankment, peeling off the sweater I just put on a short time ago and throwing off my sneakers and socks. My warm feet sank into the sand; its chill needled my feet then zinged up the back of my legs, all the way up my spine. The hair at the base of my skull bristled. I plunged into the lake. The icy water struck me like a giant ping-pong paddle. My body stalled. My heart thumped. Adrenaline took control. I kicked my legs and came up for air.

Echo Lake was reverberating worse than I ever remembered. Wally was still bellowing, "Ruth! Becky! Laura! Call 911!" I heard a splash and knew Wally had dived into the frigid water behind me.

I swam toward the overturned rowboat. Halfway there, I noticed Brutus dogpaddling towards me. I had to stop him. He'd climb on top of me, trying to get out of the water. He'd shove me under the water and we'd both drown. Through chattering teeth, I commanded, "Brutus, home."

The terrorized Doberman kept coming.

What was the right command? I shouted out every combination that came into my head. "Brutus, at ease. Brutus, go home." Brutus this; Brutus that. One of the commands must have been the right one, because abruptly, the Doberman turned for shore. He swam past Wally whose powerful breaststroke brought the man to me.

My frozen jaws produced twisted feeble screeches. "Get Tom! I'll find Mike!"

I dove beneath the capsized boat and surfaced within the hollow space of its frame. Only drips of water and my own frantic respiration disturbed the eerie silence.

I sucked in air then plunged straight down - down into cold that got colder - down past schools of minnows - down into the darkness that got darker as the sky faded above me. I couldn't see my hand in front of my face. How was I ever going to find Mike? I surfaced to get my bearings. Treading water, I looked toward shore. My legs were scarcely keeping me at the surface. Treading.

Ruth was wading out into the water. At waistline, she reached Wally. Together they brought Tom to safety. She was close to hysteria, chattering away about how everything was going to be okay, we'll all be safe and sound and in our warm beds in no time at all - anything that popped into her head. Tom's orange life vest glowed in the twilight. Thankfully, it served its purpose.

Becky came running from the direction of the house, her arms full of towels.

Mike! raced through my head.

Brutus was still shaking off the water as he took off after Laura Gray. They disappeared up the lane to the main road. She was going to hail emergency volunteers who must be on the way.

Mike…

I had to do my part. I filled my lungs then dove, deep, fast, conserving my air. Time was running out for him. There wasn't enough time for me to surface again.

Mike…

It was hard to decide just where to focus my eyes when I couldn't even see. What if I missed him? I neither had the time nor air to miss him.

Mike…

Like a giant hand, hysteria took hold of me, squeezing, crippling my body. Hysteria rejected my demands to know where he was. Hysteria purged the air from my lungs.

I had no choice. I had to surface.

Sinister laughter echoed all around me.

I breached the surface and sucked in air. Sinister echoes cackled all around me, riding the whitecaps that buffeted me. Everything was blurry. I made for the form of the capsized boat. I held onto it, my body convulsed from fatigue and cold. Waves surged into my mouth, choking me, denying me of air.

A male voice, "Did you see Mike?"

"Everything's so blurry."

"Elizabeth! Pull yourself together! It's me! Wally!"

"Wally?" I hacked.

"Did you see Mike?"

"N-n-not u-un-der the… b-boat…"

"Let's fan out!" A shadowy hand rose out of the water, finger pointing. "You look over that side of the boat and I'll look on this side. Meet you at the bow."

Panic was zapping my energy, I knew that. Panic added to the numbing chill. I wasn't thinking clearly, I knew that. I had to pull myself together. If I didn't, I was done for. Okay… Okay…

Yesterday, Tommy Gray Drowned

I forced myself to think. Exactly where did Gerald find Tommy? I studied the surface. Gerald… Exactly where was Gerald found?

Think, 'Lizbeth.

Where were Tommy and Gerald found?

Think, 'Lizbeth.

I squinted in one direction then another and another. Was that the place? I blinked. Fireflies?

A voice boomed inside my head: Yes! There! The voice came at me like a giant loudspeaker, full and resonant, vibrating the bones of my skull.

Without a shred of a doubt, I knew exactly where Mike Anderson was. I screamed for all I was worth. "He's over here!" Letting go of the boat, I filled my lungs to capacity then dived deeper and faster than I ever had in my entire life. Intuition led me through the murky, black and white world. With every stroke, cold currents numbed my arms, my legs, my entire body. I seemed to descend like a lead weight.

"There he is!" I cried, my words transforming into meaningless bubbles that slid past my cheek. Cruelly, it seemed to me, the bubbles meandered to the surface. Cruelly, minnows schooled around me. Didn't they get it? These cryptic depths were holding Mike Anderson prostrate, suspended like a helpless blue-faced puppet playing out the drama of death at the will of Echo Lake. I wanted to scream: You can't have him! But my lungs were burning wicked bad.

I looked up at the surface. It wasn't that far, but at that moment, I could hardly see the surface. It seemed miles away. I could make it to the surface with Mike. I knew I could - at least I was pretty sure I could. Thinking about that was a waste of time, so I forced my muscles onward. Sheer determination battled the disabling cold as I latched on to the front of Mike's red and black flannel shirt. A red button popped and flitted down into the blackness. My lungs were on fire!

Surface!

I planted my feet into floor of Echo Lake. Muck oozed between my toes then rose into a filthy cloud that intensified the darkness. I bent my knees, getting ready to spring then pulled

Mike to me. His thick hair wafted indifferently across my face. I set my jaw. Pop goes the weasel! With all my limited strength, I straightened my legs. Mike and I torpedoed up as if Jack-in-the-boxes. Towards the faint glimmer above.

Up!

The faint glimmer above brightened. Air deserted my lungs.

Up.

Momentum slowed. I held onto Mike, gritting my teeth, scissor-kicking. Come on! Come on!

Up...

I struggled with my load and limitations. No longer did we rise. We hung there, suspended between life above and death below. Minnows surrounded us. Move muscles! Move!

My air was gone. We were going down. Not enough strength left... Help! Please, help us! There's nothing more I can do!

A warm surge enveloped me. A boost!

Up!

Daylight got closer, brighter.

I burst through the surface, my lungs expanding like a blacksmith's bellows. I coughed out water, gagging, my heart pounding. My nose was clogged. Everything was blurry, spinning. I floundered.

Suddenly, somebody was there, grabbing Mike Anderson by the arm. I wanted to fight off that somebody - I had to save Mike Anderson - but I could hardly hang on to him at all, never mind yank him away from that somebody.

Things seemed awkward. I was being towed. My entire body was solidified mass, my arms refusing to move, my legs refusing to kick. I hacked so bad, my lungs were on the brink of collapsing.

A whirling flash struck my fading eyes. Shadows running, diving. Splashing. Mike Anderson was plucked from me.

His weight had somehow sustained me. Now it was gone. I had nothing to cling to. Nothing existed within me to save myself. I dropped beneath the surface. I couldn't stop going down. I had nothing to hold onto even if I could. Minnows surrounded me, picking at my frozen, immobile fingers and toes. Nothing for me to do but allow gravity to bring me down. I sank into a profound relaxation. Darkness closed in. I was no longer aware of my limbs at all. Down… Cold, senseless silence… Down… Desperate for air, my lungs expanded involuntarily. Freezing water invaded every lobe, icing blood vessels, becoming avalanches of red coursing through my veins and enveloping my brain like a liquid ski mask.

This was what it feels like to drown…

"Sandman, I'm so alone…" Tommy Gray was singing behind the trees. "Don't have nobody to call my own."

I joined in, my right hand sloshing rhythm in the clarity of Echo Lake. "Please turn on your magic beam." I spread my fingers of my left hand then held them still. Silvery minnows nibbled at my fingers. "Mister Sandman, bring me a dre…"

My collar was choking me. Stop! Somebody's got hold of my collar! No! I want to stay here! My voice! What happened to my voice? Leave me alone! My arms! I can't move my arms. Tommy! Tommy! Tommy…

Waves battered my face. I could barely feel my toes dragging across sand.

I was laying facedown.

Someone yanked my arms over my head.

Leave me alone!

Pressure on my back. I was rolling over.

Stop!

Trouncing on my chest. Again. Again.

Water belched out my mouth and nose. I was wedged upright. My vision was greenish, concentrated, hard to see through.

A blanket! Oh, it's so warm.

A thermometer jammed into my mouth, making noises against my teeth and rattling in my brain. I felt dizzy. I might throw up.

Someone kept asking me: You all right? I wasn't. I nodded. Hot fingertips on my wrist, digging for my pulse. Something squeezed my arm, tighter and tighter.

It's okay, 'Lizbeth.

"It's only the blood pressure armband."

I coughed up water. The thermometer rocketed into oblivion.

Another heated blanket.

Across from me was a figure, swaddled in blankets, hunched over, an exhausted, dazed look on his face. I squinted at him.

"It's me, Elizabeth. Wally."

I recognized Ruth. Her arms were wrapped around... Who's that guy? I had trouble concentrating. Ruth and that guy were rocking back and forth.

Go to them.

I tried to get to my feet. Somebody pulled me back. My frozen left arm pushed the somebody. I crawled in sand, reaching out. Ruth and I touched fingers. I collapsed in the sand, sobbing with energy I did not have.

"You and Wally saved them!" Ruth cried, laughing at the same time. "You did it!"

I sobbed some more, glaring at Echo Lake. Your sinister clutches won't take anybody today.

A warm hand patted my shoulder then a voice soothed my rage: "Everything's going to be all right." I looked up into the eyes of Mrs. Gray. She took me into her arms and cradled me - and I clung to her.

"Come on," Mrs. Gray said. She coaxed me to my feet. "Let's have a doctor take a look at you."

The ambulance strobe light blinded me. I felt as though I were back in the water. I panicked and pulled away from Mrs. Gray. "Mike Anderson!" Another blinding flash. I shielded my eyes. "Mike!"

Mrs. Gray took hold of me. "It's all right, Elizabeth. They're putting him into the ambulance right now with Tom."

Yesterday, Tommy Gray Drowned

"Tommy Gray?" I cried. "He's okay?" I collapsed against Mrs. Gray. "Tommy didn't drown! Tommy didn't drown!"

WEIGHTED DOWN

The wall phone in Ruth's kitchen rang. And rang. And rang.

I jammed the pillow against my ear. "Somebody answer the phone."

The persistent bugger just would not stop ringing!

I yanked the pillow away from my head and squinted at the clock on the nightstand. 11:37 a.m.

Ring. Ring. Ring.

I threw off the covers. "Better not be a salesman." I hauled myself out of bed. "Oh man, I am so achy." I felt jittery as I opened the bedroom door.

The house was silent.

Ring. Ring. Ring.

A crawly feeling slithered over me. I ran my hands up and down my arms. "I better not be catching a cold."

Ring. Ring. Ring.

I grunted and headed for the kitchen. My life had been such a bore after Peter left, but being here in Echo Lake it seemed every time I turned around…another catastrophe. What's it this time? I passed Ruth and Wally's bedroom. The door was closed. "Humph. Still asleep."

Ring. Ring. Ring.

"Oh, shut up." I turned the corner into the kitchen then unhooked the mouthpiece. "Hullo!"

"Elizabeth? This is Laura Gray." Her voice was almost too affable for someone who had just faced losing more loved ones; almost too affable for someone like me just waking up.

I crumpled onto a chair then braced my elbow on the table to hold up my aching head.

"Can you come over here to Becky and Mike's later on this afternoon?" Laura asked. "And tell Ruth and Wally to come, too. There is something I think you all should know about."

The boating accident last night flashed across my mind for the umpteenth time. An onslaught of adrenaline bolted me onto my atrophied legs. Suddenly wide-eyed, I feared the worst. "Mike and Tom! Everybody okay?"

"They are all doing just fine, Elizabeth. Chief Parker brought Tom and me back here, oh, must've been somewhere around two this morning. Becky stayed with Mike. They got here a little while ago. They are lying down right now."

I sighed with relief. "Thank goodness for that!" I sagged onto the chair.

"Can you be here at five o'clock?" Laura asked. "We will have that dessert we never got to last night."

That afternoon, Ruth and Wally followed me into the Anderson's kitchen. Mike was sitting hunched over the table, contemplating his folded hands. Pale and drawn, he appeared awfully downtrodden - like a withered old man. Not at all the teen-aged smart aleck I once knew or the gorgeous hunk that habitually set my heart atwitter. His frail blue eyes glanced up at me. Suddenly the thought of him suffering like that became more than I could bear. I wanted to run to him, hold him, love him, tell him everything was going to be all right.

But then Tom zoomed into the kitchen with Brutus nipping at his feet - back to their old selves. A whirlwind of kid and fur circled the table then spun out the back door.

As Mike watched the antics, a spark of fatherly love invigorated his worn-out demeanor. He gave me a thin smile.

I went over to him and kissed him on the forehead. "Nice to see you, guy," I said.

He took hold of my hand and squeezed it. His touch was cold and lethargic; his voice weak and raspy. "Thanks for pulling me out of there, you guys."

"All in a day's work," Wally breezed, stepping around me to shake Mike's hand. He boxed Mike's shoulder, making light of the circumstances.

Mike heaved a faint chuckle then motioned for us to have a seat.

"What happened out there last night?" I asked, believing it was too coincidental, his boat overturning almost in the exact same spot where Gerald and Tommy Gray drowned.

"A fish took Tom's line," Mike said, rubbing his palms together. "Pretty good sized one too. Foolish thing yanked the pole right out of his hands. Tom grabbed for the pole but stubbed his toe on the tackle box and took a header into the lake." A sour expression sheeted Mike's face. "I went to haul him back in but then went over myself. Bashed my head against the rail. I can't remember anything else except hitting that cold water." He shivered as his head rocked side to side. "How could I have been so clumsy?"

Ruth and Wally made eye contact with me. We shifted. What could we say? Was there any rhyme or reason to the near tragedy? Goose flesh spiked my skin as I recalled the frigid water enveloping my body, what it felt like to be out of air, lungs collapsing, involuntarily sucking in ice cold water. At that point, even water was better than nothing. But then it surged into my lungs, icing my blood. I still could feel it worming through my body, zapping the life out of me. My brain screamed, surface! But my muscles refused to obey. Impotent, I hovered, awaiting my end.

Muffled sounds of kitchen activity snapped me back to the here and now. As the flashback vanished, I heaved a trembling breath, listening to Ruth and Becky. Their chatter was less than usual and much more subdued.

Mrs. Gray was at the buffet table, making herself busy, artfully arranging pastries and other sweets on a crystal serving platter. She set the colorful array on the table in front of us. None of us made a move for it.

Yesterday, Tommy Gray Drowned

"Who's having coffee?" Becky asked brightly. Her fingers entwined the handles of several mugs that clinked together. She was putting on a brave front, I could tell.

Laura waved her off, but Wally and I disconnected mugs then held them up for Becky to fill. She filled Wally's cup. Halfway through filling mine, her eyes caught my stare. Her brows furrowed. Momentarily the stream of coffee stopped. Her lips quivered. I guess mine did, too. Both of us realized we nearly lost a man who meant a great deal to us. She finished filling my cup then turned away. I felt as if someone shut off the light switch.

"What'll it be, Mike?" Wally asked, offering the dish of pastries.

Mike wrinkled his nose then ran his hand through his hair. "Believe it or not, a glass of ice water."

Becky chuckled. "Coming right up."

We made small talk until Laura Gray cleared her throat and straightened herself. "I have come to the conclusion that all of us around this table have not put my son's death to rest." She looked me square in the eyes, not angry, not critical, but in a way that let me know she understood. She sighed. "I thought I had, but I know now that is not the case. I believed that thinking about Tommy so much and how he died was a part of the grieving process. Perhaps it is. But for so many years? Then conversations I had with all of you in recent days gave me reason to reconsider my grief. And then last night…" She zeroed in on me again.

I had seen that look before, one of astonished horror, and it suddenly came back to me: last night, Laura corrected my senseless blathering; it was not Tommy Gray in the ambulance, it was little Tom Anderson. My stomach turned. How could I have been so insensitive? Still, if only it were true: Tommy Gray was in the back of that ambulance; he didn't drown after all.

Becky stared intently into her mother's dark eyes. "What are you getting at, Mom?"

Silence befell the room as Laura poured herself a mug of coffee. She added milk, took a pensive sip.

250

Sounds of Tom and Brutus horsing around in the backyard joined the ticking of the mantle clock in the living room.

Laura set her mug down on the table. Her hands cupped it as she gazed into it. "Last night, after I got home from the hospital and put Tom to bed, I came out here in the kitchen." She glanced around the table at the intent faces staring back at her. "I saw the computer paper lying on the table. I read about crystal violet. Well, I got to thinking…" She held up the printout and pointed to the first paragraph. "It says here, 'Ingestion: Do not induce vomiting; If the victim is convulsing or unconscious, do not give anything by mouth; Ensure that the victim's airway is open then lay the victim on his side with the head lower than the body; Immediately transport the victim to a hospital.' Well now, I thought, what if Tommy drank crystal violet? You know, he was in agony from all that infernal itching. Maybe he figured it might help if he drank some of it."

Moments passed.

Mike spoke guardedly. "I saw Tommy do some strange things - so did you, Laura. You yourself caught him putting mayonnaise all over his poison sumac to see if the itch would stop. I was there, too; yet I didn't see him drink any of that purple stuff. But neither you nor I watched his every move." Mike hesitated, searching her face. "Come on. He wasn't stupid enough to drink that stuff."

"If he didn't drink it," Laura said, "how about this: Rick Morton… Maybe *he* had a hand in the mix? You said yourself that Tommy saw some of what happened in the graveyard that night. After that, Rick threatened to kill Tommy if he didn't keep quiet about it, right? What if Rick convinced Tommy he wasn't after him anymore? Rick may have tricked Tommy into trusting him and then gave him something, perhaps a candy bar - a peace offering laced with slow-acting poison that eventually killed my son."

Mike ran his hand through his hair. He looked skeptical.
So was I.

251

Yesterday, Tommy Gray Drowned

But then the image of two guzzling inebriates squatting on that ledge behind the waterfall blasted into my mind. Impatiently awaiting nightfall to pitch me into that waterfall, Rick Morton and Rusty Kane would have murdered me without a second thought. I never would have known why until they let the cat out of the bag when they thought I was out of it. They assumed I knew the meaning of the graveyard sketch; however, that was not the case. They admitted to murdering Linda Benson - and they were out to murder me, too. Linda and I were just trash under their feet. Tommy Gray was no different. I saw Rick Morton fall backwards into the waterfall. He feared nothing and nobody; even Death was not going to get in his way. Yes, Rick Morton definitely was capable of killing Tommy - but the question was: How?

"It is a bit farfetched," Mike said. "But I wasn't with Tommy twenty-four hours a day and he surely didn't tell me everything. Remember, Laura, Tommy never let on to me about what Gerald did to him either - neither did you or Becky."

"You were upset enough," Becky said. "I didn't want to make it worse."

Mike pursed his lips while scratching his unshaven chin between his thumb and forefinger.

"So how do we find out what really happened to Tommy?" Ruth asked.

"If Rick Morton did such a terrible thing to Linda and got away with it for all these years," Laura said, "what makes us think that he didn't think up a scheme to get rid of Tommy?"

"So, alright, tell us what you're thinking," Mike said.

"I guess what I'm thinking is: I want an answer, a real answer." Determination was written all over Laura's face. "So I've decided to have Tommy exhumed."

Someone gasped. Perhaps it was me.

Laura continued, "I am surer than sure that an autopsy will provide us answers. I already made a few calls. This matter will be put to rest once and for all, so we can all get on with our lives. It's been thirty years. How much longer must we go on tormenting ourselves?"

Uneasiness settled over everyone sitting around that kitchen table. Unspoken questions raged. Could any of the scenarios that Laura mentioned actually occur? Was it right to dig up Tommy after all these years? Didn't Tommy deserve to be left alone - no matter what really happened?

I picked at a fingernail mangled during the watery ordeal last night. Maybe Tommy wanted this. My heart palpitated. Maybe an autopsy was the right thing to do - lingering questions should finally be put to rest. Still the whole idea seemed sacrilegious. And yet...it also possessed a degree of sanctity, because Tommy would be free to go on to eternity, just like Linda. But if he did go, all I would have left of him would end - and that really ate at me. Tommy would leave my thoughts. Sadness swamped me. Tommy would never come back to me again.

The silence - thick as the fog that socks in Boston Harbor when air masses shift - weighed me down. My fingers toyed with the mug still half-full of coffee. It almost spilled. The smell of the caffeine sickened me. I shoved myself away from the table then stepped over to the sliding glass doors. I stood there, watching Tom racing across the backyard. Oh, how much he reminded me of my fourth-grade classmate.

Tossing a yellow Frisbee into the air, Tom hollered for Brutus to fetch it. The Dobie leapt at the spinning disk and plucked it out of midair just before it descended into Echo Lake. Tom ran up to Brutus and yanked the Frisbee out of the Dobie's mouth. It was a miracle Brutus had any teeth left.

I looked off into the distance. Echo Lake lay still, motionless, a viper awaiting prey. I leered at the cursed water, so tranquil, so inviting. It almost took the life of another child yesterday - and his father. But Wally and I put a stop to that evil.

I slid open the screen door then stepped out onto the deck. A steady current of cool evening air fanned my burning face. Fine strands of my hair fluttered in front of my eyes. I wasn't dressed warm enough, but no way was I about to go back into the house for my lavender sweatshirt. I crossed the deck then slumped down on the top step. I pressed my fingers into my temples then rotated them. I had a headache - but I didn't.

A barn swallow swooped down a short distance from me, aiming for the lake. The tips of its wings skimmed the surface. Nothing below snatched the bird. Up into the air it soared, this way and that, ever so gracefully.

If only I was that bird. I'd take wing away from here in a heartbeat. Go far, far away. Hover high above the earth and look down upon all the turmoil. Turmoil could not touch me way up there. Weightlessly, I would glide in big, wide circles, my arms stretched out wide. Round and around I would soar without a care in the world. Up over marshmallow clouds. I would take the hand of Tommy Gray and...

The slider opened behind me.

My lavender sweatshirt was being draped across my shoulders. I made no move to put it on.

Laura Gray sat down beside me. "That grandson of mine is the spitting image of my Tommy," she whispered, pride mixing with melancholy.

Sullen and withdrawn, I took in the view. The sky was fading. Budding trees rustled slightly. A solitary spring peeper sang a half-frozen song of unrequited love.

"Those mares' tails hint at a change of weather," she said. She drew in a full breath. "Spring is coming early this year."

I lifted my face to the breeze and said, "Just like thirty years ago."

Laura took my sweatshirt off my shoulder and helped me to put it on as though I were a child of ten again. "Tell me what is on your mind."

I hesitated. Rarely did I reveal my true inner feelings. Doing so opened me up to ridicule. I looked into her eyes.

"You can tell me, Elizabeth."

"I-I guess I just don't understand." I tried not to whine, but it sure sounded that way.

"What don't you understand?"

I hesitated again.

She tucked a lock of hair behind my ear.

"Well…" I faltered. My voice sounded so childish, so maudlin. "I just don't understand why Tommy had to die. He was my friend - I know he was. That day with the newspapers - it was all a big mistake, and I never got the chance to tell him how bad I felt about it; and I didn't know he was going to die; and I didn't know I'd never talk to him again. If only I could go back and make things right. If only…" I burst into tears that were thirty years in coming.

Tommy Gray's mother put her arms around me and rocked me. "Shh… Everything is going to be all right. I am sure he was just as sorry about what happened between you two as you were."

"Oh, why did Tommy have to die?" I sobbed bitterly.

"God called him to His side, dear. It was his time." Laura was weeping. "There is nothing you nor I nor anyone else can do to change all that. And no matter what they find when they examine Tommy, nothing will ever bring him back. It will only help those of us he left behind to understand what really happened. We owe him that - and ourselves. So we can heal."

I felt the love of a mother - the very thing I needed as a ten-year-old. When Tommy Gray drowned, I needed a big person to explain away death to me. Not my peers. Not the local hoodlums.

"I've been so angry and sad and…" I babbled on and on, miserable, making no sense at all. "Why on earth did Echo Lake do such a mean thing? Look at it out there, just waiting, lurking. It's a monster. It's going get somebody again - I just know it."

"Water can be deadly," Laura said. "But at the same time it brings us so much pleasure. Like almost everything in nature, we enjoy so many things water blesses us with. However, we always must remember to be careful. That is all we can do. Unfortunately, sometimes, a person makes a terrible mistake and…"

"Do you think that something is out there?" I pointed. "In the lake? Doesn't it seem awful strange that everything happens in the same place?"

Yesterday, Tommy Gray Drowned

Laura pondered the idea for a moment. "Well, I never thought of it that way, dear. Still, I cannot imagine anything like that to be real. Everything that happened out there has a logical reason. My husband drowned there quite simply because he was drunk. And that's all there is to it. Gerald was drunk. That terrible thing that happened last night was an accident. It could have happened to any one of us the same way it did to Tom and Mike. It was just one unfortunate accident. I thank God you and Wally were there." She hugged me. "I thank God you and Wally are okay. And soon we will find out why Tommy drowned that day." Laura got to her feet and took my hand. "Come on." She led me to the beach. "Look out there, dear. Can't you just feel the essence of Tommy? I can. And I'll never stop feeling that way. He was my son, and he was a good boy, even when he was not such a good boy. That's all that matters to me. What should matter to you is how you feel about him. Tommy was your friend, even when he was not such a good friend. Look out there, Elizabeth. Don't you feel his friendship, his love?"

Beneath tear-swollen lids, I peered out over the placid water just like the bewildered ten-year-old girl of long ago. I blinked several times then rubbed my waterlogged eyes. My grief eased. Yes, my dear friend was gone but he would always be with me. I felt myself expand with calmness, like a balloon inflating. A half a smile lifted my pouty lips. Tommy was going to stay in my heart forever. Tommy was never going to leave me.

Waves of warmth brushed my cheeks. "Never leave 'Lizbeth."

LIES

I drove out to Walpole State Prison where Rusty Kane was serving time as an accessory to murder. I told Ruth that I had business to take care of in Brighton. I felt guilty about my little white lie; however, this was something I wanted to do alone. If I could prove that Rick had a hand in Tommy Gray's death, Laura might change her mind about the autopsy and all this nonsense would be over and done with. I wanted Tommy to stay right where he was, undisturbed - even if that meant lying beside his abusive father; even if that meant I had to lie to Ruth. Rick Morton was responsible for Tommy's death - in my mind there was no doubt about it. All I had to do was prove it.

During a taped confession, Rick's wannabe gave the gory details of the drunken savagery that went on in the graveyard that night. In addition, Rusty owned up to other crime sprees over the years. All involved Rick Morton. Rusty described one such incident that went down eight years ago in upstate New York where an old man caught them breaking into his isolated cabin. Rick got the drop on the old man and after a night of heinous torture, strangled him - with one hand, which Rusty found hilarious. Rusty helped Rick dispose of the old man's body down a deserted mine shaft located just over the Vermont state line.

Vermont state police investigated Rusty's story. Sure enough, the old man's bones were found in the mineshaft.

I turned into the entrance of the state prison and stopped at the gate. As I rolled down the window, an icy blast smacked my face. It gave me the creeps, which only worsened when the guard said, quite briskly, "License and registration, please."

Yesterday, Tommy Gray Drowned

I rummaged through my purse for my wallet. "Uh-h-m, I'm here to see Rusty Kane."

"You a relative or attorney?"

"Neither," I said, latching onto my wallet. I pulled my license out of my wallet the handed it to the guard, quite satisfied with myself.

"Registration?"

I gave him a dumb look. Then it hit me: he had asked for *both* my license and registration. I leaned over to the glove compartment and got out the registration. I handed it to him.

"Your reason for seeing Mr. Kane?" the guard asked.

"I need him to shed light on a friend's death," I said.

"One moment please." The guard stepped back into the guardhouse and picked up the phone.

I rolled up the window. I gnawed the inside of my cheek. I looked at the guard standing behind bulletproof glass. His mouth moved silently. It seemed as if he was reading information off my license. I scraped my palms on the steering wheel. What if he didn't let me in? And if I did get in, how was I going to persuade Rusty to open up about Rick Morton and Tommy Gray?

The guard sat down at a small desk and impatiently tapped my license and registration on the desk. That didn't look good to me. I might just get turned away right here at the entry gate. I sighed. "Maybe coming here was a dumb idea."

I mulled over this business of digging up dead people - something that never even remotely crossed my mind before going back to Echo Lake after thirty years. Exhumation and autopsies usually transpired in movies - ghoulish rites that rarely happened in real life - certainly not in the circles I traveled. Sure, I had heard, from time to time, media reports of exhumations to prove guilt, innocence, or actual identity, but that happened elsewhere, far from the realm of possibility in my life.

The guard tapped at my window.

I snapped to life. I jammed on the button that rolled down the window.

The guard made like he didn't see the sheepish grin on my face as he handed back my license and registration. He explained the visitation authorization and then handed it to me. "Keep this with you at all times."

"Yup," I said. Man, did I sound stupid.

He directed me to a parking area near the main entrance then stepped back and waved me through.

As I drove up to the mammoth jailhouse, the morning sun reflected off the windows. Temporarily blinded, I reached my hand up and shoved down the visor.

I parked between two yellow lines marked "Visitor" and then shut off the engine. My fingers gripped the key. To think, most of those interred in this black hole would never leave. "Black hole," I mused as the memory of a red rosebud lying on polished mahogany came back to me: Sunlight was gleaming off Tommy Gray's casket and his mother was placing a rose on the lid of polished mahogany. My ten-year-old brain railed with unfathomable sadness as six men in black suits slackened the ropes and the coffin descended slowly, gently, smoothly, never touching the edges, into that black hole. The rose embraced the casket and never let go. I peered down into the semi-darkness, my mind a deep, black hole. Mourners edged past me, scooping up handfuls of earth. Grains of earth plinked on the casket. A few people lingered; others just walked away. And then I found myself standing there, loathe to pick up dirt; even more so to open my fist and drop it on Tommy lying in that casket. As the breeze ruffled my hair, I gazed down at the speckles of earth defacing the red rosebud and the shiny mahogany. The perfection of that rose should have lived on for a very long time - just like my ten-year-old friend - if not for that heartless fiend, Echo Lake. That was the moment I actually realized Tommy Gray was not going to be picking up the newspaper from me anymore. My immature body curdled. Grief the likes of which I never before experienced owned me.

Thirty years later, my mind insisted that only God had the right to raise Tommy Gray again. My grief was also sacred. I owned it and no exhumation or autopsy was going to take it away from me. I yanked the key out of the ignition and got out of the car.

Inside a stark conference room at the Walpole State Prison, a heavy steel door at the far end opened. In shuffled Rusty Kane. A guard followed. The door closed. The guard took up a spot, his body barricading the door. His arms crossed. His eyes were ever vigilant upon Rusty and me.

Freshly showered and shaved, Rusty wore pressed green prison garb. The cleanest he's been in years, I thought. His carrot-red hair had been shaved off. No more head lice, I thought.

Upon recognizing me sitting on the other side of the glass barrier, Rusty stopped in his tracks. His face contorted.

I felt vulnerable, even though thick shatterproof glass separated us. Shaking off insecurity, I drew a deep breath and straightened. Whether I liked it or not, I had to face this bully who tried to kill me. I had to do it for Tommy's sake.

It looked as though Rusty might turn around and leave. What if he did? Suddenly a defiant air came over him. He strutted over to the window then plunked down onto the metal chair. He yanked the handset off the wall then slid down on the chair, spreading his legs wide apart. He hooked his free hand behind his neck. He was egging me on; I knew it. It was impossible for me to kick the option he was displaying in front of me - and he knew it. I pursed my lips. Such thoughts were not going to get me anywhere. I grabbed the phone on my side of the window and put it to my ear.

He put the phone to his ear. "What're ya snoopin' 'round here fer?"

"They're exhuming Tommy Gray," I said, hiding all emotion.

"Hey, good times." His voice was so sarcastic.

I gritted my teeth.

He gnawed on his thumbnail.

"Exactly what did Rick do to Tommy?" I was bluffing, pokerfaced. I knew nothing about what happened between Rick and Tommy, but Rusty didn't know I didn't know.

Rusty became quite agitated. His teeth pulverized a piece of fingernail. "Whaddaya tink?"

I got down to his level. "Hey, man, don't babble ta me with all your harebrained riddles. I'm not in the mood. The D. A.'s itchin' to get his grubby paws on scuttlebutt like I got, so I ain't got any problem at all spilling the beans. So 'fess up, jailbird. Tell it to me…or the D. A… Your choice."

Rusty eyeballed me, gnawing on that foolish piece of fingernail. "Phshh," he puffed. His face twisted up as he sucked at his nasal cavities, weighing his options. He hucked a blob of fingernail-laden sputum at the bullet proof glass. "Threatened the kid; that's all Rick 'n' me done."

The guard at the door hollered.

Sputum driveled down the glass.

The bald redhead scoffed.

The guard uncrossed his arms and took a step towards Rusty.

Rusty raised a submissive hand then slouched lower.

The guard backed off.

Now was my chance to finagle more information out of this arrogant jerk. "Only threatened the kid… You expect me to swallow that bull?"

Rusty snorted. "Eat dog fer all I care. Ain't got no reason ta tell tales. Look at me. No way am I ever gonna see the outside this snake pit. I ain't got nothin' ta lose by tellin' it like it is, so take that and shove it where the sun don't shine."

Rusty Kane certainly was aware of his lot in life. With every passing day, prison time was stacking up against him, which made chances for parole during his life on this earth more than just slim. When Rick Morton plummeted over the waterfall, innumerable victims surfaced. No longer threatened by Morton, victims were spouting off about heinous acts of intimidation and violence perpetrated by Rick and his cohorts. Victims burned for revenge - and were getting it - against Rusty. Because Rick and the other bullies were dead now. Hourly, new charges against Rusty were being filed. But was he going to lie to me? Or give in and tell me what actually happened? So I ventured, "You mean to tell me Tommy Gray saw Rick Morton do in Linda Benson and Rick only threatened him? And Rick didn't follow through with it? Sheesh!" I waved off Rusty and half turned away. "Gimme a break!"

"Listen here, bimbo!" Rusty snapped, jumping up. His phone flew in the air as his metal chair crashed onto the floor behind him. Shock waves rippled the glass between us then his palms flattened against it.

I jolted backwards.

"Rick had his plans fer the Gray kid!" he bellowed. Even though the phone was nowhere near his ear, I heard him loud and clear on my phone still pressed against my ear. He grinned sadistically. "No sense denyin' it! But..." Slowly he turned to upright his chair - and there was the guard standing right over him. They exchanged words. Rusty raised his hands submissively then up-righted his chair. He seated himself and resumed that spread-eagle pose of his. He made no move for the phone.

I waved my phone at him.

He heaved then hunted for his phone. Upon locating it, he put it to his ear. "Whaddaya want?"

"Rick had a plan..." I snarled.

Rusty grunted. "Turns out, afore we gits to it, the kid did hisself in." The redhead leaned back so far he almost toppled backwards. His arms flailed as he caught himself.

The guard barked.

Rusty brushed off the guard with the wave of a hand.

"W-o-w..." I sneered. "Rick planned to take down Tommy Gray but never got the chance... Is that the pile of dog you expect me to eat?"

"Yep," he scoffed, turning sideways in his chair.

I looked him straight in the eye. "Know that fer shur, do ya?"

"Yep."

I detested his one-word answers. "How do you know? I suppose you were with Rick every blessed second between the time he killed Linda Benson and Tommy Gray drowned?"

"Every last stinkin' minute," he sneered, drawing up his weak chin.

I struggled to maintain my outward composure, but inside frustration built so much that I ached to get my hands around his scrawny neck.

"Ya see," Rusty continued. "Me and Rick, we tooled up ta the woods o' Na Hampsha jes' about that time. 'Bout at da Canady border we was. Sick 'n' tired o' Echo Lake, that we was. Bullshit always happenin' 'n all. Talk about pissed off - sheesh-ya. 'N den Linda craps out on Rick… Jes' because he slugged her? Well I have ta tell ya: her crappin' out trashed Rick somethin' awful." Rusty wedged his elbows on the counter opposite the glass enclosure. His fists propped up his chin. Within colorless irises, pupils dilated, shooting black evil in my direction. He leaned towards me. "Rick had nobody but me. Jack Whitaker took off - sheesh, yeah. 'N I gits scare't 'cus I'm athinkin' da pigs'll nail us fer Linda. Soz, me and Rick gits up north fer a time. Got ta drinkin' ya know'd. Kilt us some game. Even jacked us a deer one night." Rusty savored the thought - not the taste, but the thrill of the kill. "Countin' on ever'thin' bein' blown over by da times we gits ourse'ves back ta Echo Lake. Soz what happens next is when me and Rick hauls in dat Sunday, siren's blarin' away ta beat da band 'n ever'one's bombin' up ta da lake. Soz, we follers 'em. It's like nobody even notices we wun't in town in da firs' place. Ha! Soz theres we was, at da lake and whaddah ya knowd? Ol' man Gray hauls his kid outta da water! Soz Rick turns ta me and says, 'Well, punk, dat's takin' care o' nice and tidy fer us, now ain't it?'"

Rusty was not exactly a pillar of truthfulness, but I tended to believe his twisted story. A sinking feeling came over me: Laura Gray might be right after all; perhaps Tommy did drink the crystal violet and it spawned convulsions. If that were the case, less than a half an hour elapsed, because that was the last time Mike saw the jar of the purple stuff and it was full - well, except for the small amount that Tommy's mother dabbed on Tommy and Mike.

I mulled over the possibilities all the way back to Brighton. By the time I pulled into my driveway, I had come to the conclusion that the autopsy was the only way to provide the answers everyone needed to put Tommy's death in perspective. "Tommy's got to be exhumed - no matter how I feel about it." The thought lingered in my brain as I put the key into the front door lock and then entered my house.

I checked the answering machine first thing.

"William Tanner here. No news from Vietnam. I'll keep you posted."

"So what else is new," I muttered.

"Hi Mom. Call me when you get in. Don't worry. Nothing important."

"What's more important than my, er, our... For crying out loud, Peter! Our daughter is having our first grandchild!"

I thought about Mike, safe and warm in Becky's arms. I had given him up to her. It was the right thing to do. But here I was - alone. Funny, it didn't feel as bad as I thought it would.

The last message was from Ruth. "Just checking in to make sure you got home okay. Give me a call."

Shoot, I should have told her I was going to Walpole. What possessed me to go there all by myself? Well, it's water over the dam now. If Ruth had been there, I would not have acted as scrappy as I did.

I phoned Julie. Ken was still boozing and freaking out, but Julie was planning to go to see Kurt Shirlington about it. Kurt was Ken's longtime friend - and a doctor - so I was confident that everything was going to get straightened out with them in no time. One thing didn't set right with me though: Julie mentioned something about a candy-colored-clown. I couldn't figure out what she was talking about. I sloughed it off. She probably wanted me to buy a candy-colored clown to put in the crib I bought for the baby.

I dialed Ruth. My confession about going to see Rusty Kane didn't bother her as much as I thought.

"Too bad Rusty denied Rick's involvement," Ruth said. "I don't like the thought of digging up poor Tommy any more than you do, but Laura is bound and determined to go through with it. I hear it's scheduled for day after tomorrow."

I winced. "That quick?"

"Uh-huh. And speak about quick! Mike got a reply from the Selectmen already! If we are willing to incur the expense of restoring the graveyard, the town will maintain it in the future. And Chief Parker promises regular patrols to monitor activity, day and night."

"Hey, that's great," I said. "So now what?"

"Mike and Wally are getting things underway as we speak," Ruth said. "Cleanup starts this Saturday morning."

"I'll be there," I said.

Yesterday, Tommy Gray Drowned

FLIES

Mike was already working when I got to the graveyard on Saturday morning. So were Ruth and Wally.

A flatbed truck pulled up behind me. It was loaded to the hilt with the white wrought iron fencing, grass seed, and other supplies Wally ordered last week.

While we unloaded the truck, other people flooded in, tools in hand, and rolled up their sleeves. The deteriorated graveyard was about to get a long overdue facelift.

"Look at all the people," I said.

How wrong I had been about the citizens of Echo Lake. They weren't so mean-spirited after all. Looking back, my mind - my ten-year-old mind - had made things worse than they actually were.

"News media gave the project great publicity, huh?" Mike said.

"Unsolicited money and supplies keep pouring in," Ruth said. "Some as far away as California."

"There's enough money to maintain this graveyard for years," Wally said.

"Speaking about media," I said. "Here they come now. I'm outta here!" I melted into the crowd of volunteers.

The cleanup went incredibly fast with Wally at the helm. Like any great leader, he became the brunt of jokes. Slave driver, tyrant, boss, master, those were some of the names he put up with throughout the day. One time, when I poked fun at him, he motioned to me. I thought I was in deep pooh for sure. Under his breath, he said, "Before you overhear people talking about it, you should know that last night, Chief Parker stopped in to check on Squire. He saw Squire sittin' there on his front porch glider earlier in the day and then just around sunset. Bottom line is: Squire kicked the bucket."

I felt like the earth quaked beneath my feet. "Forgive me for saying this, Wally, but it's about time."

"I hope the pervert rots in hell," Wally said.

"Probably will," Ruth said, sidling up to us. "Imagine going to your grave with that hanging over your head?"

"At least young-uns won't put up with the likes of him anymore," Wally said.

"Laws against sexual predators are pretty strong these days," I said.

"But laws are only as good as the people who enforce them and the community," Ruth said.

"I'm sure you two will keep an eye out for any other scum like Warren Squire," I said, squeezing Wally's muscular arm.

Wally had a handle on what Squire did to him. So did I. Facing my own memory of what that dirty bird did to me helped me realize why I turned out the way I did. I certainly did not have the greatest childhood, but lots of people don't. So what if the other kids poked fun at my name? Or I didn't have a lot of nice clothes? Kids will always find something to pick on each other about. Besides, Elizabeth is a great name - straight out of the Bible, just like Ruth, Mary, Ann. I must like my name, because I never took one single legal step to change it. Which side of the tracks I grew up on will never change either. My life from here on in was going to be the best I could make it. I got guts enough to put the past in its place.

Ruth's voice shattered my introspection. "Chief Parker! What are you doing here?"

"Well, you see, I was on my way over here to help out for a few hours and ran across these two vagrants walking alongside the road." Parker's thumb pointed over his shoulder at Becky and Tom. "So, I picked 'em up and shook my good finger at 'em. Goin' directly to the slammer, I tells 'em - that is, unless they do time here today."

Tom ran up to Mike. "Dad! Guess what? I rode in the squad car! Chief Parker let me radio in to the station and give our location!"

Wally laughed. "Don't tell me Brutus rode in the Chief's car, too."

"Are you kidding?" Becky covered her mouth, squelching giggles. "Brutus was the first one in when the Chief opened the door!"

Parker snorted. "Weaseled himself way up in the back window, too. That he did." Parker scanned the enormous amount of work already done. "Look at this place! How long have you been here?"

"An hour and a half," Ruth crowed. "Can you believe this amount of people showing up? It's just terrific!"

Chief Parker winced. "Expected to fight off the media."

"They gave up," I said.

"Not sensational enough," Wally said.

Mike tapped Wally on the shoulder. "Hey there, *Capo de Tutti Capo*, what are we supposed do with all the brush piles?"

"See that dude?" Wally said, pointing toward the back of the graveyard.

"In the brown jacket?" Mike asked.

Wally nodded. "That's Fred. He told me yesterday he's bringin' a mulcher. Go and see if he did."

Mike saluted and then marched away.

Wally sneered at him. He turned to Ruth. "Why don't you take the wagon and go refill the water containers? Got a thirsty bunch here."

"I'll go with you, Ruth," Becky said.

Chief Parker called after them, "Bring back some donuts and coffee, will ya?"

Fred got the mulcher going and I helped Mike broadcast the pulverized material behind the graveyard where the woods pitched down to the backwash of Echo Lake. Tom and Brutus were halfway down the embankment.

The second pile of brush was nearly history when Brutus howled. Then Tom scurried up the embankment. "Dad! Dad!"

Yesterday, Tommy Gray Drowned

"Tom!" Mike dropped everything and ran to his son. He bent at the knees and opened his arms.

"Dad!" Tom cried, smacking into Mike. "Someone's down there!"

Wally signaled Fred to shut off the mulcher.

Suddenly aware of the silence and their own shouting, volunteers stopped in mid-sentences. The only sounds were the wind in the trees and the out of breath boy who pointed down the embankment. "Behind that log, Dad!"

Chief Parker raised an index finger. "Hold it, everybody! Lemme get my tools and I'll go down 'n have a look-see." He hustled off to his patrol car and shortly thereafter, came back strapping on his gun belt. The leather griped as he passed me, which sent chills up and down my spine.

"Stay with Wally, Tom," Mike said, trailing after Parker.

Chills up and down my spine intensified.

Low-growing brush and overhanging tree limbs made the going rough. Parker stepped down the steep incline sideways, slipping and stumbling, holding on to anything at hand. Mike, however, was not as cautious. He lost his footing on some leaves and acorns. His arms counteracted a forward plunge; as a result, he fell backwards. He caught himself with his right palm. From then on, Mike kept a steadying hand on every tree he passed.

The whole town seemed to congregate behind me as I squinted though the trees, watching the two men edge cautiously closer and closer to the log where Brutus was standing guard, right front knee crooked in mid air. Not one muscle moved. Even at my distance, I could see his red eyes targeting his prey. Canines glistened exactly the way they did the first time that Dobie and I first got acquainted at the edge of Echo Lake.

"Wait!" I cried.

Mike and Chief Parker froze. They looked back at me.

I leaned in for a closer look then bolted upright and dug my fingers into the arm of the stranger standing next to me. "That shirt!" I said, grasping my chest. There for a minute, I thought my heart was going to explode right through my ribcage. "I recognize that shirt!"

As the stranger plucked my fingers out of his arm, I bellowed, "Watch out, Mike! Rick Morton is behind that log!"

The crowd gasped then shrunk back. Mike and Parker instantly crouched. Echo Lake repeated, "Rick Morton behind that log! Behind that log!"

Chief Parker whipped out his gun and leveled it on the log.

My heart raced. I dug my nails into my palms and let out an agonized moan, "When will this nightmare ever end?"

"We know it's you, Morton!" Parker shouted. "Come on outta there, hands up!"

Only Echo Lake answered, "Hands up! Hands up!"

As Brutus stood his ground, ice shot through my veins. That mutt had become very dear to me. Shaking like a leaf, I mumbled, "Oh, please Mike, call off Brutus. Please. He's going to get hurt."

The stranger beside me patted my shoulder as Parker's voice rang out again. "Rick Morton! This is Chief Parker! Give it up! Right this instant! Or I'll be obliged to come on down there and get cha m'self!"

"Get cha m'self!" echoed again and again.

Everything was happening in slow motion. I wanted to speed things up. I wanted this over and done with. I wanted Rick Morton rotting in State Prison - but not with Rusty - never, never with Rusty. After all the heinous thing those two did, they didn't deserved the company of one another.

"What's goin' on?" Ruth asked. Before I could answer, I heard her gasp. She grabbed my arm.

Becky elbowed herself between me and the stranger on the other side of me. Her hand smothered her horror at the sight of Mike and Chief Parker, gun in hand, contriving a plan.

Mike and Parker nodded at each other. Once again, the Chief hollered, "Get yourself outta there, Rick Morton! No more screwin' around!"

"Screwin' around," echoed the lake.

Mike bolted to the tree closest to the log.

I held my breath. I heard Becky praying, "Please God, don't let anyone get hurt."

Leaning out from behind the tree, Mike took a closer look. He straightened then gave a hand signal. Chief Parker dashed to the tree next to Mike. They jabbered back and forth. Moments passed. Mike issued a command to Brutus.

The Doberman took slow deliberate steps towards Rick. Right foot. Left foot. Just beyond the log, Brutus stopped. He extended a paw. Tap. Hordes of flies peppered the air. No other movement. Another tap. More flies. Nothing else.

Chief Parker kept his pistol leveled on the log as he and Mike inched away from the safety of the trees. Parker stepped to one side of the log while Mike craned his neck on the other side to see over Brutus. Their hands brushed away flies. Mike spun away, stroking his furrowed brow. He looked kind of green.

Parker circled the log, brushing away flies. He knelt down on one knee, squinting. He stood up and holstered his gun. He motioned to Mike. They clambered back up the embankment. Brutus dashed ahead of them.

"Rick's body is down there," Mike announced as Becky and Tom ran to his side. "For quite some time, I'd say." Mike kissed his wife on the forehead then patted his son on the head.

A sigh of relief rustled through the crowd.

Chief Parker shook his head. "Can't believe Morton survived those falls; much less, makin' it halfway up that incline. Guess I better go radio the coroner." He headed off to his patrol car, unbuckling his gun belt and then slinging it over his shoulder.

"Where on earth was Rick going?" I asked.

Ruth pointed at a rundown house choked by trees not far from the graveyard. "Rusty Kane's house."

MEMORY BOX

A few weeks later, Wally and I small talked on his back porch while waiting for Laura Gray to arrive. The morning sun streamed through the open windows where zephyr animated the pale yellow café curtains and specks of dust. Wally was balancing a saucer and half-eaten donut on top of his coffee mug, gazing out the back door. "Another awesome April day," he mused.

I was about to add, very much like those in April 1959, when Ruth stepped into the picture. "More coffee?"

"I've had enough caffeine for one day," I said, my hand covering my mug.

"Let me guess," she said, shaking a finger at me. "You didn't eat a blessed thing before you left Brighton."

I gave her a weak grin. "Laura's phone call last night wrecked my appetite."

Ruth scrunched up the side of her face. "I know what you mean."

Wally frowned. "I'm on edge about Laura's face-to-face with that medical examiner. Bet that's how come she wants all of us here."

"She was quite adamant about going over the autopsy only once," I said.

"Whatever," Ruth said. "She's upset - I just know she is."

"With the potential of doing the same thing to the rest of us," Wally added.

Ruth sank into the chair beside me then instantly was on her feet again. "Oh, here she is now!" She rushed off then came back with Laura Gray.

Yesterday, Tommy Gray Drowned

Wally offered his chair to Laura. She gave him a small hug then set a time-worn shoebox on the coffee table and sat down.

Mike, Becky and Tom came in and while they settled themselves, I helped Ruth put out more donuts and coffee. In a heartbeat, Tom snatched one of the sugarcoated morsels then sped off with Brutus to the living room. Making themselves at home in front of the TV, they were intending to consume the donut while watching the florescent shenanigans of Saturday morning cartoons.

Laura got right down to business: "I brought Tommy's memory box. We will share its contents a bit later, but first of all, I want to read the medical examiner's report."

Ruth and I exchanged glances as if to say, well, this is it. She sat down next to Wally on the wooden glider and latched onto his hand. I still had none to hold. This was not going to be easy; I just knew it.

Laura opened crisp white bonded documents, which had been folded into thirds, and flattened them as best she could. She scanned pertinent entries then gave a faint sigh and began: "The official cause of death is drowning, brought about as a result of previous trauma."

"Previous trauma?" I echoed.

Ruth and Wally exchanged horrified glances. Becky covered her mouth.

Ignoring our reactions, Laura read, "No evidence of intense peripheral vasoconstriction or vagal slowing of the heart due to sub-freezing water. Abuse is clearly evident, having occurred sporadically throughout the ten years of the decedent's life. Eleven previous fractures, contusions, and cicatrix are duly noted."

I winced. "Cicatrix is scar tissue."

"Bethie's a nurse," Ruth said. "Well, used to be."

Laura hesitated. Her dark eyes met mine then fled to the heavens as she fought the tremors that wracked her body. After a time, she refocused on the paper. "Subdural hematomata are observed in the cranium. Evidence of past hematomyelia - perhaps within a six-month time frame before death."

"Bleeding in the spinal column," I said, choking back anguish.

Her brows twitched as Laura scanned our faces. Her eye contact was shallow. She drew in a couple of labored breaths then resumed the grisly account in her own words: "Tommy's right arm - the one Gerald broke - was not set correctly and so it didn't heal properly. At the time of that injury, hairline fractures weakened several of his ribs - one broke completely. His spleen ruptured, too. All this happened when Gerald kicked Tommy in the stomach with those big ugly clodhoppers of his."

Laura shuffled through the legal documents. "This report speculates that Tommy endured an enormous amount of pain from these injuries. The spleen superficially healed itself, but when Tommy dove down, water pressure ruptured it. Evidence of internal bleeding, both old and new, scar tissue on the spleen, and a tear in the wall of the spleen affirmed the examiner's opinion that massive bleeding and excruciating pain undoubtedly crippled Tommy so bad that he would not have been able to save himself. Water in lung tissue indicated that Tommy struggled valiantly for his life. Excess carbon dioxide in brain tissue and lack of oxygen suggested he fought for air but then blacked out." Her voice trailed off as Laura got to her feet and went to the back door.

"So his lungs took over the process of breathing automatically," I said. "His lungs inhaled, heedless of the fact it was water and not air."

Laura stared at the back yard. A cloud whisked across the sun, draping her face in an eerie shadow. Her eyes closed as sunlight once again bathed her face.

None of us spoke, but I heard Ruth sniffle and Mike clear his throat. Becky was grinding her teeth. And I wished I were anywhere else but here.

Laura turned back to us then leaned against the door. "The medical examiner told me that, with today's technology, Tommy may very well have lived."

"That's because Echo Lake was still extremely cold from the winter and Tommy was so young," I said. "These days, children are revived who have been in frigid water much longer than Tommy was."

Wally nodded. "Immediate medical attention increases chances of survival. Unfortunately, when Tommy was brought out of the water, the general consensus was that it was too late - even though Pop tried anyway."

"Even if Tommy had been taken to the hospital," I said, "nothing would have been done to bring him back."

Wally hung his head, waving it side to side, as he said, "Plus, ol' Doc Morgan pronounced Tommy dead at the scene."

I could no longer sit there and watch anguish rip Laura to shreds, so I got up to comfort her. But words failed me. All I could do was put my arm around her shoulders. All I could do was lay my head against hers.

"And then...the mortician took my son away..." Laura reeled.

"Come sit down," I said. I helped her onto a chair then pulled mine up next to hers.

She gazed at the coroner's report. "Tommy did not ingest crystal violet. Nor did he have any adverse reaction to topical application. The medical examiner found no evidence of poisoning factors." She looked into my eyes.

"So Rusty told me the truth," I said. "Rick had nothing to do with Tommy's death."

Becky jumped to her feet, flailing her arms. "So, Dad's the one who killed Tommy? All because he tripped over my baby doll? If that simple, stupid, insignificant blunder didn't piss him off...if that never happened...he wouldn't have come after me? And Tommy wouldn't have stepped in? He never would have kicked Tommy? Tommy could've saved himself and he'd be here today! Tommy is dead because of me!" She collapsed, sobbing in Mike's arms.

I hung my head to conceal my bitterness. If only I had known about the abuse. For crying out loud, I saw Tommy's broken arm. Why didn't I at least ask him about it? There must have been some way to stop more abuse - stop all those despicable events that led up to my classmate's death.

Laura got to her feet and stepped over to Becky. She cupped her hands around Becky's cheeks, gazing into her eyes. "You must listen to me. You were only five years old. Children that age cannot be held responsible. Do you know for sure your father tripped over your doll? Because he said so? Did you actually see it happen?"

Becky shrugged.

"Yeah, well," Laura huffed. "I never said this before, but Gerald Gray was a brainless alcoholic clod. He never took a lick of responsibility for any of his actions. Whenever something happened - because of his own self-imposed drunkenness - he flew into a rage. Nobody but him dumped that booze in his mouth. If he took the slightest thing the wrong way, the nearest person took the heat for it. Unfortunately, the day of the baby doll incident, that person was you, Becky." Laura embraced her guilt-ridden daughter then kissed her forehead. She turned to Mike. Her eyes searched his. "How in the world could you have known the terrible things Gerald did to his family? Tommy never let on."

A tear budded in the corner of his eye then trickled down his cheek. He made no attempt to brush it away.

Laura grasped Mike's hand. "There was simply no way for you to help. You were only thirteen years old."

Mike groaned and hid his face in his hands. "But I should have searched for him sooner."

"Mike…" Laura gently pulled his hands away from his face. "You cannot go on blaming yourself."

He gazed up at her.

She smiled. "My son was a great swimmer and had the ability to stay underwater a very long time. You know as well as I do the little devil fooled around all the time. None of us could ever tell whether he was kidding or not. You know that, Mike."

He gave a faint nod.

Laura kissed his cheek then patted it before stepping back. Her eyes shifted to mine, giving me that same heart-felt compassion I had seen as a ten-year-old. "'Lizbeth," she cooed, crouching down in front of me. "My son's fourth-grade friend..." She took my hands in hers. Her hands felt so warm and mine so cold. "You thought that if you had not lost his friendship that windy March day, somehow things would have turned out different. Well, you know, dear, you never lost his friendship. That is the very reason you are here today. He called you back to Echo Lake."

I squinted at her.

"I truly believe Tommy called you back," Laura said. "Because of the secret friendship you two had for each other. All of us are here in this room, today, because of you, Elizabeth. Now we can all let go of the terrible burdens we have carted around all these years. And best of all, through you, Tommy helped Linda Benson. From now on, she will rest in peace with her sweet little one."

Laura squeezed my hands then let go and stood up. She straightened her back then eyed us. "I want all of you to listen to me very closely. I know each and every one of you well enough to know what you are thinking. You blame yourselves - unjustifiably so. There is absolutely nothing any one of you could have done to save Tommy. If anybody in this room carries responsibility, it is me. The first time Gerald pushed me around, I should have gotten out of that ramshackle firetrap." Her head drooped. When she spoke again, her tone was steeped in self-reproach. "But I didn't leave. My children and I should not have lived like that. I don't know how I loved that mean drunk. I lived where he wanted me to live, isolated and alone, because that's the way Gerald Gray wanted it. I took his abuse and drunkenness and he gave nothing in return." Laura snickered. "Well, that man surely turned over in his grave the day I got his life insurance from the merchant marine union."

"How did he expect us to live without it?" Becky spat.

Laura scratched her head. "We didn't live much until after he died and that check came in. I had it in my mind that I deserved what he did to me, but for the life of me, I could not figure out what I did wrong to set him off. I tiptoed around, trying not to do whatever it was, and thought I could predict when he would blow up. I should never have tolerated that monster striking my children. I hate myself for not protecting Becky and Tommy. Until yesterday, I had no idea how much Tommy endured. Gerald had to have gotten at Tommy when I was not around. But how? Why didn't I know?"

"The medical examiner claimed Tommy had a very high tolerance for pain," I offered. "How else could he hide it so well?"

"Still, I'm his mother. I should have known. There were so many injuries. If anyone is to blame for Tommy's death, it's me. Only me."

Becky went to her mother's side. "This autopsy puts an end to the torment we've all been going through - once and for all."

Drawing a laborious breath, Laura gave Becky a very tired smile. Then she reached for the time-worn shoebox. "It's time we remember Tommy in good ways. For that reason, I brought his memory box to share with you - good memories." She removed the lid of the collection she saved since the day Tommy was born. On top was a yellowed newspaper clipping. Beneath his faded fourth-grade picture, heavy black headlines: "Yesterday, Tommy Gray Drowned." Laura slid the clipping face down underneath the memory box. Then, one by one, she passed around rest of the contents.

In reverent silence, we touched the objects.

And Tommy Gray touched us.

Laura held up two tiny hospital identification bands and smiled, "Tommy wore these on his ankle and wrist after he was born." Next, she took out an infant's mint green sweater, which was part of an angel outfit that included hat, mittens without thumbs, and booties. She caressed her cheek with it. "I knitted this set while I was pregnant with him. Good Lord, if Gerald knew how expensive this angora yarn was…" She trembled with the thought.

Next, Laura picked out a yellowed envelope, unevenly torn open. She removed a card of congratulations. "My mother and father sent this. Tommy was their first grandchild. We only saw them when Gerald was at sea."

My eyes fell upon some grainy unbleached stationery with double-spaced, faded blue lines.

"Go ahead," Laura said, "Take a look."

Gingerly I picked it up and eased open the fragile creases. My voice was barely audible when I spoke. "Mrs. King gave this writing assignment to our fourth grade class." Mother had thrown mine away. She claimed writing was a bunch of malarkey.

"Tommy wrote that essay the week before he left us," Laura said. "The day after the funeral, Mrs. King made a special trip out to the shack to give it to me."

I gazed at a crude picture of Echo Lake that had been used as a cover. Royal blue waves with white chalk peaks rippled on a light blue surface. Cotton-ball clouds drifted across the uncolored sky where crayon birds soared: some black; others brown with orange bellies; one dark blue.

"That is Tommy's own handwriting," Laura said.

I contemplated the choppy penmanship on the grainy blue-lined stationery. Was that due to his right arm not healing properly? Did that injury also cause him to lose control when he latched onto my newspapers that March day?

"Won't you read it out loud for all of us, dear?"

I fingered the pages. My broken heart choked me. I didn't think I could read it aloud. I looked at Laura.

She nodded at me.

My voice cracked as I began. I faltered. I began again:

Echo Lake

By Tommy Gray

I live in the red shack next to the lane going down to the beach at Echo Lake. The roof leaks when it rains. In the wintertime, my family sleeps with jackets on, because it gets very cold inside the shack. In the summertime, all kinds of insects and brown field mice with coal-black beady eyes crawl up through the holes in the rotten floor. The shack leans to the side real bad.

One day, my mother, sister, and I went outside and wedged a log up against the wall, so it cannot tip over any farther. At least, we hope so.

I like to be outdoors every minute of the day. I can sit for hours on old trees that fall down in the wintertime. If I sit very still, sooner or later, I hear rustling sounds and then a forest creature comes along. I move only my eyes to watch it and try not to breathe. If one single muscle of mine twitches, the creature suddenly looks up at me. Its eyes get big and scared. Then it scoots off.

I am the best swimmer in all of Echo Lake. Echo Lake is why they named our town Echo Lake. Sometimes, Echo Lake turns all silvery. It only looks that way because schools of minnows swim around in it and then suddenly zip in a different direction real fast. If you dangle your feet over the boat dock, the minnows nibble at your toes. It tickles a lot.

Most of all, I like the feeling I get when I jump off the wharf and dive real deep. The water is so crystal clear that the rays of the sun go straight to the bottom. The deeper I go, it turns colder and colder. Lots of times, I pretend I am one of those minnows and go real fast. I wiggle this way and that. It would be fun to be a minnow.

My friend Elizabeth and I make believe we are Jack-in-the-boxes. We crouch on the bottom of the lake and listen to the music in our heads. When we get to the part about pop goes the weasel, we spring with all our might. Up and up we go. When I look up, I can see sunlight sparkling on the surface and it looks like the tinsel on a Christmas tree I saw once in a store window in Worcester. I really like that.

Yesterday, Tommy Gray Drowned

My mother's name is Laura Gray. She has dark brown eyes and a very even temper. Sometimes I do bad things and that makes her mad, but she hardly ever yells at me.

I have a little sister. Her name is Rebecca. We call her Becky for short. My favorite thing about her is her long brown hair. My mother calls it chestnut brown. I like to watch my mother comb it. The comb makes lines in it. What I like best is when my mother makes a fat braid down the middle of Becky's back.

When I grow up, I am going to build a great big house right there beside Echo Lake. It will have lots of windows. My mother likes windows. I will make sure it is always warm in the wintertime. Becky will have her own bedroom and so will my mother. I will too. Lots of friends will come to visit us.

The End

I folded up the essay and held it to my heart - afraid to breathe - afraid that one single breath might take my friend Tommy Gray away from me.

A thought occurred to me: Never once did Tommy mention his father, Gerald Gray.

MARCH WINDS IN AUGUST

Upon finishing up a late lunch, I told everyone I had to get back to Brighton, because Julie and I had made plans for this evening.

Laura seized my hand. "Before we go our separate ways, there is one more thing." As all eyes converged upon her, she cleared her throat. "You all did such a fine job fixing up that graveyard down the road from here," she said. "I like it so much that I purchased two plots." She took a resolute breath. "Tommy is not going back next to Gerald." Her lips pursed.

Becky smiled. "You're the best, Mom."

"Where are the plots?" Mike asked.

"In the corner that overlooks Echo Lake," Laura said. "To the West is the backwash and beyond that is where the shack used to be."

"The sunset is beautiful from there," I said.

Laura looked at me. "I sure would be pleased if you placed Linda Benson to rest there, Elizabeth. Next to Tommy."

Her unexpected offer overwhelmed me. From then on, whenever I thought about Tommy Gray's mother, I pictured her as she looked at me at that very moment. Her kindness and generosity of self was always the first thing that entered my mind. My memory of her bellowing over my head thirty years ago vanished like March winds in August.

Backing out of the driveway, I waved to Ruth, knowing full well that our goodbyes were not forever. I steered towards Echo Lake one last time before heading back to Brighton. At the lane that led down to the beach where Tommy Gray drowned, I stepped on the brakes. The heavy rusted chain that blocked the lane was gone. The no trespassing sign had been taken down. Mike Anderson had taken them down a while back, proclaiming that this summer the happy voices of children playing in the sand and water were going to echo across the lake once again. I could almost smell the campfires and hot dogs already. I visualized a new wharf and a mishmash of boats alongside of a new boat dock - Mike and Wally were handy at constructing such things.

I chuckled as I pictured this forty-year-old body of mine lying across the roughhewn planks of the new dock, my fingers dangling in the crystal clear water. One way or the other, I was definitely going to do that. Then, as if I were actually lying on that new dock, I started to sing: "Mr. Sandman, Bring me a dream, Make him the cutest that I've ever seen..." I began to hum - because I forgot some of the words.

An ethereal lilt chimed in: "Mr. Sandman, I'm all alone. Ain't got nobody to call my own..."

The song ended. Quiet. A breeze rustled the budding trees. It fanned my cheek. I sighed then put my car in reverse and backed into the lane to turn around. I hesitated. Instead of putting my car in drive, I put it in park and switched off the key. I chucked my sketchpad under my arm and got out of the car.

Perched upon the same decaying tree stump where I had sat when I first came back to Echo Lake, I opened up the sketchpad. Tommy Gray's grave. Incredibly clear; a lot more than when I first drew it. Now, I knew the reason for the dark chaos that enshrouded the grave: Throughout his short life, Tommy was constantly subjected to Gerald's violence. The torment continued after death, because the person who caused his death was buried in the very next grave. I was sure Tommy had stopped my hand from clearing up the gravesite. Tommy craved freedom.

Somewhere, a voice purred: Freedom.

Everything around me seemed to glow, vivid, alive. Specks of light flickered like fireflies. I wasn't nervous at all. No. Because I sensed the presence of Tommy Gray. Happiness filled a long-empty void within me. "The times I peddled papers past the cemetery, I heard you."

You...

The voice was soft, mellow, but clearer than if breath had taken them to wing. I sensed no tribulation - not anymore.

"I understand now, Tommy. You needed me. And just like other times throughout the years, you drifted into my mind because you wanted me to come back.

Come back...

"You found a way to me, Tommy - through my sketches. Only I could get you what you wanted - and that was the truth."

Truth...

"The sketch of the shack - Gerald beat you in that shack.

Shack...

"The overgrown graveyard and Pierce's Grocery Store led to Linda."

Linda...

"That sketch of you and me chasing newspapers thirty years ago had nothing to do with your death. The sketch was about you and me. I thought we weren't friends anymore. I was wrong.

Wrong...

Before my eyes, pools of hazel veiled by flaxen tresses rippled like endless waves. "I saw friendship in your eyes."

Eyes...

"Your face in the lake...half above the water, half submerged...so transparent... Clues that your death was not as it seemed. Gosh, Tommy, so many lives messed up by guilt: Mike's; Becky's; your mother's... The only one to blame was Gerald. It was his beatings that caused your insides to burst, so when you dove into the water, joking around with Mike Anderson, you couldn't surface. You couldn't save yourself."

Save yourself...

"This last sketch... Squire's front porch..." My insides revolted. "Me, Tommy. That sketch was all about me and my past. I needed to know that subconsciously I was carrying around the past. I needed to consciously let it go."

Let it go...

Yesterday, Tommy Gray Drowned

"Even though I love Peter with all my heart and soul, I have the strength to survive with or without him. It's been there all the time."

All the time...

The song swelled in my brain once again.

Streaks of yellow mist took shape into a wavering transparency.

"Tommy," I breathed, blinking at his sandy hair scattered across his hazel eyes. At first, I thought he was an illusion, but then I realized that as a child, I had seen Tommy Gray so many times and I always dismissed him for the same reason - an illusion. Whether alive or dead, he was always an illusion. Now here he was again. This time, I was not going to dismiss him. I reached out to touch his face. A fuzzy yellow enveloped my fingers where I should have felt solid flesh and I heard sounds - kind of like bubble wrap popping. I tingled, feeling as if I were a child again. Bashfully we gazed into each other's eyes. A broad smile lifted his cheeks. Dimples drilled so deep I thought a hole was about to appear and any second now, spit was going to ooze. My heart swelled. Happiness sheeted over me like tropical rain on a summer afternoon as I listened to him sing.

Mr. Sandman, Bring me a dream...

"Why did you stop, Tommy?"

Watch over Mike and Tom.

"Mike and Tom?" I gawked at my surroundings. I was alone. I scratched my head "I'm losing my mind." I looked down at my sketchpad. Were those sketches just my way of releasing unpleasant childhood issues? Like Emma told me? I thought about it. Perhaps. And yet, I liked Emma's way of thinking that out-of-the-blue thoughts about someone more often than not had meaning. I pursed my lips. Perhaps I was not talking to Tommy just now. I smiled. Still, it made me feel better thinking I was. And so I answered Tommy Gray: "Sure, I'll watch over Tom - and everyone else - the best I can. But if I ever become lost, Tommy, you better show your face to me. You better show me the way."

I heard loud popping. A car was coming! Just out of sight, its tires were crushing sticks, acorns, and other debris. The hair on the back of my neck bristled as kneejerk reaction yanked me back to another time when I was walking in a downpour, alone on this deserted road. Fear blinded me to current facts: Rick Morton was dead; the dregs of his sorry butt turned up behind the refurbished graveyard; Rusty was incarcerated. Not one of those facts mattered one iota as I bug-eyed the road, expecting to see Rick's hunk-of-junk truck. Run! Hide! Too late, there it was! My heart seemed to stop in the middle of a beat. That's not Rick's truck… It's… No… My eyes were deceiving me…

Peter's car pulled up beside me. "Want some candy, little girl?" His voice low and raspy.

I couldn't believe it was him. He was unshaven and unusually unkempt, but yes, "It is you!"

Tears of happiness swelled as I replied quite coyly, "No, sir. My only desire is my globetrotting husband."

"My only desire is my ever-faithful wife," he said, hopping out of the car.

As we rushed to each other, my sketchpad fell to the ground. I melted in his arms, crying, "Don't you ever - *ever!* - go away from me again!"

"From now on, my sweet little morning eyes will be right beside me everywhere I go," he vowed.

I backed away, brushing away my tears. I shook my finger at him. "I'm holding you to that, mister."

He grabbed hold of me and squeezed. "Oh, Bethie, all that time in the jungle without you I was like a ship lost at sea searching for land. I dreamed of holding you in my arms and hated myself for not holding you a whole lot more."

I gazed into his cocoa eyes, brindled with amber. "No amount of time can ever be enough."

"I had no right to leave you again," he said. "I'm so sorry I…"

I pressed my fingertips against his lips. "Hey, I survived."

"My heart and body ached for you, Bethie, more than I could bear."

"How terribly romantic that sounds, Peter."

We both laughed. Then he said, "We do fit each other so perfectly, don't we?" He smiled that silly grin of his as he caressed my cheek.

I leaned into his burning fingertips. "We're two pieces of a puzzle," I said. "Never whole without each other." Pleasure raced through me. I wanted him so much. By the look in his eyes, I knew he felt the same. I flashed him a smile as notions of the unmentionable kind perked in my mind, brewing like fresh morning coffee. "Let's go home, Peter. I got a few things to tell you."

"And I you, Bethie."

I scooped up my sketchpad and got in my car. I waited for him to turn his car around, looking forward to a little rest and a whole lot of Peter Blair.

In the distance, spring peepers were singing a grand harmony of love renewed. It won't be long before, within quiet shallows, the eggs inside gelatinous masses were going to hatch, witnessed by two naïve ten year old kids bending at the knees. One was going to scoop up newly hatched polliwogs and extend his hands to the other who claps hers in delight. I smiled. "Just like Tommy and me, so long ago."I started my car. "So many good things I forgot about, Tommy - or didn't want to remember."

Ever so slowly, I drove out of the lane, gazing at the spot where Tommy Gray yanked the Evening News from my paper bag. What a cluttered life I had led, carrying so many grudges around with me. It was a relief to be rid of it all - like March winds in August. I never would have imagined my life turning out this way.

A horn tooted.

"Coming, Peter." But before I stepped on the gas, I blew a kiss to my forever friend in another place and another time. "Good-bye, Tommy Gray."

B-y-e... L-i-z-b-e-t-h...

About K Spirito

Born and raised in New England, K Spirito, always the history buff, loves to browse through microfilm of old newspapers. Noting articles of human-interest, she then weaves them into a variety of fiction—all set in New England.

Visit: www.kspirito.com

Other Books by K Spirito

FATHER SANDRO'S MONEY - *Historical Fiction*

The LaRosa family leaves Italy and lives through 30 years of real events spanning 1908 through 1930 in East Boston, MA, New England and the world.

- Available in print, on CD, Kindle & Nook

TIME HAS A WAY - *Inspirational Fiction*

Emma LaRosa loses her husband Seth after fifty-two years of marriage and feels her life is over. She discovers Julie brutally beaten and life takes on new meaning. Mutual need creates a strong friendship and brighter futures for Emma and Julie.

- Available in print, on CD, Kindle & Nook

YESTERDAY, TOMMY GRAY DROWNED - Murder / *Mystery*

- Available in print, on CD, Kindle & Nook

CANDY-COLORED CLOWN - *Thriller*

Life is perfect for Julie Waters—great husband, gorgeous hundred-year-old brick manse perched upon a broad precipice overlooking the open Atlantic off Cohasset, Massachusetts, friends, family... Then she gets pregnant. Great husband, Ken, descends into a constant state of fretfulness, slugging down single malt Scotch and pacing about the manse that he and his first wife Regina restored just before the plane crash that took her and their only child Katrina.

- Available in print, on CD, Kindle & Nook

Spiderling - *Thriller*

The White Mountains of New Hampshire is the setting for this Thriller. While attending Ecology Camp, Katrina Waters gets caught up in a terrorist sleeper cell. All she wants is her own identity and destiny—not the one her father wants for her and not the one terrorists intend for her.

- Available in print, on CD, Kindle & Nook

PISCATAGUA - *Adventure /Romance*

Seventeen-year-old Chas Riley who is no taller than the average five year old seeks the love of Katrina Waters. Chas struggles with self-esteem issues, a heart condition, and the aftereffects of terrorism. Will Katrina view Chas as a real man? Or will she pursue tall, bronze-toned Bert Moro, an FBI mole who is never around when she needs him? This sequel to *Spiderling* is set in the White Mountains of New Hampshire, Maine, and Massachusetts.

- Available in print, on CD, Kindle & Nook

Summer And August, A *Cape Cod Murder Mystery*

Yellow Umbrella Books is one of several Chatham locations featured in this great summer read. Eric Linder, Yellow Umbrella Books owner, plays himself in *Summer and August*; And Debra Lawless, reporter for The Cape Cod Chronicle, plays herself. There are twists and turns along the road to the end of this rainbow you will never expect!

"If you want to peek behind the idyllic setting of summer on Cape Cod to a place filled with secrets, deception, and a dead body or two, read *Summer and August*, a saga of genealogical consequence and intrigue."

-Debra Horan, Owner of Booklovers' Gourmet, Webster, MA

- Available in print, on CD, Kindle & Nook

Works in Progress

Kathleen - *Fiction—Historical Journal*

You meet Kathleen in **Father Sandro's Money**. Then you learn much more about Kathleen in **Summer And August**. And now you get to know the entire story of what happened after Armand was gunned down. Follow Kathleen and her two children on the path life leads them, through the intimacy of her journal.

www.ingramcontent.com/pod-product-compliance
Lightning Source LLC
Chambersburg PA
CBHW020233260626
47156CB00002B/655